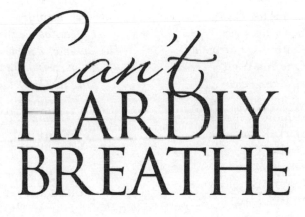

Can't HARDLY BREATHE

GENA SHOWALTER

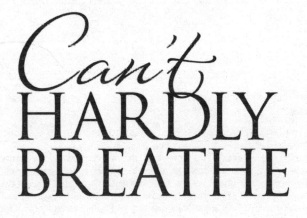

Can't HARDLY BREATHE

HQN™

HQN™

ISBN-13: 978-1-335-14287-0

Can't Hardly Breathe

Copyright © 2017 by Gena Showalter

This edition published by arrangement with Harlequin Books S.A.

For questions and comments about the quality of this book, please contact us
at CustomerService@Harlequin.com.

® and TM are trademarks of Harlequin Enterprises Limited or its corporate affiliates.
Trademarks indicated with ® are registered in the United States Patent and
Trademark Office, the Canadian Intellectual Property Office and in other countries.

www.HQNBooks.com

Printed in U.S.A.

To Jill Monroe, the best friend a girl could have.

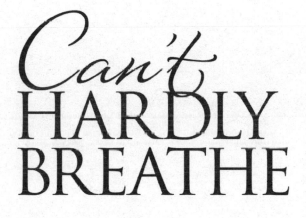

PROLOGUE

Some people excelled at high school. Other people…didn't.

Dorothea Mathis sucked so hard she made everyone else in the "didn't" category look like rock stars.

Fighting the urge to vomit, she entered the hallowed hallways of Strawberry Valley High, home of the mighty Stallions. Today marked the first day of her sophomore year.

I'll do better this go-round. No matter what. She would be strong and brave and stand up to Harlow Glass, the school bully; she wouldn't run away. She would talk to other students at lunch, and she would make new friends; she wouldn't hide in the band room. Somehow, she would convince everyone to use her given name rather than the nickname her family had cursed her with—Dottie.

Or Spotty Dottie. Or Dot dot dot, followed by laughing and pointing at the freckles on her face. Or her personal favorite, Dottie the wannabe hottie.

Today she forged a new path. *I can do this!*

Oh, crap! *What if I can't do this?*

Insults she'd heard adults whisper behind their hands claimed center stage in her mind.

Bless her heart. Her face would turn milk into sour cream.

Poor girl. She could make a freight train take a dirt road.

Heaven's above. She's probably got to sneak up on a glass of water just to get a drink.

What did looks matter? So she was technically considered obese. So her eyes were too big for her face, and her teeth were crooked. Well, her teeth *used to be* crooked. The braces were definitely helping. So she had a mass of frizzy corkscrew curls and looked like the human version of a Dalmatian. So the heck what. She was a good person with a good heart. Nothing else mattered.

I can *do this*, she repeated.

Squeals of happiness rang out as kids reconnected with friends. Dorothea smiled and waved at everyone, whatever their clique, but hardly anyone acknowledged her. No biggie. Right? Improvement took time. RIGHT?

She forced herself to trudge on, head high. If only her besties were here. Lyndie Scott and Ryanne Wade. They would build her confidence.

You're beautiful.

You're so freaking smart.

You have the best sense of humor around.

A few months ago, Lyndie's dad married Ryanne's mom. They were a real family now, sisters on paper as well as heart. This year, the lucky girls were being homeschooled. Ryanne's mom enjoyed having her only daughter nearby, and Lyndie was so quiet and reserved she functioned better in a contained environment.

When Dorothea had asked *her* mom about the possibility of being homeschooled, Carol had responded, "In order to feed and clothe you and your sister, I have to work two jobs. I can't take on another responsibility, honey."

Carol owned and operated the Strawberry Inn. Unless there was a festival in town, very few guests ever stayed overnight.

For extra spending money, she waitressed at the all-night diner just down the street.

Dorothea had pouted. "You don't understand, Momma. Without Lyndie and Ryanne, I'll have no friends. I'll be tormented."

Carol had looked at her with compassion. "I'm sorry, honey, but girls like us have to learn to be as tough as nails. It's the only way we can find happiness."

Girls like us. Different? Unattractive?

Dorothea's attention returned to the present as the gorgeous, popular and oh, so cruel Harlow Glass stepped into her path. Two other gorgeous, popular and oh, so cruel girls flanked Harlow's sides. Madison Clark and Charlene Burns.

"Mirror, mirror on the wall, who's the ugliest girl of all?" Harlow asked.

"Spotty Dottie," Madison piped up.

"The wannabe hottie." Charlene smiled a cold smile.

Despite the heavy thud of her heartbeat, Dorothea stood her ground. *Want change? You have to be the change.* "My name is Dorothea."

"Oh, my bad. Dorkthea." Harlow held up a can of whipped cream as if it were a weapon of mass—

Wait. Had the vicious brunette just called her *Dork*thea?

Dreams of a successful school year began to implode.

Harlow sneered at her. "Are you going to cry? You look like you're going to cry."

Madison and Charlene giggled.

As Harlow sprayed a stream of whipped cream into one girl's mouth, then the other, she said, "Look, Dorkthea, I'm not going to sugarcoat the truth because you'll probably eat it. You *are* a dork. And ugly. And fat. Face it. You're a disgusting she-creature."

Dorothea's cheeks blistered with humiliation, her lungs deflating. She'd tortured herself all summer, running five miles every morning. *Still* she carried extra weight.

Be strong. Be brave.

"I won't sugarcoat the truth, either," she said, lifting her chin. "True beauty isn't the size of your body but the size of your heart. *Your* heart is small, making you the most hideous girl I've ever met."

Sky blue eyes glittered with venom.

Madison and Charlene huffed and puffed with indignation.

Score! Harlow-1, Dorothea-1. All tied up.

"Ask any boy in school to choose between the pretty girl and the *nice* one with a heart of gold," Harlow grated. "Heck, ask any boy in the world! Guess who will win every—sin-gle—time."

Be strong. Be brave. Stand up for yourself! Easier said than done. Harlow had a way of stripping a girl of her humanity and leaving a wounded animal.

"Who a boy chooses doesn't matter," Dorothea said, know-ing deep down it was true. "With your own words, you proved boys can be as ignorant as you are."

The girl's mouth opened and snapped closed.

All right. Time to go. Before things got worse!

Could *they get worse?*

Yes! Dorothea took a step backward, intending to run… when she smacked into a wall. No, not a wall, but a person, she realized with a gasp. As strong hands settled on her waist to steady her, she glanced over her shoulder to see—

Daniel Porter!

Her crush. Her eternal flame. Her one and only. A senior just as beautiful on the inside as he was on the outside.

She'd adored the boy since the first day of kindergarten, when she'd skinned her knee during gym, and he'd come to her rescue, acting as her crutch while she limped to the nurse's station.

Today he was taller, of course, and cut with muscle…and he was peering at her with the most beautiful gold eyes framed by thick black lashes. Peering at *her*. Not the other girls. But… his hands still rested on her waist. He could probably feel the fat rolls underneath her shirt.

Tensing, Dorothea jumped away from him to sever contact.

He frowned at her. "Everything okay here?"

His voice! So low and husky. Her heart leaped into her throat, making it impossible to breathe or speak or even pretend to be cool.

Unaffected by his presence, Harlow flipped her dark hair over her shoulder. "This is a private conversation. Move along, Daneroni."

Two years ago, when Harlow had given him the nickname—Daniel plus pepperoni—he'd had a problem with acne. But he didn't have a problem anymore. The summer sun had cleared his skin, bronzing him to perfection. In his black T-shirt and faded jeans, he was the guy every girl dreamed of dating.

An-n-nd he stepped in front of Dorothea…acting as her shield? Her eyes widened as he leaned down, going nose to nose with Harlow. "You're the queen bitch. Everyone gets it. Don't be surprised when someone pushes you off your throne."

The color drained from her majesty's cheeks, but she gave her hair another flick, as if she'd never been more confident. "You obviously lost brain cells when you gained biceps, so I'm going to let this infraction slide. Just know this is a once-in-a-lifetime opportunity. Now—move—along."

He crossed his arms over his chest. "How about you give me a once-in-a-lifetime opportunity I'll actually like and move to a new town?"

Dorothea gaped. Daniel Porter, the hottest boy ever born, had just out-bullied Harlow Glass.

Forget crushing on him. There, in that moment, Dorothea fell madly, deeply and passionately in love with him. *My hero!*

Harlow kissed the tips of her fingers, then blew him a kiss with only the middle one extended. "Come on, girls," she said as she shouldered him out of the way. "Let's give Daniel time to think about the error of his ways."

The group marched off. Madison glanced over her shoulder to wink at Daniel.

Something dark rolled through Dorothea. Jealousy? She moved, blocking the love of her life from the blonde and perfect cheerleader's view. "Thank you. For everything."

He bestowed his full attention on her, and *oh, my stars*. She almost melted into a puddle of goo. His eyelashes! They were so long they curled at the ends.

When he smiled at her, revealing straight, white teeth newly freed from braces, she forgot how to breathe.

"Don't let Harlow's cruelty get you down," he said. "She likes herself, which means she has terrible taste. I think you're perfect just the way you are."

Her still-thumping heart dropped into her ankles. Perfect? *Her?*

He gently chucked her under the chin. "See you around, Dottie."

He knows my name! A nickname she suddenly loved.

As he strode down the hall, she called, "Yes! I'll see you around!" Then her cheeks blistered with humiliation. Shrieking at him like a banshee? Not cool.

And oh, wow, had he seriously called her perfect?

Waves of feminine pride flooded her, something she'd never before experienced. Shoulders squaring, chin lifting with more attitude, she made her way to her new locker and dropped off her backpack.

A senior—Jessica Kay Dillon—had the locker next to hers. Tears welled in Jessie Kay's eyes as she wiped whipped cream off the door. Dorothea caught the remaining letters—*L-U-T*—and swallowed a groan. Harlow must have spelled *slut*.

Jessie Kay had a reputation as "easily had and easily forgotten," and Dorothea's heart suddenly ached for her. The pretty blonde and her sister Brook Lynn had lost both of their parents. Their uncle had come to stay with them, but he must not have had any money to spare, because Jessie Kay's clothes were ill fitting and threadbare.

Dorothea repeated what Daniel had just said to her, because—obviously—the words had the power to change *everything*. "I think you're perfect just the way you are."

"Like your opinion matters," the blonde snapped before stomping away.

A little of Dorothea's newfound confidence wilted. *I'm strong. I'm brave. I'm perfect.* Daniel wasn't a liar.

She floated to first period on a cloud of euphoria. What if she flirted with him? How would he respond? Would he ask her out? What if *he* fell in love with *her*, they got married and had a million babies?

Dorothea smiled. She had two long-term goals: become a meteorologist, and have a large family. She'd always been fascinated by weather, in all its many forms, and the more kids she had, the more people who would be obligated to adore her. Now, however, she added a third goal: enchant Daniel.

What career did he want for himself? What college did he hope to attend?

As her teacher droned on and on, Dorothea watched the clock, desperate for lunch hour to arrive so she could see Daniel. What if he invited her to sit at his table?

What if his friends teased him about spending time with her?

Her stomach twisted into sharp little knots. Maybe she should admire Daniel from afar. Just until she'd changed her social status from dead to alive.

But shouldn't he like her regardless of her station?

By the time first…second…and third periods ended, she'd worked herself into a lather about whether or not to approach Daniel. Was she reaching too high too fast? Oh, crap, she was, wasn't she? When had anyone ever wanted her?

Dorothea trudged to the cafeteria. When she spotted a smirking Harlow, she whipped around and rushed to the band room, her sanctuary, as if her feet were on fire.

She would be brave tomorrow.

She glanced over her shoulder as she turned the doorknob. Spotting Jessie Kay, who may or may not have noticed her, she quickly and quietly shut herself inside. The lights were out. Good. If Harlow *had* given chase, she might not think to look here. And if she *did* look here, she might not see Dorothea in the shadows.

Coward! Shame coated her skin like a sticky film. *This isn't strong, and this isn't brave.* Daniel would never fall for—

A low moan drifted through the air.

Oh, crap! Someone had beaten her to the hideaway. Someone injured?

Dorothea rounded two rows of ceiling-high shelves, each stacked with different musical instruments and—

"Mmm, that feels good."

The voice dripped with pleasure, not pain, and struck Dorothea with the force of a lightning bolt. Madison Clark.

"You like that, sweetheart?"

Ice crystalized in her veins. *That* voice belonged to Daniel. The love of her life…the boy she'd hoped liked her back.

He was here with Madison Clark. And he'd called the cheerleader *sweetheart.*

"Yes, oh, yes," Madison said, and moaned again.

Dorothea's hands balled as she continued trudging forward. She had to see this. Had to see Daniel's betrayal up close and personal.

What betrayal? She didn't know. Only knew her insides were shredded.

When she reached the end of the shelf, she peered through two flute cases—and swallowed a cry of despair. Daniel had Madison pinned against the wall. He towered over the girl, his wide shoulders engulfing her delicate frame.

"Where did you learn— Oh!" Madison liquefied in his arms. "Don't stop."

Daniel chuckled. Or purred. Dorothea wasn't sure which. She fought for breath, her lungs pulverized like two slabs of chicken. This boy...he was the reason her heart beat, and the reason it broke into a million little pieces.

He didn't choose me. He chose her.

He's a fool. Just like Harlow.

Worse, he *was* a liar. Dorothea *wasn't* perfect. She would never be the girl a boy like Daniel desired.

She sniffled, then slapped a hand over her mouth. Unnecessary. Neither Daniel nor Madison stopped what they were doing, too wrapped up in each other...

This was for the best, Dorothea decided with a nod. If she and Daniel had dated, their names would sound stupid together. Daniel and Dottie. No, she hated Dottie all over again. Daniel and Dorothea. Dorothea and Daniel. The double Ds.

Yeah. Stupid!

A tear slid down her cheek.

Daniel traced the tip of his tongue over Madison's lips. "You made me chase you all summer, naughty girl."

"And now you're going to punish me?" Madison dug her manicured nails into his nape to tug him closer.

"No. Now I'm going to *reward* you." His hand—

Oh, my stars! His hand delved between Madison's legs!

Dorothea spun, her chest burning as if she'd been doused in acid. She needed to leave the band room. She needed to leave *the building*. Now.

"Don't stop," Madison said. "Pleeease. I want my reward."

He gifted her with another husky chuckle. "All right, but I'm skipping lunch to do this for you…which means *you'll* owe *me* a reward."

Dorothea forced one foot in front of the other. Somehow, she managed to exit the room as quietly as she'd entered. Jessie Kay leaned against the bank of lockers across from her. The blonde opened her mouth to speak, but Dorothea ran. Just ran. There was no sign of Harlow—not that it mattered anymore.

Harlow had hurt her pride. Daniel had hurt her soul.

CHAPTER ONE

Present day

Dorothea Mathis studied the last room on her cleanup schedule and groaned. The bed had been wrecked, the comforter and pillows tossed haphazardly on the floor. A pair of panties hung from a bedpost. The TV remote had been busted, the pieces scattered across the nightstand. Wet towels created a path to the bathroom door, and the trash can...

Oh, gag me! The trash can contained used condoms.

The place needed to be decontaminated by people wearing hazmat suits.

Am I up to date on my vaccinations?

With a sigh, Dorothea anchored earbuds in place, keyed up her iPod and donned a pair of latex gloves. One—germs. Gross! Two—she was protective of the green nail polish she'd applied only that morning.

She selected color based on mood. Green = irritated.

Somehow she'd *known* today would suck balls.

Her mom must have checked in Mr. and Ms. Pigsty last night after Dorothea had gone to bed. Since she had a 4:00 a.m.

wake-up call, she tended to hit the sack by 9:00 p.m. Granny hours, her sister, Holly, liked to tell her.

Dorothea picked up the dirty towels, removed the panties from the post, emptied the trash, changed the sheets on the bed, straightened the pillows and covers, and tossed the remote remains, planning to bill the Pigstys for a new one.

Time was limited this morning. She'd promised to drive her mother into the city in— Crap! Less than an hour. She rushed through dusting and began vacuuming. As the machine swallowed dirt and debris, she tried not to envy her mother. Carol would soon be enjoying her fourth "singles retreat" of the year. Her fourth, but certainly not her last. She stayed at the Michaelson, a five-star hotel owned by the richest guy in Strawberry Valley, Dane Michaelson. Dane was married to a local girl Dorothea had gone to school with, and he allowed Carol to stay free of charge. No doubt about it, she took full advantage, attending speed-dating sessions, mixers and a plethora of themed parties.

Her busy love life was just one of the many reasons she'd given the Strawberry Inn to Dorothea.

The wheels on her cart suddenly squeaked, the sound louder than her music. Yanking out the earbuds, she spun.

Surprise expelled the air from her lungs, leaving her gasping. This so wasn't happening right now.

It *couldn't* be happening.

Nightmares didn't really come to life. Nor did pornos. Not that she watched those…very often. But dang it, this had to be one or the other.

The sexiest man on the planet had just stridden into the room. He was shirtless, sweat glistening on his eight pack— and his name was Daniel Porter.

The Daniel. The childhood crush she'd never forgotten. The first boy to break her already fragile heart.

She gulped. What was he doing here?

Wait. Like she really needed to ponder this one. *Welcome back, Mr. Pigsty.*

Her hands trembled as she yanked the vacuum cord from the electrical socket, the room descending into silence as the engine died.

I think you're perfect just the way you are.

She smoothed her trembling hands down her "uniform," a pair of blue scrubs that could take a licking and keep on ticking. "Uh, hi. Hello." Oh, wow. Could she be any lamer? Definitely in a nightmare, not a porno. "Welcome back."

He pulled the earbuds from his ears and gifted her with a small smile that failed to hide the lines of strain around his mouth. "Sorry about the mess. I planned to clean up before I checked out." His gaze darted throughout the room, and he cringed. "I also plan to pay for the remote."

What kind of sexual acrobatics had placed the poor remote in harm's path, anyway?

Oh, my stars. A warm flush poured over Dorothea, threatening to overheat her. She almost fanned her cheeks for relief, barely stopped herself.

Look away! She tried, she really did, but Daniel was just so freaking beautiful. He was even taller now, and stronger, with a rough, tough face. His cheekbones were sharp, and his nose boasted a small notch in the center. Been broken a time or two? Dark stubble dusted his angular jaw, though the shadows couldn't disguise the fine tracery of scars on his left cheek.

He was a modern-day warrior—literally. After high school, he'd joined the army, defending the country he loved.

This wasn't the first time Dorothea had seen him since his return to town a few months ago, but her body reacted as if she'd never seen *any* man, heating and tingling in all the naughtiest places.

Act naturally. He's just a customer.

A customer who'd wrecked a room during his most recent stay, but whatever. He was waiting for her to respond to his offer.

Let's do this. "Yes, thank you. Payment would be appreciated." She wound the vacuum cord around her arm, her motions clipped. "As for the room, I just need to tidy the bathroom, and I'll be done."

With his back to her, he stuffed his toiletries into an overnight bag. "I'll get out of your way, then."

During his senior year of high school, he hadn't just slept with Madison Clark; he'd slept with a string of beautiful, popular girls, as if banging-and-bailing had finally been dubbed a national sport.

Good thing Dorothea hadn't pursued him. He would have taken all her firsts and discarded her like garbage.

Instead, Jazz Connors had taken all her firsts and discarded her like garbage.

Anger boiled her blood until bitterness swept in, leaving a glaze of frost. Fire and ice. This wasn't the first time they'd battled it out, and this wouldn't be the last. The biggest downside? They ensured the wounds inside her hollowed-out chest never really had a chance to heal.

After graduation, she'd moved to the big bad city, enrolled in the University of Oklahoma's meteorology program, met Jazz and gotten hitched, just as she'd always dreamed…only to return home several years later with a divorce and no degree.

A washed-up has-been by the age of twenty-four.

Daniel, having served multiple tours of duty, had come back a hero.

His life had meaning, hers didn't. He and two of his friends had started a security company right here in Strawberry Valley. He took care of his ailing father, and in his free time he dated a plethora of city girls.

Dorothea knew about the girls because he'd stayed at the inn every time a date had ended…successfully.

Her flush returned full force as she considered the other five rooms he'd wrecked since his return…all the pleasure he'd been having…all the pleasure she wished *she* could experience.

Not with him, of course. With someone she liked and respected. Someone who liked and respected her, too, despite the fact that she was still too round for society's unhealthy standards, a lot too freckled and trapped in a dead-end job.

Daniel Porter would never qualify.

Dorothea found him attractive, yes, but to her, appearance would never outshine personality.

My man must be my equal. She had a lot of love to give. She'd even grown to like herself…kind of. Maybe. Fine, she was *trying* to like herself.

Avoiding Daniel's gaze, she said, "No, you stay. I'll go." Words her mother had drilled into her shouted inside her head: *the customer comes first.* "I'll finish your room later." She rolled the vacuum toward her cart.

"You live here, right?" he asked. "You own the inn?"

"I… Yes." Technically she lived in the attic. The more rooms she had available for guests, the more money she would make. At least in theory.

Money was the number one reason she cleaned the pigsties herself, rather than hiring a maid. She was saving her pennies to turn every plain, ordinary room into a themed paradise. Then Strawberry Valley residents would happily pay to stay just for fun.

Again, in theory.

So far she'd decided on six themes. (1) Four seasons—the weather, not the hotel chain. (2) An enchanted forest. (3) A techno dance club. (4) The underwater world of Atlantis. (5) A royal palace. And (6) an inner sanctum, aka a superhero's wet dream.

Also up for consideration? A beach hut, an igloo, an insane asylum for her more daring patrons and a desert oasis.

With twenty-three rooms in total, she needed other ideas fast. And more money. A *lot* more money.

Maybe, when the transformations were completed, the feeling of accomplishment would finally chase away her anger and bitterness. Maybe she would feel alive. Happy.

"If any part of your stay was subpar," she said, "I will personally—"

"No, everything has been great." He looked over his shoulder and winked at her. "Just wanted to make sure you weren't going to get into trouble with the boss."

Every pulse point in her body leaped with excitement. He'd winked at her. Her!

I think you're perfect just the way you are.

Red alert! She would *not* read more into his words than he'd intended. Not this time. He was a flirt, plain and simple. Always had been, apparently always would be.

"Why would I get in trouble?" she asked.

"For not finishing the room."

Oh. Right. "Well, as long as you plan to come back to the inn, I won't fire myself. Not because I'm desperate to see you or anything," she added in a rush. "I'm not." Dang it! "I mean, I'm always glad to see you here. I mean, I just want your money." Okay. Enough!

He laughed, his amber eyes twinkling.

Air caught in her throat and sizzled. He had the sexiest laugh on the planet. His entire face softened. He pulsed with new life; fresh and vibrant, he was the epitome of spring.

Then he frowned, as if he couldn't believe he'd found humor in, well, anything.

Her brow furrowed with confusion. Why the doom and gloom?

"In that case," he said, his tone flat, "I think I'll stay another night."

"Really?" She licked her lips. "What about your girl-friend?"

He stiffened. "She isn't my—"

"No, don't tell me. I'm sorry I asked. Your love life isn't my business."

"I live in Strawberry Valley. My love life is everyone's business."

His wry tone made her chuckle, and he stiffened all over again. Great. What had she done wrong this time?

"I'll be alone tonight," he said, looking anywhere but at her. "Apparently I hover over my dad when I'm home, so he's asked for another night off. But I swear to you, this room will be clean in the morning."

She snorted. "I'll believe it when I see it."

The corners of his mouth twitched. "Doubting Dottie." A pause, then, "Would you like a cup of coffee before you go?"

"Oh, uh, no, thank you." While she no longer viewed Daniel through the wounded eyes of high school betrayal—he'd been a nice boy doing a nice thing for a vulnerable girl in desperate need of a white knight—she'd endured too much heartbreak over the years to risk getting to know him better and reigniting her crush.

Look at the way she'd reacted to him already.

He appeared...disappointed? No, of course not. A trick of the light, surely. "Well. See you around, Daniel."

"Yeah. See you around, Dottie." He returned his attention to his toiletry bag, dismissing her.

Irritation had her snapping, "My name is Dorothea."

Before he could respond, she stepped into the hall and closed the door with a soft *snick*. Hands trembling, she hooked the vacuum to the cart and rolled the cargo to the supply room...where her younger sister Holly was smoking a ciga-rette.

Coughing, Dorothea claimed the cigarette and stubbed the tip into an ashtray.

"Hey!" Eighteen-year-old Holly glared at her. "I wasn't done."

"You mean you weren't done giving our guests lung cancer and stinking up the inn?"

"Exactly." Ever the smart aleck, Holly tossed a piece of gum in her mouth and popped a bubble in Dorothea's face. "Besides, we don't really have guests, now, do we? Since you took over, only four people have stayed here. Mayor Trueman and his side slice, and Daniel Porter and whatever bimbo he happens to be banging."

Not true! A few months ago, Dorothea had hired Harlow Glass, and everyone in town had rented a room to witness the former bully's downfall.

Good times.

Dorothea hadn't wanted to like Harlow, but dang it, something bad had happened to the girl in the years since high school, and she'd changed. More than that, Harlow had done everything in her power to make amends, and eventually Dorothea had warmed up to her.

Now the beautiful brunette was married to reformed playboy Beck Ockley. The happy couple were expecting their first child in a few months.

A razor-sharp pang cut through Dorothea. *Won't think about my own—*

Nope. Slam the breaks.

To ward off the oncoming pity party, she drew in a deep breath…slowly released it… Good, that was good.

She focused on her sister. Holly had pinned back the sides of her jet-black hair, the remaining locks tumbling all the way to the metal links anchored around her biceps. She'd paired a crimson corset top—her first pop of color in months—with a ruffled black skirt, ripped fishnet stockings and combat boots caked with mud Dorothea would have to clean from the floors.

In a town as small as Strawberry Valley, Oklahoma, Holly was a legend. Unique.

"My inn, my rules," Dorothea said. "No smoking. Ever." Besides, she suspected the teenager only ever lit up to aggravate her. Not once had Dorothea witnessed an actual puff.

"You're worse than a Mogwai that's been fed after midnight."

A *Gremlins* reference? Seriously?

"No wonder Jazz left you," her sister added.

Air hissed between her teeth. Holly might hate her guts, but the teenager loved to insult her, and this barb hit harder than most.

Rather than waiting for love, as Dorothea had dreamed, she'd settled for companionship, marrying the first guy to pay attention to her. Worse, she'd believed his words rather than his actions. *I adore you and only want what's best for you...for us.*

Jazz Connors had been a master at manipulation. He'd cajoled and charmed...and then he'd cheated.

Holly had no idea. To this day, she idolized him and blamed Dorothea for the split. And that was the way Dorothea preferred it. The girl distrusted too many men already. Starting with their snake of a dad!

When Joe Mathis divorced their mother to marry his side slice, as Holly liked to say, he'd cut all ties with his daughters. Dorothea had been hurt, but Holly...she'd cried herself to sleep for weeks.

Carol had shut down so completely Dorothea was ultimately forced to step up and act as both mother and father. A role she'd played until the day she moved to the city.

Biggest mistake of my life.

She'd promised to stay in constant contact, but every time

she'd visited, every time she'd called, Holly had treated her like, well, this. Insults and rancor had abounded.

Eventually Dorothea stopped coming around, and even stopped calling, unwilling to deal with a new bombardment of vitriol…not realizing until too late that young Holly had interpreted her move as yet another rejection.

Now Dorothea longed to repair their broken relationship *without* damaging her sister's perception of Jazz. The two were like siblings. *Loving* siblings.

Jazz called Dorothea at least once a week to report the things Holly texted him—and also to beg Dorothea to give their marriage another chance.

He missed her worship and adoration, nothing more.

After saying "I do," he'd somehow—and easily—convinced her to drop out of school, work two jobs and support him until he graduated. That way, he could get a job at a news station and one day become the state's premier meteorologist. Then Dorothea could return to school. And after *she* graduated, Jazz would do her a favor and recommend her to his boss.

I'm such a fool. He'd finished school and gotten a job, no problem. But before *she* could return to school, he'd also gotten his side slice.

"Jazz and I didn't love each other," she finally said, whisper-soft. "Love is the difference between success and failure."

"Love is a myth," Holly said, her tone as dry as the last two Oklahoma summers. She arched a brow, the silver hoop pierced at the edge glinting in the light. "Sex is what makes or breaks a relationship."

"Holly!" Dorothea had lost her virginity to Jazz. In freaking college. "You're too young to be having…you know." She thought of high school Daniel and his parade of girlfriends. "Teenage boys are fickle. They come and go, and leave heartbreak in their wake."

Her sister rolled her eyes, eyes the same bright green as

Dorothea's. "You aren't my mom, and this isn't a teaching moment. Stop acting as if you care about me."

"I do care." She reached out, intending to hug the girl. "I care a lot."

"Too bad, so sad." Her sister darted out of range and popped another bubble. "*I* don't care about *you*."

Dorothea spun so quickly she'd probably experience whiplash in the morning. Tears burned her eyes, and she blinked rapidly, hoping to prevent a spill down her cheeks. She'd been hurt many times in her life. She'd faced rejection after rejection. But this...

"I stopped caring when you decided to act like Dad," Holly added, her tone flat.

Her sister had scented blood, hadn't she? Had gotten hold of an emotional knife and intended to twist the blade while it was buried deep inside Dorothea's heart.

"I know I've said this before, but I'm sorry." She wrapped her arms around her middle. "I should have come back to see you more often. I should have called more often. Going radio silent just to prevent another fight was cowardly and—"

"Thanks, but no, thanks. I'm not interested in hearing this again." Holly popped another bubble. "Your *should have* is too little, too late."

Twist. Dorothea decided to change course before she bled out. "Shouldn't you be at school?"

"Shouldn't you stay out of my business?" Holly marched out of the room. The door slammed shut behind her.

Twist, twist.

Feeling a hundred years older and a thousand pounds heavier, Dorothea pasted a smile on her face and headed to the lobby to place the Be Back Soon sign on the reception desk. Then she dialed Mrs. Hathaway's room. The widow took over guest services at odd times in exchange for room and board.

"I'm headed out," she said. "Can you—"

"Sure, sure. Just got to find my denture cream."

Dorothea muttered a hasty goodbye as Carol rounded the corner, her bag rolling behind her. A dark bob framed her ageless features, and a bright green dress flattered her larger figure. If Dorothea wore that dress, she'd look like a watermelon. While she'd inherited her mother's not-quite-delicate bone structure, her shorter height did her no favors.

I think you're perfect just the way you are.

For a moment, she fought the urge to run into her mother's arms and sob. Carol loved her and always found a way to comfort her on the worst days of her life.

"I'm single and ready to mingle!" Carol's sunny smile only brightened when she met Dorothea's gaze. "Life is good."

This woman…oh, this woman. She was so wonderful, kind, loving—and utterly clueless. *Purposely* clueless. When the going got tough, Carol got going, retreating to her room or even out of town to check out mentally, leaving Dorothea to deal with everything on her own.

"Mom, did you know Holly ditched class this morning? Worse, I caught her sm—"

"Let me stop you there. She didn't ditch. I gave her permission to stay home. Everyone deserves a break now and then." Carol patted her shoulder. "Are you ready to go? I don't want to miss the welcome reception."

Translation: *I don't want to deal with sibling rivalry.*

"Fine. Let's go."

During the entire hour-and-a-half drive to the city, Carol chatted about nothing important. Only when they reached the luxurious hotel did she change her tune, leaning over to kiss Dorothea's cheek. "Do something fun while I'm gone. Something spontaneous and maybe even wild. Okay?"

Dorothea flinched. "I'll try."

"Don't try. Do."

The entire drive home, she remained thoughtful. *Fun, spontaneous* and *wild*. Three words no one had ever used to describe her. In fact, her friend Ryanne had referred to her as Doro Downer since her return, and Lyndie had teased her about being a fuddy-duddy. They'd invited her to multiple girls' nights, shopping sprees and spa days, but she'd always said no. Holly and the inn came first.

And look where that mind-set had gotten her. Hated, broke and miserable.

Maybe her mother was right. Maybe it was time for a change—time to be fun, spontaneous and wild. To put *herself* first. For once!

No, not maybe. Definitely.

But I don't wanna be fun, spontaneous or wild, part of her cried. With change came risk. With risk came failure. With failure came hurt.

Or...with risk came success. With success came joy. She could use a little joy in her life.

She wasn't feeling particularly brave or strong, but dang it, what did she have to lose?

To achieve a different result, you had to do something different. She desperately craved a better life. No, not just better, but the complete opposite of what she had. Therefore she had to do something different.

Maybe...maybe it was time to go against her instincts and do what came *unnaturally*.

Yes. Yes! That was what she would do. What came unnaturally. Starting today.

CHAPTER TWO

Out with the old Dorothea, in with the new Dorothea. It was time to shuck off the chains of her past and walk, no run, to a better future.

Yeah! Long past time. She paced the length of her attic room, her hand pressed against the rose tattooed over her heart. A thorny vine twined with Christmas holly and wrapped around her entire breast, forming a complete circle. A constant reminder of the best and worst moments of her life.

Love and loss.

Fresh start…fun…spontaneous…wild. No more regrets.

What should she do?

Old Dorothea would spend the night texting her sister apologies. New Dorothea would…

Stop apologizing? Yes! For sure. What was done was done. New Dorothea would stop trying to rebuild a relationship she'd ruined and start trying to build a stronger one. No, not trying. Doing. She wouldn't sulk or cry. Ever. She would go out. Finally. Maybe to a bar.

Definitely to a bar!

Ryanne owned the Scratching Post and drew crowds from

Strawberry Valley as well as two neighboring towns, Blueberry Hill and Grapevine. New Dorothea would dance, meet
good-looking men and actually flirt.

Is that a wallet in your pocket or are you just happy to see me?

She would charm, well, everyone, her beguiling wit on
dazzling display.

A girl could dream, anyway. In reality, both New and Old
Dorothea had never flirted with anyone, and charm was beyond her.

So. Slight tweak to her plan. Instead of going to a public
place, she'd stay here.

Old Dorothea would stay here. You're New Dorothea.

Yes, but there *was* an eligible bachelor two floors down…

She sucked in a breath. That was right. Daniel Porter. The
one who'd gotten away. The ultimate conquest. The star of
her wildest fantasies.

I think you're perfect just the way you are.

Problem: he'd been with a woman just last night. There
was a little bit of an ick factor. What was the term? Oh, yeah,
sloppy seconds.

Okay, that was pretty offensive.

Forget his past. The present situation was simple. Her crush
couldn't be reignited—because it had never died. The shy
high schooler trapped inside her still wanted him. So did the
needy girl who'd never tasted fruit from the forbidden tree.

Truth was truth. Only Daniel would do.

Biggest obstacle: she hadn't magically morphed into Daniel's type. He dated ex-cheerleaders. Thin beauties who belonged in the pages of a magazine. Successful women who'd
actually finished college and now enjoyed high-powered ca-
reers, or at least had prospects.

Were successful women better in bed? Yeah. Probably.
Confidence was sexy, no matter a person's sex.

Dorothea had nothing to offer. Except maybe an orgasm.

Or twelve. But then, orgasms were the point, the whole point and nothing but the point.

A tremor of excitement and nervousness swept through her. *Mmm, orgasms…*

Small obstacle: she'd never had a one-night stand. She'd only ever been with Jazz, so it had been a while. Some nights she ached so badly, so deeply, *nothing* assuaged her. Ached for an orgasm, yes, but mostly companionship. Having strong arms banded around her, holding her close, the rest of the world a distant memory…yes, please and thank you.

A night with Daniel could be fun, spontaneous and wild, far beyond her most wanton dreams. And really, what man would turn down a no-strings encounter, even with a woman he had no interest in dating?

No one!

Was she going to do this?

He would be alone, ripe for the plucking.

Why not? she decided. What did she have to lose? Besides her pride. And her peace of mind.

You have no pride or peace of mind.

True. She wiped damp palms on her scrubs, her mind continuing to whirl. To win him, she would have to do something epic. Tiptoeing to his door, softly knocking and stuttering as she tried to form a complete sentence would only turn him off.

Maybe she should call him and— No. Too impersonal.

She could show up at his door with a pizza and— Nope. Too friend-zoney.

She could show up at his door wearing lingerie, and only lingerie…

Wrong! She owned…oh…*zero* pieces of lingerie. Pretty bras and panties were too expensive for a woman with no one to impress.

Dang it, showing up in a T-shirt and jeans wasn't fun,

spontaneous or wild. Neither was her standard after-work attire—pajamas.

What if she showed up at his door in a raincoat and a (fake) smile? As nervous as she'd be, fake was all he'd get.

Straight men responded to a woman's nakedness, right? Before her accident, Jazz had seemed to like her body. A lot.

Once inside Daniel's room, she could drop the coat, revealing her body to him. Her soft, now scarred body. In the light. All of her flaws would be spotlighted.

Nope. No way. Never. *Can't do it.* Won't *do it.*

Coward! If you want a different life, you have to *do* something different. *Be strong. Be brave.*

So, yes, she would do this.

Next problem: she owned the inn, and he was a patron. Also, they lived in a small town, and there would be talk. They would see each other tomorrow…and the next day… and the next. There would be no avoiding the one-night stand who'd seen her flaws.

And what would happen the next time he wrecked a room with a thin, successful date?

Air wheezed from her as her footsteps quickened. Back and forth. Back and forth, going from the couch she'd found discarded on a curb to the wall covered with pictures she'd taken of clouds, hail, rain, tornadoes, sunrises and sunsets.

How badly did she want to be held…to laugh with a lover? To forget the rest of the world? How badly did she want an orgasm?

No risk, no reward.

Very well. She *was* going to do this.

Dorothea hurried through a shower, repainted her nails yellow and orange—hopeful and nervous—and spritzed herself with an essential oil body spray she'd created, the mist settling in places the sun had never seen.

It was time to lady-nut up or shut up.

★ ★ ★

Daniel Porter sat at the edge of the bed. Again and again he dismantled and rebuilt his Glock 17. Before removing the magazine, he racked the slide to ensure no ammunition remained in the chamber. He lifted the upper portion of the semiautomatic, detached the recoil spring as well as the barrel. Then he put everything back together.

Rinse and repeat.

Some things you had to do over and over, until every cell in your body could perform the task on autopilot. That way, when bullets started flying, you'd react the right way—immediately—without having to check a training manual.

Sometime during hour two, he reached for his pack of smokes, only to remember he'd quit weeks ago. Every time he'd lit up, he'd seen his dad's disappointed face, heard worried words.

Gonna put yourself in an early grave, son.

He'd also replayed the day Dottie Mathis had spotted him outside, taking a drag, and wrinkled her pretty nose. Other people's opinions usually held no sway, but for some reason, her reaction had stuck with him.

My name is Dorothea.

Today she'd spoken in a soft, heartbreaking voice that had made him feel as if he'd taken a knife to the gut.

Forget her. She doesn't matter.

By hour three, his eyelids were heavy. At last he placed the gun on the nightstand and stretched out across the mattress. But as one hour bled into another, he merely tossed and turned. Though he wore a pair of boxers, nothing more, and had the air conditioner cranked to icebox, sweat soon drenched him.

Staying at the inn without a woman hadn't been one of his brightest ideas. Sex kept him distracted from the many horrors that lived inside his mind. After multiple overseas military tours, constant gunfights, car bombs, finding one friend after another blown to pieces, watching his targets collapse because he'd gotten a green light and pulled the trigger…his sanity had long since packed up and moved out.

Maybe he should ring his buds, Jude Laurent and Brock Hudson. They'd talk him off the ledge.

The two had served with him as army rangers in an elite unit known as the Ten, so they understood him in a way others never would. Like him, they'd had trouble acclimating to their lives as civilians; to help him out—and each other—the two had decided to move to Daniel's hometown. Together they had launched a new security firm: LPH Protection.

What if both men were having nights as bad as his? He'd rather die than add to their troubles.

Daniel scrubbed a clammy hand over his face. Maybe he should call Kate. She'd return for a second night of debauchery, zero hesitation.

Not just no, but hell no. To her, a second night would be a sign of commitment, no matter how clearly he stated otherwise. She'd already texted to drop hints about a possible future.

We had so much fun together, Dan. How about one more night— or two? Doesn't have to mean anything if you don't want it to…

If *he* didn't want it to mean anything, she'd said. What about her?

Whether she admitted it or not, she would assume the aberration in his routine proved she was special. And when he failed to call in the days and weeks to come, she would be hurt.

Been there, done that.

Hurting a woman wasn't his jam.

But who else could he call? He only dated women who lived in Oklahoma City, about an hour and a half away from Strawberry Valley. Preferably ice queens. The colder the woman, the more hyper-focused he became on a concrete goal: melting her resistance and setting her on fire with desire.

He'd developed a routine. Two to four weeks spent winning the woman over, distracting himself and delighting her. One night of total hedonism. Afterward, they both moved on. No harm, no foul. No tangle of emotions. No love, no pain.

He would then move on to his next challenge. His next distraction. Without one...

In the quiet of the room, he began to notice the mental chorus in the back of his mind. Muffled screams he'd heard since his first tour of duty. He pulled at hanks of his hair, but the screams only escalated.

This. This was the reason he refused to commit to a woman for more than a night. He was too messed up, his past too violent, his present too uncertain.

A man who looked at a TV remote as if it were a bomb about to detonate had no business inviting an innocent civilian into his crazy.

He'd even forgotten how to laugh.

No, not true. Since his return to Strawberry Valley, two people had defied the odds and amused him. His best friend slash devil on his shoulder Jessie Kay West...and Dottie. No, Dorothea.

Don't think— Oh, what the hell.

She'd been two grades behind him, had always kept to herself, had never caused any trouble and had never attended any parties. A "goody-goody" many had called her. Daniel remembered feeling sorry for her, a sweetheart targeted by the town bully.

Today, his reaction to her endearing shyness and unintentional insults had shocked him. Somehow she'd turned him on so fiercely he'd felt as if *years* had passed since he'd last had sex rather than a few hours. But then, everything about his most recent encounter with Dorothea had shocked him.

Upon returning from his morning run, he'd stood in the doorway of his room, watching her work. As she'd vacuumed, she'd wiggled her hips, dancing to music with a different beat than the song playing on his iPod.

Control had been beyond him—he'd hardened instantly.

He had yet to recover.

He'd noticed her appeal on several other occasions, of course. How could he not? Her eyes, once too big for her face, were now a perfect fit and the most amazing shade of green. Like shamrocks or lucky charms, framed by the thickest, blackest lashes he'd ever seen. Those eyes were an absolute showstopper. Her lips were plump and heart-shaped, a fantasy made flesh. And her body.

Daniel stopped tossing and turning and grinned up at the ceiling. He suspected she had serious curves underneath her scrubs. The way the material had tightened over her chest when she'd moved…the lushness of her ass when she'd bent over…every time he'd looked at her, he'd sworn he'd developed early onset arrhythmia.

With her eyes, lips and corkscrew curls, she reminded him of a living doll. He really wanted to play with her.

But he wouldn't. Ever. She was too warm, too sweet, and non–ice queens tended to cling after sex. Plus, she lived right here in town.

When Daniel first struck up a friendship with Jessie Kay, his father had expressed hope for a Christmas wedding and grandkids soon after. The moment Daniel had broken the news—no wedding, no kids, they were just friends—Virgil teared up.

Lesson learned. When it came to Strawberry Valley girls, Virgil would always think long-term, and he would always be disappointed when the relationship ended. Stress wasn't good for his ticker. He'd had a heart attack last year and needed absolute calm to facilitate a full recovery. Daniel loved the old grump with every fiber of his being, wanted him around as long as possible.

Came back to care for him. Not going to make things worse.

And yet, in a moment of absolute insanity, Daniel had entertained a desire to laugh again, to feel normal for once, which was why he'd asked Dorothea to stay for coffee. Thank the good Lord she'd turned him down.

Bang, bang, bang!

Daniel palmed his semiautomatic and plunged to the floor to use the bed as a shield. As a bead of sweat rolled into his eye, his finger twitched on the trigger. The screams in his head were drowned out by the sound of his thundering heartbeat.

Bang, bang!

He muttered a curse. The door. Someone was knocking on the door.

Disgusted with himself, he glanced at the clock on the nightstand—1:08 a.m.

He frowned. As he stood, his dog tags clinked against his mother's locket, the one he'd worn since her death. He pulled on the wrinkled, ripped jeans he'd tossed earlier and anchored his gun against his lower back.

Forgoing the peephole, he looked through the crack in the window curtains. His gaze landed on a dark, wild mass of corkscrew curls, and his frown deepened. Only one woman in town had hair like that, every strand made for tangling in a man's fists.

Concern overshadowed a fresh surge of desire as he threw open the door. Hinges squeaked, and Dorothea paled. But a fragrant cloud of lavender enveloped him, and his head fogged; desire suddenly overshadowed concern.

Down, boy.

She met his gaze for a split second, then ducked her head and wrung her hands. Before, freckles had covered her face.

Now a thick layer of makeup hid them. Why would she *ever* want to disguise them? He liked those little dots, and sometimes imagined—

Nothing.

"Is something wrong?" On alert, he scanned left…right… The hallway was empty, no signs of danger.

As many times as he'd stayed at the inn, Dorothea had only ever spoken to him while cleaning his room. Which had always prompted his early-morning departures. There'd been no reason to grapple with temptation.

"I'm fine," she said, and gulped. Her shallow inhalations came a little too quickly, and her cheeks grew chalk white. "Super fine."

How was her tone shrill and breathy at the same time?

He relaxed his battle stance, though his confusion remained. "Why are you here?"

"I…uh… Do you need more towels?"

"Towels?" His gaze roamed over the rest of her, as if drawn by an invisible force—disappointment struck. She wore a bulky, ankle-length raincoat, hiding the body underneath. Had a storm rolled in? He listened but heard no claps of thunder. "No, thank you. I'm good."

"Okay." She licked her porn-star lips and toyed with the tie around her waist. "Yes, I'll have coffee with you."

Coffee? "Now?"

A defiant nod, those corkscrew curls bouncing.

He barked out a laugh, surprised, amazed and delighted by her all over again. "What's really going on, Dorothea?"

Her eyes widened. "My name. You remembered." When he stared at her, expectant, she cleared her throat. "Right. The reason I'm here. I just… I wanted to talk to you." The color returned to her cheeks, a sexy blush spilling over her skin. "May I come in? Please. Before someone sees me."

Mistake. That blush gave a man all kinds of ideas.

Besides, what could Miss Mathis have to say to him? He ran through a mental checklist of possible problems. His bill—nope, already paid in full. His father's health—nope, Daniel would have been called directly.

If he wanted answers, he'd have to deal with Dorothea… alone…with a bed nearby…

Swallowing a curse, he stepped aside.

She rushed past him as if her feet were on fire, the scent of lavender strengthening. His mouth watered.

I could eat her up.

But he wouldn't. Wouldn't even take a nibble.

"Shut the door. Please," she said, a tremor in her voice.

He hesitated but ultimately obeyed. "Would you like a beer while the coffee brews?"

"Yes, please." She spotted the six-pack he'd brought with him, claimed one of the bottles and popped the cap.

He watched with fascination as she drained the contents.

She wiped her mouth with the back of her wrist and belched softly into her fist. "Thanks. I needed that."

He tried not to smile as he grabbed the pot. "Let's get you that coffee."

"No worries. I'm not thirsty." She placed the empty bottle on the dresser. Her gaze darted around the room, a little wild, a lot nervous. She began to pace in front of him. She wasn't wearing shoes, revealing toenails painted yellow and orange, like her fingernails.

More curious by the second, he eased onto the edge of the bed. "Tell me what's going on."

"All right." Her tongue slipped over her lips, moistening both the upper and lower, and the fly of his jeans tightened. In an effort to keep his hands to himself, he fisted the comforter. "I can't really tell you. I have to show you."

"Show me, then." *And leave.* She had to leave. Soon.

"Yes," she croaked. Her trembling worsened as she untied the raincoat...

The material fell to the floor.

Daniel's heart stopped beating. His brain short-circuited. Dorothea Mathis was gloriously, wonderfully naked; she had more curves than he'd suspected, generous curves, *gorgeous* curves.

Was he drooling? He might be drooling.

She wasn't a living doll, he decided, but a 1950s pinup. *Lead me not into temptation...* She had the kind of body other women abhorred but men utterly adored. *He* adored. To his shock, and delight, a vine with thorns and holly was etched around the outside of one breast, ending in a pink rosebud just over her heart.

He wanted to touch. He *needed* to touch.

A moment of rational thought intruded. Strawberry Valley girls were off-limits...his dad...disappointment... But...

Dorothea's soft, lush curves *deserved* to be touched. And licked. The freckles on her body were visible, the perfect treasure map for his tongue.

I'll start up top and work my way down. Slowly.

She had a handful of scars on her abdomen and thighs, beautiful badges of strength and survival. More paths for his tongue to follow.

As he studied her, drinking her in, one of her arms draped over her breasts, shielding them from his view. With her free hand, she covered the apex of her thighs and, no shit, he almost whimpered. Such bounty should *never* be covered.

"I want...to sleep with you," she stammered. "One time. Only one time. Afterward, I don't want to speak with you about it. Or about anything. We'll avoid each other for the rest of our lives."

One night of no-strings sex? Yes, please. He wanted her. Here. Now.

For hours and hours…

No. No, no, no. If he slept with the only maid at the only inn in town, he'd have to stay in the city with all future dates, over an hour away from his dad. What if Virgil had another heart attack?

Daniel leaped off the bed to swipe up the raincoat. A darker blush stained Dorothea's cheeks…and spread…and though he wanted to watch the color deepen, he fit the material around her shoulders.

"You…you don't want me." Horror contorted her features as she spun and raced to the door.

His reflexes were well honed; they had to be. They were the only reason he hadn't come home from his tours of duty in a box. Before she could exit, he raced behind her and flattened his hands on the door frame to keep her inside the room.

"Don't run," he croaked. "I like the chase."

Tremors rubbed her against him. "So…you want me?"

Do. Not. Answer. "I'm in a state of shock." And awe.

He battled an insane urge to trace his nose along her nape… to inhale the lavender scent of her skin…to taste every inch of her. The heat she projected stroked him, sensitizing already desperate nerve endings.

The mask of humanity he'd managed to don before reentering society began to chip.

Off-kilter, he backed away from her. She remained in place, clutching the lapels of her coat.

"Look at me," Daniel commanded softly.

After an eternity-long hesitation, she turned. Her gaze remained on his feet. Which was probably a good thing. Those shamrock eyes might have been his undoing.

"Why me, Dorothea?" She'd shown no interest in him before. "Why now?"

She chewed on her bottom lip and said, "Right now I don't really know. You talk too much."

Most people complained he didn't talk enough. But then, Dorothea wasn't here to get to know him. And he wasn't upset about that—really. He hadn't wanted to get to know any of his recent dates.

"You didn't answer my questions," he said.

"So?" The coat gaped just enough to reveal a swell of delectable cleavage as she shifted from one foot to the other. "Are we going to do this or not?"

Yes!

No! Momentary pleasure, lifelong complications. "I—"

"Oh my gosh. You actually hesitated," she squeaked. "There's a naked girl right in front of you, and you have to think about sleeping with her."

"You aren't my usual type." He couldn't get involved with a Strawberry Valley girl and risk hurting his dad. No matter how badly he wanted the girl in question.

She flinched, clearly misunderstanding his meaning.

"I prefer city girls, the ones I have to chase," he added. Which only made her flinch again. Okay, what the hell was wrong with him?

Tears welled in her eyes, clinging to her wealth of black lashes—gutting him. When Harlow Glass had tortured Dorothea in the school hallways, her cheeks had burned bright red but her eyes had remained dry.

I hurt her worse than a bully.

"Dorothea," he said, stepping toward her.

"No!" She held out her arm to ward him off. "I'm not stick thin or sophisticated. I'm too easy, and you're not into pity screwing. Trust me, I get it." She spun once more, tore open the door and rushed into the hall.

This time, he let her go. Even though his senses devolved into hunt mode, just as he'd expected, the compulsion to go after her nearly overwhelming him.

Resist!

What if, when he caught her—and he *would*—he didn't carry her back to his room but took what she'd offered, wherever they happened to be?

Biting his tongue until he tasted blood, he kicked the door shut.

Silence greeted him. He waited for the past to resurface, but thoughts of Dorothea drowned out the screams. Her little pink nipples had puckered in the cold, eager for his mouth. A dark thatch of curls had shielded the portal to paradise. Her legs had been toned but soft, long enough to wrap around him and strong enough to hold on to him until the end of the ride.

Excitement lingered, growing more powerful by the second, and curiosity held him in a vise grip. The Dorothea he knew would never show up at a man's door naked, requesting sex.

Maybe he didn't actually know her. Maybe he should learn more about her. The more he learned, the less intrigued he'd be. He could forget this night had ever happened.

He snatched his cell from the nightstand and dialed Jude, LPH's tech expert.

Jude answered after the first ring, proving he hadn't been sleeping, either. "What?"

Good ole Jude. His friend had no tolerance for bull, or pleasantries. "Brusque" had become his only setting. And Daniel understood. Jude had lost the bottom half of his left leg in battle. A major blow, no doubt about it. But the worst was yet to come. During his recovery, his wife and twin daughters had been killed by a drunk driver.

The loss of his leg had devastated him. The loss of his family had changed him. He no longer laughed or smiled; he was like Daniel, only much worse.

"Do me a favor and find out everything you can about Dorothea Mathis. She's a Strawberry Valley resident. Owns the Strawberry Inn."

The faint *click-clack* of typing registered, as if the guy had already been seated in front of his wall of computers. "Who's the client, and how soon does he—she?—want the report?"

"I'm the client, and I'd like the report ASAP."

The typing stopped. "So this is personal," Jude said with no inflection of emotion. "That's new."

"Extenuating circumstances," he muttered.

"She do you wrong?"

I'm not stick thin or sophisticated. I'm too easy, and you're not into pity screwing. Trust me, I get it.

"The opposite," he said.

Another pause. "Do you want to know the names of the men she's slept with? Or just a list of any criminal acts she might have committed?"

He snorted. "If she's gotten so much as a parking ticket, I'll be shocked."

"So she's a good girl."

"I don't know what she is," he admitted. Those corkscrew curls...pure innocence. Those heart-shaped lips...pure decadence. Those soft curves...*mine, all mine.*

"Tell Brock this is a hands-off situation," he said before the words had time to process.

What the hell was wrong with him?

Brock was the privileged rich boy who'd grown up ignored by his parents. He was covered in tatts and piercings and tended to avoid girls who reminded him of the debutants he'd been expected to marry. He preferred the wild ones... those willing to proposition a man.

"Warning received," Jude said. "Dorothea Mathis belongs to you."

He ground his teeth. "You are seriously irritating, you know that?"

"Yes, and that's one of my better qualities."

True. "Just get me the details." Those lips...those curves... "And make it fast."

CHAPTER THREE

For three days, Dorothea sported blue nails—for sadness— as she struggled to rebuild her decimated self-esteem with healthy living. She jogged an extra five miles every evening, the increase in oxygen making her feel stronger. Even smarter! She avoided sugar with the same indomitable willpower she used to tune out her sister's insults, improving her mood. And last but not least, she worked from sunup to sundown, taking pride in a job well done.

Why should she care whether or not Daniel Porter desired her? He was shallow, and she had depth. She had shucked off her fears and gone after what she'd wanted, while he had clung to old habits. *No regrets!*

To be honest, she was glad he'd turned her down. She'd never had a one-night stand, had only suspected she would despise running into Daniel after they'd hooked up. Now she knew beyond a doubt.

They hadn't kissed or touched, but he'd seen her naked, and that was plenty bad enough.

After she finished cleaning her last room of the day, she strode to her own, ready to gather her gear and run another five miles. No, she would run an extra *ten* miles tonight. The more she sweat, the more toxins she would expel and the better she would feel.

When she reached the top of the stairs, she spotted Daniel in front of her door and froze. He was here. Why the heck was he here?

The horror of her imagination had failed to do this first sighting justice.

"Open up," he said, not yet realizing she stood behind him. "We need to talk."

Talk? Face-to-face? *Now?*

No. Not now, not ever. He looked too good. Good enough to devour. His dark hair stuck out in sexy spikes, and the thick stubble on his jaw suggested he hadn't shaved since their last interaction. A leather band covered each of his wrists, and his black tee hugged his muscular biceps, the cotton stretched to the max. Ripped jeans and steel-toed boots only added to his appeal.

Meanwhile, she wore scrubs stained from a hard day's work. There wasn't a drop of makeup on her face, and several wayward curls had escaped the messy bun on the crown of her head.

Oh, what the heck. An encounter had to happen sooner or later. They lived in the same small town, for goodness' sake. Why not get his apology over with? And that was why he was here, wasn't it? To apologize for his boorish behavior. So she looked her worst. So what? She would be checking a worry off her ever-growing list.

Brave and strong, she took a step forward.

Her knees almost buckled as the look of horror he'd donned when she'd dropped her raincoat constantly refreshed in her mind.

Nope. Can't do this.

Heart karate-kicking her ribs, she tiptoed down the steps.

At the bottom, she leaped into a full-blown sprint, racing down the hall and through the lobby, the outdated decor making her cringe. The peeling wallpaper boasted strawberry vines that had faded just enough to look like dangling testicles. Anything wooden had nicks. Only the chandeliers were new, the gorgeous ruby and emerald crystals shaped to resemble wild strawberries. A Christmas gift from Jessie Kay West for hosting a last-minute party.

Holly sat behind the reception desk and called her name. Dorothea skidded to a stop, willing to risk anything—even a confrontation with Daniel—to help her sister.

"Is something wrong?"

"Just wanted you to know I'm taking tomorrow off," Holly said.

The good times never stopped. "Mrs. Hathaway has a doctor appointment in the morning, so I need you here." Tomorrow was parent-teacher conference day at Strawberry Valley High. For once, her sister could work an entire day, allowing Dorothea to attend in their mother's place. "Without you, I'll have to close the inn."

"How cute." Holly popped a bubble as she stared down at her phone, her fingers dancing over the keyboard. "You thought I was asking for permission."

"This is a family business, Halls. We—"

"Aren't a family. We're strangers."

Only five words, but they utterly *shredded* Dorothea. She whispered, "I want to be more. I'm *striving* to be more."

"Well, you can quit that like you quit Strawberry Valley, college and your marriage. As soon as I graduate, I'm gone, and I'm not ever coming back."

Dorothea swallowed a cry of despair, a countdown clock appearing in the back of her mind. Three months. She had three months to win her sister…or she would lose her forever.

"I love you, Holly. I'll always love you."

Her sister swiveled the chair in the opposite direction. Message received. The conversation had officially ended.

"However you feel about me," she persisted, a lump growing in her throat, "you still have to work tomorrow."

Silence. Thick, oppressive silence.

Disheartened, Dorothea strode outside. The bell over the door tinkled, and cool air embraced her. She'd go…somewhere. She was New Dorothea, after all, and she would do something other than wallow.

She made her way to the parking lot across the street. Her car keys—

Were still in her room. Crap! She switched direction, heading for the town square. What she'd do when she got there, she had no idea. Every shop had already closed for the night.

The scent of wild strawberries wafted from the fields that surrounded the entire town, resurrecting what should have been happy memories. As a child, she'd run through those fields, laughing merrily, untouched by troubles as her dad gave chase.

He'd loved her then.

At least, she'd *thought* he loved her. If he had felt the smallest bit of affection for her, he would have stayed in contact after he'd divorced Carol.

For a long time, Dorothea had blamed herself for his abandonment. She'd wondered if her appearance or weight had disappointed him. But then, she used to blame herself for Jazz's infidelity, too. If only she'd worked harder to bring in more money, fixed her hair a different way, lost more weight, tried harder in bed, cooked better, offered more stimulating conversation, something, anything, she would have been enough.

But the fault didn't rest on her shoulders. Even though she was the one constant in all her failed relationships.

Fighting a wave of depression, she focused on the hodge-podge charm of her surroundings. Four-bulb lampposts illuminated historic buildings intermixed with modern ones. While the inn possessed the elegance of an antebellum structure, the local grocery store was housed in a metal warehouse with a tin roof. Across the street, a row of box-shaped homes contained a hardware store, a "gourmet" café, an antiques store and a dry cleaner. The theater had a copper awning, and gargoyles perched along a balcony.

A whitewashed bungalow was home to Rhinestone Cowgirl, the town's premier jewelry store. Around the corner was Lintz Auto Shop. Just down the street was Strawberry Valley Community Church, a white stone chapel with massive stained-glass windows.

Out of habit, her gaze lifted to the sky. No stars in sight, the bright pinpricks of lights obscured by cirrostratus clouds. A whitish veil with a smooth sheetlike appearance.

"Dorothea!"

A car idled beside her, she realized, Lyndie Scott behind the wheel.

Warm relief washed through her. "Hey, you. What are you doing out so late?"

The strawberry blonde was as beautiful as ever with wide amber eyes and flawless porcelain skin, but…she looked sad. She always looked sad, even when smiling. At the age of twenty-one, Lyndie had married the police chief of Blueberry Hill. By twenty-three, she had become a widow.

Dorothea had only seen pictures of her friend with Chief Carrington; their relationship had taken place during her years away. She hoped they had loved each other deeply, madly, the way Dorothea had always yearned to be loved, but she suspected the couple had had their fair share of problems. Otherwise Lyndie would have kept her married name? Maybe?

"I actually came by the inn a few hours ago." Lyndie gazed at her with concern. "Are you all right? Your sister said you didn't want to be disturbed because you had a case of—" she glanced over her shoulder and whispered "—raging diarrhea."

Dorothea nearly choked on her tongue. "Holly lied." What else had the girl told the townspeople? Chronic flatulence? Hemorrhoids and anal fissures? "I promise I'm perfectly healthy."

Lyndie pressed her lips together only to burst into laughter. "I'm sorry! I am. But oh, wow, your sister is a character."

"Yeah, a character in a horror novel." Though Dorothea had done a lousy job of keeping up with her dear friends while living in the city—she'd worked too much and foolishly poured all her free time into Jazz—the two had called and texted her often. Tidbits here and there about what they were up to, or inside jokes about their high school days. For instance, the time they created the ten commitments for any relationship, even though they were invisible to boys.

A boy shalt not.

Lie to anyone, ever, not even to flatter;

Cheat with so much as a look;

Steal even when desperate;

Harm others in any way;

Make excuses for bad behavior.

He shalt:

Compliment when merited;

Help when needed;

Treat others with kindness, always;

Consult you when making big decisions;

Do his best, not just what's good enough.

Looking back, she comprehended Lyndie and Ryanne had seen through Jazz's charisma to the slimeball within. By reminding her oh, so subtly of the list, they'd hoped *she* would see the truth.

She had, only far too late.

"Ryanne has the night off," Lyndie said, "and she's fixin'

me breakfast for dinner. Of course, by 'me' I mean 'us.' You're coming, and I won't take no for an answer."

A fun, spontaneous night with friends? "You don't have to drag me kicking and screaming. I'm in!" She climbed into the passenger seat and buckled up.

They drove to the Scratching Post a few miles outside of town, once owned and operated by Ryanne's fourth step-dad, Earl.

Her mother—Selma Martinez-Wade-Lewis-Scott-Hernandez-Montgomery—had married Earl after divorcing Lyndie's father for reasons neither girl had ever discussed with Dorothea. In fact, both girls tended to act cagey whenever the subject came up, so she'd stopped asking questions. Eventually she'd stopped feeling hurt by the secrecy, too.

Whatever had happened, the two had obviously been hurt deeply. Dorothea flattened her palm over her tattoo. Some hurts worsened when they were discussed, never able to heal.

Ryanne lived directly above the bar. She'd moved in a couple years ago to take care of Earl, who'd later died of cancer.

What seemed to be millions of cars littered the parking lot. Inside the smoky, two-story warehouse, crowds of people stretched wall-to-wall. A few months ago, Ryanne had begun selling a house-made fruit cocktail moonshine; now patrons came to the Scratching Post in droves.

Directly behind the counter, a narrow hallway led to offices as well as a secret stairwell guarded by a weathered door and some kind of weird-looking digital lock. Lyndie punched in the code known to very few people, and together they climbed to the top, where they found another lock. This time, Lyndie knocked.

When you lived above a bar, you had to take precautions.

"Come in," Ryanne called from inside.

Lyndie punched in a second code and entered the apartment, Dorothea at her heels. The sound of clanging pots and pans drew them across the great room and into a spacious, industrial kitchen with state-of-the-art appliances, everything chrome or stainless steel.

The scent of maple and bacon saturated the air, and her mouth watered. Her stomach growled.

The gorgeous Ryanne bustled from stove to sink. She had long, dark hair, even darker eyes and flawless golden-brown skin. In a pink tank top and skinny jeans, her hourglass figure was on perfect display.

A cloud of steam rose from the pan, painting her in a dreamy haze as she looked up and smiled in welcome. "Good girl, Lyndie. You managed to corral us a wild filly."

Me? Wild?

"Yes, ma'am, I surely did." Lyndie patted herself on the back. "I didn't even have to hog-tie her."

Dorothea loved seeing the reserved redhead come out of her shell. "I'm not that bad," she said, only to sigh. "Okay, I'm worse. Sorry."

"Hey. Don't worry about it. We understand." Lyndie gave one of Dorothea's fallen curls a tug. "Your heart is still in the process of mending."

She offered a half smile, which was all she could currently manage. Lyndie and Ryanne knew the bare bones about her past: she'd gotten married and divorced after Jazz cheated on her. The pair had no idea she'd discovered the affair only because Jazz's girlfriend had wanted Dorothea out of the picture. They had no idea she'd walked in on the couple mid-act and had run out of the apartment in horror—only to fall down a flight of stairs.

And lose her baby.

A knot tangled in her throat. *Don't think about the baby.*

Too late. The memories had been banging on the door of her mind, waiting for a chance to overtake her. She'd been five months pregnant, but because of a wonky cycle and a few extra pounds, she had only just found out.

Falling down the stairs had caused her to deliver her precious baby prematurely. Though the little girl was already dead, she'd had to give her a name. She'd chosen Rose. Rose Holly Connors.

Rose…dead…beyond hope.

A pang in her chest. Dorothea flattened a hand over the tattoo on her breast. She would forever carry her baby close to her heart.

If Rose had survived, she might be walking by now. *Pang.* If she'd gone to term, she might be crawling. *PANG.*

"Are you sure you're all right?" Lyndie asked her.

"Excuse me. I need to use the bathroom." Fighting tears, Dorothea shut herself inside the small enclosure. After splashing cold water on her face, she breathed in and out with purpose until her heart rate calmed and the pangs subsided.

By the time she rejoined her friends, she had her wayward thoughts back under lock and key.

Lyndie smiled at her before settling on a chair behind the counter. "You and me, Dorothea, we're the first two members of the very exclusive Broken Hearts Club. Ryanne, honey, you need to pick a man, marry him, then have your heart broken by losing him. Then you can join us."

Ryanne munched on a crunchy piece of bacon. "Sounds like a perfectly sane reason to begin and end a marriage. Consider me on board."

Dorothea sat next to Lyndie and raised her hand, as if she were a student eager to give an answer. "Oh! Oh! I get to be your maid of honor, and I get first pick at the groomsmen."

Her dark eyes sparkled. "Sorry, *chica*, but me and my imaginary guy are eloping. There's no way I'm doing the white dress and flowers thing." She shuddered with distaste. "I'm saving my money to travel the world and— Wait a sec. Did you say you want to do a groomsman?"

"Ohhh. Good catch." Lyndie bumped Dorothea's shoulder. "Spill!"

"Okay, okay, but first…" She extended her hand to shake. "Let me introduce you to New Dorothea. I'm fun, spontaneous and wild, and I plan to hook me a man-fish. A really hot one!" Daniel had turned her down, yes, but there were other man-fish in the Testosterone Sea. "My first requirement is easy. He has to live in the city."

No one else in Strawberry Valley would see her naked. That way, she could walk the streets with her head held high rather than cringing in embarrassment.

"Hook you a—" Ryanne burst out laughing, and Lyndie grinned.

The sight of her friends' amusement warmed Dorothea. As much as she'd missed the town, she'd missed this. No, she'd missed this more. Since her return, she'd mostly stayed cooped up inside the inn, too afraid to live, blaming her shattered relationship with Holly and her failure with Jazz. No more!

"You got anyone in particular in mind?" Ryanne asked.

Her cheeks flamed with heat. "Not yet." Next time, she would pick a *sure thing*. For a relationship, not just sex. She would prove to Holly—and herself!—that men could stick around for the long haul.

Lyndie leaned over to snag a piece of bacon. "How can we help?"

"I don't know. Point out the good ones, I guess?" So far, her bait had only hooked a shark.

"Whoa." Ryanne spread her arms. "You're saying good guys aren't just a myth, like assassin werewolves and millionaire vampires?"

Lyndie snorted. This time, Dorothea was the one to laugh.

Ryanne had always loved video games involving fantastical nocturnal creatures.

"Good can be a mask for evil," Lyndie said when Dorothea sobered. "If you find an honorable man—hello, oxymoron—never let go."

"I won't have to worry about hanging on to him," Dorothea replied. "Because he'll be too busy clinging to me!"

Ryanne wiggled her brows before pouring a glass of orange juice. "I bet there will be plenty of hotties at the spring festival next month. You guys going? Way I hear it, Daniel Porter's company is overseeing security, and Jase Hollister, Beck Ockley and Lincoln West are bringing friends to run the kissing booth."

Beck Ockley, the husband of Harlow Glass.

He's so rich, her mom once said, *he buys a new boat whenever he gets the old one wet. Too bad he's as dumb as a box of rocks. Only a fool would choose to spend the rest of his life with a woman like Harlow.*

Carol refused to believe Harlow had changed. "Maybe," Dorothea finally said. Not to see Daniel in action, of course, but to check out that kissing booth. "Scratch that. Yes." She nodded. "I'm going, and you guys are, too."

Lyndie's nod held a scootch less enthusiasm. "Fine. I'll be your incompetent wingwoman."

"Bet I'll be more incompetent than you." Ryanne grabbed a carton of milk and a stick of butter from the fridge and asked Dorothea, "How do you want your eggs?"

Mimicking a meme she'd read earlier, she said, "In a cake, please." She'd run five miles this morning, and she had internal wounds in need of soothing. Why not indulge her sweet tooth for once?

Ryanne snickered. "I have a chocolate ice-cream cake in the freezer."

"You've got a chocolate ice-cream cake on the premises?"

Lyndie jumped to her feet and basically shoved Ryanne out of the way mid-race to the freezer. "Gimme!"

Ryanne gathered three spoons. "I've never seen this chocolate-addicted side of you, Scott."

"I usually only unleash her in private. But the fact that I'm willing to share with you should make you feel special."

As soon as Lyndie placed the dessert on the counter, Dorothea crumbled the maple-glazed bacon over the top.

"Hey! What—" Lyndie began at the same time Ryanne said, "You can't—"

"Trust me," Dorothea interjected. "You're about to weep with rapture. Bacon makes everything better, even cake."

They dug in and moaned with bliss, Dorothea a little more heartily than the others. The salty-sugary treat went straight to her head in a dizzying, delicious rush.

"Who knew pigs in cream would rock so hard?" Ryanne said.

"I did." Control nowhere to be found, Dorothea shoveled in another bite. "This is heaven on Earth."

"Agreed." The familiar voice startled—and horrified—her.

Heart thundering in her chest, she jumped to her feet. "Daniel." Daniel Porter. Here. "I don't understand."

A glaring Ryanne extended her spoon as if it were a weapon. "How did you get in?"

"I knocked. You didn't answer, but I heard voices and knew you were back here." He shrugged, unabashed. "Your lock is a joke, by the way."

"You actually dismantled—" Dorothea shook her head. "But why?"

He ignored her, saying to Ryanne, "I've already called the man who will replace the outdated lock with something even I can't bypass. He's tall, blond and has blue eyes. His name is Jude. Please don't hurt him with your deadly spoon."

"I don't care what he looks like, or what his name is. If

he shows up, he'll be trespassing, just like you, and he'll get locked up. I'm calling the…cops," Ryanne finished lamely, shooting Lyndie an apologetic look.

Lyndie stared down at her wringing hands, her cheeks now chalk white. Fear radiated from her.

Fear? Just how bad had things been with Chief Carrington?

"Don't worry, I'm leaving." Daniel's intense, amber gaze finally locked on Dorothea. "But first I'd like to speak with you."

The air in her lungs turned to steam and evaporated; she began to wheeze, the urge to both fight and flee screwing with her head. "No, thank you? I mean, no. I'm having a girls' night." Translation: leave! *Please.*

He crossed his arms over his chest. "One way or another, I'm picking up where our last conversation ended. You sure you want to have an audience for that?"

He wouldn't dare!

Who was she kidding? He would probably dare in a heartbeat.

"You guys had a *conversation*?" Ryanne lowered her spoon and arched a brow at Dorothea. "I'd love to hear the main topic…or were you guys too busy grunting to use actual words?"

Lyndie's eyes widened like saucers. "Is he the *raging diarrhea* you were having?"

Kill me. Kill me now. Could this night get any worse?

She'd known a meeting had to happen sooner or later. Postponing it had been a mistake. If she allowed Daniel to say his piece now, she could say goodbye. Forever.

"Fine. If you'll follow me…" Chin high, the rest of her trembling, she strode past him.

Heat pulsed from him as he followed her. Goose bumps broke out over her skin.

Once she reached the front door, hopefully out of the others' hearing range, she faced him. Crap! He was so close she could have tripped over his shadow.

Bones threatening to melt, she moved two steps back. "How did you find me?"

"How did you know I was looking for you?" he countered. "Did you, perhaps, see me at your door and run?"

"I... Well..." She licked her lips. His hooded gaze followed the motion of her tongue, and the heat he was throwing off cranked up about a thousand degrees. In the next instant, he was looking at her as no man ever had. Not even her ex-husband. As if she were a mystery he had to solve. A dessert he wanted to eat. A treasure he expected to claim.

Her hands fisted. Someone needed to tell him a look like that made promises he couldn't keep. And dang it, she hated that look almost as much as she loved it. It meant nothing to him but everything to her.

"Dorothea," he prompted, "did you run away from me?"

Lying would lead to complications. How could she be expected to keep falsehoods straight when she could barely remember her name in this man's presence? Still, there was no way she would admit to her cowardice.

"What I did or didn't do doesn't matter." As she spoke, she waved her hands through the air to punctuate each word. A bad habit she'd fought most of her life, whenever her emotions got the better of her. "Tell me why you're here."

He closed what little distance separated them, and she backed up another step, then another, determined to remain at arm's length. It wasn't long before she smacked into a wall, and crap, he just kept coming until they were only a whisper apart.

A dark, dangerous whisper...

Her tremors redoubled as she breathed him in. He smelled like her favorite mix of essential oils: sandalwood, lavender and vanilla. And there was a good reason for that. She made soap as a special gift for the inn's guests. A mistake, she realized now. She wanted to breathe him in forever.

"I'm here for you." He wrapped his fingers around her wrist and brought her hand to his mouth. Out came his tongue, licking away a smear of chocolate. "I want to take you back to the inn and give you that orgasm you asked for—plus a couple more."

What! *He's here to* pleasure *me?*

"I didn't… I mean…" Wet heat branded her core. "You're too late? Stop tasting me?" Questions? Really?

"Mmm. You sure you want me to stop?" His voice deepened to a sensual purr. "Let me assuage my curiosity and find out if you're this sweet all over. Let me see the exquisite body that haunts my dreams."

The—exquisite—body in question experienced a thousand different reactions at once, namely tingling skin, hardening nipples and a quivering belly. Ohhhh! Her blood began to sizzle in her veins.

Daniel Porter had *not* just implied he wanted to go down on her…right? She was mistaken?

"I don't understand what's happening," she said.

"Tell me you still want one night with me." He kissed her knuckles, leaving a white-hot ember behind. "This time my answer will be yes."

CHAPTER FOUR

Having braved enemy territory in the bright light of day and in the dark of night, Daniel had learned to recognize the signs of impending danger.

Dorothea was stiff as a board, her hands balled into fists. Tension crackled from her.

Incoming!

She beat at his chest. "You…you…prick! Three days ago, I wasn't worth a pity screw, and now that you're desperate for sex, you decide to turn on the charm, expecting me to thank you for the scraps you toss my way?"

He took a moment to admire the pale blue paint on her nails. Adorable.

He had a feeling he would like her nails even if they were puke green or bowel-movement brown.

Ever since she'd flashed him, he'd been *turned on*, unable to turn off.

Earlier today he'd walked past the inn. Through the window he'd seen her leaning over the reception desk, her pants pulled tight over her ass, and his decision to avoid her had crashed and burned. He would have paid any price to stand behind her, rub against her and hear her purr with satisfaction.

Throughout the rest of the day, his desire for her had only grown.

Time had had the opposite effect on her.

"I'm sorry, Dorothea. I *never* thought of you as a pity screw, as you put it. You misunderstood, and the blame is mine. First, when I said you aren't my usual type, I meant you are a Strawberry Valley girl. I've avoided locals ever since my dad learned about my friendship with Jessie Kay and started planning our wedding. I won't disappoint him again. Second, I'm not desperate for sex right now. I'm desperate for *you*. Since you came to my room, I've done nothing but fantasize about your beautiful curves."

Her shamrock eyes went wide and her breathing quickened, but she said nothing.

The past three days had been at times heaven and at others hell. He hadn't slept, but he hadn't tossed and turned as he usually did, either. Again and again, his mind had returned to Dorothea Mathis. To her incomparable body and the freckles he wanted to lick. To the eroticism of her movements. To her ability to make him laugh.

Yes, miracle of miracles, she'd made him laugh. But he hadn't returned the favor. No, he'd done the opposite.

He *needed* to return the favor.

"To be blunt," he said, "sex is easily had. I can drive into the city and set up an assembly line of potentials in less than an hour."

It was true. No matter where you were, there were always people who craved some kind of connection, even if that connection was nothing but a mirage that lasted a single night. He would have felt sorry for the poor saps—if he hadn't been one of them.

"Dating for dummies, by Daniel Porter," she muttered.

"Step one. Don't bother getting to know the other person, just get naked and screw the first available rando you find."

Rando? "The other night I didn't hear you asking what I like to do in my spare time."

She opened her mouth, closed it, opened it again. Her shoulders stooped. "You're right. I'm sorry."

"I forgive you, Dorothea," he replied without pause. "Now it's your turn. Say, *I forgive you, Daniel, and I would love to sleep with you. I think you'll taste better than bacon.*"

Her eyes narrowed, and he tried not to smile.

Then her sweet lavender scent intensified, as if she was somehow—purposely—attempting to lure him closer, and his good humor fled.

Want her.

He planted his hands on the wall, caging her in. Lust threatened to engulf him. Well, well. He'd never enjoyed pinning a woman in place—until now. Light streamed over his shoulder to bathe her delicate features. Tonight, she'd nixed the makeup, and he could have shouted with relief.

"I'm not sure I believe your apology." She chewed on her plump bottom lip, an obvious nervous habit, and he had to swallow a groan. "If you wanted to keep your women a secret from your dad, why stay at the inn, where anyone in town could witness your...rendezvous?"

"His health is fragile. I stay close, especially at night. And I never flaunted the women. I sneaked them in and out."

She glowered at him. "I told you I wanted one night, nothing more. No one would have found out about our...whatever, especially your dad."

He glowered right back. "For all I knew, you planned to tell everyone in town the next morning."

"And you're certain I'll keep quiet now?" Her dry tone had edges so rough they could have cut the insides of his ears. "You know me better?"

"Yes." Jude's report had come in about an hour ago. The final nail in the coffin for his control.

Dorothea had been married to a weatherman who might or might not have cheated on her with a coworker. She had a grand total of zero social media pages, and no one in town or otherwise had ever posted anything about her love life.

How Daniel interpreted the info: (1) she knew how to keep her relationships private and (2) his dad would never find out if Daniel spent the night with her.

As soon as realization had struck, he'd rushed to the inn, then followed her trail to the Scratching Post. But in a moment of startling clarity, he'd understood just how deeply his rejection had hurt her. *He* wasn't adorable to *her*. He was going to have to work for her.

Game on.

"*How* do you know me better?" she demanded.

Admit he'd done a background check on her? Yeah, not gonna happen. She would rage. Well, rage more. "Maybe I had a little sense knocked into me."

"Doubtful. As you previously admitted, you like the chase, that's all, and I'm suddenly a challenge." She gestured to the door with a trembling hand. "Leave. Please."

"Leave…or stay?" He brushed the tip of his nose against hers, and she sucked in a breath. "I know which one gets *my* vote."

Her gaze locked on his mouth. He thought—hoped—desire for him was rising inside her, a tide she couldn't ignore. Then she flattened her chocolate-smeared hands on his chest and fisted his shirt to shake him.

"You're being nice to me, and I don't like it," she grated. "Stop."

"No, I don't think I will. My momma told me I could catch more flies with honey."

"First, you realize you just likened me to a fly, right? Second, why would you ever want to catch one?" Her nose wrinkled at the sides. "FYI, you can also catch flies with a dead, rotting carcass. Your own, to be exact."

A laugh brewed in the back of his throat, astounding him. Clearly Dorothea had a superpower; the ability to amuse him, even while his body *burned* for hers.

"I'd rather catch *you*," he told her, his voice going low and husky. "Say yes, and I'll spend the first hour in bed making you come over and over again, doing anything you want. *Everything* you need. The second hour, I'll make the first one look like amateur night. By the third, there's no place on your body I won't have explored—no place you won't ache for me."

"Hours?" She melted against him only to stop, blink up at him and bare her perfect pearly whites. "Look, I'm going to give you a bit of advice, okay? Most guys get lucky *after* they get to know the girl, but that isn't a good strategy for you. Your face attracts us, but your personality repels us. Stay quiet, and you'll stay lucky."

Ouch, that stung—mostly because it was accurate.

He wrapped his fingers around her wrists and caressed his thumb over her racing pulse, internal wound forgotten as he marveled. Compared to his, her bones were small and delicate. Her skin radiated pure, silken heat.

"*Am* I going to get lucky tonight?" he asked.

Her gaze remained on their hands, where they touched. "No?"

A question rather than a statement of fact. What sweet progress. "I'll take your no as a maybe."

"Don't. I—"

"Too late. Besides, if I were in the habit of giving up easily, I would have died the time I took five slugs to the chest."

She gasped. "You almost *died*?"

"Multiple times. Kiss my scars and make them better?"

Now a strangled sound left her. "I... You—" She drew

in a deep breath, slowly released it and visibly calmed. "You know what? Let's never discuss this again. Next time we see each other, let's pretend we're strangers."

"Counteroffer. Let's discuss this all night. Next time we see each other, let's pretend we're lovers and we're allergic to our clothing."

Her lips pursed. "I'm not playing games with you, Daniel."

"Not yet." He ghosted his knuckles along the curve of her jaw, relishing her softness and warmth. "But soon, I hope."

She leaned into him, realized what she'd done and batted his hand away. "Your sudden desire for me—"

"Trust me, it isn't sudden."

"—is insulting," she finished. "Wait." She shook her head, as if she needed to reset her brain and replay his words. "What?"

Why not tell her about the first time? "I remember driving past your bus stop one morning back in high school. You were watching your feet as you kicked a pebble. The rumble of my truck's engine drew your attention, and you glanced up, smiled shyly. You even blushed." Just like now, this moment. "I got hard just looking at you."

"You did?" Wonder lit her eyes, the air between them charging with electricity. Then she growled and stomped her foot. "You haven't changed. You always say the right things, building up a girl's hopes, then you crush her with disappointment."

"Always? Name one other time I've crushed your hopes." And he *had* changed. Losing loved ones had chipped away at his happiness. Killing enemy soldiers had left a stain on his soul, even though the government had sanctioned his actions.

"In school you—"

When she said no more, he prompted, "What?"

"Never mind. If you want me now," she said, "you're going to have to prove it. And I don't mean with a hard...you know."

"You know?" He snickered. "Say it. Tell me what it's called."

"You don't think I will? Fine." Up went her chin. "Penis. Penis, penis, penis."

He laughed—again—and then she laughed. Their eyes met and they both quieted. Tension mounted quickly. Lightning strikes of sensation shot through him. Perhaps her body acted as a conductor; she jolted as if she'd just been hit.

"You should go," she croaked, stepping to the side.

Leaving held no appeal, but there was a time for war, and a time for retreat. If he continued to push, he'd only orchestrate an ambush—for himself.

"This isn't over, Dorothea. We'll talk soon."

"No, I—"

He pressed a finger to her lips, saying, "Soon." Then he left the apartment before she could contradict him.

Outside, cool night air failed to temper the heat of his desire.

He was used to being turned down by ice queens. At first. In the past, he'd always loved to romance a succinct no into an enthusiastic yes. But Dorothea wasn't made of ice. She couldn't be. She smoldered. And yet he suspected turning her no into a yes would be far more satisfying—even if he'd rather have her yes now than later.

He climbed into his '79 Chevy pickup and headed into town. Twelve years ago, he and his dad rebuilt the engine. The thing guzzled gasoline like Brock guzzled beer, but it was part of his family.

Out of habit, or instinct, whatever, he parked in the lot across from the Strawberry Inn. Then he remembered he hadn't rented a room tonight. Why not jog home and burn off a little excess energy?

Couldn't hurt. He exited, popped the bones in his neck and took off.

By the halfway mark, his heart rate finally spiked for a reason other than desire or even his usual PTSD. Tension seeped from his pores, and his mind cleared of every thought but one. Since his honorable resignation from the military, he'd moved from one woman—or life raft—to another. Should he really drag Dorothea into his crazy?

He remembered how sweet the chocolate tasted on her soft skin.

Yes, he really should drag her into his crazy. Wasn't like she had to stay with him. One night wasn't a big deal. No harm, no foul. Although...

Maybe he could convince her to give him two nights? Possibly a week. An aberration from his usual MO, sure, but *she* was an aberration. Someone he'd known since childhood. He shouldn't just bang, bail and oh, well. And it wasn't like she had her hopes and dreams pinned on a commitment. The night she'd come to him, she'd asked for sex, nothing more.

A wealth of oak and hickory trees replaced the line of buildings. The tops seemed to reach the sky, shielding the golden glow of the moon. He—

Snap.

The sound of a breaking limb.

Daniel dived to the ground, at the same time reaching for his Glock. Over the years, his eyesight had grown accustomed to the dark; he could now pick up details other people missed. Though he expected to see enemy forces marching closer... he saw a dog? He—she?—hobbled out from behind a bush, spotted him and froze, utterly petrified.

He took a moment to breathe as his too-tight throat loosened. This wasn't hostile territory. No threat advanced. But someone *did* need his help.

As he stood, the dog bolted, only to whimper and stop.

Cooing in a gentle voice, hoping to soothe the animal, he closed the distance. A Chihuahua. He/she cowered and peed in the grass.

"I'm not going to hurt you, little guy…girl?" Daniel used the flashlight app on his phone. Girl. Both of her back legs were mangled but scabbed. She'd been attacked, probably days ago.

What had gotten her? Coyotes ran rampant out here. So did shit humans willing to use innocent animals as bait in a dogfight.

Rage scalded him. Another whimper; she must sense the darkness of his emotions.

Daniel breathed in, out, and forced himself to calm. He knew nothing about dogs, but he'd dealt with plenty of scared, wounded soldiers. Easing beside her, he started talking. He told her all about his day, even about Dorothea, allowing her to get used to his presence. After a while, she stopped cowering and weakly nuzzled his hand.

Right—that—second. She broke his freaking heart. How long since she'd been petted? Or fed?

His mother had been afraid of dogs, no matter their size, and he remembered one of his high school girlfriends complaining about her parents' pet. *Filthy creature*, she'd said with a sneer. *Always chews on my shoes and poops in my closet.*

Actions unhurried and measured, he picked up the dog, his grip as light as possible. She couldn't weigh more than five pounds. He decided to take her to the local vet. Dr. Vandercamp lived a few streets away from his dad.

"What's your name, little girl?" She wore no collar. "I bet it's something menacing like Killer or She-beast. You Chihuahuas are known for your tempers, right? Well, I'm going to call you Princess." Nicknames mattered. Just ask Dorothea. Nicknames built you up or tore you down.

Jude was once called Priest. While some soldiers had girlfriends in every port, he'd remained faithful to his wife. Happily so.

Brock was sometimes likened to a bulldozer. The Broc-dozer. He'd tended to mow down anything in his way.

Daniel was known as Mr. Clean. When a situation got dirty, he rushed in and cleaned up the mess.

Irony at its finest. He couldn't clean up the mess he'd made of his life.

When Daniel reached his dad's neighborhood, he quick-ened his step. The housing subdivision had three streets and a grand total of twelve homes, each centered on a one-acre plot. Some of the homes resembled barns, while others were more traditional two-story colonials.

Dr. Vandercamp lived in one of the barns. The porch light was off. To discourage visitors? Oh, well. Daniel knocked on the door. Hard.

Several minutes passed before the lights flipped on and the old man—

Nope, not the old man, but his son, Brett, who was Dan-iel's age. Right. He remembered Virgil telling him that Brett had become a vet, just like his dad, and that he'd taken over the old man's practice.

Brett wore a pink T-shirt that read "Save the Boobies," a pair of boxers and a scowl. "What do you want, Porter?"

Far from intimidated, Daniel said, "I found this little beauty a few miles back. She's injured. Do you have the tools to care for her here, or do you need to go to your office?" Subtext: Princess was getting treatment *tonight*.

Brett's gruff exterior was suddenly replaced by caring con-cern. "Poor darling. Don't you worry. I've got what I need here."

Good. "I'll pay for everything."

An-n-nd goodbye concern. "Considering you made a house call in the middle of the night, you're lucky I'm not going to make you pay double." The guy looked the little Chihua-hua over with a critical eye. "She's malnourished, and she'll need to be hooked to an IV for the rest of the night. Maybe tomorrow, too."

Daniel reluctantly handed her over, knowing she would be terrified of the new human as well as the new situation. And he was right. She peed on him.

"You're going to be okay, aren't you, sweet girl? Yes, you are. Oh, yes, you are." Brett's hazel gaze flipped up to Daniel. "I'll call you in the morning."

"You don't have my number."

"Do you really think getting it will be difficult?" The door shut in his face.

"Thank you," Daniel called.

He jogged to his dad's house. When he'd first arrived in town, the colonial had been a run-down mess. Before starting LPH, Daniel had redone the trim, replaced the roof and painted absolutely everything.

A quiet entry proved unnecessary. Jude and Brock sat in the living room, exactly where he'd left them. They spent a lot of time here, discussing work and watching Virgil whenever Daniel had to be gone for an extended period.

"Why do you reek of urine?" Jude looked him over and frowned. "Better question. Why do you have a streak of blood on your shirt?"

The guy noticed *everything*. "I found an injured dog and took her to the vet. Where's my dad?"

"In bed. Told us to use our inside voices or he'd put buckshot in our asses." Brock grinned a sinner's grin. Completely unrepentant. "Does he not know he's partially deaf and wouldn't be able to hear us if we shouted?" Of course, he shouted the question.

No bellow of warning came from Virgil's bedroom.

Daniel stalked to the kitchen, grabbed a beer and returned to the living room, falling into one of the chairs. What a day.

Beside him, Jude balanced a laptop on his thighs, his prosthetic limb propped against the coffee table. With his pale, shaggy hair, navy blue eyes and golden tan, he could have passed for a surfer—if there had been anything lighthearted about him. The right side of his face bore the same shrapnel scars Daniel possessed, though Jude's were worse; one cut through his lip, giving him a permanent scowl.

"How'd it go with your girl?" Jude asked.

My girl. Not really. "I failed worse than Brock when he tried to pick up an entire bridal party."

Brock, who occupied the other end of the couch, laughed and fluffed the cushion under his neck. He kept his jet-black hair cut close to his scalp and, no matter how often he shaved, always sported a five-o'clock shadow. His eyes were so pale a green they sometimes appeared neon.

"Why are you grumbling about a rejection?" the guy asked. "You're no longer on the sidelines. You're now in the game."

Next time we see each other, let's pretend we're strangers.

Daniel drained half the beer. "Her defense might be stronger than my offense."

"Gotta admit," Jude said, casting the beer a death glare. "She's not your usual type."

The glare, Daniel understood. A drunken frat boy was the one who'd killed his family. The idiot had driven one hundred miles per hour down an overpass at night and slammed into Constance Laurent's minivan.

But Daniel wasn't a frat boy, and he wanted to help his friend get past his past, not coddle him.

He drained the rest of the beer and said, "I know she's not my usual type. She's better." Sexier, with a fiercer temper.

"Dude. If you're this enamored of her after...what?" Brock spread his arms. "Two conversations with her? You're in trouble. Take it from me. I've been divorced twice—"

"From the same woman," Daniel interjected.

"Still counts. Anyway. The three of us, we are high maintenance, no doubt about it, and we're never going to make a romantic relationship work long-term until we get our heads screwed on properly."

"I have no interest in making a romantic relationship work long-term," Jude grumbled.

Grumble was all he did anymore. But then, he wasn't living; he was surviving.

Daniel had been doing the same, hadn't he? Moving from girl to girl. He sighed. "You implying *my* head is on crooked?"

Brock gave him a pitying look. "My friend, I'm flat-out telling you. Your head is only hanging on by a thread."

Maybe, maybe not. But probably. Funny thing, though. He'd never been more certain about a woman. He wanted Dorothea in his bed, but he also wanted to talk with her, to laugh with her...

Unfortunately, he had a feeling he would do almost any thing to get what he wanted. Consequences be damned. Which proved Brock's claim. Daniel's head *was* hanging on by a thread.

But no matter. He wasn't a freaking mansel in distress, waiting for his white knightress to come and save him.

He'd have fun with Dorothea, be distracted by the chase. If she succumbed, great. If not, no big deal. One way or another, he would move on. As always.

CHAPTER FIVE

Huffing and puffing, Dorothea increased her speed for the final mile of her morning run. She'd decided to go ten miles rather than her usual five, hoping to energize her body and clear her mind. Daniel's offer? Not even a blip.

Okay, maybe a blip.

He'd said he *fantasized* about her. He'd called her curves "beautiful." Told her that her body haunted his dreams.

Maybe I should give him a chance?

Ugh! What are you doing? Softening? Stay hard!

Last night Daniel had been as hard as a rock for her…

Shivers danced through her limbs, and she swallowed a groan. Come on! She wasn't special to him. He would use and discard her.

You planned to use and discard him first.

Yeah, well, that was different, because—why?

Just because!

A cramp in her side slowed her, but her mind continued to whirl. Daniel confused her. He'd rejected her but had later claimed to desire her. He'd offered her a single night of passion only to leave when she finally began to maybe kinda sorta consider it.

Enough! Give no more thought to this.

The more you thought about something, the more power it had over you.

When she reached the inn, she decided she wasn't ready to adult yet and paced along the sidewalk. Would Holly be stationed at the counter, as commanded? Or had her sister abandoned her, as threatened?

With Dorothea's luck? *I was abandoned without a moment's consideration.*

With a sigh, she leaned against a large white column and watched as the sun rose in the distance. The cloudless sky blazed with magnificent shades of gold, pink and purple. Such beauty! The air wasn't hotter than a goat's butt in a pepper patch, or colder than a penguin's balls.

Break out those short shorts, y'all, but keep a raincoat within reach.

This evening, a thunderstorm would roll in, no doubt about it, and it would be the first of many. Tornado season had officially kicked off, and the possibility of a cyclone would only strengthen throughout the week.

The greater the storms, the more time Jazz would spend on TV screens throughout Oklahoma. Resentment flared within her, the urge to punch something—or someone—strong.

No more regrets. *Let go of the past and march into the future.*

Right. Dorothea drew in a deep breath. As she released it, she straightened. She would adult whether she wanted to or not. She would shower and—*whimper*—she would interact with other people.

A loud rumble suddenly assaulted her ears, growing in volume, and the inn began to shake. Earthquake! Dust plumed. Her heart galloped into a faster rhythm.

She stumbled but managed to remain upright. A second later, the shaking stopped, but her heartbeat failed to slow.

While Strawberry Valley only registered the bigger ones, quakes had become a way of life. Some people blamed fracking. Others blamed a previously undiscovered fault line.

At long last, Dorothea entered the inn. She'd painted her nails red this morning—anger—and now flattened her palm over her tattoo as she studied the interior, searching for any damage. Nothing appeared to be broken and Holly—

Wasn't behind the counter.

Dorothea gnashed her molars as she phoned Mrs. Hathaway, who'd promised to man the desk until her doctor appointment, to ask if she could come sooner and return sooner, as well. Then she set up the Be Back Soon sign and stalked to her room. After a quick shower, she dressed in a pale green cotton blouse to match her eyes, and a pair of stonewashed jeans she'd cut into shorts when the denim had ripped at the knees. Recycling old clothes was a great penny saver.

She drove to the high school for the parent-teacher conferences. According to her mother, there was no reason to go and a thousand reasons to avoid it, because every teacher she met would complain about Holly, and Dorothea's blood would boil. But she was determined to grin and bear it. Someone had to keep up with Holly's life to ensure she wasn't being bullied for her unique wardrobe choices. Someone had to check her academic progress, offer support and show her just how deeply she was loved.

Unfortunately, the first four meetings rolled out exactly as Carol had predicted. The teachers complained about Holly's lack of focus.

"I'll talk to her," Dorothea vowed to each one.

When anyone mentioned Holly's terrible attitude, she said, "We're working on it."

When her sister's abysmal grades came up, she said, "I'll find her a tutor."

When Holly's constant threats to drop out and become a streetwise hooker with secret hopes of being rescued by an icy billionaire only she could melt was mentioned, Dorothea said, "It's good to have goals, yeah?"

Mr. Jonathan Hillcrest, the fifth and final teacher, saved the day. Even though he was a few years older than Dorothea, they'd played in the band together when they were in high school. The popular crowd had considered him a nerd, just like her. *Kindred spirits unite!*

While Dorothea had retained her supposed "nerdiness," he'd grown out of his. Tall and lean with sandy-colored hair, he had a construction worker's tan, and adorable laugh lines around his eyes and mouth. His nose was a little too long, but it worked in his favor, giving him an aristocratic vibe.

She thought she recalled a rumor that he and his girlfriend of two years had broken up a few months ago.

"I have to tell you, Dottie. Holly has so much potential. She's so smart. She just needs to apply herself." He sat at his desk, the surface cluttered with papers. "Any tips for how I can reach her?"

She decided not to correct his use of the hated nickname. The meeting wasn't about her. "Are you kidding me? *I* need tips."

He chuckled, and she grinned.

"And please, call me Dorothea."

Twining his fingers over his middle, he leaned back in his chair. "I think this is the first time I've ever seen you smile."

Her eyes widened. He'd noticed her? Before this?

Then he shocked her further, saying, "It looks good on you."

What! It did?

"Thank you," she replied, her tone soft, her cheeks burning. "That's very kind of you to say."

"Not kind. Honest." Now unwilling to meet her gaze, he cleared his throat and stacked a set of papers at the corner of his desk. "Anyway. We were talking about Holly."

"Right." Dorothea hooked a lock of hair behind her ear. How to explain she'd been back home for nearly a year, but her sister had yet to forgive her for leaving in the first place?

"I know your family owns the Strawberry Inn, and I wonder if Holly maybe…works too much?" His hesitation lessened the sting of his words. "She rarely turns in her assignments. I've offered her numerous extensions, but she always declines, stating she's far too busy to pencil me into her schedule."

Guilt pricked at Dorothea. Holly had zero free time, the way Dorothea had once had zero free time. The way she now had zero free time. And she had only perpetuated the problem.

When her sister asked for a day off, she should have given it to her. She remembered the teenage horror of being forced to turn down every after-school invitation. Not that she'd been invited anywhere by anyone other than Ryanne and Lyndie.

Making a split-second decision, she said, "Consider Holly fired, effective immediately." The theme rooms could wait. Every penny she'd saved could be used to hire a new receptionist. "I want the best for her. Underneath her insults, she has a good heart."

He nodded as she spoke. "I agree."

Those two swords fertilized Dorothea's hopes, helping them grow. If she and Mr. Hillcrest teamed up, surrounding her sister with love and acceptance, Holly would have nowhere to run.

Together, they brainstormed ways to help Holly engage with the class. At one point, he stopped Dorothea to ask for her number. "So I can keep you apprised of my progress."

How kind. She rattled off the digits.

A harried knock echoed inside the room, and they jolted in unison. The door swung open, an irritated-looking woman stalking into the classroom. She tapped on the screen of her phone. "My meeting was scheduled to begin six minutes ago. I've been pacing the hall, waving at you through the glass partition, doing my best to be patient, but I have a job, too, and I can't be late."

"I'm so sorry." Dorothea jumped to her feet. "I lost track of time. I'm sorry," she repeated. "I'm leaving." She extended her hand to Mr. Hillcrest. "Thank you again, Mr. Hillcrest. I—"

"Call me Jonathan. Please."

She inclined her head before darting into the hall. As she left the building and made her way across the parking lot, her gaze lifted to the sky out of habit. Over the past few years, Oklahoma had been dubbed the home of the quakenado. Storms, tornadoes and earthquakes, oh my! She loved to predict what would come next.

The thunderstorm she'd predicted now brewed, a thick wall of cloud stretching as far as the eye could see; the heavy veil of humidity suggested there would, in fact, be tornadic activity, too.

A horn blasted.

She yelped and skidded to a stop. A minivan sped past her. Yikes! She'd been so wrapped up in weather-watching she'd lost track of her surroundings.

"Sorry," she called.

Heart thudding, she settled behind the wheel of her car. The same car she'd had since she was sixteen years old. A granny mobile, kids had called it. Once, those same kids had used shoe polish to write the words *oink oink* on her windshield.

Ugh. No more thinking about the past.

Since she planned to fire Holly later today, she needed to stop at Copy Copy to create the perfect flyer for a new hire...

Wanted: Receptionist for the Strawberry Inn.

If you can:

★ Speak to strangers
★ Answer a phone
★ Show up on time
★ Type complete sentences

You have the skills we need.

Contact Dorothea Mathis to schedule an interview.

Excellent! Up next, posting the flyers and setting Holly free. Would Dorothea be met with hugs or insults?

She heaved a sigh. Like she really had to wonder.

Dorothea returned to the inn and stopped short in the lobby. Her little sis had actually listened to her! Holly rather than Mrs. Hathaway manned the desk. If "manned" was defined as staring at a cell phone and chewing gum. Still, it was progress.

"Good afternoon." Dorothea approached her sister the way she would approach a wounded animal.

Holly popped a bubble. "Daniel Porter came by to see you."

The air gushed from her lungs. "What'd he want?"

"He looked *tee-icked*, but he wouldn't tell me what the problem was. I bet he's going to complain about his last stay."

Or discuss his offer.

Head fogging, she said, "Enough about Daniel. Let's talk about you."

"Nope. I'm busy."

"Too bad." *If it's broken, fix it.* Dorothea braced herself for an onslaught of insults and said, "I met with your teachers today."

"So? Would you like a medal?"

Ignore. Continue. "I was told you haven't been turning in your assignments."

Holly never even glanced up. "That sounds like a me prob-lem."

Anger sparked. "I'm giving you the rest of the school year off. That means no more working this desk. Now you can devote yourself to your studies." Good. Her tone remained calm, collected. "You can use your free time to get caught up…and afterward you can have a little fun."

Holly pressed a button on her phone with enough force to crack the plastic case, ending the game. Her emerald gaze jerked up at last and narrowed. "You're firing me?"

"Yes."

"You *can't*."

"I can, and I did."

"Well, I'm hiring myself back. You aren't the boss of me."

"Actually, I am," Dorothea said with just enough sneer in her voice to shock them both. "Mom gave the inn to me, not you, and my decisions are final. You're fired, little girl. You're welcome!"

Holly hurled her phone across the lobby—the phone Dorothea paid for—and leaped to her feet. "You're being stupid. You *need* me."

Was she freaking kidding? "You are lazy, incompetent, destructive and entitled. In what way do I *need* you?"

Uh, maybe take it down a notch?

No! New Dorothea didn't take crap.

Holly pointed an accusing finger at her. "You're just desperate to get rid of me. Admit it!"

"I'm not—"

"You *are*!" Foot stomp.

Sweet Lord in heaven. Knife fighting with a serial killer would have been easier than arguing with a teenage girl. "I'm desperate to repair our relationship, Halls. I'm desperate to do right by you. I'm desperate—"

"I don't care!" Once again her sister stomped her foot like a five-year-old child. "You and Mom worked here during your school years. Therefore *I* will work here during *my* school years. Got it?"

So much fury trapped inside one little body, her usual antipathy toward Dorothea nowhere to be found. *I'm actually... getting to her?*

"No," she said with a shake of her head. "When tradition does more harm than good, it's time to try something else."

Holly bristled. "Tradition isn't the problem. You are. You're miserable, and you want everyone around you to be miserable, too. I bet that's why Jazz left you."

Wow. Low blow. Jazz had been happy with her…at first. And he'd truly seemed to love her. He'd called and texted anytime he was away, just to tell her how much he missed her. When they were together, he'd watched her as if the sight of her gave him great pleasure. If she'd been near, his hands had been on her.

But it had been a trick, only a trick. A long con.

After everything had gone down the toilet, she'd wondered if he'd married her because she'd been the only woman in creation dumb enough to quit school in order to pay his bills. If she'd been a free ride—in more ways than one.

Sure, he still called her at least once a week to talk about Holly and beg Dorothea for a second chance, saying he'd made a mistake, blah, blah, blah, that he missed her more every day, that he'd lost the best thing that had ever happened to him, that he'd only slept with Charity Sparks—his coanchor—because he'd feared she would get him fired if he refused her advances. As if he were a Victorian maiden with a pushy beau. He'd said he needed his job in order to provide for Dorothea and the baby.

If that were true, why had he insisted she continue to work, saving money, rather than return to school?

Truth was, he hadn't wanted Dorothea to return to school— to become competition. Now he just wanted to keep her on the hook. Well, good luck with that. He'd made her feel like garbage when she was a prize. More than that, his actions had led to the worst day of her life. He meant nothing to her. Less than nothing.

Holly glared at her. "You want to run the inn without me. Fine. Do it. When you fail, and you will, I'll laugh in your face, not just behind your back. Meanwhile, I'll be sure to get caught up in my favorite class. Assholeology 101."

Can't win. She hadn't reached her sister at all, had she? Rather than wilt, she forged ahead. "If today is any indication, you're well on your way to a solid A plus."

Her sister's jaw dropped. Dorothea walked away before she said something to further widen the gulf between them.

Once enclosed in her room, she pressed her palm against her rose tattoo and focused on her surroundings—her sanctuary. She'd decorated the space with Grandma Ellie's antiques: a floral-print couch, a pink velvet settee and a royal blue porcelain side table painted with...of course...roses. Those flowers were the reason she'd named—

Sickness churned deep in her stomach, and she forced her thoughts back to Grandma Ellie, who lived in heaven now; the woman was probably speaking with angels right this very second. *You go down there and slap some sense into my former son-in-law. He's actin' nuttier than a Porta Potty at a peanut festival. No one treats my grandbabies like that!*

Dorothea missed her spunky grandmother with every fiber of her being.

Disheartened—again—she showered and dressed in a clean pair of scrubs; they were made to survive daily washings and vast amounts of bleach. This pair happened to be purple, one of her favorite colors. She swiped her lips with cherry-flavored lip gloss before heading to the storage closet on the bottom floor. Along the way, she anchored her thick mass of curls into a sloppy, wet knot on the crown of her head.

As she cleaned the first block of rooms, music spilling from her iPod and setting the pace, she tried not to lament her initial attempts to improve her life. With Holly...and Daniel.

Time to figure out what to do about him.

To be fair, he wasn't exactly a failure. He'd offered her exactly what she'd asked for—a single night of pleasure.

Not enough for me. Not anymore.

Just once, Dorothea wanted to be the girl the guy desired

deeply, madly…and long-term. She longed to be first choice, the prize and not the consolation. She yearned to *matter*. To mean more to a man than his job, his bank account or the opinion of his family. What she *didn't* want? To sleep with a man and later see him fawning all over another woman.

Been there, done that.

What had a lot better odds of success: the local tackle shop selling bait and calling it sushi.

A hard knock sounded, jolting her. She ripped out her earbuds and spun. A common occurrence lately. This time she had to swallow a yelp or a moan, she wasn't sure which. Daniel had pushed her cart aside, giving her a full frontal view of masculine perfection. His black tee stretched across wide shoulders and hugged well-defined biceps while his dark jeans did naughty things to his lower body. The wind had left his hair in charming disarray, and her fingers ached to comb through the strands. His beard stubble had grown thicker, making him look rough, tough and bad to the bone.

He looked so danged good, like a sexy outlaw who followed no rules but his own…and he was seeing her in her scrubs and without a speck of makeup.

Oh, what the heck did it matter? She no longer had any interest in catching his attention. Did she?

She lifted her chin, all *drink me in—but don't you dare touch*.

Daniel smiled at her, slow and devastating and utterly wicked. Pleasure unfurled deep inside her, delicious warmth spilling through her whole body.

He held a large bouquet of dew-kissed roses. One of every color, with the exception of pink, which had two buds.

The moisture in her mouth dried, and she shook her head. The roses couldn't be for her. He couldn't know what that particular flower meant to her.

And according to Lyndie and Ryanne, flowers were cliché, a generic gift given without much thought for the recipient.

"Hello, Dorothea."

"Hi." To mask her sudden cascade of tremors, she ripped the sheets from the bed. Cooter Bowright had checked in last night and, though he didn't know it, he'd competed with Daniel for the title of Worst Guest Ever, wrecking the room. "Holly mentioned you wanted to speak with me."

"Among other things." The huskiness of his voice proved to be a weapon as powerful as any touch. "These are for you. I thought your favorite color might be pink, because of your tattoo, but decided to cover all the bases, just in case, because of your fingernails." He walked around her, placed the flowers on the nightstand and helped her fit the clean sheet around the edges of the mattress.

The roses are *for me. And he noticed my tattoo* and *my nails.* Goose bumps spread from head to toe.

Dang him! "They're beautiful." *Like my curves?* "Thank you," she muttered. She gathered the supplies she needed and headed to the bathroom. A hint for him to leave.

Hinges squeaked. Then a soft *snick* sounded. Then an ominous *click*. She sucked in a breath. He'd just shut and locked the front door, hadn't he?

He appeared in the bathroom doorway and crossed his arms over his chest. Before she could protest, he said, "You smell amazing, like lavender and...what's the other scent?"

"Scent*s*. Sweet marjoram and ylang-ylang. I like blending essential oils." Those particular scents happened to be known for relieving stress...and stoking desire. Which had nothing to do with her choice to basically soak herself in them. Of course.

"I like *you*. I want to start over with you, Dorothea. I want to go on a date with you, get to know you better."

Her heart leaped with excitement... "What about your dad?"

"We'll have dinner in the city. He'll never know."

...only to fall into her ankles.

There was no denying the truth any longer. She still wanted Daniel. Actually, she wanted him more than ever. He hadn't just called her curves beautiful; he'd backed up his words with actions; he'd chased her, bringing her a gift. Something Jazz had never done. And she understood Daniel's reasons for wanting to hide their association from his dad. She really did. But that understanding failed to soothe the fears and hurt his answer had sparked. What if, deep down, he was simply ashamed of her?

What if he only liked the challenge she represented?

For a moment, only a moment, Dorothea allowed herself to ponder what things would be like if Daniel were *proud* of her. They'd go to dinner, but not in the city. No, he would surprise her with a picnic in the middle of Strawberry Valley. Then they would go hiking. Oh! *Bowling.* They would trash talk, of course, and decide the winner would receive a bone-melting kiss…in the location of his or her choosing.

"One date," he said. "Give me a chance."

"No, thanks," she croaked. "I'm not interested." The words resounded inside her head, shaming her. Lies were Jazz's thing, not hers. "Fine. I'm interested, but what I want isn't what I need. I *won't* date you."

He listened to her without reaction, seeming to ponder her words. "Tell me why."

"Why?" she parroted like a fool.

"Are you afraid I'll hurt you?"

"I *know* you'll hurt me." As soon as he finished with her, her hard-won self-esteem—if she had any left—would take yet another beating.

His gaze hardened, pinning her in place. "If we discuss the terms of our relationship up front, the chances of either of us getting hurt diminish significantly."

Please! As if *she* would ever be able to hurt *him*. "We wouldn't have a relationship, not really. And I can already guess your terms. One, we'll sleep together and never speak again. Two, see term number one." And oh, wow. The bitterness in her tone astounded her. She had once *demanded* he have a one-night stand with her, zero strings. Now she hated him for offering the same to her?

When had she become such a hypocrite?

"We'll sleep together once…twice…a dozen times." He hiked a shoulder in a shrug. "The number is negotiable as long as we both accept where the relationship—because yes, we'd have one—is headed. But why must we never speak again?"

"A dozen times?" She struggled to breathe. And she understood where the "relationship" would be headed, all right. Nowhere.

"Or more," he said. "Like I told you, I'm flexible. I'm also waiting for an answer to my question. Why must we never speak after we have sex? I happen to like speaking with you."

He did?

Thou shalt compliment when merited.

Red alert! Danger, danger.

She cleared her throat. "Please don't take this the wrong way, Daniel, but *I* don't like speaking with *you*." Truth. Conversations with him tended to end disastrously for her.

Again he gave no reaction, as if he'd expected resistance and had come prepared to forge ahead regardless. "I'm happy to do all the talking, then." He held out his arms, the last sane man in the universe. "See how easy I am to get along with?"

Double dang him! He was too charming for his own good. No, he was too charming for *her* good.

He tapped two fingers against the stubble on his chin. "I have a brilliant idea. Which happens to be the only kind of idea I ever have. Why don't we focus on getting to know each other today, and speak about sex tomorrow?"

I'm not delighted by his persistence. And his ego is absolutely, positively not charming.

She grabbed the glass cleaner and a new rag. See Dorothea fake nonchalance. "No way, no how."

"All right, then, we'll talk about sex *today*."

She nearly choked on her tongue as she faced the mirror. Her reflection had enormous green eyes and bright pink cheeks. Soft, open lips, ready to be kissed…

Spray, spray, spray. Wipe, wipe, wipe.

"I don't know about you," he said, the husky note back in his voice, "but I'm imagining you seated on that counter… naked."

This. This was the tone he would use in bed. The one he would use to whisper into a woman's ear, driving her wild with raw, primitive passion.

"Your legs are spread, and I'm—"

"Fine!" she blurted out. "You can get to know me today. Okay? All right?" Anything to shut him up. If he continued to weave such an intoxicating picture, her resistance would shatter. She would end up in his arms, the consequences an afterthought. "What would you like to know?"

His eyelids were heavy, almost drowsy. "For starters, what's your favorite color?"

Spray, spray. Wipe, wipe. Could he see how fervently she trembled? "I like pink in the morning, blue in the afternoon and gold in the evening."

The corners of his lips quirked up, as if a smile was attempting to sneak past his usual frown. "That's pretty specific. I would have guessed red, the color of your fingernails."

"Well, my color favorites change according to the position of the sun. And the nail colors aren't based on what I like but on my mood."

One of his brows winged up. "Please tell me red is for passion."

She fought a smile of her own. "Nope. Red is anger. I don't actually have a color for—" She pressed her lips together.

Crap! She'd basically admitted passion had no identifier and therefore no place in her life.

He could have teased her. Or come on to her, flirting more obviously. Instead, he quieted, different emotions whirling behind his eyes. Intrigue. Desire. Confusion.

"What do yellow and orange mean?" he finally asked. "Actually, tell me all the colors."

Why not? "Yellow is hopeful, orange nervousness. Green is irritated, pink happy. Blue is sad, purple determined." She stopped, pressed her lips together. Sharing these details made her feel exposed. Wanting the spotlight taken off herself, she said, "What's *your* favorite color?"

"Yellow. No matter the time of day."

"Why?"

"Because it's bright? Mellow?"

"You don't know?" To her, yellow represented the rise of the sun. The start of a new day. A clean slate.

"Never really thought about why. I like what I like." He crossed his arms, his biceps straining the tee. "How'd you get the nickname Dottie? Those adorable freckles?"

"Adorable? As if! But yes, that's exactly why, and I hate it. I've always hated it."

"I think it's endearing. More than that, Dorothea doesn't fit you. It's the name of a ninety-year-old crazy cat lady. So why have you stuck with it?"

"Never really thought about why," she said, mimicking him. "I like what I like."

His grin bloomed full force, causing her hormones to sing and dance with bliss. "Well, I'm a rebel, so I'm gonna mix things up and call you... Thea. Yeah. Thea. Short and incredibly sweet."

She gulped. *He* was incredibly sweet. Feigning nonchalance, she said, "All right. I'll call you Danny."

He laughed with delight. "Look at us. We've got pet names

for each other already." Then his amusement died a swift death, his smile fading.

Why the change?

"Did you always want to run the inn?" he asked, switching gears.

"No," she replied, and cringed. Her mother would be devastated if she found out Dorothea saw the job as, well, a job rather than a passion. "I wanted to be a meteorologist."

"So why aren't you a meteorologist?"

Let me count the ways… "It's a long story." Her guts churned as years of bad memories whisked through her mind.

"No worries. I've got time."

"Too bad. I've got no inclination."

He thought for a moment, nodded. "That's fair. There are things I never share with others."

"Never?" Not with anyone?

"Never." Did he realize his gaze had glazed over, the color seeping from his cheeks? Did he know he was rubbing a small scar on his cheek?

That scar…she thought she remembered his dad talking about Daniel's face being lacerated by shrapnel.

Did his secrets have anything to do with his many missions overseas?

She ran the rag over the faucet, the inside of the sink. "Did you always want to be in the military?" Wait. She had to stop asking him such personal questions. Nowhere in her Make Daniel Go Bye-Bye plan did she get to know him better.

"As a little boy, I ruthlessly and relentlessly led my toys into war. Stuffed animals against action figures. I'd be working my way to general if my dad's health hadn't deteriorated."

Her heart melted as she pictured little Daniel commanding his furry or plastic troops. She'd played with Barbies, sending them into rainstorms and tornadoes—the washing machine and the dryer.

Red alert! Softening toward him…

Okay, time to move the conversation along. "Now you run a security firm?" She exchanged the glass cleaner for bleach, a toilet brush and a pair of latex gloves.

"Yes. With my friends Jude and Brock—have you met them? Good guys. They've been in town for a while."

"I've heard of them but haven't officially met them." She spent most of her time here. When she *did* get out, she tended to keep her head down.

"We do security for companies and individuals, setting up cameras, running background checks, offering cyber and even physical protection. We're full-service. We have offices in Oklahoma City as well, headed by former army rangers."

So young, so successful. Like the women he preferred to date. "You guys are providing security for the spring festival, I hear. Though you probably should have declined. Half the women in town will end up catfighting just to get your attention." And she wasn't jealous about that. Nope. Not even a little.

He snorted. "You have more faith in my appeal than I do."

"Yes, well, I'm most excited about the food trucks." Everything from fried ice cream to fried butter. "I always allow myself a treat."

Now he frowned. "Only one?"

How had he locked on the singular? She soooo did not want to discuss her weight, but he'd asked a question and she needed to reply. "I'm on a diet," she muttered, and offered no more. She'd been on a diet for over a decade.

Some days she dreamed of being trapped inside a candy store and never coming out. Oh, to die buried in a pile of M&Ms.

"Why?" His gaze slid down, down her body and heated with…awareness and admiration? Her kryptonite. "I believe I mentioned the beauty of your curves."

Maybe he believed those words. Maybe she *was* attractive in his eyes. But he would never be proud to date her. He would never want anything more than a lay or two.

"I think we've gotten to know each other well enough to prove our incompatibility." With all the dignity she could muster, she pulled on the gloves and knelt in front of the toilet. "Please leave."

CHAPTER SIX

Another failure. Daniel wanted to punch a wall. Then he'd have to repair the hole he left behind, an excuse to spend more time with Dorothea. If she didn't run away from the maniac who'd thrown a temper tantrum.

But what else was he supposed to do? The woman with lips made for kissing continued to turn him down flat.

Forget playing chase for a few weeks. He would much rather have this woman in his bed, screaming "Yes, yes. Please, Daniel, please." Now *and* later.

Not only because she made him laugh. Somehow affection overshadowed his memories of war every time he neared her. She intoxicated him. *I'm already an addict.* She made him want to give more than he took.

Today, as he'd once again watched Thea dance while she cleaned, molten desire had consumed him, burning any lingering reluctance to ash, leaving him raw, agonized…vulnerable.

She was like a priceless piece of art. The more he studied her, the more mysteries he uncovered—and the deeper depths his fascination reached.

He loved that she painted her nails to match her mood; he planned to buy her a new shade ASAP. Something to represent passion.

"Leave?" he finally said, his voice low. What'd a guy have to do to break through her defenses? "When I'm far from satisfied?"

The most spectacular shade of pink bloomed on her cheeks. *Screw yellow, I like pink.* His fingers itched to touch her, to find out how warm her skin had become…to discover just how far the flush had spread.

Keeping her back to him, she said, "Bad weather will hit in an hour or two. Go home, Daniel. I'm tripling room rates tonight."

"Does the triple rate come with cuddle time?"

Slowly she craned her head around to meet his gaze, and it was like something out of a horror movie. Scary as hell. And yet for some reason it made him want to smile.

"No cuddles," she said, "but I can make sure your stay comes with a knee-to-crotch introduction."

Do not laugh. "Yeah, baby. Talk dirty to me. Filthy."

A giggle bubbled from her. Then she sucked in a breath, as if shocked by her amusement.

He stared at her, riveted by the sight of her glowing features, as addicted to the sight of her as he was to, hell, everything else about her. Arousal had simmered inside him all day. No, since she'd flashed him. Seeing her like this pushed him over the edge. He ached. He burned, and he shook.

Somehow, just kneeling there, she was hotter and more inherently female than any woman he'd ever met.

He balled his hands to prevent himself from doing something stupid, like reaching for her before she was ready. Her eyes were like open wounds right now, filled with uncertainty and fear.

Did she fear her feelings for him, or did she just fear *him*? The things he was capable of... She must have heard rumors.

"You really want me to go?" *Ask me to stay. Please.*

She licked those porn-star lips, her pretty tongue leaving a glistening sheen of moisture behind. With her wealth of dark curls pinned to the crown of her head, he had a perfect view of her elegant neck. At the base, a pulse hammered wildly, a match to his. Desire like this...he'd never before experienced it. This was all-consuming. A fire in his bones. A drug in his veins. He was quickly becoming obsessed.

"Yes," she finally whispered. A croak. "Go."

The rejection was a brass knuckle punch of disappointment to the stomach. For the first time in...ever, he resented the need to chase a woman. He would rather have Thea in his arms, his mouth pressed against hers, his hands exploring her luscious body...her legs wrapped around his waist.

He should kick his own ass for sending her away the night she'd shown up at his door. What could he do to make her willing again? Eager? To make her warm, sweet and languid.

The moment she agreed, he would carry her to bed, and he wouldn't allow her to leave until she writhed with desire, the way she did in his dreams.

He still wasn't able to sleep, but at least he now enjoyed the hours he spent lost in his head.

"I'll be back," he told her. And this, he decided, was the last time he would allow either of them to retreat. "I won't give up on you. Or us." He walked backward, keeping her baby-doll features in his sights until the last possible moment. In her eyes, hope and longing replaced the uncertainty and fear. Did she *want* to be chased?

I can chase the hell out of her.

No man gave better chase.

But first, he needed a plan. To plan, he needed more information. Who better to help him than Jessie Kay?

He texted the feisty blonde and, after buying glittery white nail polish for Thea—the new representative for passion—met Jessie Kay at Lazy Susan, an old train car that had been transformed into a Victorian teahouse. The walls were paneled with royal blue velvet and cherry woodwork, and from the ceiling hung a crystal chandelier. Stained glass windows filled the cart with colored prisms of light.

Lazy Susan wasn't located in Strawberry Valley. None of the patrons cared about what he or Jessie Kay said.

She sat at a table in back, eating from multiple platters of food. Beside her, two cups of coffee steamed.

He kissed her cheek and slid into his chair. "Do you know Thea Mathis?" he asked, treading carefully.

Jessie Kay blinked at him as she buttered a piece of toast, her brow creased. The beautiful blue-eyed blonde had the sassiest mouth in the South—not counting Thea—and had once been touted as Strawberry Valley's wildest wild child. "Who?"

"Dorothea. Formerly Dottie," he said. "But do not, under any circumstances, call her Dottie. In fact, wipe the nickname from your mind. Call her Dorothea." She hated her childhood nickname, so he would put an immediate end to its use.

"Why can't I call her Thea? And why do you care what I call—"

"Because I do." Thea was his nickname for her. His alone. "And because she's…my friend." Not that she would agree. Yet.

"Whoa." Jessie Kay held out her hand, palm up. "Let's backtrack a little. We're talking about the freckled girl from the inn, yes?"

He gave a single, curt nod, not liking that she'd reduced Thea to "the freckled girl from the inn."

As slow as molasses, she set her toast on a plate. "If you're asking 'cause you're planning on nailing her, I'm gonna knock your testicles into your throat. I like her, and I don't want her hurt."

"For your information, I like her, too." He shook a blueberry muffin over her head, smiling as the crumbs settled in her hair. "Why would you want to hurt my testicles, anyway? You'd deprive everyone of my manly prowess."

"Manly prowess?" She rolled her eyes. "I've seen the way she looks at you. You date and dump her, and you'll devastate her. And since I'm the patron saint of mending broken hearts and breaking callous MARTS, I will—"

"Marts?" he interjected, even as he reeled. Other people had noticed the way Thea looked at him? The want and need hadn't been wishful thinking on his part?

"It's an acronym, and it stands for a *Male* who is an *Asinine, Rotten, Two-timing* piece of *Shit*."

"In my case, I think you mean *Male* who is *Adorable, Remarkable, Talented* and probably a *Superhero*. Because I've never two-timed anyone, and never will." To cheat, you had to lie. He refused to lie.

He remembered the one and only time he'd fibbed to his parents. Virgil had smacked his butt and said, "Don't you piss on my leg and tell me it's rainin', boy. I'll lose all respect for you, and you'll prove you've never respected me."

His mother had remained silent, peering at him with disappointment, cutting him to the quick.

"Hate to break it to you," Jessie Kay said, "but you're still asinine. You'll hurt her, guaranteed, and I'll be forced to mass produce bronzes of your penis with a designer line of dresses he can wear. And maybe hats. Everyone in Strawberry Valley—heck, the world—can have a Danny Jr. on their mantel."

"I would never hurt her." He snapped the words, defensive. "Not purposely. But I *would* like one of those bronzes."

Wicked pleasure brightened Jessie Kay's features as she leaned back in her chair. "Well, well, well. Daniel Porter is smitten, and not with an imaginary bronze. I might have to help you rather than hurt you." Her Southern drawl thickened when she added, "Now, don't you go gettin' a big head about this, but Miss Dot—*Dorothea* has had a crush on you since our glory days in high school."

Thea had wanted him for *years*? "How do you know this?" If curiosity hadn't run the show, his eagerness would have embarrassed him. He might as well have been a sixteen-year-old girl with a crush and overactive ovaries.

Laughter rumbled from the merciless Jessie Kay. "Want to come to my slumber party tonight? We can stay up all night gabbing about boys and having pillow fights."

He drew his cell from his pocket and spoke as he typed. "Dear West. Your woman needs a spanking. Take care of it." Send.

Smug, she withdrew *her* cell. "Dear West. I do hope you'll take Daniel's advice and spank me. I look forward to having your palm print on my butt."

Daniel snorted. Incorrigible girl. "Tell me about Thea. Please with a cherry on top."

"Fine. The first day of my senior year, I said something hateful to her. And don't you dare chastise me for it. I've chastised *myself* a million times. Harlow had just called me a slut, and I— Never mind. I digress. I planned to apologize to Dorothea at lunch, but she rushed into the band room. I didn't want to interrupt whatever she was doing, so I waited for her. When she rushed out, she had tears in her eyes. I sneaked in to find out what had hurt her...and there you were, making out with Madison Clark."

Seeing him with another girl had reduced her to tears? Poor, sweet Thea. "I barely remember Madison."

But he clearly remembered the way Dorothea had once looked at him in the halls of Strawberry Valley High. Of course she'd crushed on him, he thought now; he'd just been too stupid, or too hormonal, to see it.

He'd been too young and inexperienced to appreciate her then.

He wasn't too young or inexperienced now.

A wanton smile kicked up the corners of his mouth.

"Look at you," Jessie Kay said and tsk-tsked. "You're the cat who just caught the mouse. I never would have guessed plain, ordinary Dorothea Mathis—"

"Plain? Ordinary?" His voice increased an octave, drawing the notice of their waitress. She stepped toward them, but he waved her back. "Are you kidding me? Thea is *gorgeous.*" The sexiest woman on the freaking planet.

Jessie Kay gaped at him, as if he were insane. And yet, for the first time in years, he felt...almost at peace. His warrior instincts were fully engaged, the prize incomparable. Thea enraptured and amused him. She tantalized all five of his senses. She challenged him but also soothed him. Soon he would have her.

"What about your dad?" Jessie Kay asked, dead serious now. "He'll have your wedding planned by the end of date one."

"I'm going to see Thea in secret. Dad will never know." If he and Thea ever decided to take the next step—

Whoa! What kind of thought was that? Next step? Him?

"Oh, Daniel." She flattened a hand over her heart. "You are *such* an idiot. And I mean that from the bottom of my heart."

His cell phone rang, saving him from having to offer a reply. The name "Dr. Vandercamp" appeared on the screen. Daniel held up a finger, indicating a need for silence, and answered. "How is Princess?"

"The dog is doing well. She isn't chipped, so I wasn't able to find the owners. However, I've posted photos online. Miss Princess will be ready for pickup after three. At the clinic, not my house. And I told you I'd have no problem getting your number. I just left Style Me Tender. Your dad was there, and he looked pale." *Click.*

Wow. What a conversationalist.

Jessie Kay fluttered her lashes at him. "High five to whoever put a burr under your saddle blanket."

He forked a bite of her eggs, despite the food he hadn't eaten on his own plate. "I'm taking off. Got to check on my dad." He'd looked pale? Why?

"Fine. Abandon me. Tell Dorothea I said hi. Maybe give her a kiss for me." She wiggled her brows. "Use tongue. I would."

Daniel parked in the town square, near Style Me Tender. Virgil would be playing checkers with his best friend of forty years, Anthony Rodriguez. Or rather, pretending to play checkers while people-watching and gossiping like an old hen.

As Daniel strode down the sidewalk, several groups of older women attempted to chat with him, but he never slowed. He was a man on a mission.

Finally, he spotted his target in front of the shop, seated at a small, square table. As a young man, his dad had been stacked with muscle. Now he was far too thin, verging on fragile. Life had weathered his skin, leaving its mark.

To Daniel, he was still one of the most beautiful people on the planet. Virgil was gruff but kind, always honest, and for too many years he'd worked two jobs in order to give his only child the finer things. Nice clothes, money to take his dates to fancy restaurants in the city and a reliable mode of transportation.

Now it was Daniel's turn to give back. His mom would expect nothing less.

Bonnie Porter had been a true Southern belle. She'd cooked every meal from scratch, just like her mother and grandmother before her, and she'd never raised her voice in public. She'd never cussed, even in private. She'd considered wrinkled clothing a sin and sweatpants the devil's invention. Most of all, she'd refused to work or clean on Sundays.

Even the good Lord rested, she'd liked to say.

She'd died over ten years ago when a vat exploded at Dairyland, a plant in Blueberry Hill, where half the residents of Strawberry Valley had once worked. Many people in town had lost loved ones in that explosion, not just Daniel and his father.

Even still, a light had been extinguished inside Virgil that day. Daniel, too. He'd learned no matter how much you loved someone, you couldn't stop Death from demanding his due.

" take over the receptionist desk," Virgil was saying. "But dang it all to heck and back, she's so poor she couldn't jump over a nickel to save a dime. Who's gonna sign up for long hours and little pay?"

"She just needs to make do for a few more weeks," Anthony replied. "The spring festival is coming up, don't you know? Those rooms are gonna go like hotcakes at a Sunday brunch, and she'll be sitting pretty on a fat stack of coin."

The rooms. The inn. Had to be Thea. Daniel's blood flashed white-hot.

He struggled to maintain a neutral expression. "Hey, Dad. How you feeling?"

Both men smiled in greeting.

"Feeling good, son. Feeling good."

Daniel noted the color in his cheeks and breathed a sigh of relief. Whatever had caused the old man to pale around Vandercamp must not be a problem anymore.

Since Daniel was here, he might as well work. "I'm going to finish installing the cameras inside." Considering how much time his dad spent at the salon, he'd decided to monitor the shop, free of charge.

When Daniel had first mentioned putting in a security

system, Anthony had said, "In all my years, I've never been robbed."

Daniel had replied, "You were robbed, you just didn't know it. Every time I visited, I stole the hearts of your customers."

That had settled that.

"If you want, I can go buy you guys a box of tampons first," Daniel said now.

Virgil spewed a drink of iced sweat tea. Anthony snorted and slapped his knee.

"You calling us women?" Virgil demanded.

"And insult women? No, sir." Daniel shook his head. "I'm calling you puss—"

"Hey, hey. Is that any way to talk to your father?" Anthony asked.

"Pussycats," Daniel finished.

Virgil snorted. "For your information, we've been *detecting*."

Detecting, huh? "What mystery are you trying to solve?"

"Well, it's like this." Anthony moved a red checker into a new box. "Dottie Mathis—you know her, don't you, boy?"

Every muscle in his body tensed. Had they heard something?

No, no. They couldn't have heard *anything*. After all, there was nothing to tell. They were just playing matchmaker.

Tread carefully. "I do know her. She's my friend. And she prefers her given name. Dorothea. You hurt her feelings every time you call her Dottie."

Anthony looked properly horrified. "I never meant to hurt no one's feelings."

"Why didn't she say nothin' to us?" Virgil tossed up his hands.

Daniel hiked a shoulder in a shrug.

Anthony cleared his throat and pulled at his shirt collar. "*Dorothea* was passing out flyers this morning. A position has opened up at the inn, you see, because she fired her sister."

"And…" Daniel prompted, doing his best to hide his insatiable curiosity that had nothing to do with her reasons for firing Holly.

The girl had checked him in on multiple occasions without ever speaking a word to him. She'd merely glared at him, as if he'd threatened to torch the place.

When he'd asked her, "Have I done something to offend you?" she'd popped a bubble in his face.

"*And* she squealed when she spotted me. She even tried to run away." Virgil gave Daniel the stink eye. "I had to clutch my heart and holler for help to get her to come back. Poor thing wouldn't meet my gaze, and it got me to wondering. Did something…maybe…happen between you two?" he asked with a glint of hope in his expression.

This. This was the very circumstance he'd wanted to avoid. Getting his dad's hopes up, only to watch the old man's features darken with disappointment.

"Women," he said, as if that one word explained every mystery in the universe. "Nothing happened between us." And that was the absolute truth. Nothing had happened…yet.

"A good sweet girl, our Dot—Dorothea." Detective Virgil moved a checker across the board, watching Daniel from the corner of his eye. "She'll make someone very happy."

Tread—carefully. Expression blank, he said, "Yep, she's as sweet as sugar." In more ways than one. "And you're right. She'll make someone very happy." His stomach suddenly clenched with…something he wasn't ready to name. He patted his dad on the shoulder, momentarily taken aback by the seeming brittleness of bone. "I better get to work."

Jude and Brock arrived a short time later, and as they helped install the cameras, they quietly doled out more deets about Thea's ex. Employees whispered about an upcoming promotion that would launch Jazz Connors, the storm chaser, into a prime-time in-studio position.

No accounting for taste.

Jazz's relationship with his coworker had, by all accounts, started while he was married and ended roughly two weeks ago.

The affair had most likely wounded Thea's feminine pride. She'd probably come to Daniel—whom she'd wanted since high school, thank you very much—for a self-esteem boost. Instead, he'd knocked her down another couple of pegs.

Despite his apology, a fresh tide of guilt eroded his new-found confidence. What if he'd hurt her too deeply? What if he couldn't win her?

No. No! He would *show* her how much he wanted her. With his mouth and his hands. Words would never be enough.

"What's this?" Jude snatched up a piece of paper next to a hair dryer. "Our little Dorothea is in need of a receptionist?"

My Dorothea, he almost snapped. *Mine. All mine.*

Brock snickered. "A second job could do me some good, teach me a few hard lessons about responsibility. Maybe I'll apply at the inn. And by 'maybe' I mean definitely."

"You'll do no such thing," Daniel grated.

His friends looked at him, then each other, then Brock laughed and Jude snorted. A second later, the bastards raced out of the shop. Jude's prosthetic gave him a slight limp, but it didn't slow him.

"Assholes," Daniel muttered and gave chase. "I'll be back, Dad."

The pair blazed down the sidewalk, pushing and shoving each other before rounding the corner and soaring into the inn. Daniel remained close on their heels.

Thankfully, school was in session and there was no sign of Holly. "Hello?" Brock called.

Silence. No sign of Dorothea, either. And no sign of Mrs. Hathaway, who usually slept behind the desk whenever she was on duty.

Daniel looked around. The spacious lobby was clean but worn. The laminate countertop blocking patrons from the desk had a crack in the center. The carpet had several thread-bare spots. However, the chandeliers were new and probably worth thousands. Did Thea know Daniel had helped Jessie Kay pick them out?

Jessie Kay had wanted to say thank you for hosting her then-boyfriend's company Christmas party last minute but hadn't known what to buy.

Thea needed a camera in here STAT. Multiple cameras, actually, to monitor the entire area and deter thieves.

He could connect the feed to her cell phone, allowing the cameras to act as a secondary receptionist. That way, she could use the new employee to help her clean all those rooms, rather than manning the desk with a snoring Mrs. Hathaway, freeing up precious time.

Time she could spend with Daniel.

Whenever the front door opened or someone entered the lobby, her phone would beep or buzz, and she could send the employee to take care of things.

Yes. He liked this idea. It might take a week or two to get the parts. Until then, *Daniel* could help her out...

"Dorothea," Brock bellowed. "Someone? Anyone?"

"I'm here, I'm here." A harried Thea raced into the lobby.

Daniel experienced a swift gut punch of lust. Multiple curls had slipped from the knot on top of her head and now framed her face. Perspiration caused her skin to glisten as if she'd taken a dip in a glitter-filled hot tub. Her shirt pulled tight over plush breasts he longed to palm.

Her shamrock eyes found Daniel, and a little gasp left her.

How is she more beautiful every time I see her?

"I'm, uh, sorry for the wait," she said. "How can I help you?"

He made the introductions and said, "They'd each like a room." Then he glared at both men. "Wouldn't you?"

Brock smiled an unrepentant smile.

Jude pursed his lips before giving a clipped nod.

"Really?" Thea brightened. "I mean, of course. Let me check to make sure we have vacancies."

As she typed, Brock propped his elbows on the counter and leaned forward. "So you're the infamous Dorothea Mathis. Daniel has mentioned you a time or twenty. Now I understand why."

The color drained from her cheeks, making her freckles stand out. As she focused on Daniel, she radiated anger and incredulity. "How could you!"

Confused, he spread his arms, all innocence. "How could I what?"

"Tell them about…about… Oh!" She type, type, typed, jamming her fingers into the keys. "They can stay. You can go."

"I didn't tell them *that*. I wouldn't. I won't." The memory belonged to him, and him alone.

"And so the plot thickens." Brock canted his head. "Tell us what, exactly?"

Daniel punched him in the arm and said to Thea, "Before you sign them in under the names Shithead and Dickhead, I'd like to speak with you privately."

Brock nonchalantly replied, "Shithead is actually pronounced Sha-thead."

Thea frowned at Daniel. "No, thanks. Customers come before…whatever you are."

No way was she getting rid of him this time.

"Yeah." Jude nudged his shoulder in a very un-Jude-like move. "Customers come first."

"Then I'd like a room of my own," Daniel announced. "As a paying customer, my happiness is now your top priority."

Thea stared at him, looking pouty, irritated and excited all at once.

He reached out and curled his hand around hers, drawing another gasp from her—and a soft hiss from himself. A handful of calluses marred her palm, the friction sparking a thousand fires inside him.

He could have used this heat every time he'd spent a cold, dark night in the desert, waiting for a target to appear.

"As the owner," she said, a catch in her voice, "I have the right to refuse potential patrons."

"I'm afraid I have to insist, Thea. On the room, *and* the conversation." Before she could issue another refusal, he stalked around the corner and gently but firmly ushered her into the hall, out of view.

That moment, that very second, he caged her against the wall and nearly forgot the reason he'd demanded the meeting. Those shamrock eyes were wide again, her irises glittering with challenge. Her lips were wet—she'd licked them.

My turn.

Not yet, not yet.

Her curves melted against him, the scent of her teasing his nose. His favorite scent in the world. She'd added vanilla to the mix this time.

"What are you doing?" she asked, deliciously breathless.

Besides drinking her in and wishing he were already inside her? "For starters, I'm blackmailing you."

She gulped. "To blackmail, you have to have leverage. You have none."

"Don't I?" His gaze slid over her slowly, languidly, and she shivered. "You came to my room naked, sweetheart. I'd say I've got *major* leverage."

Before his eyes, her nipples beaded. She pressed her legs together, as if she couldn't assuage a sudden ache.

That gut punch of lust? Merely the first round.

This time? TKO.

"One, you have no proof," she said, her voice a rasp of silk. "Two, you don't want your dad to know."

"One, I don't need proof. It's my word against yours. Two, my dad will commend me for acting like a gentleman and sending you away." Virgil would also slap him upside the head and mention all the pretty babies Daniel could have with the Strawberry Valley girl.

"You...you..." She beat her little fists into his shoulders, a catapult of feminine fury. "You better keep quiet. You said you'd never tell."

"And I never lie. But I do change my mind upon occasion."

The pulse at the base of her neck raced, just as before. "Why are you doing this?" she asked softly.

"I told you," he said, and gentled his tone. Just how deep did her hurt and insecurities run? "I'm desperate for you, which means I can't play by the rules. So. To buy my silence, you've got to date me."

"What!"

"Let me clarify. You've got to go on five dates with me." Good number. Too few, and he'd get nowhere fast. Too many, and it would be tough to convince either of them he wasn't interested in something long-term. "I'll pick the days, times and locations. I'll even pick what you wear," he said, fighting a smile. Let her worry about changing the details of their dates rather than canceling altogether.

"Are you freaking kidding me? No way, no how."

"Let's negotiate, then. What do you want? Ten dates?"

She sputtered for a moment. "No, I don't want—"

"Ten dates, and I'll work here free of charge for a week, so you can search for Holly's replacement without worry."

Her mouth snapped closed, and she rubbed the spot above her heart, where her tattoo was hidden underneath her shirt.

This wasn't the first time she'd performed such an action. What did the image mean to her?

Images *always* meant something. Jude had gotten a tattoo of a heart with daggers on his chest to memorialize his wife and daughters. Brock had sparrows tattooed on his shoulders, though he refused to talk about why.

"Five dates," Thea said, "for five weeks of work."

Playing right into my hands... "Five dates, three weeks. But I have to take this Friday and the next two weekends off. I have jobs in the city."

Surprise flickered over her expression. Because he'd upped the ante? "Three dates, three weeks," she said. "That's only fair."

"How right you are. Very well, then. You've got a deal. I'll even help you find Holly's replacement. But your flyer requires a few more qualifications. Like being kind to customers, not chewing gum while talking on the phone and not drawing severed heads on the bills. Oh, and the ability to type legible sentences rather than a series of symbols and emoticons."

"Holly doesn't— Never mind." Thea's fists opened and, as she dropped her arms to her sides, her fingertips traced the center of his T-shirt, snagging in the cotton. "What if I can't find a suitable replacement within the three-week time frame?"

I won't rock my throbbing erection between her legs. I won't... "I'll work an extra week or two, depending on my schedule, to give you whatever time you need, and for every extra week, you'll give me another date. Or two. We can renegotiate if it becomes necessary."

The surprise deepened. She *softened* against him. He stepped back—perhaps the most difficult thing he'd ever done—and held out his hand.

"Deal?"

She peered at the offering before smiling up at him with a feline confidence she'd never before displayed. "You think we're done with our negotiation, don't you? How cute."

A sizzling bolt of lust sent him stumbling another step backward. What had caused the change?

Did it matter? If he touched her again, he would kiss her. If he kissed her, he would strip her. If he stripped her, he would take her against the wall. Damn the consequences.

The official motto for this girl.

"I'll pick the days, times and locations of our dates." Just to be contrary, he was sure, she added, "I'll also pick what *you* wear. And you can't tell *anyone* about *anything* that happens between us. Not even your friends."

"You'll control *one* of the dates," he said, his tone firm. "I'll control the other two. And I won't breathe a word about us to anyone."

"Well, of course you won't!" she snapped.

He blinked with confusion. She was ticked that he'd given her exactly what she'd asked for?

"You won't tell anyone…unless you change your mind, right?" she added.

"Trust me." *Please.* "I won't change my mind."

She crossed her arms over her middle in a clear effort to hide her beaded nipples. "I'll control *two* dates."

And insist he wear a hazmat suit? "One date with you in charge," he said, "and you can double my room fee tonight. And Jude's and Brock's."

Dollars signs practically flashed in her eyes, and he had to swallow a laugh.

"Fine. But while you work here," she said, "I get to refer to you as my he-ceptionist."

"Assistant," he countered. "Or favorite person in the world."

Eye roll. "And just so you know, he-ceptionist, nothing is

going to happen between us on those dates. You're going to a lot of trouble for no reason."

"Oh, something will happen between us, guaranteed. Desire as strong as ours can't be denied for long." He did touch her then. The warmth and satin of her cheek. Took every bit of strength he possessed, but he didn't allow himself to press closer to her...or kiss her. "But guess what? Spending time with you is reward enough. You, Thea Mathis, are sweet, intelligent, witty and charming."

A tremor swept through her. Her breathing turned shallow.

Triumph overtook him. "So? Do we have a deal or not?"

She closed her eyes, her shoulders rolling in. "We...do."

If he weren't such a self possessed man, her reluctance might have hurt him. But he was, and it didn't.

Even still, his tone contained a bit of bite as he said, "Why so gloomy? If you don't want me, you'll have no problem resisting me."

She studied him. Understanding passed over her exquisite features, and compassion wasn't too far behind—compassion that ripped up his freaking heart because it spoke of all the times she'd been rejected in her life.

"You are a wonderful man, Daniel." How kind she sounded now. How contrite. "You just aren't the one for me."

"I don't have to be the one." Determined to regain the advantage, he held out his hand, and this time, she took it. Calluses...friction. He brought her knuckles to his mouth and ran his tongue over the ridges. "I just have to be the one *right now.*"

Goose bumps broke out along her arm. With a yank, she freed herself from his grip and pressed her hand against her chest, using the other one to rub the spot where he'd kissed.

I'm not the guy for you, honey? Think again.

"I can check in Jude and Brock today, but afterward I have a few errands to run before I can officially start my duties." Namely, he had to buy supplies for Princess and print flyers about her, just in case her owner lived nearby. Oh, and he had to beat his friends bloody.

"Okay. All right." She pulled at the collar of her shirt. "I'll take you on our first date…tomorrow. After work. I'll be in charge."

Resolved and hoping to get their first romantic interlude over with as soon as possible? Her mistake. He'd gained a tactical advantage today, and he would utilize it to his full advantage.

He unveiled his wickedest smile. "Shall we seal our deal with a kiss?"

She bristled, saying, "Sure. If you want to kiss my butt."

"Yes." He fought a grin. "I accept. Bend over."

Her jaw dropped, and she leaped away from him, pointing a finger at him. "You stay away from me, you hear?"

"Yes, ma'am. For now." He withdrew the small bottle of nail polish from his pocket. "This is for you. A new color."

The starch drained from her, and she looked up at him through the thick fan of her lashes. "White with glitter?"

"To represent passion. Soon you're going to lust for me, and you need to be prepared."

A sharp intake of breath, her bee-stung lips parted. He leaned closer, intending to kiss her. *Can't resist a second more.* Just a peck. A precursor for the things to come. Without another word, she spun and darted down the hall, disappearing around the corner. A door slammed.

"I won't count this as a retreat," he called. Since he'd already solidified their dates. "I'm pretty sure you're running away so you can prepare for tomorrow. You know I like to be wined, dined and sixty—"

Her screech echoed down the hall. "Shut your piehole, Porter!"

He laughed with genuine amusement. And it felt good. Odd, but good. They needed to discuss her tendency to bail on him. Or maybe he should give her a reason to stick around?

Yeah. That one.

As good as done.

Whistling like a carefree boy he couldn't remember being, he headed to the lobby to deal with his asshole friends.

CHAPTER SEVEN

Dorothea stayed up all night watching online radar, hoping an F-1 or F-2 would blow through the barren fields on the outskirts of town. No one would be hurt and nothing would be damaged, but she'd have a legit distraction from thoughts of Daniel.

Alas. The storm passed without dropping a single piece of the predicted hail.

When finally she lay down, thoughts of her tormentor continued to, well, torment her. Why had she agreed to his negotiation? She should have cultivated discord instead of welcoming him closer.

Face it. I'm about as sharp as a marble.

Nowadays the only person she could count on was herself, but even she was unreliable.

Could she really blame herself, though? The lure of free labor had tantalized her. Almost as much as Daniel.

Thou shalt help when needed.

Today, when Daniel had looked at her, she'd felt like the most beautiful woman on earth. She'd felt desired. Heck, she *was* desired. The man was coming at her guns blazing, determined to seduce her into his bed. He was working to win her, as if she were a prize. It was a first for her.

Sighing dreamily, she clutched a pillow to her chest and rolled to her side.

Before the bare-her-body-and-soul incident, she would have accepted whatever he offered with a *please* and *thank you*, grateful for his attention, no negotiation necessary. But no matter what she'd told him—or herself—she would have crumpled like a tin can when they parted.

He wouldn't have been a memory to cherish but another nightmare to add to her collection. The newest guy to take what he wanted from her and leave. Unfortunately, such an abysmal outcome wasn't a proper deterrent for her hormones; they hungered; they wanted to devour him.

They said: *Sleep with Daniel once, as originally planned. Or twice. Probably three times. He can be your guilty pleasure. The first you've ever had. You'll enjoy nights of ecstasy. What do consequences matter?*

All she had to lose was her pride. No big deal, right? Been there, done that.

Except, Daniel planned to hide his association with her, as if he were ashamed of her. So really, more than her pride was at stake. He could destroy the entirety of her self-worth.

Yes, he wanted to protect his father from disappointment when the relationship ended. *When* it ended, she reiterated. Not if. Daniel *believed* the relationship would end, and what he believed would influence every decision he made, dictating the course of his life. Meaning everything he did and said would serve a single purpose: the perpetration of the expected end.

They would be doomed from the start.

When the end ultimately came, she would be alone...would feel like a woman without worth.

I'm worth something, dang it! Her heart was bigger than her thighs. And she might not have a college degree, but she owned a business. Maybe not a successful business, but one with great potential.

Besides, she wanted to be more than a challenge to a man. She wanted to be special, beloved even. A treasure worth fighting for. Finally! She hadn't been special to her husband, and she certainly hadn't been special to her father.

Joe Mathis had remarried as soon as the ink dried on his divorce papers. Dorothea and Holly hadn't been invited to the wedding. Certain there'd been some kind of mistake, she'd driven Holly into the city; her sister had been so eager to see their dad and excited to meet their new stepsiblings. His new wife had a son and a daughter of her own, both close to Holly's age.

Neither Dorothea nor Holly had a chance to even get out of the car. Dad and the kids had been playing a game on the front lawn. He'd laughed and tossed a ball with the boy before twirling the girl through the air. When he'd spotted his girls in the rust bucket, he'd sent the other kids inside a pretty house with white shutters over the windows, closed the distance and crouched beside Holly's open window.

"Go home, girls," he'd said. "I've started over, and so should you. I don't need reminders of my past."

No *I love you*. No *I miss you*. Just a basic *I'm done with you*.

That day was forever branded in Dorothea's mind. It was the last time she'd seen her sister cry. Because, the moment her dad said *Go home, girls*, all hope had died in Holly. The color had faded from her cheeks. Her lips had pressed together, and her eyes—*so like my own*—had hardened.

It was as if Holly's tender side had been cleaved from her soul, leaving her cold inside.

Remembering, Dorothea fought a sob.

Men sucked. Why did she even want one?

She didn't! So. She would continue to resist Daniel. But…

if a miracle happened and someone worthy of *her* came along, she would pursue a relationship with him. Because, dang it, she did want one.

Sharp as a marble.

Her alarm screeched to life. Ugh—5:00 a.m. Dorothea groaned, rubbed her dry, burning eyes and stretched her arms over her head. This was a new day. A new opportunity to succeed in areas she had previously failed. Today, her nails would be solid yellow.

She brushed her teeth and checked her radar apps. A cold front had moved in. She dressed in warm clothes and hooked her iPod to her bicep before heading outside to start her morning run.

The sun hadn't yet risen, the sky filled with stratus and nimbus clouds. Rain clouds. The stratus were flat and spread out, while the nimbus were puffy and dark. A hint of moisture suggested a new storm system brewed.

By the time she hit her sixth mile, a crack of thunder boomed. She should return to the inn before she experienced an outdoor shower, but Daniel would be working in the lobby today, and she slowed her pace. *Not yet ready to see him.*

Wait. Hold up. What the heck was she doing? Daniel Porter wasn't going to chase her away from her own business. Well, not again. Not ever again. On principle, she increased her speed.

About two blocks away from the inn, a truck pulled up beside her, the breaks squeaking. A squeak she'd heard before. *Don't be Daniel. Don't be—*

"Hey, Thea." The vehicle remained at her side, the window rolled down. Daniel hooked an arm over the door, a little tricolored Chihuahua nestled against his chest.

He had a dog? A tiny creature he nurtured and loved? *Be still my heart.*

No, no. Stay strong! "Hi, Daniel." Her heart thumped against her ribs. Because she'd overexerted herself, no other reason. "Headed to the inn to report for your he-ceptionist duties?"

When she stopped to catch her breath, the truck stopped. Intending to tell him to mosey on, she faced him…but no words escaped. The sun was in the process of rising at last—directly behind him. Of course! The storm clouds hid most of the golden rays, but a few managed to escape and frame Daniel, as if drawn to him.

This just in: the sun is female.

"You mean my *assistant* duties. And the answer is yes. But what are *you* doin', darlin'?"

His exaggerated Southern drawl was sexy as heck.

I'm huffing and puffing like the big bad wolf, sweating and generally looking like crap. "Take a wild guess."

His grin was slow and wicked, making her shiver. "This isn't a guess so much as a statement of fact, but you are definitely turning me on."

No way. Just no way. "You are not turned on," she blurted out.

His grin only widened. "I'll stop the truck and show you. Just say the word."

"No!" Thankfully, there were no other cars on the road to witness her mini heatstroke. "I'll pass."

"You sure? My *you know* would love to show off."

She hesitated. She actually hesitated. "Very sure," she finally said with a nod. No reason to throw the ultimate temptation into her influx of problems.

"You sure you're sure? I'm sensing doubt."

Rather than answer him—and possibly lie—she focused on trudging uphill. When she reached the top, the town square would be visible. The real world. Daniel would stop flirting. Anything to keep his secret, right?

"Do you jog every morning?" he asked.

"Yes." Changing the subject before he could invite himself along, she said, "Cute dog."

"I found her. Something or someone mauled her back legs. I couldn't leave her alone in a strange house, especially while I'm searching for her owners."

A big strong guy taking care of a poor, injured dog. Was there anything sweeter? "What's her name?"

"Princess." One of his brows winged up. "Animals are allowed at the inn, right?"

Her mom had always issued a No Pets Allowed policy, but Dorothea overrode it, effective immediately. "Princess will be a welcome addition to the staff."

He began to protest, only to shut his beautiful mouth. Expected a completely different answer, had he? "You aren't worried about your desk being used as a chew toy, or finding poop in your filing cabinets?"

"Why would I worry? One can be fixed and the other cleaned. By you. My he-ceptionist." And now, they'd reached the top of the hill. She picked up the pace, and this time, he let her move ahead.

In fact, he never accelerated past her but remained on her tail. Looking out for her, without publically associating with her.

Great! They weren't even dating, and he'd already made her feel worthless.

When she reached Main Street, she moved to the sidewalk. She passed Daniel's dad and Mr. Rodriguez, who were setting up the table and chairs they used for their daily round of checkers. Both men hollered out a greeting, and she waved without looking over. The last time she'd come across them, they'd done nothing but praise Daniel.

He's grown into a handsome man, hasn't he?

His wife will be a lucky lady. There's no man more faithful. Bet his kids will be cute as buttons.

Oh, there'd been one bit of hinting/leading, too.

He's troubled and needs a woman to soothe him. (nudge, nudge)

Troubled? Daniel? Ha! Except...

The night she'd propositioned him, there'd been a haunted glaze in his eyes when he'd opened his door. A glaze she'd overlooked in her panic but hadn't forgotten in her thousand and one mental replays. Sweat had beaded over his brow and upper lip, and his breathing had been accelerated.

Every morning for the past week she'd jogged past his dad's house. Because it was located along the best route, no other reason. Daniel had been up while the rest of the town had slept. He'd paced back and forth in front of the window.

Considering his military background, he'd probably seen and endured horrors she couldn't even imagine. Did memories plague him?

He idled his truck in front of the salon, chatting with his dad, taking the focus off her, and she gratefully raced around the corner, soared inside the inn and—

Stopped, incredulous. Holly sat at the reception desk, ignoring the ringing phone while playing on her cell. She should have been getting ready for school.

Dorothea's temper—utterly—exploded. She stomped over and pushed Holly out of the chair. As her sister crashed to the floor—then jumped to her feet—Dorothea pointed to the hallway. "Go! Gather your school supplies and get your butt to class. Now!"

Defiance crackled in Holly's eyes. A look Dorothea had never seen in her own. "I won't, and you can't make me."

"I can drag you kicking and screaming, and I'll do it without a qualm. Go!"

"You think you're stronger than me?" Holly actually drew back a fist, intending to...punch Dorothea in the face?

She braced, ready to take the blow. Maybe, after hitting her, Holly would finally feel vindicated. They could start fresh.

The bell over the front door tinkled just before her sister struck. A second later, Daniel stood between them, his arms extended to hold them at a distance, Princess barking at his feet.

"We use our words, ladies, not our fists." His hard tone demanded immediate submission. "Back away, Holly."

"Whatever. I'm out of here." Holly flicked her dark hair over her shoulder and flounced out of the room. The back of her T-shirt had two bold letters: *F* and *U*.

Nice.

A scowling Daniel focused on Dorothea. "Tell me what that was about before I blow a gasket."

He was mad at *her?* He had no right! "*That* was private business and—" Dorothea deflated with disappointment as questions raced through her mind. Would Holly ever speak to her again? Or would her sister spend the day building stronger walls? "You shouldn't have interfered."

"Are you freaking kidding me? She was going to hit you, Thea." The words lashed from him, his anger only seeming to grow.

"Afterward she might have talked to me. Thanks to you, I'll never know."

Oh, yes. His anger was definitely growing. Steam practically wafted from his nostrils. "Let's get one thing very clear. No one hits you. *No one.* Not for any reason. Ever."

His vehemence thrilled her to the core. Which ticked her off! He was military, the need to protect branded in his bones. This wasn't romance; this was White Knight Syndrome.

"Don't act as if you care," she said. "I'm too tired to sift through—"

His big hands framed her cheeks in a tight grip, silencing her. He leaned down, getting in her face. "You're the woman I want in my bed. Of course I care."

Her knees shook to the same rhythm as her jacked-up heart rate. *Resist him!*

This was a practiced move, had to be. And after Jazz, she was immune to moves. She was! "You need to let me go, Daniel. Anyone could walk in. If we're seen like this, gossip will spread. Your dad—"

"Thinks we're friends, nothing more." His thumbs caressed the rise of her cheekbones. "Tonight's our first date. The one you're planning. Where are you taking me?"

Oh…crap. Their date! Yesterday she'd thought, *Get it over with.* Today she thought, *I'm in trouble.* He'd brought his A game.

Well, she would just have to ensure they were never alone. On tonight's menu? The Scratching Post. And maybe Dorothea would use him. Not for pleasure, but for practice. Maybe she would attempt a few flirting techniques so that, when her Mr. Right finally came along, she would be ready.

Yeah, talk about a foolproof plan with zero flaws, she thought drily.

"I, uh, need to shower." She *hated* the breathless quality to her voice. "And you need to get to work."

He crossed his arms over his wide chest. "Before you go, tell me about my new duties."

Right. She moved around him, careful not to touch him, and tapped the keyboard to wake up the computer. "Whenever a customer checks out, you do a quick survey. Like any good he-ceptionist would. Ask how they enjoyed their stay, how likely they are to return and, most important, what type of theme room they'd find most exciting." Something Holly was supposed to have done.

"You considering doing theme rooms?" Daniel looked around, as if seeing the inn through new eyes. "That's a brilliant idea. Both SV residents and out-of-towners will stay for the experience as much as the convenience."

She tried not to flush with pleasure. Yeah, she tried. "One day, yes. Every room will have a different theme."

"What's stopping you *today*?"

"What else? Money."

"You don't need money to get started, sweetheart. Not much, anyway." As she sputtered with incredulity, and secret pleasure that he'd called her sweetheart, he added, "What's *your* favorite theme?"

Easy. "The four seasons. And I'm not talking about the hotel chain, but winter, spring, summer and fall."

"Then that's the one we'll start with."

Hope fizzed in her blood for the first time since taking over the inn. "How?"

"How else? We'll barter with the locals."

Barter. As in, offer overnight stays free of charge in exchange for goods and services? "That's even more brilliant," she admitted.

"Yeah, yeah. I'm an amazing person, and you can't get enough of me. Stop fawning. You're embarrassing us both." Daniel gave her a little push toward the hallway. "Go take your shower. Let your assistant—"

"He-ceptionist."

"—handle the details."

Daniel spent the bulk of the morning on the phone. First he called Harlow Glass. Well, Harlow Ockley now. The woman created magic murals with her paintbrush.

He told her what he wanted—four different murals in a single room—and she said, "For Dottie Mathis? I'll do *anything*. I'll even buy the paints, and I'll do the murals for free."

The girl had certainly changed since high school. "First, her name is Dorothea. Second, how soon can you start?"

"How about tomorrow? Beck has been overprotective ever since we found out—"

"Even better," he interjected, uninterested in swapping life stories. He had too much work to do. "Thanks."

Her chuckle drifted over the line. "No small talk, huh? Got it. Have Dot—Dorothea call me so we can discuss her vision, okay?"

"Will do." He hung up and called his supplier to order the parts he needed for the inn's new security system. It would be his "I'm an ass, I'm sorry, but hopefully my actions speak louder than my words" gift to Thea. Romance at its finest. After listing everything he wanted mailed to the inn, he spent a little time in one of the unoccupied rooms, measuring walls and windows. Then he called Jessie Kay, who owned an online dress shop—Jessie Kay's Closet. He gave her the specs and asked her to sew a king-size comforter and a set of curtains at no charge.

She threatened to charge double until she heard the pieces would be the crowning glory of the Strawberry Inn's first theme room.

"If I can pick the theme of the second room," she said, "I'll sew two comforters and two sets of curtains at no charge."

"Done." He figured she'd want the second room to be themed Jessie Kay Rules the World. If Thea wasn't on board, well, the two women could work something else out.

"Perfect. Send me links to the kind of material Dorothea wants, and I'll get started on the comforter right away."

"I'll do better than that. I'll bring you the material tonight." After work, but before their date, he would drive Thea to the city. Fabric shopping wasn't exactly his idea of a good time, but he couldn't stop smiling as he imagined her surprise and delight. "And thank you."

"Yeah, yeah," Jessie Kay said. "I'm awesome. I know. And I already know how I'm going to theme my room. I'm calling it Daniel's Downfall."

Lord save me. He hung up on her.

During the next half hour, two people called about the reception job. So soon? He told both the woman and the man to call back in a week. And he didn't feel guilty about it. He'd just started, and he needed more time to do his thing. Besides, Thea needed to save a little money.

Excited by the new developments, he jumped to his feet. He'd hunt her down, tell her all about the favors he'd done her. Maybe he'd catch her dancing…

Or maybe not. Word of his new job had already spread, and multiple people stopped by the inn to "check on" him.

Why you working here? You short on cash, boy?

Did your security business already fail? Bless your heart. I remember when Jed Goodfellow tried to open that fancy sour cream store. You 'member that? He called it yogurt, but I know sour cream when I taste it.

You rack up a big bill last time you stayed here? Them pay-to-view movies can be expensive. I reckon I should have asked to work the counter in exchange for that porno I accidentally ordered.

No one asked if he was sweet on Thea, at least, which he'd expected. And it pleased him that nobody asked, of course it pleased him, but it also troubled him. Could *no one* picture them together?

Unwilling to answer any questions, he diverted everyone's attention to Princess. She was a cute little thing with both back legs wrapped in bandages. Not that she cared for the attention; she growled at every newcomer.

All the while, Daniel remained on alert for Thea. He couldn't *not* watch her whenever she appeared; every fiber of his being was attuned to every fiber of hers. Damn, she was gorgeous. She'd piled her dark curls on the crown of her head, and praise be to God above, she'd once again forgone makeup. His favorite freckles were on display.

She wore a pair of purple scrubs, and even with her Barbie doll features—those big eyes and plump lips—she looked about as innocent as a Sunday-school teacher.

He knew the decadent curves hidden underneath her clothes, a carnal secret he shared with no other man in town.

His gaze lingered on her delicate hands. She'd added red polka dots to her nail polish. Hopeful and angry.

Angry at him? Or Holly?

Either way, thoughts of war had no chance to intrude. The memory of Thea standing in his room, exquisitely naked, remained front and center in his mind all day, threatening to fry every brain cell he possessed. Well, fry his brain cells *more*.

The lack of workable circuits might explain his rush to protect her from a hundred pounds of goth fury, as if she were about to be murdered with an ice pick. But he'd simply reacted. The woman who'd blushed as she propositioned him deserved hugs, not slugs.

He was petting Princess when Thea peeked her head around the corner.

"Um, about our…" She licked her lips, obviously nervous, and glanced behind her to ensure no one stood nearby. "Evening together," she concluded in a whisper. "Since we don't want anyone to know about us, you'll have to meet me at the Scratching Post."

He swallowed a laugh, knowing she wouldn't understand his amusement.

Didn't think he'd make a move in a crowd? Challenge accepted.

"Fine. I planned to take you into the city to pick fabric for the theme room. If you'll send me links to what you like, I'll pick it up myself. Then I'll meet you at the bar. What time?"

"Nine?"

"You want me to decide? Are you ceding control to me already?"

"Already? Try never." She scowled at him, a little kitten

pretending to be a tiger. "Meet me at nine." A firm statement this go-round.

He experienced a familiar rush of excitement, exactly what
he'd lived for since leaving the military. But underneath the
excitement? A hint of impatience and a dash of irritation. He
wanted this bundle of delicious contradictions *now*.

"I'll be there," he said with a nod. Nothing would keep
him away.

The bell above the front door tinkled, and Dr. Vandercamp
strode inside the lobby. Princess didn't growl at him, but she
didn't rush over to greet him, either. *That's my girl.*

"I'm headed back to the office," Vandercamp said, "and
thought I'd check on our pup."

The word *our* raised Daniel's hackles.

Thea took a step forward, wringing her hands, the scent of
her fogging his head. "Brett? Brett Vandercamp?"

The doctor looked her up and down and brightened. "Dottie. Hi."

"Her name is Dorothea," Daniel snapped.

She ignored him. "How are you, Brett? I'd heard you
moved back to town to take over your dad's veterinary hospital."

"I'm well, and you heard correctly. How about you? What
have you been up to?"

She played with a loose tendril of hair, the curl coiling
around her finger. Her color was high—because of douche-
nozzle Vandercamp?

"I'm even better now that you're here," Thea said with a
tremulous smile. "You look good."

"So do you. Very good."

What. The. Hell. Were they *flirting*?

"I didn't realize you two were friends," Daniel grated.

"I tutored Brett," Thea said, her gaze remaining on the
vet. "Thanks to me, he made an A in history."

Vandercamp rested an elbow on the counter, leaning toward her as if he had every right to invade her personal space. "I haven't seen you around, had no idea you'd grown even prettier."

"Really? You think so?" She blushed the loveliest shade of rose. "I mean, *of course* I've grown prettier. Thank you for noticing."

When Daniel had complimented her, she'd called him a liar.

Annoyed, he inserted himself between the pair. "Are you here about the dog or trolling for a date?"

"Why not both?" Far from intimidated, Vandercamp picked up and examined Princess. He changed her bandages and said, "What do you say, Dot—Dorothea? Want to go out sometime?"

Her breath caught in her throat, as if she couldn't believe something so wonderful was happening to her.

Say no. She had better say—

"Yes. I'd like that."

Daniel gripped the edge of the counter with so much force he feared he would crack the wood. As Thea exchanged numbers with Vandercamp, he focused on his breathing. In, out. In…out.

When the vet left at long last—good riddance!—Daniel glared at the flustered Thea. "You're dating *me*."

His little kitten showed her claws, hissing, "I'm dating you *under duress*. We are *not* exclusive, Mr. Room Wrecker. If we were, then and only then could you warn me away from Brett."

I will not punch a wall. She was the only woman he wanted, and he expected to be the only man *she* wanted. "What would you like me to wear for *our* date?" The words shot from him, as sharp as daggers.

Her gaze slid over his white button up and dark slacks. His

Sunday best, as his momma used to say. "Wear a T-shirt and jeans. No, sweatpants." She waved a finger over him. "And make sure both are baggy."

The motion startled Princess, who snarled at her. To his surprise, Thea stuck out her tongue at the dog. A second later, she covered her mouth with her hand, those shamrock eyes wide. Then she giggled. Soon the giggle bloomed into an all-out laugh. The amusement lit her entire face, making his chest ache.

She's mine, and I won't share. But she's right. If our relationship is to remain a secret, I can't warn Vandercamp away.

He bit the inside of his cheek until he tasted blood.

A boom of thunder rattled the building, and Princess quieted. She began to tremble. He pressed her against his chest. Sometimes, in the heat of battle, explosions and gunfire raging all around him, he and his buds had to lie down and press together in the shadows, waiting for the opportunity to strike... or for death to strike them. Feeling another's heartbeat had been their only tether to life.

"Finally! We're getting some action." Thea messed with her phone. "There's a ninety-five percent chance of hail." She skipped to the door to...record the storm?

"You like hail?"

"Don't be silly. Only crazy people like hail," she said—while grinning. "Maybe a freak snowstorm will blow in and a tornado will hit. We could have a snowquakenado blizzard. Do you know how awesome that would be?"

"Only crazy people like hail, but sane people wish for a snowquakenado blizzard?" The incongruity of her statement somehow eased the tension inside him. "Sweetheart, I'm getting mixed signals from you." In more ways than one.

Another giggle, and hell! He wished she had stayed quiet; the sound of her good humor only enchanted him more. "If everything goes as predicted, the sun will show up in about an hour and the storm will move on." She opened the door and stepped outside, saying over her shoulder, "You'll be safe here, so there's no reason to worry."

Who *was* this girl? "I'm not worried."

She'd wanted to be a meteorologist but had dropped out of school after getting married. He wondered why.

He wondered about *every* detail of her life, and it disconcerted him. Curiosity had never before factored into his romantic pursuits, but the more he learned about Thea, the less he realized he actually knew.

Daniel carried Princess to the front door and peered out the glass, watching as Thea spoke into her phone, wind whipping around her, rain soaking her hair and plastering her scrubs to her skin. Her nipples were hard.

A sense of possession riveted him in place, invaded his blood, his bones.

Secret or not, she's mine. No other man will have her.

He walked away before he gave in to the temptation to join her outside. He could wait for their date to make his move. Barely.

CHAPTER EIGHT

What the heck was going on?

Yesterday Dorothea had woken up with no way to create her first theme room and zero dates. Now she had a theme room in the works and three dates. Three! Daniel, Brett the vet and John, Holly's teacher.

John had texted her about an hour ago. I haven't stopped thinking about you since the parent-teacher conference. Or sister-teacher conference LOL :) It would be an honor to take you to dinner on Sunday. Any interest?

She responded with, Dinner would be lovely.

A totally suave answer, breezy rather than flabbergasted. Meanwhile she'd had a panic attack on the inside. *He likes me, and he can't stop thinking about me. He's clearly insane! No, no. He's smart, and he has good taste. I've got a good heart, remember? And I have prospects. But I just agreed to go on a date with him, which means I just agreed to talk to him with food stuck in my teeth, because that is totally going to happen!*

Brett had called about twenty minutes after John texted. "Look, I don't know what you've got going with Daniel Porter—"

"Nothing," she'd assured him in a rush, ignoring the twist of…something dark in her gut.

"Good. How about dinner on Sunday?"

For the first time in her life she'd gotten to say, "I just made plans with someone else." What were the rules for dating multiple people? Was she supposed to tell Brett who she'd made plans with? "How about dinner on Saturday?"

"Great," he'd said. "I'll text you Saturday morning with details."

At that point, she'd almost canceled on Daniel. Two men? Alert the presses, she was a wanted woman. Three men? She was a glutton.

In the end, she'd let things stand. A deal was a deal. Three dates with Daniel meant three weeks of free labor. Only a fool would pass up such a delicious—uh, advantageous opportunity.

She spent the next half hour on the phone with Harlow, planning the murals and exchanging ideas, and her excitement skyrocketed. The four seasons theme room would be better than she'd ever dreamed. And so would her love life!

Tonight would be a dress rehearsal for the other, more important, dates.

She'd go all-out and scale back as needed.

With that in mind, she donned her most feminine outfit: a white baby doll dress with lace straps and a lace trim that ended just above her knees. Her once-treasured wedding "gown," special only for sentimental reasons. It had been the best she could afford the day she and Jazz eloped. For her feet, she selected ballerina slippers with ribbons that crisscrossed up her calves.

Both items were completely nonsensical, maybe even out of fashion, okay, definitely out of fashion, but so what? She'd never been a trendsetter.

I am who I am, and Brett and John like me anyway. What an amazing day!

She considered painting her nails with the glittery white polish Daniel had given her. Problem was, he would consider it a sign she wanted to sleep with him. She did, but she wouldn't. Then she toyed with the idea of painting her nails solid yellow, Daniel's favorite color. But again, he would consider it a sign. She selected a pale gold to represent her nervousness. What? Gold could pass as orange. Just because the color resembled Daniel's eyes, well, that meant nothing.

Her cell phone buzzed, Holly's face appearing on the screen, and she hurried to answer.

"I'm going to the city with friends," her sister said in lieu of a greeting. Laughter rang out in the background.

"What are—" Dorothea began.

Click.

"—you guys going to do in the city?" she finished lamely.

She sighed and stuffed her cell in the pocket of her dress. At least her sister had deigned to call and tell her. But still, the rift between them had widened, no doubt about it, and Dorothea hadn't yet come up with a plan to build a bridge.

Not going to worry about it. Not tonight.

As she'd proved, time was the difference between despair and glee, zero dates and three...the death of a relationship and the start of a new one.

With her head high, Dorothea strolled into the Scratching Post. Her heart raced, and perspiration dampened her palms. Through a thick veil of smoke, she saw a sizable crowd congregated at the bar. Wednesday wasn't really a let's-party night, but Ryanne was on duty, hustling to fill drink orders, and the guys couldn't get enough of her.

Dorothea noticed a man she'd met but had never truly conversed with—Brock Hudson. He was heavily tattooed and pierced in several places, his dark hair shaved military short, the shadow of a beard darkening his jaw. A woman perched on either side of his lap, making him the picture of debauchery. Though he smiled at one, then the other, he seemed more aware of his surroundings than his companions.

It was a trait Daniel shared.

Brock stubbed out a cigarette, and she grimaced. At least he'd used an ashtray. Daniel used to smoke outside the inn. But he hadn't done so the last few times he'd stayed, she realized now. Had he quit?

A blond man gave her a thumbs-up. She recognized him but couldn't remember his name. Yet another man whistled at her, and her head lifted a little higher. There was no sign of Daniel, but then, she'd gotten here fifteen minutes early and he'd had errands. He'd driven to the city to buy material for the theme room, as promised; afterward he would be taking Princess to his dad's.

His devotion to the little dog astounded Dorothea. And okay, okay, it made her chest throb with feminine appreciation.

Thou shalt treat others with kindness.

He was such a good guy. In one day, he'd done more for her first theme room than she'd done in an entire year. He'd encouraged her to live her dream. Not tomorrow—tomorrow wasn't a guarantee—but today. He'd proved obstacles could be used as opportunities.

She thought Daniel could maybe possibly become her friend. *If* she learned to control her physical reactions to him. The cascade of warmth every time she looked at him. The tingles and tremors. The elevated heartbeat…the surge of lust low in her belly.

He was the human equivalent of a brownie. Yummy, but oh, so bad for her.

Ryanne twirled bottles as if they were batons and poured

the contents into glasses. Noticing Dorothea, she smiled. "Wow! You look amazing."

I do? Wait. *That's right, I do.* "Thank you." Dorothea fluffed her hair.

At the other end of the bar, a man shouted for her friend's attention. Ryanne held up a finger, saying to Dorothea, "What would you like to drink?"

"Something tasty but light." Too much sugar caused sluggishness, and she needed to remain on high alert.

"All right, then. I'll make you a Moscow Mule. It has vodka, which is made from potatoes. Potatoes are practically a salad."

Suddenly a wall of white-hot heat pressed against her backside and wrapped her in a force field of masculinity. "Make that two salads, please."

Daniel's rough, husky voice stroked her ears an-n-nd, yes, she experienced an intense and undeniable physical response to him. Tremors raked her, and tingles erupted in select places.

She turned to face him and promptly lost her breath. Primal hunger blazed in his amber eyes and also painted fine lines around his mouth. His dark hair stuck out in wind-rumpled spikes. He wore a black T-shirt and sweatpants as requested. The problem was, the shirt fit well. Too well. He'd ignored her orders, and he would be punished. Or not. Definitely not, because the thought made her shiver. The pants bagged a little, at least, hanging low on his waist, but wow, they still managed to look good on him. Her plan to camouflage his hotness had backfired. His muscular physique was on spectacular display.

"What are you doing?" she whispered, planting her palm on his chest to push him back.

Strong as steel, he remained in place, his heart drumming against her hand. "I'm admiring you. You are…" His gaze slid over her, hooded, then traveled over her a second time at a more leisurely pace. "Absolutely exquisite."

Thou shalt compliment when merited.

How was she supposed to respond to such blatant appreciation?

Easy. By focusing on tonight's goals. Shedding her shyness, learning to flirt and saving herself for a viable candidate.

He took her hand in his and studied her nails. "Gold?"

"A version of orange," she said, a little defensive.

"You're nervous, then."

Ugh. She never should have told him about her polish. "People can see us, Daniel. You need to back off."

A muscle jumped beneath his eye. "People should mind their own business. Besides, there's nothing wrong with a little flirting." He leaned toward her, becoming all she could see, all she *wanted* to see. "Fair warning, sweetheart. Tonight my main objective is getting my hands under that dress...and into your panties."

Her world tilted, her mind abuzz with a tempest of warring emotions. *Say something!* "I... You... Tonight the only hands in my panties will be mine." She sucked in a sharp breath. She hadn't just implied... *Oh, my stars.* She had. She really had. *Kill me.*

Daniel's pupils expanded in a rush of pure lust. "May I watch?" His voice had evolved into a growl, barely audible over the erratic pulse of music. "I'm willing to beg for the privilege."

"I didn't mean—" Oh, what the heck? *You're here to flirt, so flirt.* "No, you may not watch me," she said with what she hoped was a sultry pitch. "But you have my permission to imagine..."

The response must have been appropriate—or tantalizingly *in*appropriate—because he moaned. "In my mind, you're going to scream my name when you come."

The panties in question? Suddenly drenched.

Thankfully, Ryanne pressed two copper mugs against the back of Dorothea's arm, drawing her attention and saving her from having to think up a response.

"Okay, my pretties. These are on the house," her friend said. "My way of saying *thank you* for the show."

The show. Aka Dorothea's near capitulation, all because Daniel had uttered a few flattering words. Dang it, she needed to beef up her resistance to him.

I can do better. I will do better.

Daniel nodded a greeting at her friend. "Good to see you again, Rye-anne."

"It's Rye-in, and you know it. And you, too, Danny boy." The mouth that had inspired the poems written on the bathroom walls curved into a sugary sweet smile. "By the way, your friend Jude is a turd on the half shell."

"Yeah, he gets that a lot," Daniel said.

"I'm sure you all do." Ryanne waved a hand through the air, dismissing the subject. "If you hurt Dorothea, little pieces of you will end up scattered all over town."

Oookay. A groan slipped from Dorothea.

Daniel gave her friend a jaunty salute. "Warning received."

"You mean *promise* received," Ryanne corrected.

"Well. Hello, there, beautiful." Brock sidled up to Daniel and grinned at Ryanne. His companions remained at his sides, petting his chest as if they'd been paid to adore him.

Had they?

Daniel motioned to him with a tilt of his chin. "Ryanne, have you met my friend and business partner Brock Hudson? Brock, I'd like to formally introduce Ryanne Wade, the owner of the bar."

"I've already had the displeasure." Ryanne batted her lashes at Brock. "Mr. Hudson is a regular pain in my butt."

The still-smiling Brock released his cargo—now pouting

cargo—to cross his arms over his chest. "Every weekend I ask Miss Ryanne to play fifteen minutes in heaven with me."

"And every time I tell him to kiss my go-to-hell," she said without heat…but maybe with a little sisterly affection?

He laughed the huskiest, sexiest sound on the planet—when not compared to Daniel. But seriously. That laugh was like a mating call heard on National Geographic.

The girls stopped petting him and started pawing at him. Seriously, had he paid them, or maybe fed them a magic aphrodisiac? More important, where could Dorothea get a magic aphrodisiac?

Brock gave both women a little push. "Wait for me over there, pretties."

The girls twittered with disappointment but left as requested. As soon as they were out of hearing range, Dorothea said, "Be honest. They're hookers, right?"

"Nah. We're playing a game. Whoever fawns over me the most and the best wins a—"

Daniel hit him in the chest, and he quieted.

A *sexual* game, then. Envy wafted through her—followed by a sublime flicker of bliss when her gaze met Daniel's ponderous one. What would it be like to play—

Nope. Not going there.

To Ryanne, Brock said, "Baby, kissing your go-to-hell is what I'll be doing for twelve of your fifteen minutes in heaven."

"Lucky me." She pretended to gag. "By the way, your dates are wearing pants so tight I can see their religion."

"I saw you bend over earlier. Yours are tighter, doll." His gaze swept over her, his eyes twinkling. "Tsk-tsk. Haven't been to church in a while, have we?"

Okay, now *that* was flirting. Except, Dorothea felt no real sparks between them. No underlying tension.

Oh, you're an expert on chemistry now?

Someone bumped into Daniel. He stiffened, reaching around his waist to—

Abruptly he stilled. His arm lowered, his hand fisting, and a shuddering breath leaving him. The guy responsible stumbled away without realizing how close he'd come to a beat down.

Concerned, Brock patted Daniel on the shoulder. He also cast Drunk Guy a look laden with violence, his smile gone.

Acting on instinct, Dorothea cupped Daniel's beard-shadowed cheeks. Was his past threatening to gobble him up? Remembering a pickup line she'd heard in meteorology school, she said, "I'm not a weather girl, but I'm predicting you'll get six or seven inches tonight."

Brock spewed the drink he'd just taken. Ryanne snickered behind her hand.

Daniel focused on Dorothea, his jaw slack. Then he threw back his head and laughed with genuine amusement, and she nearly collapsed under a great wave of relief.

"I think you're underestimating tonight's storm," he told her. "I'll be getting *zero* inches. You, on the other hand, will be getting ten—"

"Ten?" she squeaked.

Overheating, she pressed a hand over his mouth before he could say anything more. He nipped at her, and she yelped.

They shared a smile as he gathered their drinks.

"Come on." He ushered her to a darkened corner in the back.

For some reason, Brock followed.

Ever the gentleman, Daniel set down the drinks and held out a chair for her. He claimed the seat at her right while Brock took the one at her left, as if...

Realization struck. He was a cover, she realized with a surge of disappointment. That way, no one from Strawberry Valley would suspect this was a date.

"I'm going to ignore Brock, and I hope you'll do the same."

Daniel traced a fingertip over the top of her hand. "You and I are the only two people who matter."

"Words hurt, Danny," Brock said, though he didn't sound upset.

"So do fists." Daniel's gaze remained on her. "Okay with you?"

I think you're perfect just the way you are.

Her nails dug into her knees. "Depends on what we're going to do. Stare at each other all night?"

"I'd like that." He threaded one of her curls around his finger. "But you're in charge tonight. Whatever you want to do, we'll do."

Right. In desperate need of a distraction, and maybe a little liquid courage, she tasted the drink Ryanne had made her. Vodka and...ginger ale? Absolutely delicious. Refreshing, with a sweet burn. Dorothea emptied the copper mug in only a few gulps.

All right. *Let's do this.* "I want you to teach me how to flirt without blushing or stammering."

His eyes darkened with pleasure. "I never blush or stammer."

"I mean me."

"Trust me, sweetheart. You know how to flirt. Your hook is baited, and I'm dangling from the end."

"But I want to catch other fish," she admitted quietly. Truth was truth, and if it created a shield between them, great. Perfect.

Daniel flinched.

Such an intense reaction from him...confused her.

Cautiously, she said, "We're not going to last. Your words, not mine. Not that we've started anything."

He drained his mug.

"It'll be easier for us both if we *never* start anything," she said.

Brock pulled a cigarette from a pack and a lighter from his pocket.

Daniel grabbed the cancer stick and snapped it in two. "No smoking."

"Hey. I'm not the one who quit because some woman wrinkled her nose," Brock replied, but he set the pack and lighter on the table.

Who had wrinkled her nose at Daniel? Dorothea had always been careful to blank her expression and hide her aversion, and she was pretty sure she'd succeeded each and every time.

Daniel kicked his friend's seat. "Quiet, you. The grown ups are talking."

"Besides," she interjected, picking up their conversation as if it hadn't lagged, "you told me I'm not your type."

"You told her she's not your type?" Brock gave his friend the stink eye. "She's sex in a dress."

I am?

"I know she is," Daniel grated.

He does?

He peered at her with the heat of a thousand suns. "I also told you how deeply you misunderstood my words. You *are* my type. You are my *favorite* type. Right now you're my *only* type."

She nodded, clearly surprising him. "Of course I am. *Now.* I'm a challenge."

He pinched the bridge of his nose. "Chasing a woman saves me from the horrors trapped in here." He gave his temple a series of taps. "It gives me a goal. A purpose. Nothing more, nothing less."

I was right, she thought. She'd wondered if multiple overseas tours had affected him adversely, and now she knew. Yes, oh, yes. He used women and sex as a distraction…which meant he would always be searching for the next conquest.

"With you," he said, "I don't want to chase. I just want."
Softening...

Fight this! "Um, knitting can give you a goal and a purpose, too," she said, a tremor in her voice.

Daniel pursed his lips. "Have I mentioned you are more of an irritation than a challenge?"

"Hey!"

"You think the worst of me," he continued, "while I think the best of you."

"What do you mean, the best?"

"You are gorgeous, sexy, smart and kind. Amusing and enchanting."

A hand fluttered over her heart. Her? Enchanting?

Meanwhile, Brock pulled a Ryanne and pretended to gag.

"I don't think the worst of you," she told Daniel, realizing she must have hurt his feelings. "You, too, are gorgeous, sexy, smart, kind and amusing." And yes, even enchanting, which was why she had to guard her reactions to him.

And dang it, she'd been hard on him long enough, she decided. He'd messed up and said the wrong thing at the wrong time. So what? How often had she done the same?

No more thoughts about using him. Instead, she would work *with* him.

"We just want different things," she told him, and patted his hand.

His eyes narrowed. "When you came to my room, you wanted—"

"I know." She licked her lips. His gaze followed the path her tongue had taken, making her shiver. "But then I changed my mind. A pop and drop isn't enough for me."

He blinked at her, incredulous. "A pop and drop?"

"You know, a one-night stand. A hit-and-run. A bang and bail." Dorothea twined her fingers with his, ignoring the wonderful warmth and delicious friction that sparked between them. Daniel had scars. Jazz had smooth skin, and she'd thought she liked it, preferred it—until now.

Fight!

"You are a wonderful man," she said. "And I want to be your friend."

A moment passed in crackling silence. Brock was forgotten. Heck, the rest of the world was forgotten. Adrenaline surged through her, as potent as any drug. Tension tightened her skin over aching bones.

"I can't be your friend, Thea." His tone was grave.

"But why?" A lance of disappointment and dismay cut through her. "You're friends with Jessie Kay."

He flashed his teeth, his features twisted into a fierce scowl. "Yeah, but I don't want to sleep with Jessie Kay."

Daniel was trapped in a nightmare worse than any combat situation he'd faced.

Thea had rejected him yet again. And she'd done it with unwavering certainty.

He should have rejoiced. Talk about a new and intense challenge. Instead, he hurt. He fumed. Not only had she rejected him, she'd asked him to teach her to flirt—with other men. As if she needed to do more than bat those long black lashes or pout those lush red lips. Actually, showing up at a man's door wearing nothing but a raincoat would get her whatever she wanted. Only a grade-A asshole with shit for brains would turn her down.

Did she have her sights set on Vandercamp? Probably. Damn it! Daniel's guts twisted into a thousand little grenades.

"Let me put this another way. I don't *want* to be your friend, Thea." Her features darkened and fell, a sight he despised. Worse, she released his hand. "I want to be your lover."

"But—"

No buts! "You promised me two more dates, and I'm going

to demand you keep your word." He had to shout to be heard as the live band began a new song. "If you want to give flirting a shot, go for it. I'll be honest and tell you what works and what doesn't. But know this. Where you're concerned, expect it to work, whatever it happens to be."

She stared at him, as if confused.

"Fluttering your lashes at me? Check. It works." In spades. "Next."

"I wasn't… I was fluttering my lashes?" How pleased she sounded. How damned enchanting.

Her eyes glittered as she smiled at him. A smile that should have been illegal in every state. It was dangerous. Too bright and far too hot—likely to cause localized swelling in men.

"I'll attend the other two dates as promised," she said. "But we can't go out this Saturday or Sunday. I have plans. And I must emphasize, again, that I won't end up in your bed."

"On the floor or in the car will be just fine." Her cheeks reddened, and like every time before, he found himself wondering, again, just how far the color spread. A mystery he *had* to solve. "What plans?"

"Well." Nibbling on her bottom lip, she squirmed in her seat. "I…have dates."

Absolute rage detonated inside him, shrapnel embedding in his heart. Both his jaw and hands clenched. "With whom?"

The squirming got worse. "Brett Vandercamp and Jonathan Hillcrest, respectively."

In the past, competition had excited Daniel. Right now he would gladly raze the entire world so that he and Thea could be alone, and the reaction stunned him. He felt this strongly, this quickly? Ridiculous! He'd gone years without giving the woman a second thought.

But he'd since watched her dance and seen her naked. He'd laughed with her. Noticed the purity of her heart. Her kindness toward others. Her dedication to her sister. Her quirks—

like her love of nail polish and rainstorms. Her heartbreaking vulnerability.

If he somehow convinced her to cancel her other dates, she would grow to resent him. Maybe even wonder what she was missing.

Stay calm. A successful mission started with a concrete plan.

Step one: touch. He traced a fingertip over the rise of her cheekbone.

She leaned into the touch, a bliss all its own. Then she straightened, her spine so rigid he feared she would snap in two.

Step two: engage.

"Why do you want to stop blushing?" he asked. "It's pretty."

"No, it's even more embarrassing than whatever made me blush in the first place."

Again he asked, "Why?"

"Because… Just because! You wouldn't understand. You've been accepted your entire life."

How often had she been rejected throughout *her* life?

Step three: another touch paired with a compliment. He shifted, leaning toward her while brushing his knee against her thigh…loving her gasp of surprise. At her ear, he whispered, "Your blush gives a man ideas. Very naughty ideas. I vote you keep doing it."

She shivered against him, exciting him—before she pushed him away, disappointing him. "This is *my* date," she said primly, "and I've decided we're going to sit in silence for the rest of the evening."

Step four: give her a glimpse into his deepest fantasy.

"I won't say another word, sweetheart. I'll be too busy imagining your dress on my floor and your ass bent over my bed."

CHAPTER NINE

Daniel marched inside his dad's house, Brock behind him. He would much rather be marching into the inn, with Thea, but at the end of the evening, he hadn't even won a kiss.

All his tried-and-true steps, and he'd failed.

He expected his dad to be sound asleep. Instead, Virgil reclined on the couch, his fingers woven together, locked behind his head. He'd waited up.

Jude sat on the floor, playing with Princess, who spotted Daniel and bounded over. Her excitement soothed him. After his date with Thea, well, his pride was nothing but tatters.

He picked up Princess and let her rest her head in the hollow of his neck while he rubbed her belly. "Everything okay here?"

"No, everything is not okay." Virgil stood. He used to be several inches taller, but the stoop in his back had shortened him. "First of all, you smell bad enough to gag a maggot. All that smoke on your clothes is going to give me the cancer. And what's this I hear about you taking sweet little Dorothea Mathis to the Scratching Post?"

Well. News had certainly traveled fast. But who the hell had told his dad?

Of all the bar's occupants, only Ryanne would have had any interaction with his father, but she and Thea were as close as sisters. There was no way she'd narced.

"I didn't take Thea anywhere," he said, inwardly lamenting. He'd been so careful. Well, sort of careful. He'd have to do better next time. "I was there. She was there. We spoke." True, true and true.

His dad bristled. "Son, you're waking up my inner coyote. Did I not teach you better? Are you not attracted to her? If I were thirty years younger, I'd get her into bed as soon as possible. No one wants to roll over and wonder if he's lying on a hammer or his girl's leg. You should have whisked her out of there, taken her to a nice dinner and paid the check, even if she ordered the surf and turf."

How was he supposed to respond to that?

Jude continued to frown, as usual.

Laughter glimmered in Brock's expression as he patted Virgil on the shoulder. "Bars are the devil's den."

Virgil gave a hearty nod in agreement. "Way I hear it, women throw brassieres and bloomers at the band and men throw shirts at sweet little Ryanne Wade whenever she sings."

To Virgil Porter, every girl from Strawberry Valley was "sweet" and "little."

"Speaking of sweet little Ryanne Wade." Brock stroked his fingers over his jaw, the picture of curiosity. "What's the story on her?"

Daniel had known the man would make a play for her, despite a lack of chemistry. She was his type. Street-smart and hardened by life. The fact that she could mix his favorite drinks didn't hurt.

"Type" doesn't mean shit if what you want isn't what you need.

He rubbed his temple to shut his brain up.

Virgil brightened like a lamp with a new bulb. "You just dilled my pickle. You take a shine to our Ryanne? She's got the voice of a cigar-smoking, whiskey-chugging angel, that one. She's single, and I think that's the way she likes it, so it's gonna take a special man to break through her walls."

"Or dynamite." Brock winked. "I'm *very* good with dynamite."

"Good, good," Virgil said. "We can host the wedding right here in my backyard. And since that sweet little girl ain't got no daddy to call her own, I'll be happy to walk her down the aisle."

Brock flinched as if he'd just taken a punch to the gut. "Wedding?"

"Of course. That *is* the natural progression of a relationship, is it not?"

Welcome to my world, Daniel wanted to tell his friend. Instead, he threw the guy a life raft, saying, "Brock isn't looking to get married, Dad. Neither am I."

If he were a better son, he'd do it. Marry a hometown girl and settle down. But a sham marriage wasn't the answer to his dad's happiness. Or Daniel's. He would still battle PTSD. Maybe on a larger scale. No challenge, no distraction.

And what if the wifey poo decided to divorce him? Virgil's heart would break once and for all. Even worse, what if the wife died unexpectedly?

People died every day.

"You sure you don't want to wed Dorothea Mathis?" his dad asked. "Your eyes light up every time I mention her name."

"They do not."

"Dorothea Mathis, Dorothea Mathis, Dorothea Mathis."

Okay, maybe they did.

He scrubbed a hand down his face, hiding his eyes until he was sure they were as dull as a rusty tin can. "I'm doing security for the inn. I'm even working reception until she hires someone to replace Holly." Again, all true. "Thea and I, we're...friends." The word tasted foul on his tongue. "But you have my word, the next time I see her at the Scratching Post, I'll pick her up and carry her out fireman-style." Eventually.

Virgil heaved a heavy sigh of disappointment. "You're a good boy, Danny, and I love you."

A stab of guilt, straight through the heart. *Never wanted to disappoint this man.* "I love you, too." And maybe Thea was right. Maybe they were better off as friends.

Every cell in his body screamed in protest. *Crave her. Must have her.*

Yeah, but then what?

"All right, boys. This old body needs some rest. You young'uns make sure you keep it down, now, you hear?" Virgil patted Daniel's cheek before padding off.

Princess struggled for her freedom. Daniel set her down and strode to the kitchen to fix a midnight snack. His friends followed him, the dog at their heels, and gathered around the table.

"You want a critique of your performance tonight?" Brock asked him.

"No, thanks." He spread a little mayo over two slices of bread and slapped slices of turkey in the middle. "I'm good."

"Too bad. At first I thought your caveman approach might just be the golden ticket. Then, when you realized you were floundering, you went with stalker-clingy." Brock gave him a thumbs-down. "I was embarrassed for you."

Wonderful. "Thea wants me to teach her how to flirt with other men. In fact, she has a date on Saturday *and* Sunday. With two different guys."

"Count your blessings. You're better off alone." Jude opened a bag of sausage-and-gravy-flavored potato chips. "A solitary life is underrated."

Brock spread his arms wide. "Dude. Your cynicism is show-ing and it's ugly as hell."

"We can't all be beauties," Jude replied, tapping his cheeks.

With a sigh, Brock focused on Daniel. "Give me names, and by tomorrow afternoon the other dates won't be a problem."

Jude popped a chip in his mouth, chewed and swallowed. "Your inner serial killer is showing."

"And he's one of those beauties you mentioned, I know," Brock said.

Daniel polished off his sandwich. "You guys staying here tonight?"

"Nah. I'm going back to the Scratching Post," Brock said. "Got dates of my own."

He'd already slept with the two women he'd had on his arms when Daniel first arrived. He'd escorted the pair to the bathroom and returned fifteen minutes later with his clothes askew, lipstick on his neck.

"I'll go with you," Jude said, surprising both his friends. He usually avoided bars. Only ever showed up when Brock called for a ride. "I'll be your on-site DD."

"You should come with us." Brock waved a finger in front of Daniel's face. "I don't like what I'm seeing here. Bruises under the eyes, lines of tension around the mouth."

"Nothing a few beauty z's can't fix." If he were normal. But he had no desire to return to the scene of Thea's crime against his masculinity. No desire to pick up another woman, either.

Jude stood and pulled Brock to his feet. "Leave the man alone. He probably wants to stroke his *ego* in private."

Brock chortled.

"You guys suck," he called as they strode from the kitchen.

Not liking the sudden silence, Daniel carried Princess out-side. He was tired—hell, he was *always* tired—but he wasn't ready to dream.

While the dog played on the porch, the area spotlighted

by a single bulb, he worked out. He kept his hands and arms rough and tough, spending a good, solid hour honing his ability to strike. Fingers, knuckles, forearms. He threw each against a tree over and over again. The bark scraped his skin, preventing him from getting too soft now that overseas missions weren't happening on the reg. Or at all. He also used a dagger, knowing that maintaining his dexterity was important. Strength could carry you. Weakness would always fail you.

When he finished, he closed himself and Princess in his bedroom. A small space with a full bed, a dresser he'd built in shop class and, his pride and joy, a nightstand he and his mother had painted together.

He showered, which only made his desire for Thea flare. After his last stay at the inn, he'd brought home one of the soaps. Now he had the scent of her all over him, exactly where he wanted it. But it wasn't enough.

Like a puss, he sat down on his bed and flipped through his yearbooks, searching for pictures of Thea. While other kids were captured playing football and other sports, swinging on the monkey bars and doing cartwheels, she only ever stood on the sidelines. Her eyes, which had been far too big for her face back then, radiated sadness and longing.

Had anyone ever invited her to join the fun? He damn sure hadn't, and he was suddenly and deeply ashamed.

Jude was wrong. Solitary living wasn't underrated. It wasn't even living.

The only time Thea had smiled, revealing a mouth full of braces, was when Ryanne and Lyndie had been with her. However, during her sophomore year, the two had opted to be homeschooled, and Thea had truly had no one.

His heart suddenly felt as if it had been flayed with a butter knife. He wished he could go back in time. He would shake his younger self and say, "Real friends are rare. Kindness is rarer. Be nice to that girl. One day, you're going to want her more than air to breathe."

At last he crawled under the sheets. He didn't want to fall asleep, didn't want to be plagued by nightmares, but Princess was exhausted. She burrowed under the covers and curled up beside him, seeking his warmth.

For over an hour, his mind refused to settle. Thea seemed to think all he had to offer her was a torrid one-night stand. And that was certainly true...to an extent. What if he were willing to give the relationship thing a try, as long as they kept emotions out of the picture and their association on the down low? When things ended—and they would—they could be friends, just like she wanted. His dad would never know they'd been more, never get his hopes up, never experience a moment of disappointment.

It could be a win-win with absolutely no downside.

Yeah. He could do it, no problem. He even *liked* the idea of having something more, something solid, between them, without having to worry about either one of them falling in love or walking away unexpectedly. They'd know the end would come. But until it did, Thea would belong to Daniel, and he would belong to her.

While they were together, he would be devoted to her. He wouldn't lie to her, cheat on her or, hell, even look at another woman. Why would he need to? No other woman compared to her.

Finally, blessedly, a sense of contentment overtook him. One he hadn't experienced since his mom died. And yet underneath it was a sense of...wrongness, as if there was a flaw in his plan.

He combed through every detail once, twice, but nothing set off an alarm.

Eventually, he drifted to sleep. A gradual process. Then, in a snap, screams erupted inside his head. The air around him was thick with smoke as well as the pungent aroma of blood and emptied bowels. The scent of death. Despite the constant stream of gunfire, he heard the soft *click* of a pin being pulled from a grenade.

Whoosh. Boom! The ground shook beneath his feet, already unstable buildings threatening to topple. In the distance, fire blazed and smoke clouds drifted. Dust plumed. But even in the hellish darkness, he could see the worry in Brock's face.

"We're going to be okay," he told his friend.

"Not if we stay here. Go on. I'll cover you, and you can come back with help." Brock had taken a bullet to the calf as he'd dragged a bleeding Daniel into this hidden pit. Now they were both injured. "Go!"

"Like hell." The shards of metal embedded around his ribs sank deeper with every move he made. "Our help is already KO'd." Earlier their friend Felix had tripped a Bouncing Betty. The land mine had shot into the air and exploded, ensuring the shrapnel inflicted maximum damage to nearby soldiers. "We wait until the trouble passes."

Jude was hunkered in front of a makeshift window, staring outside with night-vision binoculars. He was the only one without a gusher. "Sorry, bro, but it's not going to pass us. Not for hours yet."

"Then *I'll* cover *you*," Daniel told Jude. *Already lost my mom. Would rather die than lose a friend.* "Leave your battle-rattle here and get Brock to the medic."

Boom!

Debris rained over their hideaway, the roof caving in. Through the ringing in his ears, he detected a storm of footsteps. The enemy approached. He readied his weapons for a final stand and—

Sat up, gasping for breath he couldn't catch. Sweat drenched him. Princess licked his hand, reminding him that he wasn't alone, that he'd survived the battle and, more important, his friends had survived, as well.

He drew his knees to his chest and rested his head on top. People wondered why it was so difficult for soldiers to acclimate to "normal" life. Forget the nightmares. Often Daniel had to retrain himself from speaking in "command voice," a tone that demanded an immediate response; a tone that scared…everyone. And that was the least worrisome reason.

He stood to shaky legs, showered and dressed in a T-shirt and jeans. A glance at the clock revealed it was 3:13 a.m. Unlucky thirteen. Whatever. He had no fear of a man-made superstition.

Fear wasn't a friend but a hated foe. Time and time again, he'd seen men freeze in battle anytime a shot rang out, making themselves a perfect target. Fear could act quickly or slowly, but if left unchecked, it would always take control of your life.

Fool! You're letting fear make your decisions with Thea.

What? No. Hell, no. He didn't fear a relationship with her. He wanted it with every fiber of his being. And he didn't fear his dad's reaction to the inevitable breakup. Not really. He simply preferred to stop a punch before it was thrown.

Though it was a little too early to head to the inn, staying here was no longer an option. He could smell the taint of war, could hear the faint echo of screams. He needed Thea's scent around him, calming him, and not just from her soap, but from every piece of fabric and furniture he encountered. He needed the excitement of watching every corner, wondering when she would round it and finally enter his line of sight. He needed the joy of hearing her voice and seeing her face…her body, a bounty of softness. A treasure.

Freckles mark the spot.

"You want to go with me?" he asked Princess.

She barked and ran circles around his feet.

"I'll take that as a yes."

On the drive to the inn, he realized he needed to buy Princess a doggy car seat. Or maybe a travel crate? Was that an actual thing, or did he need to build one? Either way, better safe than sorry. If something were to happen to his dog—

He shook his head. She wasn't his dog.

Her owner would show up eventually, and he or she would have a lot to answer for. Would have to pass Daniel's Do You Deserve Princess exam, too.

"Today I'm going to turn Thea's no into a yes," he told Princess as he parked in the lot across from the inn. But he felt no excitement at the prospect. What was wrong with a woman wanting him just because he was, well, him? Nothing, that's what.

Thea might not admit it, but she did want him. The way her breath hitched when he touched her...the way her gaze lingered on him... He just had to remind her of her feelings, and *that* was what excited him.

The front door was locked, saving Thea from a lecture about safety. Even small towns had crime. He used his key. The one he'd had made before yesterday's date. In the lobby, a soft lamp glowed on the counter, highlighting a sign that read "Office hours 6:00 a.m.–12:00 a.m. To report a problem, call 405-555-6892."

Thea's cell phone number.

Not on my watch.

Daniel hid the sign in a drawer and taped a new one to the counter. "Office hours 7:00 a.m.–10:00 p.m. If there's a problem after hours, take care of it yourself. You're an adult."

He sat at his desk and worked on answering questions sent from the inn's website. Another job Holly clearly hadn't done. There were hundreds of messages from people raving about their stay, complaining about the rude receptionist and asking about reserving a block of rooms for different festivals.

There were also two new applications. He placed them both in a To Be Read Later folder without reading a single word. He would look everything over in three weeks, when his tour of duty ended.

You're welcome, Thea. Thank me with a kiss.

He answered the questions as best he could, apologized for Holly's behavior and promised the new beefcake behind the counter was much nicer.

When he finished, he headed for the kitchen, Princess trotting behind him. The door was unlocked, the room empty. Guests could walk in and take anything they wanted with no concern about the money the food cost Thea.

He started a list of things he needed to buy for the inn, and digital locks took the number-one spot.

Harlow would begin painting her murals in the first themed-out room today, but not for hours yet. He might as well tape the door frames and windows, allowing her to concentrate on the main event. Again Princess trotted behind him, his own little shadow.

He frowned when he noticed the bright light spilling from beneath the door. Hadn't he turned off everything before he'd left? Yeah. Definitely. He hadn't wanted to add an extra expense to Thea's electric bill.

Very quietly, he used his master key. The door—which would look cool with a twister carved in the center—swung open to reveal Thea in a T-shirt and raggedy jeans, her mass of curls piled atop her head. She had earbuds stuffed in her ears, and as she wrote on the wall, her hips bumped and ground just the way he liked.

A bolt of lust slammed into him, the trials of the night fading from his awareness. He wanted to groan and laugh at the same time. Such a gorgeous, silly girl, his Thea.

He flipped the light switch on and off to alert her to his presence. With a gasp, she yanked out the buds and spun.

"Daniel." Her emerald gaze swept over him—and heated. "What are you doing here?"

Looks like I'm stoking a fire in you, my sweet. The same fire he'd noticed when they were at the Scratching Post, and Brock had mentioned playing a sex game with his hookups.

"I couldn't sleep," he said, hopeful for the first time in forever, it seemed. Finally he had a weapon to use to his advantage. "I figured I'd get started on the room."

Compassion softened her features.

Just like that, irritation began to claw at him. It was the total wrong response, he knew. He was the one who'd told her there were horrors in his mind. Something that had shocked him as much as it had shocked Brock. They had an unspoken rule: Sharing Is Scaring. Civilians didn't need to know the things they'd witnessed...the things they'd done.

"I couldn't sleep, either. I was too excited." She waved him over. "Come see what I've done."

He'd have to be a stronger man to resist her. He eagerly closed the distance.

"Each wall will represent a different season but also different weather patterns, with a single tree spreading its branches across all four," she said. "This one will be a winter wonderland with an ice storm...this one is a rose garden with a tornado...this one is a pumpkin patch with noctilucent clouds... and here, where the bed presses against it, a lush summer forest with rain showers. I'm hoping you'll build a headboard in the shape of a tree. The branches can stretch out over the mattress, and I can drape them with a canopy of green fabric. Like the walls, different branches can represent different seasons."

"Me? I'll build a headboard?"

"Well, you took a woodworking class in school..."

She'd known his schedule?

He masked his pleasure by donning the most severe expression he could muster. "You want me to build a tree...you'll have to negotiate."

CHAPTER TEN

Negotiate. like everything Daniel suggested, the idea was both a threat to her peace of mind and a delight. He wanted her in his bed. He'd made that clear…and it was growing clearer by the second. His jeans were unable to hide the *massive* evidence as he hardened right before her eyes.

A fact that didn't embarrass him. No, he ran a hand down the entire length of it, as if he was *proud* of his reaction to her.

She swallowed in an effort to moisten her suddenly dry mouth. There was no way she'd give up her goods and services for a headboard…right? That would be bad? Right!

I'm worth more, blah, blah, blah.

"Provide the headboard," she said, breathless, "and I'll put your name on the plaque that will hang outside the door."

His look was as pitying as it was carnal. "You think I'm going to spend days…weeks…constructing the headboard of your dreams just to have my name put on a plaque? Think again, pinup girl."

Pinup girl? What a delicious nickname!

Do. Not. Soften. "You can stay in this very room, no charge, once a month for the next year." And if he brought a woman with him? "Alone," she added, and her cheeks began to burn.

"Now you're just embarrassing yourself, sweetheart."

Ugh! "You build the headboard, and I won't tell Jessie Kay you made me cry."

He pursed his lips. "You wouldn't."

"I so would." Dorothea went in for the kill. "Jessie Kay texted to tell me she'd heard we'd hooked up at the Scratching Post, and that I should let her know when you mess up. When, not if. Said she'd take care of the problem—you—lickety-split."

"Wait." He shook his head, his expression twisted with horror. "I made you cry?"

Head slap. Why hadn't she kept that bit of info to herself? "Not recently, no. And never you mind about that. Concentrate on the headboard."

"I am concentrating, but you're going to have to give me something *I* want. Make the backbreaking manual labor worth my while."

"I'm not going to offer sex, if that's what you're hinting at." The very idea should probably offend her, yet here she was, trembling like a teenage girl with her first crush.

Because Daniel *was* her first crush.

The look he gave her was ravenous. "The sex you'll give me for free. Admit it, you crave me as much as I crave you. But there are other things we can do in the meantime…"

Other things? "I will not give you a…a…blow job. Do you hear me?"

One corner of his mouth curved up. "Someone has a very dirty mind, doesn't she? But don't worry. You'll give me a blow job free of charge, too. And I'll reciprocate. Gladly. For the headboard, I'm thinking…a kiss. Right here, right now."

Butterflies with razor-sharp wings took flight in her stomach. "A kiss? Just one?" *What! Don't tell me you're considering this, Dorothea Mathis.*

"Just one. Right here, right now," he repeated huskily.

Well...something short and sweet shouldn't be a problem. A dry peck, even. Loophole! He'd stated no particulars.

"Are we agreed?" He took a step toward her and, as if reading her mind, said, "It'll be openmouthed. With tongue."

Dang him! Shivers danced through her. "How long will it last?" Was that needy tone really hers?

"Ten minutes."

What! "Ten minutes?" she squeaked. She and Jazz had kissed, stripped, had sex and cuddled in that amount of time. "Five minutes, and that's my final offer."

He laughed with masculine appreciation, as if he knew something she didn't. "Done. Five minutes." He took another step toward her, then another.

This was happening. This was really happening. "Wait! I meant two minutes."

"Too late. The deal has been made, the conditions settled. No backing out now." He stopped, only a whisper away.

Her heart erupted in a crazy rhythm. "What are you going to do with your hands?"

"Now, that's a real good question, and one you should have asked before we finalized our negotiations." He rested the hands in question on the wall, caging her in like he'd done the first time she'd come to his room. Obviously he liked being the predator, and making her the prey. She liked it, too. His shoulders were so strong and wide she felt engulfed by him—possessed by him. "I'm going to put them all over you. And I'm going to put my fingers inside you."

Her panties basically liquefied. "N-no?" A question? Come on! "No." Better. "Your hands have to stay above my waist."

Oh, wow. *Way to restrict him, Dor.*

"Very well." He rubbed his nose against hers. A reward?

Because she'd given him exactly what he'd wanted? Now he had permission to play with her breasts...pinch her nipples...

He set a timer on his watch, saying, "I'm not going to let you short me of a single second."

"Be honest. You can't really kiss a woman for five whole minutes. You'd smother her."

"Let me set the scene for you. We're going to pretend we're at school, and the bell's about to ring."

How is he feeding my longest-standing fantasies? Her limbs trembled as the rest of her heated.

"I'll be real careful not to wrinkle your clothes, sweetheart." Peering at her with eyes on fire with lust, he hovered his face over hers, not touching her, not yet.

She waited, wrapped up in an agony and ecstasy like she'd never known.

Why wasn't he kissing her already, dang it?

"I don't care about my clothes," she told him.

"You don't care if the other students know what we've been doing?"

"The students." Her shivers returned, redoubled. Heat bloomed in her chest and swiftly spread through the rest of her. Breathing became a chore, her airways restricted, oxygen too thick. Her heart only raced faster. "Yeah, be real careful."

"Promise." But still he hovered...

There was anticipation, and there was torture. They'd reached the torture stage.

"Daniel," she rasped, willing to beg for his kiss.

"There she is." He pressed his mouth into hers, and she opened eagerly. Somehow, when his tongue brushed against hers, it was a shock to her senses. He was hot, his lips soft, his jaw prickly. The taste of him...mint and...sin? Crack?

He kissed her deeply, dreamily, slow and easy, sweeping her up in the gentlest of storms. A soft summer rain. An exploration.

A delight—but not exactly satisfying when she longed to rip off his clothes.

All too soon, he lifted his head. He was breathing heavily. "We should stop, sweetheart."

What? No!

"The bell," he said.

Did his old girlfriends have to attend support groups? *Hello, I'm Dorothea, and I'm a Daniel addict.* "I'm your English teacher, Mr. Porter." Warm shivers tracked through her. "I'll write you a note."

He chuckled against her lips, gave a little lick. "That's why you're my favorite teacher. Just want to make sure you're giving me the A you promised me."

"Not if you keep talking." She wound her arms around him, one hand sinking into the silk of his hair, the other tunneling under the collar of his shirt. Skin-to-skin contact was essential. Absolutely critical to her survival.

"Thea." With a moan, he swooped down to kiss her again. This time, he deepened the pressure, pressing harder, thrusting his tongue against hers.

Yes! This! This was everything. Time ceased to exist. As she inhaled...exhaled, her nipples puckered and rubbed against his chest. A delicious abrasion that sent waves of pleasure straight to her core, exactly where she wanted his hands.

Where *were* his hands?

Still beside her temples, she realized. Dang him. Why hadn't he touched her yet? He had to touch her. It had been so long. Too long. She *ached*.

"Daniel." A croak this time. "Mr. Porter. Please."

Finally! He kneaded her breasts and ran his thumb over the distended crests. She gasped, her nails digging into his scalp and between his shoulder blades in an effort to hold him closer—or to ensure he never got away.

"I know I'm not supposed to wrinkle your clothes, Miss Mathis, but I'm losing my mind here."

"Daniel," she repeated, and the tone of the next kiss shifted, becoming a ravenous feasting. "Wrinkle them. *Ruin* them."

He bit, sucked and nipped. Staying still wasn't an option. She rocked her hips against him, creating a notch at the apex of her thighs. A notch he utilized to their mutual satisfaction, sliding his big, scarred hands down her sides to cup her butt.

"Wrap your legs around me. Now." Before she could obey, he lifted her as if she weighed no more than a cotton puff.

Not once did she consider denying him. As she wrapped her legs around him, he used the wall as leverage, pressing an insistent erection against her core, holding her up. The contact was bliss, rapture...but she hated their clothes, wanted him inside her, filling her, thrusting so deep. She was empty! Need consumed her, drove her. Release...she had to have a release.

He stayed true to their deal, however, his hands exploring only *above her waist*. Restrictions sucked...sucked... Oh! Yes! He sucked on her bottom lip, at the same time shoving a hand under her shirt. She jolted. His skin—white-hot!

His fingers traced a path up her quivering belly. He kneaded her breasts once again, only this time directly over her bra. Why had she worn one? Never again!

"Do you know how often I've fantasized about these plump beauties with the cotton candy nipples?"

"Please," she said, practically mindless. At the moment, it was the only word she could manage.

He kissed her chin, her jaw, then down the column of her neck, where he sucked on her racing pulse. The pressure inside her continued to build until it was nearly unbearable.

"Please," she repeated.

"I think Miss Mathis has fantasized about me, too." He pinched her nipples, gently at first but increasing the pressure.

As she cried out, needy, so danged needy, he fit his lips

over one and sucked through the shirt. Pleasure…so much pleasure. She was almost blind with it. It clouded her mind, razed her nerve endings. Clawing at him, writhing against him, she gasped incoherent words.

He pulled back the slightest bit—too far!—and lifted his head. He frowned down at her. "Thea?"

"Please," she begged, the scene forgotten by both of them, it seemed. "Please, don't you dare stop!"

His gaze slid over her, heated. "Just from a kiss? Sweetheart, you've just made me the luckiest man on the planet." He reclaimed her lips in a frenzied, possessive clash, everything she'd felt before suddenly magnified.

He played with her breasts, pinched her nipples and rub, rub, rubbed his erection between her legs. It was a sensual assault, every inch of her consumed by every inch of him… by pleasure. Her panties were soaked.

At any other time, such extreme arousal might have embarrassed her. Today? She would gladly strip and present him with the damp material as a gift. Just as long as he kept doing what he was doing!

"So close," she gasped out. "Don't stop. Don't you dare stop! You do, and I'll flunk you. I swear I will."

The bastard stopped, not easing off but stilling abruptly. She cursed him, beat at his shoulders.

He laughed, the sound strained, his features drawn tight with tension. "Let's get you more comfortable."

His stride long and strong, he carried her across the room. When he lowered her onto the coat she'd dropped earlier, her legs remained wrapped around him.

As he rose to his knees, his dark hair was rumpled around his face. His lips were kiss swollen and red, his teeth gritted. The passion she felt for him? He felt for her, she realized. He'd said the words, of course, but she'd never quite believed him until now, when there was no mistaking the truth.

She wasn't just a challenge to him; she was an object of great desire. Her. The overweight college dropout. He *liked* her.

"Take off your shirt," he commanded.

She ran her bottom lip through her teeth—*I can still taste him*—and shook her head. "No. My clothes stay on." He'd rejected her nakedness once. She wouldn't give him another opportunity. What if his passion for her died?

"Thea—Miss Mathis."

"Not unless you turn out the lights." The thought of having his naked chest pressed against hers was a temptation unlike any other.

"To turn out the lights, I'd have to let you go," he said, and ripped his shirt over his head. The dog tags and locket she'd seen before still hung around his neck and clanked between his muscled pecs.

Am I drooling? "Yes, but only for a moment."

"A moment is too long." He traced his fingers over the waist of her jeans. His knuckles brushed her navel, and she groaned. "You are so damn beautiful."

Was she? The question came automatically, and for the first time, it annoyed her. She was!

Braced on one hand, he pulled the tie from her hair and spread her dark curls around her face. Then he traced a fingertip from her brow to her shoulder, following a trail of freckles.

The task seemed to mesmerize him. It unraveled her.

"Daniel."

"Yes, Thea. Yes." He kissed her again. Deep and soul-wrenching.

She clung to him. As he arched his hips again and again, fanning the flames of her desire, she arched her own, caught up in the moment, the sensations.

"That's the way, sweetheart. Keep doing that." As he spoke, he rolled over, putting her on top of him.

They continued to grind together. He flattened his hands on her lower back, careful to remain above the waist of her jeans, and guided her into a counterclockwise rhythm. The sound of their shallow but heavy inhalations filled the room.

A single rational thought intruded: *this is a lot more than a kiss.*

Yes, and she would care. Tomorrow. "More," she commanded now. One climax. That wasn't too much to ask, was it? Then they could return to being friends. Not that he'd accepted her offer of friendship.

I don't want to be your friend, Thea. I want to be your lover.

He quickened his pace, every thrust wonderfully aggressive and frantic. Still that agonizing pressure continued to build inside her...until her body felt stretched to the max. Any second now...any moment...

"Daniel!" Her body convulsed against his. She bit the cord running from his neck to his shoulder to stop a scream from escaping. Too much! The pleasure was too much. A little quake erupted in each of her cells—millions of little ones produced a massive one. Her inner walls constricted, her bones seeming to melt.

As her teeth sank deeper, Daniel roared. He stiffened beneath her and thrust once, twice more before collapsing on the floor.

The timer on his watch beeped.

She tried to catch her breath...tried to fight the reality of what she'd just done. And with whom she'd done it.

Perhaps Daniel sensed her growing wish to leap to her feet and run away, because he rolled her over, placing her beneath him, effectively trapping her.

His features were languid and content, his eyes sparkling with pleasure.

She stared at him, fascinated. *I did this to him. Me.* And in turn, he had stoked a need over a decade old, filling her with delight. No one, ever, had looked at her like that, not even Jazz.

"You are the first woman to make me come in my pants," he told her with a laugh, and he wasn't the least bit embarrassed. "Didn't even happen when I was a horny teenager."

"Maybe that's my superpower," she said, unsure where the words were coming from. Why fight it? "Everyone has a superpower, you know."

"So…you're Spontaneous Combustion Girl?"

She giggled like the schoolgirl she'd never really been and covered her mouth. *Could I be any less cool?* "Actually, I'm the belt buckle riding champion of the world."

His sparkling eyes brightened, reminding her of a starless black sky framed by molten gold. "I guess that makes me Cowboy Creampants."

Another giggle escaped.

Wow! She couldn't believe she was sprawled on the floor with Daniel Porter. After they'd both climaxed. In their freaking pants. They were acting so at ease with each other. It was weird and nice and completely disconcerting.

"So when should we get married?" she asked, deciding to tease him.

The color vanished from his face, leaving him ashen. "I… uh… Married?"

"You *do* want to marry me, right? I mean, you don't kiss a woman like that unless you've got forever-after plans." Maintaining a serious expression proved difficult. Maybe she could handle the aftereffects of a secret affair, after all. Right now, she wasn't upset by his dismay but highly amused.

Just wait until the afterglow wears off.

"I'm thinking next winter, around Christmastime," she added. "But you better not think you can get away with combining my anniversary present with my Christmas present. You do, and there will be blood."

The more she spoke, the more he relaxed. "You are a very naughty girl. How did I not know this?"

"I'm just guessing, of course, but maybe because you never took the time to get to know me."

"Ouch."

"Truth is truth, Creampants."

"Well, here's a new truth. I was dumb, but now I'm smart. I *am* getting to know you better."

She gave his chest a *bless your darling heart* pat.

"When you relay this story to your friends—" he began.

"I would never—" she interjected, only to stop. She *might* relay some of it. But only because she needed advice about what the whole interaction meant and what she should do next. She waved her hand. "Continue."

"Be kind to me. Tell them I was so manly I took care of you, then walked away without a single concern for myself."

She snickered. "Yes, because you are *such* a giver."

"I know, right?" He traced a path down the ridges of her spine. "All I do is give, give, give."

Wanting—needing—to touch him in return, she threaded her fingers through his chains and rested her palm on his sternum. "Stay true to your nature and give me the details about your locket." He was getting to know her; it was only fair that she get to know him, too.

"It belonged to my mother." He opened the locket to show a picture of Bonnie Porter, a beautiful woman with Daniel's dark hair and amber eyes. "She used to keep a picture of me inside, said she liked to have me close to her heart at all times. When she died, I replaced the picture with one of her so I could have *her* close to *my* heart."

"I understand." With her free hand, she traced her fingertips over her tattoo. The rose she carried close to her heart. A reminder of her baby—probably her only baby. Definitely her only. According to multiple doctors, she had a one in a million chance of having another. Her body was too scarred to have another with any kind of ease.

Goodbye, afterglow.

Stop! Before you break down.

"What's wrong, sweetheart?"

Concentrate on him. He still used an endearment. But how long would it last? When would he wash his hands of her and turn his attention to someone else?

"Well," she said, and cleared her throat. *Be the one who leaves, not the one who's left behind.* "Four guests stayed at the inn last night, and they'll be getting up any moment, wanting breakfast." Which meant she would have to cook, since Carol was out of town.

"Why did you and the ex-husband split?" he asked, ignoring her comments.

She wasn't surprised he knew about Jazz. They lived in a small town, and everyone knew everybody's business. Plus, her mom had once hung wedding photos in the lobby. Dorothea had no desire to share the truth, however; it made her look pathetic. And yes, she knew her mind-set was wrong. She wasn't the one who should be ashamed.

"He cheated on me," she finally admitted.

"He's an idiot."

"Yes," she said, then changed the subject. "What made you join the army?"

"Chicks like warriors."

"So...sex?"

"Yes, ma'am. Also, I thought I wanted to escape Strawberry Valley and memories of my mom. I quickly found out those memories would see me through the worst of times."

How sweet. And unexpected. He had depths she hadn't known to plumb.

Afraid of hearing more and softening too much, she quipped, "You ready to hear my life history?"

He stiffened, confusing her. "This is probably going to make you angry, but… I did a background check on you. In my defense," he rushed on, "you'd just come to my room and asked me to ravish your gloriously naked body. I couldn't get my brain to work—still can't. I wanted to know more about you, and the check seemed like the fastest way."

Her first reaction probably shouldn't be delight and satisfaction that he'd been so curious about her, he'd gone digging for info. And yet pleasure fluttered soft wings inside her.

Shouldn't encourage him. She put as much irritation as possible in her tone when she said, "You invaded my privacy. Don't do it again."

He sat up to look at her, his brows furrowed. "You're pleased?"

"No. Yes." Deny and lie wasn't her style. She sighed. "How I feel is neither here nor there, Mr. Porter. I want a detailed report about your life on my desk first thing in the morning."

"Yes, ma'am." He saluted her, then muttered something that sounded like "Such an odd duck."

"Go ahead and leave it with my he-ceptionist. And tell him to highlight the good parts, otherwise I'm sure to be bored out of my mind."

He mock growled at her. "I'm your very manly assistant, and I'll hear you admit the truth." Merciless, he tickled her, making her squeal like a hyena.

"Fine. You're my…*receptionist.*"

"Better." He leaned down and licked her neck.

Her stomach quivered…and then it twisted. Her scars! What if his report on her mentioned her fall? Her loss?

"What did you learn about me?" she said through gritted teeth. "Tell me."

"There's the anger I expected." With a sigh, he plopped at her side. "I learned you were married and divorced, and that you'd dropped out of meteorology school."

She stared at him hard, determined to catch any minute change in his facial expression. "That's it?"

No change. "That's it."

She relaxed, but only slightly. "You invaded my privacy, Daniel." A repeat of her earlier words, though they were said with a sharper tone this time.

"I know. And I'm sorry. I won't do it again, you have my word. You mean too much to me, and betraying your trust would hurt me as much as you."

That was something, at least. Not to mention sweet as sugar—and panty-melting hot. *I'm important to him!*

Now, now. Don't you go getting a big head. Even his rescue dog is important to him.

"Why'd you drop out?" he asked. "You clearly love all things weather."

Tell him about the depths of her foolishness? Her pathetic attempt to make herself invaluable to a man who'd later proved he'd never really loved her? No, thanks.

"I just did," she said, and sat up. "I decided it was time to come home."

"I'm glad you're here." Tugging on a lock of her hair, he said, "But I'm still curious about the change. Don't tell me the reason if you don't want to, but at least give me a chance to make you *want* to tell me."

She blinked down at him, shocked. "What do you mean, exactly?" Just in case she'd misunderstood.

He sat up now, his bare shoulder brushing her clothed one. Despite her orgasm, desire for him flared anew.

Had he noticed?

Pleasure glittered in his eyes. "I want to date you," he said. "For real. Do the whole boyfriend-girlfriend thing."

Her jaw nearly dropped to the floor. "Wh-what?"

"I don't want a one-night stand with you, or even a friends-with-benefits thing. I want to be the only man you're dating because you'll be the only girl *I'm* dating."

The last words were basically growled at her. Had Daniel Porter really, truly offered her what she'd dreamed of having since the seventh grade? His unadulterated affection—long-term.

A sense of wonder wrapped her in a sweet embrace, and she began to smile. The sun was rising inside her.

"We'll still have to keep it a secret, of course," he added.

An-n-nd the sun set. "A secret," she echoed.

"I don't want my dad planning our wedding, expecting grandkids and getting hurt when things end."

When, he'd said. Again. "You expect us to fail." And she Dorothea Mathis—was to be his dirty little secret. Not good enough to tell the world *she's mine!*

Sickness replaced the sense of wonder. Well, screw him. The man she chose would want to show her off to the world, no matter what the future had in store.

"I'm being realistic," he said. "I'm not in a place where I can make a woman happy for years or even months."

"You can if you love her. Love lasts forever." Great. She'd just dropped the L word. No matter. He could deal. She didn't love him anymore, but the potential was there.

"Sweetheart," he said gently, so gently it broke the pieces of her heart that were already broken. He was like a parent telling his child that Santa wasn't real. "You, more than anyone, should know those words are simply a romanticized idea. Men and women might burn for each other, but in the end someone always gets hurt."

Was that what had happened with Jazz? Had they burned for each other until the flame died?

Maybe, maybe not. On her end, she wasn't sure she'd ever really burned for him. He'd smiled at her, and she'd felt almost drunk with her first taste of feminine power. He'd paid attention to her, spoken kind words and had genuinely seemed to enjoy her company, and she'd been grateful, not overcome by lust or love.

"If we're not going to last, why do you even want to date me at all?" she asked.

"I mentioned the part about men and women burning for each other, right?"

"You did," she grated. "But I don't want to be a dirty little secret, Daniel, as if you're ashamed of me. I've been ashamed of myself for too long, and that ends today. I might be the owner of a crumbling inn," she continued, "might not possess the ideal beauty, but I'm worth something."

Fierce and gorgeous and battle ready, he jumped to his feet. He was a thousand dreams come true...a million fantasies in the making. An illusion. He was nothing but a heartbreak waiting to happen. "I'm not ashamed of you, Thea. Of course you're worth something. You're worth *everything*."

Pretty words. Always he offered pretty words. A gift—or his personal favorite, a reward.

"Everything?" She laughed without humor. "Your actions say otherwise. And what about your love of challenges, huh? I'd date you, you'd win my affections but still keep me a secret while the flames burned out. Then you'd dump me. *Hurt* me."

"I would never hurt you. Not purposely. I only want to protect—"

"Your dad. I know. He comes first. But I'm tired, so tired, of coming in second place. My dad abandoned his wife, my sister and me, choosing to raise another woman's children instead. Did you know that? My husband put his career and his girlfriend in front of me. I won't be another man's disposable *anything*. I deserve better." Head high, she righted her clothing and walked out of the room.

CHAPTER ELEVEN

Dorothea refused to think about Daniel for the rest of the day. Or ever. Refused to think about his earth-shattering kiss, and her life-changing orgasm. *Life. Changing.* In fact, she decided to treat the day like any other. She painted her nails dual colors—blue = sad, purple = determined—and jogged ten miles and showered. She also cleaned an entire hallway of rooms as she waited for Harlow Glass to arrive.

Okay, that was new. Eagerly watching for the former bully she'd once despised. But come on! *I'm getting a theme room!*

Maybe she should have painted her nails happy pink.

Finally the brunette arrived. Nearly bubbling over with anticipation, she showed Harlow to the room. But...never again would Dorothea think of it as the Four Seasons. Try: Orgasm City. Or Five Minutes in Paradise.

But she wasn't thinking about Daniel.

Right. Dorothea told Harlow everything she'd like to see on the walls.

"All doable." Harlow rubbed her beautifully rounded belly as she listened. "I'm going to use non-toxic paint, but don't worry, it won't affect the colors."

Envy scalded her.

Envy? No! Unacceptable. Her child was taken from her, yes, but she wouldn't begrudge another woman's joy.

"Thank you. For everything," Dorothea said.

"Gotta admit, I was over the moon when Daniel told me about the theme room." Harlow toyed with a lock of hair. The gorgeous teen had grown into a stunning woman with a kind heart. Falling on hard times—and then finding love—had changed her. "I totally adore the weather premise…but what do you think of doing a romance novel theme next? Imagine it! You could do anything from the Viking era to futuristic. Oh! Did you know there are several romance series based on West's video games? You could do a Lords of the Underworld room. Or Alice in Zombieland. I'll paint it free of charge as well, if you'll let me help with the design."

West, or Lincoln West, was Jessie Kay's husband. If he kicked in on a room, too, she'd be set! And oh, wow, Daniel's barter system was one of the best things to ever happen to her.

"Jessie Kay gets to pick the second room, but she hasn't told me what she wants," Dorothea said. Before their orgasm-fest, Daniel had marched into the room she was cleaning and made the announcement. "Who knows? She could select one of West's games. Since you're helping me with the murals, you get to pick and design the third room. You can totally go with a romance novel theme and paint anything you want."

Harlow jumped up and down, clapping her hands. "Yes! Agreed."

Daniel stalked into the room with a piece of paper in hand, Princess fast on his heels. He'd changed his clothes, and his hair was damp. He must have taken a shower in one of the unused rooms.

An image of his naked body dripping with soapy bubbles invaded her mind. A spectacular image, and yet she experienced a wave of disappointment. He no longer bore the scent of her on his flesh.

She wanted her scent on his flesh.

Shouldn't think so possessively. It's wrong on every level.

He met and held Dorothea's gaze, his pupils expanding. Her body softened, preparing for another mind-blowing orgasm while her internal thermostat cranked up the heat. She was pretty sure she could warm the entire building.

The bastard noticed her reaction and smiled slowly. "What do blue and purple mean?"

Why not tell him? "Sad and determined."

His smile slipped, as if he actually cared about her mood.

Cursing him, she dug a treat from her pocket and waved Princess over. The little dog had been tentative at first but now trotted over to take the treat—only to dart out of range when Dorothea reached out to pet her behind the ears. Well, it was still progress.

"Daniel," Harlow said, clearly trying not to laugh. "It's so good to see you again."

"I know."

Oh, to have such confidence.

He handed the paper to Dorothea. "Here's that background check you demanded."

The background—on himself! She looked it over and frowned. "All it says is that you moved back to Strawberry Valley this year and reconnected with the hottest girl in school." The word *hottest* was highlighted, underlined and circled.

"Exactly. Because that's really all that matters."

"Wait," Harlow said with a shake of her head. "You had him do a background check on himself?"

"Yes. Not that it did any good." Dorothea scowled at Daniel before smiling at Harlow. "Consider Daniel your beck-

and-call boy. He'll fetch anything you need." Smug now, she stepped around him and headed for her sister's room.

On Holly's eighteenth birthday, Carol had helped her move out of their suite and into her own private living quarters, even though she was still in high school. An Enter at Your Own Peril sign hung on the door.

Dorothea knocked and pressed her finger into the peephole, knowing curiosity would get the better of the girl.

Sure enough, the door swung open. Holly spotted her and glowered. "What?"

"So kind." Today her sister wore an oversize tee that read "Play with Bed Bugs at the Strawberry Inn." Her skintight leggings were stuffed into cowgirl boots, and white lace socks peeked over the top. "Just wanted to start my day right. With your sunny smile."

Good old-fashioned surprise flickered inside those familiar green eyes.

"I love you, Halls. Have a nice day." She didn't try to push for a lengthy or in-depth conversation. Her goal was simple: let her sister know she was here, she cared, she would always care and she would always be here, no matter what. She was rebuilding trust, after all.

And she was using the very method Daniel was using on her, she realized. Close proximity, short and sweet interactions. No wonder he'd agreed to work at the inn.

Well. He really was putting everything he had into winning her over. Maybe she should—

No. Nope. Secret relationships were bad. Bad!

Deciding to take a few hours off, she phoned Ryanne, who usually worked until three in the morning…which was why she had a strict no-calls-before-noon policy. A policy Dorothea decided to ignore.

"Better be a matter of life-and-death," the girl grumbled.

"It is. I have two dates this weekend and nothing to wear. We're going shopping."

"No way, *chica*. I'm trying to sleep." Ryanne shouted the words.

In the background, Dorothea thought she heard a man muttering.

"Oh, good. You have company, so you're up. I'll be there in ten minutes." *Click.*

Dorothea changed into a T-shirt and jeans, grabbed her purse and stalked to the lobby. She passed Daniel—*won't look, won't freaking look*—and stepped outside. The too-bright sunlight made her eyes tear.

Her phone rang. A quick glance at the screen made her groan. Jazz. Ugh. This was his weekly call. "What do you want?" she said in lieu of a greeting.

"You, Dorothea." His smooth baritone drifted over the line. "I want you."

Sometimes she hung up on him without speaking. Sometimes she listened to his stream of apologies and praise. Today, she had just enough gumption to say, "You can't have me."

"Please. If you'd just listen to me—"

"You need to stop calling me, Jazz. We're over. We'll always be over, and it's your loss."

"I'm no longer with Charity. We split."

"Did you cheat on her? Or did she cheat on you?"

Silence.

Well, well. "I would have been faithful forever, you know. But nooo. You're a cheater, and you hooked up with a cheater." So how had Dorothea been the one to end up feeling like yesterday's garbage? "You guys were never going to last."

He cleared his throat. "I miss you."

"I don't care."

"I did you wrong, and I'm sorry. If you give me another chance, I'll be devoted to you. I'll never make the same mistake again. I just… I want you back. I love you. I've never stopped loving you. I miss you," he repeated.

"Again, I don't care. You aren't a prize, Jazz, and I deserve a prize."

"I'm sorry. I'm so sorry. I made a mistake."

His voice broke, as if he were crying. Maybe he was. Her heart remained set against him.

She'd forgiven him long ago, despite the anger and bitterness she still sometimes battled, but forgiveness didn't mean she would give him a place in her new life, allowing him to crap all over her a second time.

"Jazz, you know what I lost after I discovered your affair." She remembered every detail of that tragic day. She'd been at work—down to only one job thanks to Jazz's plush new position at the network. Though he hadn't wanted her to stop working and return to school yet because they'd needed to save for the baby.

She'd begun to cramp, and her boss had let her leave early.

Thrilled, she'd texted Jazz, and he'd told her to go home, that he hadn't left for work yet, so he would call in sick and give her a massage.

She'd found out later *Charity* had sent the reply. That the two had already been at the apartment, intending to head to the station together.

The news anchor had wanted Dorothea's marriage to end and had finally had her chance.

If only Charity had called her instead. *I'm boning your husband. How about you hit the bricks?*

Dorothea would have filed for divorce in a heartbeat. Rose might have lived.

That cramping…

One of the nurses had told her: *Your daughter died for a reason.*

Dorothea had almost come unglued.

Jazz had said: *God needed another angel for his choir. You and me, we can have another baby.*

Her mom had said: *Everything happens for a reason. This was meant to be.*

"Everything happens for a reason" and "meant to be" were nothing but excuses. A way to blame fate rather than the fallacy of human nature. But Dorothea understood the reason her mother believed both. When Joe Mathis had taken off, Carol had needed a scapegoat.

And Jazz's comment? Well, it made him dumber than homemade sin. God had nothing to do with her daughter's death. Evil did. And Dorothea wanted her sweet Rose.

"Please, Dorothea," he said. "I know you lost the baby, and I'm sorry. I'm so sorry. I lost her, too. But we can try again."

"I do want to try again. One day. With someone else," she said, making the decision then and there. No risk, no reward. Better to regret the things you try than the things you never do.

Yes, the odds were one in a million, but people had won the lottery with less.

"You need to stop calling me, okay? We're over, and we'll always be over." She hung up.

Her chin quivered as she shoved the phone in her purse. In, out, she breathed, searching for a happy place. Rebuilding her relationship with Holly—who was like a daughter to her already. Making a success of the inn. Even... Daniel? *You are perfect just the way you are.*

He might be partly a happy place, but he was also a complication she couldn't afford.

A craggy voice called her name. "Dorothea!"

She turned to find Virgil Porter striding toward her. He wore a pair of faded, paint-stained overalls and mud-caked boots. Despite his age, he was an imposing man. Surrounded by old buildings with exposed brick, concrete and wooden beams, he was a slice of Americana come to life.

Her nerves kicked up a fuss, but she held her ground. No more running away from tough situations. She'd kissed Daniel. Heck, she'd made him come in his pants. Spontaneous Combustion Girl could do anything.

Fake it till you make it.

She forced a smile and waved. "Hi, Mr. Porter."

He grinned in return. He hadn't just given Daniel his height and width; he'd given his son his smile, too. A mischievous smile bursting with charm.

"Heard my Danny boy is your new clerk."

"Yes, sir. And you must have raised him right, because he's a good one." It was the Lord's honest truth. Daniel did nothing halfway. He was self-motivated, finding things to fix when no guests were at the desk to ask questions and even putting a new security system in place.

Thou shalt do your best, not just what's good enough.

If only his work ethic carried over into his dating life.

Virgil puffed up with pride. "Wish I could take all the credit, but his momma was a force to be reckoned with, God rest her precious soul. She wasn't afraid to spank his bottom whenever he turned on the sass."

"So that's the secret, huh? Spanking his bottom."

Virgil snorted. "Look at you. Like a possum eatin' a sweet tater. Just don't be alarmed if he wants to spank your bottom right back."

Oh, she figured Daniel would love nothing more than to bend her over his knees and paddle her blue for giving his relationship offer the stanky boot.

For a man who claimed to relish a good challenge, he sure got crazy when things failed to go his way.

Because I'm important to him?

Nope. Not going there. The answer didn't matter. She was

no one's dirty little secret. Besides, she could never forget he expected the end to come. *Seek and you will find.*

"Well," she said, and cleared her throat. "I should probably get going."

"Where you headed?"

Welcome to small-town living. "Ryanne and I are going shopping."

"I hope you're not going to the city. No one there has the sense God gave a goose. Only thing you're gonna get is mugged."

She swallowed a laugh. "I'll take care, Mr. Porter. I promise."

"Call me Virgil. Shoot, I watched you grow up, feel like I'm your favorite uncle. I know how special you are."

The simple proclamation flipped her entire world upside down and inside out. Her own dad had rejected her, but this man who wasn't actually blood related thought she was special. The tears she'd been fighting spilled out and flowed down her cheeks.

"Now, now." He drew her in for a bear hug and gave her back an awkward pat. "I didn't mean to go upsettin' you."

"I'm not upset." Not here and now. She clung to him. "I'm happy."

"There's no need to blubber like a baby, then, is there?"

A surprised laugh escaped. "You're right."

He released her and kissed her damp cheek. "You go on now. Have fun and stay safe, and make sure you get home before midnight. Excuse my French, but by then there ain't nothing open but legs and hospitals."

She choked on a laugh. A genuine laugh. He was such a good man, and he liked her. Truly liked her. And his son—

Nope. Still not thinking about him.

Today, she'd had to deal with few ups and a lot of downs. Which one she focused on—that was what mattered. It would mean the difference between victory and defeat, happiness and despair.

I'm going to stay happy, and that's that.

She stopped at Holy Grounds, bought the strongest espresso on the menu for Ryanne, adding milk and sugar—lucky girl!—and ordered herself a cup of plain black coffee. *Whimper.* But better she wish her coffee tasted like candy than wear the milk and sugar in her thighs like saddlebags.

Miracle of miracles, Ryanne was waiting outside the bar, already dressed and ready to go. She swiped the cup of espresso and drained half the contents before Dorothea could utter a greeting.

Dorothea noticed the fluffy clouds ghosting along the sky—and frowned. Was that a man sneaking down Ryanne's stairs? The staircase that opened to the outside and led straight to her bedroom.

No, it most certainly wasn't a man. It was *two* men.

Brock Hudson and Jude Laurent, a seriously good-looking man with pale hair and a slight limp. As sunlight stroked over his bronzed skin, Ryanne stiffened.

"So you guys are having playdates with my friend?" Dorothea asked when they reached her.

Brock gave her a half grin before lighting a cigarette. Jude plucked the cigarette from his fingers and ground the entire thing into the sidewalk.

"Nothing happened," Ryanne said. "After Jude took Brock home, Brock returned and drank too much, like a teenager at his first rave, and refused to get inside a cab because the driver might—and I quote—'steal his seed.' As if he doesn't hand it out for free every night. I let him crash on my couch. Called Jude but didn't hear back from him till this morning, and he came to get Brock."

Brock spread his arms, the king of the castle. "The couch

wasn't made for a man like me. You should have invited me to share your bed."

"I was seconds away from doing just that...until I remembered I would rather cut off your balls and feed them to you," Ryanne replied.

Jude's scowl deepened. He stepped in front of his friend, blocking the guy's view of Ryanne. The action was almost... dare she say...possessive. And the tension crackling between the couple? *Oh, my stars.*

What an interesting development.

"Your hospitality sucked," he said without any inflection or emotion.

No way could Jude pass the ten commitments test. Being kind to others didn't appear to be in his wheelhouse.

"I'll be sure to mention my raging guilt in my diary." Ryanne brushed an invisible piece of lint from her shirt. "Oh. Meant to tell you. I accidentally tossed Brock's car keys somewhere in the parking lot. Y'all should probably start lookin'."

"You took the keys straight out of my pocket and said, 'I've been working on my throw. Watch.'" Once again Brock spread his arms. "Then you added, 'Expect to find those keys in kingdom come.'"

"Well, darn." Ryanne snapped her fingers. "There's another entry for my diary."

"I'll call and let you know when we find the keys," Jude said, "to ease your conscience."

She smirked. "You don't have my number."

"I found it on the bathroom wall next to the words *Gives Good Head...aches.*"

Her eyes sparkled with humor—humor?—as she hooked her arm through Dorothea's and tugged her forward. "Enjoy your day, boys. My friend and I have things to see and people to do."

CHAPTER TWELVE

Ryanne had the better car, so she drove to the city. They reached the mall in record time. The parking lot was over-crowded, big SUVs and trucks wedged into tiny slots meant for even tinier cars.

After a good fifteen minutes, her friend found an open space about a half-mile hike from the sprawling building with gorgeous glass walls. The smell of exhaust carried on the wind as they headed inside.

"So…you and Jude, huh?" Dorothea asked, deciding to probe for information at last.

Ryanne scowled at her. "No, absolutely not. He's rude."

"And yet the two of you nearly singed off my eyebrows."

"You mean like you and Daniel did to me?" Her dry tone held a note of challenge.

"I… Daniel… This isn't about me! You *never* share your personal quarters with the bar's patrons, and yet you allowed Brock—"

"Who is a total he-slut."

"—to spend the night, just so you could call Jude—"

"Who is the biggest asshole I've ever met."

"—to come get his friend. Don't try to pretend otherwise. Brock could have driven himself home this morning."

Ryanne waved a fist in her direction, all mock fury and genuine indignation. "I will punch you, and I won't feel bad or ever say sorry."

Dorothea blew her friend a kiss. "No mention of me in your diary? What a shame."

"You know I'm saving up to travel the world," Ryanne said. "I will never change my plans for a man or a relationship. Besides, you need to be hounding Lyndie. She came to the bar last night and couldn't take her eyes off Brock. He watched her, too. Well, when he wasn't screwing a woman in the bathroom."

The reserved, quiet Lyndie was attracted to the irreverent, womanizing Brock, and vice versa? Dang. The world had stopped making any kind of sense.

"This is almost more than I can process." Dorothea rubbed her temples. "The next time the boys show up at the bar, call me. I want to be a witness if anything goes to court... the court of love."

"You're cruising for a bruising, Mathis."

As they wandered in and out of stores in the too-crowded mall, Ryanne drew all kinds of male attention, considering her black leather pants appeared to be painted on. Meanwhile, Dorothea wore an oversize "Will Work For Hugs" T-shirt.

"Maybe we should go to a discount store," she muttered as she looked at the price tag on a frilly pink dress. One hundred and twenty-nine hard-earned dollars could buy fabric for a theme room. Or a graduation present for Holly. "I saw a thrift store on the drive over. Let's go there."

"No way. You aren't buying lingerie at a secondhand shop."

"I know. Because I'm not buying lingerie *anywhere*." There was no reason to do so. The next man she had sex with would never even see her. The lights would stay off from the first kiss to the last thrust.

Of course, that meant she wouldn't see him, either, and she really, really wanted to see him. Whoever he was. Because he most assuredly would not be Daniel.

"Erotic underclothes are mandatory," Ryanne said. "Not for the guy's benefit but yours. Lace will help you feel as sexy as you really are."

A girl could dream. "All right. One piece of lingerie."

Dorothea bought *three* pieces of lingerie: a lacy ice-green bra, a pair of matching panties and a thong. Aka butt floss. She'd never worn a thong, and she wasn't sure she wanted to start now, but Ryanne assured her the man in her life would thank her.

And what if she had to negotiate with Daniel again? Surely she would throw him off his game if she let him slide his hands inside the back of her jeans...and he encountered skin rather than granny panties.

Afterward, Ryanne drove her to a discount store. As they sifted through the racks, on the hunt for the perfect date ensemble, Ryanne said, "Are you moving back to the city after Holly graduates?"

"No. I've taken over the inn for good." Dorothea would always be the safe harbor her sister needed.

"You don't sound excited about that."

"I'm not *un*excited." Though part of her still fantasized about being a storm chaser.

Strawberry Valley didn't have its own news station, and the equipment she needed was far beyond her price range. Okay, okay, even free would have been beyond her price range. Equipment had to be maintained. She also needed a special vehicle that would require buckets of gas.

"Daniel Porter is your employee. Yours to boss around."

Ryanne held up a buttercup-yellow top, marked down seventy percent because of a small hole in the shoulder. "Why aren't you dancing like your feet are on fire?"

The hole she could easily sew, but the color would make her skin look sallow, so she shook her head no. "One, I don't dance. Ever." She looked like a chicken with her head cut off. "Two, he's only working for me for three weeks or until I hire someone else." And, now that she thought about it, not a single person had applied.

Did no one want to work for her? Was that the problem? Her mom had never had trouble hiring, no matter the position.

"In three weeks, or whenever you hire that someone else, transition Daniel to the position of your boyfriend. The same rules apply. You get to boss him around."

If only. "He's not interested."

"Are we talking about the same Daniel? I've mentioned I've seen the way he looks at you, right?"

"Looks can be deceiving."

"You've wanted him most of your life, *chica*, and wanting like that doesn't turn off just because you wish really hard. Take him. Let the rest sort itself out."

Could Ryanne be right? Would Dorothea always want Daniel? Even if he fell in love with another woman and married her. In front of witnesses.

Did it matter? If he got married, she would *never* act on that want, would never be the side slice. After Jazz's infidelity, she'd done a little research about why cheaters cheat, and many reasons had been listed. Sometimes the cheater justified or trivialized his actions. Cognitive dissonance, it was called. He—or she...nah, she'd stick with the male species today—convinced himself that what he was doing wasn't really that bad, that other people had done worse and really, deep down, he was a good person. There was also sex addiction, as well as the desire to feel, well, desirable. Some men felt their earning potential directly correlated with their masculinity; when a wife or girlfriend made all the money, these males sought a way to prove their prowess outside the bonds of commitment. Some men thought they loved the other woman. Some just wanted to have a good time. Some just didn't care about anything or anyone.

After a while, Dorothea had realized Jazz's reason for cheating on her wasn't important. He'd done it. Their child—the bridge between their lives—had died. They were finished.

Not even close to being finished with Daniel.

Stop. Thinking. About. Him.

In the midst of a thorough search, Dorothea found an emerald green shirt to match her eyes, with a choker neckline and an oval cutout to showcase a wee bit of cleavage. The waist cinched in while the bottom half flared to create the illusion of a ruffled skirt—though it was far too short to be classified as a skirt—with the front higher than the back. There was a black smudge on the bottom hem, but a good cleaning would definitely remove it. Considering the many stains she'd removed from sheets at the inn, she had the magic touch.

Ryanne selected a pair of short shorts. When Dorothea shook her head no, the girl nodded a yes. "Wear them with the shirt, and no one will be able to see the shorts from the back. It'll look like you're wearing a supershort dress. And from the front, the slit in the ruffle will have a peekaboo effect. This is both trendy and adorable."

Her thighs... "I need to dress for the body I have, not the body I wish I had."

Her friend ignored her. "You'll wear cowgirl boots with it, of course." She found a pair of black-and-white pants with a harlequin pattern and paired it with a shirt just like the first, only pink. "You'll wear sandals with this one."

The most Dorothea could promise? "I'll try everything

on." And then she would tell Ryanne nothing had fit—which would be the truth, no doubt about it.

Two summer dresses joined the pile before Ryanne allowed her to enter the dressing room. And the stubborn girl stayed put while Dorothea changed. Everything but the harlequin pants fit and—shocker—actually flattered her figure.

Ryanne exchanged the pants for a bigger size, and voilá, they fit, as well.

Dorothea stood in front of the mirror, spinning to study herself from every angle.

"You're about to turn me gay," Ryanne announced. "And FYI, you're buying these clothes. All of them. Well, except for the pants. I'm buying those. And a pair of hooker heels."

"I couldn't let you—"

"Actually, you can't stop me." Ryanne came up behind her, rested her chin on Dorothea's shoulder and hugged her. Their eyes met in the mirror. "I haven't always done right by you and Lyndie, but I will from now on."

"What do you mean?"

"I wasn't there for you when you needed me most. And Lyndie…her dad wasn't just a bully. Sometimes he beat the crap out of her, and there was nothing I could do to stop him."

Horror washed through Dorothea, leaving a sticky film on her soul. "I didn't know. But now… He only hit her where the bruises could be hidden by clothing, right?" she asked softly, remembering the many times her friend had flinched when innocently touched.

"Exactly right. Same deal with Lyndie's husband. It wasn't a fairy-tale marriage, but a freaking nightmare. I don't know why she picked him. He was just like her dad, always using her as a punching bag."

"I don't… I can't…" Dorothea clutched her now cramping stomach. "Why didn't you guys tell me?"

"You had enough on your plate. And there's no changing the past," Ryanne said, "only the future."

Everyone carried baggage, she realized. Some hid theirs better than others, but no one got through life without experiencing pain. And, whether you knew it or not, you were going to be the object of someone's pain. Like Dorothea was for Holly. Like Jazz was for Dorothea. But you could also be the object of someone's salvation.

Would Daniel be hers?

Wishful thought. "We will change the future," she vowed. "Tomorrow will be better than today."

"You know, I like this New Dorothea," Ryanne said as Dorothea paid. "She's willing to try new things without too much fuss, and she's got a little more pep in her step. She even smiles."

"I like her, too," she admitted.

Arm in arm, they strode out of the store, only to draw up short when a man stepped in their path.

"Dorothea." Familiar brown eyes roved over her. "You... look so pretty."

"Jazz." The stomach cramps started up again.

Sunlight poured over him. His golden hair was brushed back from his face, his jaw shaved clean of stubble. Though they'd parted a little over a year ago, and he was as handsome as ever, he appeared to have aged a decade. There were shadows under his eyes and new lines around them. The brackets around his mouth were so deep they resembled commas. However, he'd maintained his athletic build.

Have to be in tip-top shape for the camera, he used to say. And the public loved him for it. Women constantly posted about his boy-next-door good looks; they Tweeted him invitations to dinner and mailed him naughty photos. Dorothea used to sigh dreamily and think, *Flirt all you want, girls. He belongs to me. He picked me.*

Now she cringed. An emotionally healthy woman would have thought, *We're good together. He's got my back, and I've got his.* The hallmark of a good marriage. But no matter how strong, those thoughts would have been a lie. Jazz hadn't guarded her back; he'd stabbed it.

"What are you doing here?" she demanded.

He wiped his hands on the sides of his pants, as if he was nervous. But he couldn't be. He'd always tackled life head-on. It was one of the things she'd liked most about him. "I wanted to see you."

"And you knew she'd be here?" Ryanne asked softly, menacingly. "How?"

"Your phone…there's a track app. Remember?" he said, his gaze pleading with her. "You got it before our divorce."

No, she hadn't. "Or you added it when I wasn't looking so you could ensure I wasn't nearby when you wanted to sleep with other women." Fury mounting, she whipped out her phone, hunted for the app—buried on a screen she never used—and took care of the problem then and there.

He pulled at his collar, uncomfortable. "Maybe I did. I don't know."

Liar! "Like I've told you repeatedly," she snapped, "you and I have nothing to say to each other."

"I just… I wanted you to see my face and hear my tone in person. To finally understand the depths of my feelings for you."

Ryanne laughed at him. "Dude. Three out of three people agree—you're an idiot."

A fire-truck-red blush spread over his cheeks.

"Look," Dorothea said with a sigh, "I'm seeing someone else. Several someones, actually." *Am I bragging? I think I'm bragging.* Embracing the moment, she fluffed her hair.

Jazz offered her a soft, almost pitying smile. "Maybe you

are. Maybe you aren't. But that doesn't mean we can't get to know each other again."

What a rat! He thought she'd fibbed to make herself seem more desirable. Like she'd really lower herself to use a method from his bag o' tricks.

"This conversation is like a circle. Pointless. Let's go." She ushered Ryanne around him and headed for the car.

"This isn't the end, Dorothea." His determined voice followed her. "I love you, and I want you back. I'll do whatever it takes to win you."

Ryanne peered over her shoulder, calling, "Keep doing what you're doing, then. It's not creepy *at all*."

"He and the girlfriend broke up," Dorothea told her. "Now he wants to rekindle the old flame. As if there's anything left but ash," she shouted, loud enough for Jazz to hear.

All the while she wondered...

Was Daniel right? Could no relationship last?

CHAPTER THIRTEEN

Daniel worked morning, noon and night, putting security measures in place at the inn, sketching a tree-shaped headboard, playing with Princess and wondering what to do about Thea. His mind was too consumed with her to worry about the horrors of his past, a welcome change, and yet he'd never been so tormented.

Their kiss had unmanned him. He only hungered for her more, was *starved* for her.

As many women as he'd kissed over the years, he'd thought he'd experienced every possible nuance. Slow and sweet. Fast and frantic. Tender, rough. Giving, taking. Sharing. He'd kissed women face-to-face and while he stood behind them. Sitting, or sprawled across a flat surface. Twisted together or leaning over a table. He'd used props. Ice. Food. Even clothing. He'd sipped. He'd devoured. He'd worked his way down, and he'd worked his way up. But he'd never been so turned on that he'd come in his pants. He'd always stopped the play before reaching the point of no return, or better yet, he and his partner had decided to strip and go all the way.

Thea had placed restrictions on the make-out session, and

he'd obeyed. Gladly. He'd take her however he could get her. But with her, stopping at any point would have been more painful than having a bullet excised without anesthesia. And he should know!

Everything about Thea appealed to him. She drew him, had well and truly hooked him. The sounds she'd made as she'd strained against him, desperate for more. The rapturous expression she'd donned when he'd touched her breasts. The way she'd arched against him, only to linger when she'd made contact with his erection, as if she'd never get enough. The breathy way she'd called his name. Even the color of her nails. Every day he checked, hoping to see glittery white. So far she'd worn everything from red to green.

He wanted more of her—*needed* more. But she wanted nothing to do with him romantically.

A dirty little secret, she'd said. Why couldn't she see the truth? Protecting his dad had nothing to do with his feelings for her.

Feelings he would do well to ignore. With all her talk about love, she might want to get married again one day.

A growl vibrated in his chest. Thea...forever off-limits...

He scrubbed a hand down his face. When had he dipped a toe in the pool of insanity?

His friends were just as bad. Jude had warned Brock away from Ryanne, and Brock had said no problem, he'd never do a friend of Lyndie Scott's, a kindergarten teacher and Sunday-school enthusiast.

Daniel felt like he'd stepped into an alternate universe.

On Friday, he and the boys spent the night in Oklahoma City for a job, working security for a hotel downtown. A famous country singer he'd never heard of was staying there. Daniel found himself wondering what kind of music Thea listened to, and figured his taste would surprise her, since he tended to favor the old gospel tunes his mom had blasted while cleaning the house and cooking dinner.

The job went off without a hitch. His dad babysat Princess, and the two got along just fine. If "just fine" qualified as walking into the kitchen and catching the man feeding the little pup scraps from his own fork.

On Saturday, Daniel and Princess returned to the inn. He resumed his duties, and with every hour that passed, his mood darkened. Thea would be going on her date with the vet later that evening. If the bastard attempted to kiss her good-night…

No one had ever committed cold-blooded murder in Strawberry Valley, but there was a first time for everything.

Daniel should insist Thea go on one of her remaining dates with him *tonight*. Screw Vandercamp. She'd wear a raincoat and a smile, and all would be right in Daniel's world.

You will stand down, soldier. He was not Thea's boyfriend, and he had no rights to her.

By the time Vandercamp arrived, Princess had caught his bad mood. She growled at the vet as if he'd become enemy one. Because he had!

"Good news." Vandercamp leaned against the counter. "I found little Princess's family. Her name is actually Splenda."

Daniel's stomach sank when it probably should have soared. "How'd they lose her?" And why had they named her Splenda, after fake sugar? From the tips of her ears to the end of her tail, she was the real deal.

"They were driving from Dallas to Oklahoma City and stopped in Strawberry Valley to get gas. They let her out to pee and put her back in the car, but she must have seen something she liked and hopped out. They left thinking she was asleep in back. They posted pictures of her online, called shelters and veterinary hospitals. I spoke to the mom this morning, and she emailed me those pictures to prove ownership."

Deep breath in…out… "Why wasn't Princess tagged or chipped?" No way he'd ever call her Splenda. "How do we know she really belongs to them? Photos don't mean shit. I can present you with a photo album first thing in the morning, proving I've had her since she was a pup."

"I don't know why she wasn't tagged or chipped. I didn't ask because it's not any of my business. And I can't think of a single reason someone would go to so much trouble just to assume ownership of a little dog."

"The welfare of an animal isn't your business? And someone would go to so much trouble because she's a piece of heaven on earth." He petted her behind the ears, but she remained on alert, ready to snap at Vandercamp if he made one wrong move. "Has anyone ever told you that you suck as a vet *and* a human being?"

Unperturbed, Vandercamp said, "Your hostility is understandable but misplaced. I'm not taking away something you love, Daniel. I'm helping reunite a dog with her family."

"You're doing both, asshole. And if you hurt her—" He pressed his lips together, unsure if he was still talking about Princess or if he'd started talking about Thea.

"I would never hurt an animal."

Yeah, but what about a vulnerable woman?

"Look, I have their number," Vandercamp said. "They're willing to pay for your time and gas if you'll meet them halfway and—"

"Hell, no. If they really love her, they'll make the entire drive." He was being unreasonable, and he knew it. Ask him if he cared.

Vandercamp slid a piece of paper across the counter. "Here's their number. You can call and make arrangements for pickup." He studied Daniel's mutinous expression and reclaimed the paper with a forceful yank. "Never mind. I'll call."

He stepped to the side, using the phone on the counter rather than his cell phone—making a long-distance call on

Thea's dime. Bet he'd make her pay for half of dinner, too. Bastard.

A few minutes later, Vandercamp hung up and focused on him. "Good news," he said again. "They hopped in their car after talking to me. They're already on their way. They'll reach the inn in about an hour."

One hour. One more hour with Princess. His chest hurt. He wanted to curse but pressed his lips together. This was a family-friendly environment, and he'd harm Thea's business if he let loose. But damn it! Princess was his. He'd found her and helped patch her up. He'd taken care of her when she most needed care. He'd cuddled with her and fallen in love, and she'd fallen in love right back. She wouldn't want to leave him…right?

If she wanted to stay with him, he'd offer the family money. An obscene amount, if necessary. He would empty his savings. Anything to keep her.

Couldn't keep your mom. Couldn't keep the friends who died in battle. You think this will be any different?

The pain in his chest only worsened.

Vandercamp's expression brightened at the same time Daniel caught a whiff of his favorite scent. He whipped around. If he'd been standing, he would have stumbled back. Thea's dark curls tumbled to her waist. The sides were pinned back, revealing delicate earlobes pierced by silver roses. She wore a pretty top that fit her pinup body to perfection, and short shorts that revealed glorious mile-long legs. Cowgirl boots only added to her appeal.

Tonight her nails were yellow. She was hopeful. Hopeful—for Vandercamp.

Would the guy get to see her tattoo? Her exquisite curves?

Daniel bit the inside of his cheek until he tasted blood.

Never had Thea looked more like a living doll. The only

thing he didn't like, besides her nail color? A thick layer of makeup masked her freckles.

Hell, maybe the makeup was for the best. The freckles were his and his alone. They set every inch of him on fire.

Would she make Vandercamp laugh tonight? Charm and enchant the bastard?

Her eyes remained downcast during Daniel's inspection, but it wasn't long before she gathered her courage and looked up. At him, not Vandercamp. He wanted to cheer. And then he wanted to moan. Sizzling awareness arced between them.

"You look…" he began.

"Amazing," Vandercamp interjected.

Understatement. "Amazing" didn't do her justice.

She cast her gaze to her date, causing Daniel's hands to fist. He could flatten the vet with a single punch…but then he'd have to watch Thea's features darken with horror.

"Thank you," she said, and walked around Daniel. She stopped and backtracked, her brow furrowed. "I've been meaning to ask. Has anyone called about the reception position?"

He gritted his teeth. "I haven't set up any interviews." A misleading answer, yes. But the truth? Also yes. She didn't need to know there'd been interest. She'd try to get rid of him, and she'd stop saving the money she so desperately needed.

All about the money, he told himself. Had nothing to do with his feelings.

"Dang. Okay." She brushed her fingers across Princess's fur as she walked away, but she might as well have palmed Daniel's length.

Sweat beaded on his brow. *Do not touch her. Do not yank her against you.*

The good-looking couple strode out the door, out of sight, but Daniel's hunger only increased.

"Well, well. If it isn't the man who stole my job."

The voice came from the door Thea had just vacated. Holly. The sister. The girl who had never deigned to speak to him until now. She'd picked the wrong time. "Had you actually done any work, I'd agree. Since I had to pick up where you never started, I'd say I'm the man who *finally did* your job."

She flinched, as if no one had ever dared feed her a taste of her own medicine. Then she flipped him off.

"So mature." He placed Princess on the floor and filled her bowl from the box of food he kept inside the cabinet above the desk. "Did someone put on her big-girl panties today?"

"*Someone* is about to find *his* big-girl panties wedged permanently in the crack of his ass."

"And now, in the midst of her hissy fit, she spits out threats she can't possibly enforce," he told Princess. "Do you think she's...you know...so dumb she could throw herself on the ground and miss?"

Princess was too busy inhaling her dinner to respond.

"Dumb! I am *not* dumb." Holly stepped toward him as she drew back her fist. But she caught herself midway and stopped. "You aren't welcome here. You need to go."

"And *you* certainly aren't smart. Otherwise you'd be nice to your sister."

She scowled up at him. "Is this a bonding moment? Because I'd like to pass."

"Then why are you still here?"

"To make sure you quit."

"Why would I quit? I promised your sister I'd help out for the next three weeks."

Holly crossed her arms over her middle, almost as if she were—no, impossible—but...almost as if she wanted to protect herself from an emotional blow. "Why did you promise her, huh?"

"Because I like her," he said softly. "We're..." Well, hell. There was no way around it, was there? "We're friends."

The girl bristled for no apparent reason. "Do you usually violate your friends with your eyes?"

Wow. Okay. How to answer that?

Needing a moment, he petted Princess behind the ears. She finished her meal and trotted to her pillow under the counter, where she curled into a ball and promptly fell asleep. If only it were that easy for him.

"She's taken, you know," Holly said, a tremor in her voice. "She's still in love with her ex-husband. He's awesome. The best thing to ever happen to her. He wants her back, and he'll get her."

The guy might want her back. Check that. The guy definitely wanted her back—who wouldn't?—but she wasn't in love with him. Daniel had held Thea in his arms as she'd told him about her ex-husband's infidelity. He'd heard hurt, shame and self-recrimination in her voice, but not love.

He straightened and faced Holly straight on. *Tread carefully. Do not piss off Thea by spanking the hell out of her little sister.* "You're wrong. But then, you don't really know your sister. She reaches out to you, and you ignore her or insult her. Those are your only settings."

Her eyes—so like Thea's—widened.

Tread care— Oh, who cared. In about an hour, he was going to lose custody of Princess. He would have to play nice with her owners and maybe even smile when they called her Splenda.

Then he would spend the rest of the evening speculating about what was happening between Thea and Vandercamp, and would probably end up blackout drunk right alongside Brock.

"You can't talk to me like that," Holly said.

"Oh, but you can talk to me like that?"

"You're an adult," she spat at him. "You can handle it."

"So can you. You're old enough to know better, so act like

it. And cut your sister some slack. I've never seen a woman work so hard to please a less deserving person."

"You have no idea what's happened between the two of us. No idea what she did to me!"

"Did she murder your best friend? Steal your boyfriend? Run over your dog?" He put just enough derision in his tone to piss off a saint. "Did she burn your favorite collection of bubble chews?"

Holly—far from a saint—took the bait. "She left me, you bastard! She abandoned me. There. Are you happy now?" She threw the words at him as if they were weapons. "I needed her and she...she... You know what? Screw you! You've noticed my settings, well, I've noticed yours, too. You only want what's new and exciting, and you forget the one who's waiting for you. The one who's good for you, who would treat you like a king!"

"No one is waiting for me," he told her, but there was a strange churning in his gut.

"And that just proves how stupid *you* are."

Enough! "Grow up, little girl. You're a hypocrite. You accuse your sister of abandoning you, but what have you done to her? That's right. You've abandoned her."

She huffed and puffed like the big bad wolf. "You don't know what you're talking about." Then she spun, ran away, and—damn it—a whimper escaped her before she was out of range.

He almost went after her. Not to comfort her. There was no way she'd accept comfort from him. To explain a few things about Thea. Abandonment wasn't in her wheelhouse. She'd left for college. She'd gotten married. Holly had somehow equated the two with *my sister doesn't love me anymore.* And Thea had, too. She clearly carried a boatload of guilt about it.

He was also curious about the woman Holly thought was waiting for him. Couldn't be Thea. He'd offered his best, and she'd turned him down flat, choosing to be with Vandercamp and Hillcrest instead.

In the end, he stayed put. Holly's problems weren't his concern, and he wasn't going to interfere.

Daniel picked up Princess and sat on his chair, glaring at the front door, daring the family to return for his—their—dog.

Everyone was getting a happily-ever-after. Except him.

CHAPTER FOURTEEN

Dorothea sat across from Brett at Two Farms, Strawberry Valley's only "five-star" restaurant, according to the owner. Try three and a half! Overhead, an antler chandelier flickered to mimic candlelight. Around them, walls were nothing but retractable black panels. Not that they had much privacy. Their waitress had banged into the panels every time she'd come over, causing the gap between them to widen.

Now the prying eyes of other guests watched Dorothea and Brett interact. And that wasn't even the worst part! Upon their arrival, an earthquake had shaken the building, rattling the dishes, and Dorothea's only thought had been: *if the end of the world comes, I want to be with Daniel.*

A thought she had to ignore as Brett explained the meaning of Dutch treat. Basically, he would pay for his food and she would pay for hers. Anything they shared, they would split in the middle. It ruined the *he'll do anything to have me* vibe. But then, he'd selected a restaurant in the heart of Strawberry Valley. *He* wasn't afraid to show her off, as if she was a prize, so how could she complain?

Daniel looks at me like I'm a prize. Like he'll die without me.

A lie. Only a lie.

Seeing ain't believin', Grandma Ellie used to say. *Believin' is believin'*.

As they sipped wine—thirty dollars a bottle, whimper—Brett asked her about the inn, and she asked him about his veterinary practice. They kept up a steady back-and-forth chatter, and she soon discovered he had a dry wit underneath all his cragginess. A cragginess she suspected he used as a shield to protect himself from emotional harm.

When she attempted to gently lower his shield with talk of his past, he shut her down with a firm "That part of my life is off-limits."

"No problem," she said, and she meant it. The loss of Rose and Dorothea's inability to have more children without a one in a million miracle was never up for discussion, either. "Trust me, I understand."

Her words took him aback, as if he'd never heard them before. "I'm sorry if I was rude. It's just, every time I discuss the past, I feel like I'm reliving it."

"I understand that, too."

They shared a small smile.

Their food arrived a short while later.

Brett dug into his chicken potpie, saying, "Will you miss Princess or will you be happy to see her go?"

Confusion struck. "Why would I miss her? Where's she going?"

"Oh, did I forget to mention her owners have been found? They're picking her up at the inn this evening."

Poor Daniel. Whether he'd admit it or not, he'd grown to love that dog. And so had Dorothea. She adored the way Daniel kissed and cuddled the little darling. Adored the fact that he sometimes even cooed at her but usually talked to her as if she were a human. The last few days, the inn had been more than an inn; it had been a home.

He must be sick with sorrow. And oh, crap, Dorothea had just left him there to deal with the pain on his own.

The urge to go to him, to go to him *now*, overwhelmed her, and there was no fighting it.

"I'm so sorry, Brett, but I can't stay here." She folded her napkin and riffled through her wallet. After a quick calculation in her head—fifteen for the wine, ten for the Stroganoff, and thank the good Lord this wasn't a legit five-star place or she'd probably have to double the amount—she said, "Twenty-five should cover my portion, yes?" Twenty-five hard-earned dollars.

Dutch treat was fair and practical, but it kind of sucked butt.

Next time, she'd insist on eating at the inn.

Live and learn.

"You're going to Daniel." He leaned back in his chair, his expression inscrutable. "You told me you weren't seeing him."

"I'm not." She wanted to add, "It's complicated," but that would imply something was going on—it was—which would get back to Mr. Porter, which would violate the secret she'd never agreed to keep but would anyway, because anything else would hurt Daniel. "He's my friend."

"So what does that make me?"

"A very nice man," she said in a soft, quiet voice. She'd never rejected a date before. But as decent as Brett was, as handsome as he was, he did nothing for her. She'd known it the moment she'd stepped into the lobby, and her gaze had sought Daniel. She'd hoped attraction to Brett would grow, but her body had no desire to wait. Only Daniel would do.

That didn't mean she was going to date him. His we-must-stay-a-secret rule would still trample her hard-won self-esteem. But she wasn't going to date Brett, either. They had no future. She wasn't a prize to him. She was a distraction.

There was hope for John!

"I'm so sorry," she repeated. She stood, walked around the table and kissed his cheek. "I wish you all the best."

He nodded stiffly, but he didn't say a word to stop her as she rushed from the restaurant.

The sky was filled with cumulonimbus clouds, or thunderstorm clouds. They were tall, wide and heavy, shaped into clumps; if they floated down and settled over the land, they could pass for snowcapped mountains. The tops were smooth and flat with points at each side, like an alien spaceship had landed, and the bases were dark and ragged as precipitation was produced. Rain was possible tonight. Actually, rain was highly probable. Hail and tornadoes were possible.

Since she'd ridden in Brett's sedan, she had to walk the four-block stretch to the inn. Not usually a problem for her. In brand-new cowgirl boots? A huge freaking problem. Blisters had already formed on her pinkie toe and heel.

The chilly breeze caused goose bumps to sprout over every inch of exposed skin. She should have worn a jacket, but she hadn't wanted to cover up her new outfit. She looked good, dang it.

As she marched forward, her head high, she felt as if shackles of an unchangeable past were falling off her. Her dad's rejection. Jazz's infidelity. Neither was her fault. Neither was her shame.

Next, shackles of unreasonable ideals and expectations concerning her appearance fell. Before she'd known the perceived ideal of beauty, she'd been happy with her appearance. Why had she cared what anyone else thought? Happiness wasn't found in other people, especially people she didn't know or even like; happiness was found inside herself.

Finally, shackles of worthlessness fell. Her worth wasn't based on someone else's actions. How a person treated her did not speak of her value but of theirs.

I'm Dorothea Freaking Mathis. There's not another one out there. I'm one of a kind.

A raindrop splattered her forehead, the opening act. Thunder boomed, and the clouds released their bounty. A deluge poured over her, quickly soaking her hair and clothes. Laughing, she twirled. *I'm free!*

Then her teeth began chattering, ice seeming to sheen her skin and absorb into her bones. She rushed the rest of the way to the inn.

A car she didn't recognize was parked up front. Princess's family? Dorothea's newfound exhilaration received a quick kick in the nuts. As she entered, the bell tinkled, but no one noticed her, giving her time to scan the lobby.

A husband and wife in their early thirties stood off to the side, talking to a stone-faced Daniel. Two little kids, probably under the age of ten, sat on the floor, playing with an excited Princess. Oh, yes. The family.

"—morning when I made my coffee," the mom was saying, "I'd tell the kids Splenda makes everything better. So when we decided we were ready to take on the responsibility of a pet, they begged us to name her Splenda, because she made everything better." A tear rolled down her cheek. "Thank you for keeping her safe for us."

"Why isn't she wearing a collar? Or chipped?" There was no emotion in Daniel's voice. He looked cold and hard, nothing like the flirtatious charmer she'd come to know.

"Anytime we go out, we make sure she's wearing a collar. Someone could have taken it off her to use her as..." The dad coughed into his hand, probably to hide *his* tears. "Afterward, she could have escaped. Or, if no one found her, whatever attacked her could have gone for her throat."

"We'll get her chipped, Mr. Porter," the mom said. "I promise you."

Daniel faced the children and finally spotted Dorothea.

Their gazes locked. For a moment, his mask fell away, and it was like a bandage had been ripped from a festering wound. Raw agony obliterated his calm facade.

She experienced a visceral reaction and covered her mouth with her hand, afraid of what she might say if she didn't.

The couple noticed her, too, and introductions were made; their names never registered. She moved to Daniel's side and twined her fingers with his. He held on to her as if she were the only life raft on board a sinking ship.

"The storm is going to worsen and last for several hours," she said, and offered the family a room, free of charge.

For the safety of their kids and Princess—Splenda?—they agreed and thanked her profusely.

As soon as they were settled in their room, Dorothea locked the front door and flipped the sign in the window to Closed. She led Daniel up the stairs to her private chambers.

Outside, the storm continued to rage. The barrage of raindrops hit the tin roof, creating a melody she usually found soothing and even magical. She pushed Daniel onto the edge of the bed, and he sat without protest.

"I'm going to make you a cup of golden milk." Something her mom used to make her whenever she'd come home from school crying because someone had called her an ugly name.

No response.

No matter. She bustled around the kitchen, gathering turmeric and ginger powder, cinnamon, nutmeg and cardamom. After measuring the proper amounts, she mixed the spices into a pan of hot coconut milk and honey, then added half a teaspoon of virgin coconut oil to enrich the flavor.

"How was your date?" he asked. Once again, there was no hint of emotion in his voice.

"Brett and I...we decided we're better off as friends."

Some of the tension drained from him. "You mean *you* decided."

She frowned. How did he know?

"Did he make you pay for your food?" he asked.

Again she wondered how he could know. "He did. Why?"

"I read people. He's a penny-pincher. I'm not. If you were mine, I'd pay for everything. It would be my honor. My privilege."

A dangerous bolt of heat shot through her, a mimic of the lightning strikes outside. "If I was yours, you couldn't pay for anything without letting the entire town know we're dating, and *that* you would never do." She handed him a mug and, with a gentle nudge, said, "Drink."

He obeyed, his eyes widening with surprise. "This is good."

"Even better, it's good *for* you."

"Don't tell me it mends broken hearts."

"Why? Does yours need mending?" she asked softly, figuring he would either shut her down, as Brett had done, or switch to a safer topic.

Instead, he told her, "Yes. Yes it does." His shoulders rolled in, making him appear dejected, but even that couldn't detract from his appeal. Not with those sharp cheekbones, long black lashes and a nose that might have been broken once or twice.

"I'm sorry, Daniel."

His big hands gripped the cup. They were a working-man's hands, big and rough, but they looked just as comfortable holding a delicate piece of porcelain as they would look holding a jackhammer. Or a woman's breasts...

She sucked in a breath. When would her mind accept the fact that Daniel wasn't the man for her?

"I know how to deal with loss. My mom. Friends. Soldiers. Hell, my innocence." He pressed his lips together, and she thought he'd stop there. Then he shuddered and added, "Why is the loss of a dog killing me?"

He might as well have ripped out her heart with a rusty spoon.

"Princess filled a void in your life. A void you might not have known you had until now." She eased beside him, and they sat in silence for several minutes, passing the milk between them until the cup was empty. Every time she took a drink, he made sure to turn the cup so that his lips settled where hers had been. For some reason, those kisses-by-proxy helped ease him.

They had the opposite effect on her. Warmth pooled between her legs, and she squirmed, searching for relief she might never find.

"You're cold and wet," he said, his gaze lingering on her beaded nipples. "You should change. Now." A croak, the raggedness of his voice only fueling her desire for him. "Definitely now."

Just went on a date with another man. And I refuse to be a secret. I decided. Not going to change my mind because Daniel had a bad day and he looks hot sitting on my bed.

"You're right." She gathered an oversize T-shirt and a pair of sweatpants and locked herself in the bathroom. To prove she wouldn't be making a play for Daniel, she washed her face free of makeup.

Behold! Dorothea Mathis in all her freckled glory.

She exited the bathroom, her spine fused with steel. He'd abandoned the bed in order to prowl through her room. He stared at the framed ultrasound picture on her mantel—the only thing on it, actually. Acid scalded her chest. She breathed a sigh of relief when he turned his attention to the pictures on the wall. Her and Holly as kids. Her, Lyndie and Ryanne as teens.

"You had sad eyes." He turned after he'd spoken, proving he'd been aware of her the entire time. A soft smile teased his mouth as he looked her over. "I like you like this."

"You do?" Really?

"You're relaxed and soft. So damned soft. And those freckles…they give a man ideas."

She gulped, taken aback. "What kind of ideas?"

"Very naughty ones." A pause. Then, "I'd like to show you, sweetheart."

Lord save me. The way he'd said it…as if he wasn't saying "show" but "make love to." As if being inside her was the answer to every problem he'd ever had.

"I…" *Want to say yes. So danged bad.* "No." To give in was to give up on her goal. Be the prize, not the secret. "Unless you want to do this thing for real." She couldn't believe she'd been so bold, but this was important to her. And yeah, okay, she'd had a moment where she'd doubted long-term relationships could work. Maybe they couldn't, but she still wanted to try. "Do you?"

He gave her a wry stare as he unabashedly adjusted the fly of his jeans. "I want to keep you all to myself. That isn't a crime."

"I'll take that as a no." And she wasn't hurt. She wasn't! At least she'd made a play for what she wanted, right?

The sound of a hammer banging repeatedly on an anvil suddenly echoed through the room. The hail had arrived. She turned on her TV, avoiding Jazz's station. The forecaster warned of possible tornadic activity, as she'd suspected. The power flickered once, twice, before going out. Sixty seconds later, the generator kicked on.

"I need to go home, watch over my dad." He looked at the door, looked at her, then the door again. He remained in place. "I don't want to leave you."

I won't react, I won't react, dang it, I won't react. "Well, that's good, because you *can't* leave while it's hailing. You could be knocked unconscious, and your car could be totaled."

With a curse, he whipped out his cell. He had a short conversation with… Jude, if she had to guess, who was already at his dad's. By the time they hung up, Daniel's relief was palpable. "If there's a tornado, and I'm not with him…"

"He has a shelter," she reminded him. Everyone in town had a shelter. The inn had a basement. "Right now, we're in the clear, though." She pointed to the TV and explained the storm's predicted path, the clouds that covered Strawberry Valley and the movement of the wind.

Daniel stared at her with something akin to…awe? "You should have stayed in school. You would kick ass on a news station. And every man in the state would wish we had naked weather girls."

She snort-laughed.

He studied her for several prolonged moments and frowned. "You want to be behind the camera, get behind the camera. It doesn't have to belong to a news station. You can live stream for the people of Strawberry Valley. Jude can even help you with a website."

The idea had merit and gave her something to ponder. Could she? Should she? "Let me think about it," she said softly. "And thank you."

His brows knit together. "For what?"

"For taking me seriously."

"Your talent and passion are obvious. Why would I do anything *but* take you seriously?"

Softening…

Red alert! Danger zone! If she didn't do something to disrupt this tantalizingly raw moment, she was going to fall head over heels in love with him. Again!

Not that she was afraid of love. Love empowered. Love healed. It was everything else that hurt. Like rejection. Oh, how rejection hurt. Hate. Bitterness. Envy. Strife. Greed. But love…it gave without expecting anything in return. It built up, never tore down. It protected.

If only Daniel would love her back.

Emotion clogged her throat. She threaded her fingers through his—experienced a jolt of connection, a frisson of acceptance—and drew him to the screened-in porch that led to the roof, allowing them to watch the hail as cool mist brushed against their faces and dark clouds wisped over an equally dark sky.

"This is my favorite place in the world," she said, releasing him for the sake of her sanity.

But his big hand sought a new resting place, cupping her nape and massaging. "I can see why. It's as beautiful, wild and unpredictable as the woman who owns it."

Well. Disrupting the moment hadn't helped. Then and there, Dorothea Valentina Mathis fell head over heels in love with Daniel Porter, and there was nothing she could do to stop it.

CHAPTER FIFTEEN

Daniel returned home after the storm and ended up pacing all night. Not exactly a new experience for him; his mind refused to settle. Something had changed between Thea and him. Something big. Unfortunately, the particulars escaped him.

He thought back. He'd called her beautiful, wild and unpredictable, and only a few minutes later she'd ushered him out of her bedroom and into one of his own as if he'd begun leaking toxic waste.

Already he missed her. And he missed Princess. He felt like his chest had been hollowed out and glass shards stuffed inside. Every time he inhaled, those shards cut him to ribbons. His need to breathe both kept him alive and killed him simultaneously.

Dorothea was right. There was a void inside him.

One he needed to fill. Which meant he needed a dog of his own. A beloved companion. A bosom buddy.

Yeah. A dog would help his dad, too. Maybe even Jude and Brock.

Brock had returned to the Scratching Post again last night and once again drank so much he'd blacked out. An hour ago, Ryanne had texted Daniel to let him know Brock was on her couch. He'd told Jude, and the guy had taken off in a fury to collect their friend.

If Brock didn't change his destructive ways, he was going to end up in the hospital. Or worse, a casket. And Jude...the man wanted to shut himself off emotionally, but he lived with despair. Before leaving to get Brock, he'd been cleaning his gun, staring at it like it was an answer to a prayer.

The three of them were dealing with PTSD in different ways. Daniel knew it, but he hadn't realized the depths of danger until now—until Princess. She hadn't been trained as a service dog, but she'd still had a calming effect.

And Daniel needed to calm the hell down. Thea wasn't going to cancel her date with Hillcrest, and cold-blooded murder still wasn't an option.

As sunlight filtered through his window, Daniel's eyes burned, fatigue a noose around his neck. He showered and dressed and exited his room.

He drove to the inn and searched for Thea, only to find Carol Mathis bustling around in the kitchen.

She'd come back from her singles getaway early. "Ms. Mathis," he said in greeting.

"Call me Carol, please. Ms. Mathis makes me think of the poor woman currently married to my ex-husband."

"When did you get in?"

"A few hours ago. Holly's been texting me nonstop." She cast a pointed glance in his direction. "I'm needed here."

Trying to tell him that *he* wasn't needed? Well, no woman had ever been more wrong.

"Would you mind running the inn today?" he asked. "I'd like to take Thea into the city. I'm making the headboard for her first theme room, and she's got to pick out the wood." He didn't mention the dog shelter they would be visiting, lest Carol try to talk her daughter out of coming home with a pet.

Her lips pinched together. "I've been meaning to speak with my Dottie about the changes she's making around here. I don't know why she thinks a theme room is going to be profitable. I'm telling you, the inn is perfect just the way it is. Why, people like the familiar and always have. They count on us to provide a stay so comfortable they'd swear they were at home. And with the spring festival only four weeks away, we're going to fill up fast. We need every room ready to go."

He was glad she hadn't talked to Thea about this. The precious girl deserved encouragement and praise, not more roadblocks. "The room will be finished before the festival, I'll make sure of it. And everyone who's heard about the theme room seems excited for the change. Just give it a chance."

Daniel beat feet before she could protest, continuing his search for Thea. She wasn't in her room. Or rather, she didn't answer the door. He didn't think she was ducking him today. He saw no moving shadows under the crack between door and floor.

He remembered the room. He'd liked it. A lot. Had more space than the rooms below, and came with a small kitchenette. The furnishings looked as if they belonged in an old lady's house where cats ruled the roost, but Thea had added feminine touches to infuse her sparkling personality. A patchwork quilt with pictures of star formations draped the top of a floral-print chair. A velvet settee was lined with furry white pillows, as if they were clouds. Every lamp had beaded ribbons streaming from the cap to mimic rain. Beside the door to the roof was a brass telescope.

He also remembered a photo above the mantel. A framed ultrasound with last year's date in the corner. Thea had no children, and no one in town had recently given birth.

He hadn't liked the path his mind had taken—Thea's baby... lost.

The background check hadn't delved into her medical his-

tory, and he wouldn't do so now. He would respect her privacy, as he'd promised, and wait for her to share her past.

He found her in Holly's room, the door wide-open. The
two were arguing as Holly stalked from the closet to the edge
of the bed, where she was stuffing clothing into a bag. Thea
followed her and pulled out the clothes, tossing the garments
back into the closet.

"Stop that. Mom's back, and she said I could go," Holly
grated.

"Well, Mom must have had a stroke. You can't miss an
entire week of school just to go camping with your friends."

"I can, and I will. Watch me."

"Do you want to flunk your senior year?" Thea demanded.

"Why not? I can get my GED."

He knocked on the door frame to get their attention. Both
stopped what they were doing to shout, "What?"

Thea wilted, instantly apologetic. "Sorry. Is there something you need?" she asked in a gentler tone.

"Your mother is running the inn today, and after you make
me a cup of golden milk, we're going into the city to pick the
wood for the new headboard."

Relief and excitement blended in her beautiful eyes. "I'm
not making you any golden milk or going to the city with
you. You can send me a link—"

He stalked across the distance, leaned down and whispered, "You owe me a date, remember? Make the milk." If
he had to force the issue, he would. "And change into your
shortest skirt."

She glowered at him. "Fine. I'll make the milk while Holly
cancels her camping trip. She can come with us."

He knew better than to argue. "Yay," he deadpanned. "The
more the merrier."

"No, Holly cannot go with you," the girl retorted while

stuffing another shirt in the bag. "She'd rather wear a dress made entirely of vomit."

"Perfect." Thea hurled the shirt into the closet. "Vomit is your best color. Now stop being a spoiled brat and cancel that trip, or I will cancel it for you. Maybe you haven't realized it yet, but going would make you a hypocrite. You say you hate me for leaving you, and yet here you are trying to do the same to me—and ruining your future in the process, just to spite me! You have school in two days, and you will attend class. And you will be in the lobby in half an hour. With a smile! If you want to wear your vomit dress, fine, but you *will* go to the city with us, and you will help us pick wood for the headboard. I may not be the best sister in the world, but I'm *your* sister. Deal with it."

She left then, dragging Daniel with her.

He was proud of her. And he was so turned on he actually broke out in a sweat. The more she'd yelled at her sister, the harder he'd gotten. He wasn't sure what that said about his state of mind, but he was certain he didn't care.

He wanted this woman. He wanted her badly. He had to win her, which meant convincing her to date him in secret. Not for the challenge she represented—he was well past that kind of need—but for her. The woman. The pinup.

The only light in a very dark world.

To Dorothea's surprise, Holly was waiting in the lobby half an hour later, as ordered. She was dressed in a black dress with a high neck, long sleeves and a floor-length train. Old-fashioned funeral attire.

She wouldn't meet Dorothea's gaze, but she was there. Hope bloomed within her. They might be able to patch their relationship after all.

"Thank you," Dorothea said, crossing her ankles to accentuate the calf-length skirt. She'd wanted to wear pants, but because Daniel had worn sweatpants for her, she'd gone with a skirt, as he'd requested. Or commanded. Of course, she'd ignored the part about "shortest" as an eff-you to Daniel and his secret-keeping ways. However, she had worn her brand-new thong. Not that he would see or feel it, the jerk… maybe. Probably.

"Whatever." Holly popped a bubble. "Why are you dressed in church clothes?"

"Maybe I plan to pray for your soul." With a sigh, she led her sister outside. The sun glared at everyone, obviously ticked off about yesterday's storm. Daniel's truck idled at the curb, and he helped them climb inside the passenger side; Dorothea took the front and Holly the back.

"That is your shortest skirt?" he whispered so Holly wouldn't hear.

"No."

His eyes narrowed.

"But I'm wearing a thong," she said, and his fingers jerked on the wheel.

He wants me…

Maybe she should have let him stay in her room last night, rather than kicking him out. Maybe she should have scratched an itch. Even now, she wanted him right back. Despite everything, her desire remained on constant simmer, and oh, how she ached.

Her body said: *Make out with him, just once more. What would it hurt?*

Only everything! A single slice of pie would not stop a craving for the whole dang thing.

"Your nails are yellow," he said, changing the subject. "What are you hopeful about?"

Ignoring him—*no way to answer that without sounding lovesick*—she peered out the window.

He didn't push her for the deets, and she wasn't sure if

she was grateful he respected her or upset that he didn't care enough.

When he parked in front of a metal warehouse, he said, "Pick the wood you want and don't you dare look at price, all right? Promise me."

Okay, maybe he cared enough. "But—"

"No buts. This is my—" he glanced back at Holly "—you know. And I decide what we do. Plus, the headboard is my contribution to the theme room. That means I pay for it."

This. This was one of the reasons she loved him. He selflessly gave of himself, his time and his resources.

"Thank you," she said softly. "That's very kind of you."

His gaze finally slid over her, heating and hooding... He looked at her as if she'd created the moon and stars. "Absolutely my pleasure."

"Why?" Holly barked. "*Why* is it your pleasure to be kind to her? Are you guys fuc—"

Dorothea slapped a hand over her sister's mouth.

But she didn't offer a reprimand. Let Daniel respond.

He smiled, completely unabashed. "No, we aren't...screwing. I plan to hassle your sister every morning for golden milk, and I want a reason to hold over her head. 'Remember when I bought all those planks...carved that headboard...' Also, I'll be asking a very big favor of her when we're done here."

"What favor?" Dorothea asked, curiosity getting the better of her.

"I'll tell you when we're—what?—done here," he reiterated.

Argh! The wait would be torture.

The anger faded from Holly's features, and she peered at Daniel as if he were a creature from outer space. How many times had *she* peered at him that same way? Only, replace "creature from outer space" with "sex god from outer space."

Daniel opened her door for her, but not for Holly, forcing

the girl to climb over the console to exit. A difficult task in her dress. Dorothea swallowed a laugh.

What a day! She loved searching through the different kinds of wood. Loved the different colors and grains, even the different scents. A few times Holly shouted out the price, maybe to poke at Daniel, or maybe because her shock was so great.

"This one is three hundred dollars!"

In the end, Dorothea couldn't resist the black walnut. She adored the dark color and the patina on the pieces salvaged from an old barn.

As Daniel loaded the planks in the back of the truck, his muscles bulged and her heart fluttered wildly. Such a glorious man.

"You're staring at him," Holly said quietly. She stood at Dorothea's side. Willingly.

"I know. I can't help myself. He's just so…" Delicious. "Special."

"Yeah," Holly said. "The elusive unicorn."

The fact that her sister was having a real conversation with her, well, tears welled in Dorothea's eyes. That was the only reason. She would deny any others.

"He likes you, you know." Holly sounded…sad about it? Why sad?

The answer didn't require a lot of pondering. Jazz. Holly still rooted for a reconciliation. "He does like me," she whispered, "but he doesn't like me enough."

"Do they ever?" Holly replied.

A pang in her chest. "Did a boy break your heart?"

Holly opened her mouth, seemed to realize how personal the conversation had become and flounced into the truck.

"All right," Daniel said. He wiped his hands together. "We're having lunch, and then we're going to an animal shelter. I'm adopting a dog." His gaze landed on Dorothea.

"Here's the favor I need from you. See, I have a job in the city next weekend and—"

"What kind of job?" Holly interjected, leaning out of the window. "Are you a contract killer? A stripper? A male escort?"

Rather than acting put out by her rudeness, he kept his attention on Dorothea. "You know Dixie Bell-Lilly, the country singer? Her family lives in Oklahoma, and she visits frequently. This time she's throwing some kind of party, and we're keeping the peace for her."

Dixie Bell-Lilly. A beautiful blonde who would probably fall in love with him and re-create the movie *The Bodyguard*. Daniel, who wasn't dating Dorothea, would be free to sleep with her.

And that was fine. Whatever.

Bastard!

He canted his head to the side to study her more intently. "Remember the time I bought those wood planks for you? Remember the headboard I'm going to carve for you? Well, I won't be able to take a pet with me while I'm working, so…"

"So you want me to babysit." The words lashed from her. Trusty Dorothea, always the friend, never the sex object.

Uh, isn't that what I've been pushing for?

He blinked in confusion. "Whoa. You're looking at me like I'm a Yankee spy. If you don't want to do it, I'll—"

"No, no. I do. I'm sorry. I would actually love to babysit your dog. I just had a momentary brain blip." If she couldn't have Daniel, she could have moments with the creature he loved.

I'm pathetic.

He smiled at her, and dang it, she smiled back, anger and jealousy melting away. He was just so beautiful and so freaking kind.

She herself had grown bolder, tougher—but definitely not

wiser. She was allowing her love for Daniel to lead her around. She should be fighting tooth and nail to pluck him out of her heart.

Holly groaned. "You guys are gross. You should hit it and quit it like normal people. And you should really think about getting a cat instead of a dog. Cats are rude, temperamental, and spend their days plotting ways to murder their owners, but at least they aren't clingy."

"Nothing wrong with clingy." Daniel opened the truck door and waved Dorothea inside. "Some women, and I'm not naming names, should give it a try."

She narrowed her eyes at him. "Careful, Danny boy. We don't want your secret getting out, now, do we?"

"What secret?" Holly demanded.

New Dorothea came out to play, saying, "He has a micropenis. And he's impotent. And he has hemorrhoids." She patted him on the shoulder. "Go ahead and let the world know. You'll feel better."

To her astonishment, he barked out a laugh. "You are diabolical, woman."

She fluffed her hair. "And don't you forget it."

CHAPTER SIXTEEN

The best-laid plans...

Daniel entered the shelter thinking he would adopt a small dog, like Princess. *A*—a word denoting one, no more. And yet he left the shelter with two mammoth ninety-pound beasts. Adonis and Echo, brother-sister pit bull mixes. Apparently Adonis had been adopted out once before and Echo twice, and both had been returned within days of each other. They did not do well when separated.

An employee told Daniel that Adonis liked to look at himself in the mirror and bark, and Echo liked to mimic him. She also barked when anyone spoke. Or moved. Or breathed. The dogs enjoyed digging holes, escaping yards, and chasing birds and squirrels.

They'd been scheduled for euthanization later that day. In fact, they'd been on leashes, being led to their deaths, as he'd petted another dog.

Daniel had fallen in love with the pair on sight. Adonis was black with patches of white on his chin, chest and feet. Echo was white with speckles of black all over her body. In other words, dog freckles. Both were high energy and in desperate need of training, but he welcomed the challenge.

He'd enjoyed the way Thea's face had softened when she'd interacted with the siblings. Not that her opinion mattered, of course. He was doing this for himself, his dad and his friends.

After he wrangled the dogs into the back of his truck with Holly, he remained outside, looking at Thea, and she looked at a wristwatch she wasn't wearing.

"Well," she said, "we should probably head back to town. I have things to do."

Right. Like get ready for her date. The black hole in an otherwise stellar day.

Was she wearing yellow nail polish because of Hillcrest? At first he'd thought she'd worn it for Daniel. Because of their interaction last night...

"You know how I feel about you seeing the teacher," he told her in a quiet voice.

"You know how I feel about being your dirty little secret," she replied just as quietly.

"You aren't—" He pressed his lips together. No use hashing out an already hashed-out issue. Especially with her little sister inches away.

He wasn't going to change her mind, and she wasn't going to convince him they would stay together forever and his dad would never be hurt.

She wanted promises, maybe marriage. A family? He couldn't even sleep an entire night. Loud noises freaked him out. Just yesterday he'd liked the idea of committing cold-blooded murder. And if he fell for her and lost her? He'd become a shell of a man, like Jude.

With Thea, Daniel would never be able to relax his guard. Eventually their relationship *would* end. His parents had loved each other madly, but not even they had been able to defy death.

What kind of boyfriend would he be? How long before Thea tired of his antics?

But damn it. Something had to give, and soon. He couldn't live like this, wanting her but unable to have her. Desperate to escape the prison of his own making, but with no key in sight.

He helped Thea into her seat before climbing behind the wheel and starting the engine. Soon they were zipping down the highway—gagging and fanning their faces.

"What is that hellacious smell?" Holly gasped out.

"I think the dogs are *farting*," Thea said.

Daniel would bet this toxic gas was the main reason the dogs had been returned. The two were weapons of mass destruction! He rolled down the windows, allowing clean air to whip inside the cab. It didn't help. His nose was permanently seared.

Back in Strawberry Valley, he dropped the girls off at the inn and got the dogs settled in at his dad's place. He knew Virgil was playing checkers with Anthony, but where were Jude and Brock?

Until the dogs were potty trained, he decided to limit the areas they were allowed to investigate. The pair familiarized themselves with their new surroundings, sniffing everything repeatedly, including Daniel. When they were no longer leery of him, he ushered them into the backyard to play fetch. They played for hours, until the excitement wore them down. When they scratched at the back door, he let them inside and led them to his bedroom. They crawled under his bed and promptly fell asleep.

He wasn't sure how the beasts had fit, but he didn't try to coax them out. They must feel safe, maybe cocooned. One day, they would trust him enough to sleep out in the open.

What kind of lives had they led up to this point? Were they ever abused?

He rubbed the twinge in his chest. As quietly as possible,

he shut the door, wrote a note for anyone who came home before he returned and made the two-and-a-half-mile trek to the cemetery where his mom was buried. Along the way, he received a text from Jessie Kay.

What's this I hear about you & Dottie—oh, excuse me, Dorothea—spending the day in the city??? I'm your best friend. That comes with responsibilities—for you. TELL ME EVERYTHING! Are you two dating now? Huh huh? :) :)

Only a few seconds later, another text came in. WHY ARE YOU IGNORING ME?????? :)

He sent a picture of Rachel McAdams in *Mean Girls*, a movie she had forced him to watch, and typed back, WHY ARE YOU SO OBSESSED WITH ME?? I'm helping her w/ the theme room, remember?

He sent her a third text. Going to the Scratching Post tonight w/ my boys. You're invited, but you have to leave your wife at home. I mean it. He'll make friends w/ Thea & torment me the way I torment him w/ you.

He made the decision then and there. With Dorothea out on her date, he would need a distraction. Jude would agree to go only to act as the designated driver. Or maybe to watch Ryanne…

Jessie Kay: Hahahahaha! I can't wait to tell West what you said. PS if someone comes knocking on your door, don't answer. I repeat, don't answer. That'll be West. With a crowbar. Oh! And I will be there tonight, with bells on—& probably little else. Because yes, I'll be bringing West.

He snorted. Stop calling your husband by his last name. It's weird.

Jessie Kay: I do what I want and he likes it!

Like Daniel could really argue with that. He pocketed the phone.

When he arrived at the cemetery, he spotted a few other people visiting deceased loved ones, but everyone was trapped in their own heads. Or their own grief. No one paid anyone else any heed.

Daniel crouched in front of his mother's tombstone. A beautiful pink-veined marble with a cherub perched at the top. *Bonnie Teresa Porter. Beloved wife and mother.*

Underneath the years she'd lived, Virgil had carved: *The Reason I Breathe.*

After she'd died, Virgil had shut down. He'd drunk too much too often and had rarely spoken a word. Once, Daniel had caught him holding a knife to his wrist.

A scarring experience, knowing his dad wanted to die, just to join his wife.

Ultimately, Virgil had cleaned himself up for Daniel's benefit. But he'd worried so much about keeping his son safe, Daniel had often felt smothered. It was one of the reasons he'd joined the army. So, of course, guilt had followed him. His dad had only wanted to make Daniel happy. What kind of POS abandoned him?

Not me. Not ever again.

"Do you remember Dorothea Mathis, Mom? She grew into an amazing woman." Over the years, he'd had many conversations with his mom, but Thea was the first girl he'd ever mentioned. He gave a wry laugh. "You'll be happy to know she kicked my ego in the nuts."

There was no response, but he was almost certain he felt soft arms wrap around him. His mother may not be here, but he firmly believed her spirit lived on.

"She wants a relationship," he said. "Full on, nothing held

back. But when we end, Dad will be hurt. His heart can't take much more abuse. I want him happy. I *need* him happy. And yeah, okay, I know he'd be happier if I got married. But if Thea ever left me, or died, he would shatter." *And so would I.*

The arms he felt-but-didn't-feel tightened around him. He imagined his mom leaning her head against his shoulder, glossy brown hair pinned back, her dark eyes sparkling, and saying, *Does your happiness not matter? And why would your Thea leave you?*

"Why would she stay?" he asked.

Because you're a treasure.

He snorted.

All right. Fine. You're a treasure...but you have a habit of looking back rather than forward. You need a strong kick in your patootie. I have a feeling she's the girl to give it to you.

"I look back to *guard* my back. There's a difference."

Oh, my baby boy. There really isn't. Whatever life throws at you, you've got to keep walking...running...sprinting forward. You've got to love others and yourself. And for goodness' sake, Daniel, stop expecting the worst and start shooting for the stars.

She'd always told him straight. But then, she'd been a good woman with a good heart, and she'd raised her only son to the best of her ability. She'd wanted him happy the way he wanted his dad happy.

She would have busted his ass for continuing to hurt Thea. And he had hurt her, hadn't he?

Thea had struggled with self-esteem issues all her life. He knew she still ached over her dad's dismissal. Had heard the pain in her voice when she'd mentioned him. How much lower she must have fallen when the ex-husband cheated on her. But she'd gotten back up. She'd walked, run and sprinted on. Even now, she charged at life full speed.

And he wanted to hide her away? Like she was a dirty little secret?

She was the treasure, not him, and she deserved better.

Could he give her better?

"I love you, Momma. I'll come again soon."

No need. I'm always with you.

He walked home. As he slipped inside, he noted the dogs were quiet—still sleeping? Jude, Brock and his dad were seated in the living room. Shadows rimmed Brock's eyes, and lines of tension surrounded Jude's mouth.

"Something wrong?" he asked.

"No, no. I was just explaining to the boys that women don't wait forever, and if they aren't careful, someone will come along and snatch up the one they want." Virgil patted his shoulder. "Want to tell us what kind of beasts you got in your room? They almost busted down the door when I got home."

At the sound of his voice, both Adonis and Echo barked.

Daniel ignored the hard clench his dad's words had caused. "Come meet the new members of our family." He strode down the hall, opened his bedroom door.

Adonis and Echo darted into the hall. Everyone chuckled, even Jude, and a sudden sense of contentment closed around Daniel. Not quite reaching him internally, not yet, but soon. The potential was there.

He just had to figure out his next move with Thea.

"Dad," he said as the dogs played, "if I wanted to…date… someone…someone like Thea Mathis—"

Virgil's eyes rounded. Jude and Brock—the bastards— excused themselves.

"I want to point out that I said *date*. Date her. Not marry her." *Should have stayed quiet.* But he was already in the fire. Why not dance in the flames? "I don't know how long our relationship will last. Maybe a few months, maybe even a year." His longest relationship had lasted six months. Things had heated up while he was in basic training but had ended soon after he'd first shipped out. "I don't want you disappointed when things end."

His dad gave him another pat on the shoulder. "Son, I have a confession to make. I stopped by the inn today and spoke with Carol. She suspects something's been goin' on between you and her daughter, and she told me Dorothea is a fragile flower with dark secrets you don't have the strength to help her carry. Now, I took exception to that. My boy is strong. The strongest. But you have dark secrets of your own, and the two of you, you need light, not more darkness."

What secrets did Thea have?

The ultrasound photo...

"Thea is strong all on her own," he said. "She doesn't need to be carried."

"That's good. That's real good." Virgil smiled at him. "But I agree with you. About the relationship. With so many secrets between you, the two of you will never last."

What! His dad, the eternal optimist, thought Daniel would crash and burn?

"I'm worried about you, son. You haven't been living, and it pains me."

After all his hard work, everything he'd done to make his dad happy, he'd failed. From day one, he'd failed.

He'd have to do better. He'd keep going forward, as his mother would have wanted, but he'd make a new plan. He'd show his dad he could live—really live—if only for a little while.

He was going to openly date Thea. If she would have him.

Dorothea put the finishing touches on her outfit. The dress had a large heart cut out of the center to reveal another layer of fabric with black and white stripes and a bow; it accentuated her hourglass figure. At least, she hoped. The waist was drawn tight by a second bow. While one side of the hem reached her knees, the other side fell to her ankles. She wore boots and lacy socks that peeked over the edge.

For the finishing touch, she painted her nails purple. All the while, she tried not to think about Daniel. If he wouldn't risk a real relationship with her, she wouldn't risk...what? What wouldn't she risk? Her heart? She already loved him.

Just because they started in secret didn't mean they had to end that way. They could be together, and she could pour her love into him. All of it. Nothing held back. And feel as if she'd been stabbed in the chest every time he denied dating her. Every time she had to lie to her mom and sister.

Her phone rang, Lyndie's name appearing on the screen. "Hey, you," she said in greeting.

In lieu of a response, Lyndie said, "Bring John to the Scratching Post, okay?"

Revisit the site of her date with Daniel? She pushed out a heavy sigh. "Why?"

"Ryanne is singing tonight, and she could use our support. Also, her former stepbrother is in town. Do you remember Maxim?"

Maximum hotness, they used to whisper anytime he'd visited his dad. Sweet guy, if a little rambunctious.

"I do." And really, it had been years since Dorothea had supported Ryanne's amazing talent. "You had me at *Ryanne*. We'll be there."

"Thank you. You won't regret it. Or maybe you will. I guess we'll find out." She hung up.

Oookay. That was a bit odd.

"If you're going to date my teacher, you might as well make yourself useful and convince him to give me an A."

Holly had entered her room unannounced. She must have used a key she wasn't supposed to have. At least her funeral attire had been replaced by a brown top and black jeans.

The brown was as shocking as her presence. Since Dorothea's return, Holly had mostly only worn black, as if she was in mourning—over seeing each other again. Was she finally thawing?

"I hope you're not implying I—" she began.

"Bone him? I'm not implying. I'm flat-out stating it." Holly spread her arms. "Bone him and get me an A."

"I'm so out of practice, I might get you a D." Except, she remembered a time her lack of practice hadn't mattered. As she'd writhed on Daniel, her instincts had worked just fine. Better than fine.

"At least I'd pass." Holly scratched her cheek and shifted from one foot to the other. "Don't worry about the inn. Mom and me will take care of things while you're out."

The unexpected offer threw her for a loop. "I fired you."

"Well, you just rehired me to work the weekends. Congrats!"

A compromise was better than nothing, so she nodded. "Thank you. But just to be clear, you're not planning to burn the place to the ground, are you?"

"Nah. I just want to prove I'm better at managing it than you are."

"Ah. That makes sense. I look forward to coming home and finding you curled in a ball, sucking on your thumb, crying for mercy."

"In your dreams," Holly said, the corners of her mouth twitching.

They were having such a sweet moment. Zero arguing. She decided to push for a little more. "Listen, Halls, I want you to know—"

Holly exited, shutting the door behind her with a loud thud.

Abrupt beginning, and an even more abrupt end, but still Dorothea smiled with megawatt brightness. This was progress, pure and simple. While she wasn't sure what had heralded the change in her sister's attitude, she knew she would be forever grateful for it.

"Oh, and by the way, Teach is here," Holly shouted through the doorway.

Her stomach twisted. The date. With John, who was as sweet as sugar. Surely he could lure her affections away from Daniel.

Her phone beeped, signaling a text had just come in. From Jazz. Ugh.

Guess what! I'm coming to Strawberry Valley in the morning to do a special on the earthquakes and hail damage and possible tornadic activity in the coming months. I'd love to chat with you.

Jazz was coming to town? Gag!

There were no other hotels nearby, which meant he would have to stay at the inn. The idea horrified her.

Could she really afford *not* to rent him a room?

Decisions, decisions.

She had until morning. Tonight she would have a good time with a good man. They would talk and laugh and, who knows, he might kiss her at her door. Fingers crossed. That way, his kiss would be the last she'd had, not Daniel's.

That thought saddened her.

I've got it bad. And I need it good.

What on God's green earth was she going to do?

CHAPTER SEVENTEEN

Daniel experienced a series of reactions when Thea and her date walked inside the Scratching Post. The first? A near heart attack. She. Looked. Amazing. A good deal of material was cut out of the top of her dress—he wanted to undo the little ribbons at her collar with his teeth...

Next came the urge to grab his woman and whisk her away. Then the desire to strip her and take her—to brand her and slake his hunger. Last, the impulse to grab Hillcrest by the throat and teach him the error of his ways.

Never touch what's mine.

Nope, not last. Last was the need to stand on the bar and shout to one and all, *I'm dating Thea Mathis. We're a couple. Deal with it.*

But he resisted. His timing, and his methods, had to be perfect.

"You looking for a fight?" Brock asked. "Because I will wingman the hell out of a fight."

"I'll let you know." He stayed put, watching, waiting as Thea stepped deeper inside the building. She hadn't yet noticed him in the corner, playing pool with his friends.

Hillcrest draped his arm around her waist as he ushered her to the bar, where Lyndie waited and Ryanne hustled to fill drink orders. Every muscle in Daniel's body tensed. If Hillcrest spread his fingers, he would make contact with her ass.

"He's *definitely* looking for a fight," Jude said. "I wonder how many casualties there'll be tonight."

"At least two." Brock eyed the man beside Lyndie as if he'd just been issued a new government hit list, and he'd found target number one. The guy was smiling at her, tugging at the ends of her hair.

Was she on a date, as well?

Better question: Did Brock seriously want to date the kindergarten teacher who wasn't smoking or drinking or trying to pass lingerie off as clothing?

"She runs and hides from me," Brock said.

"Who? Lyndie?" Daniel asked, playing dumb.

A stiff nod. "I thought she was afraid of all men, but turns out it's just me. As if I would ever hurt a woman." Brock rubbed the back of his neck. "I did some digging. As a kid and even while she was married, she was admitted to various ERs in the city. She had a suspicious number of broken bones for being, and I quote, 'overly clumsy.'"

Daniel popped his jaw. Thinking back, he could remember all the times Lyndie had been "sick" and missed school. His senior year, she'd opted to be homeschooled.

Poor girl. "Considering the hole I dug myself," he said, "I'm probably the last person who should give you advice, but I'm going to, anyway. Start slow. Keep your interactions short and sweet, and always end on a positive note. Leave her wanting more. It'll take time, but if you want her...the ban on Strawberry Valley girls is officially lifted."

A slow song spilled from the overhead speakers, and Thea and her date moved to the dance floor. Hillcrest put both arms around her, and Daniel cursed.

"What in Sam Hill does Thea think she's doing?" he grated. "She's supposed to be a role model for the younger girls in town."

Jude arched a sandy-colored brow. "Role model, is she?"

"Yes! She's smart, kind, and that mouth..."

"Gets sassy, does she?" Brock asked.

If his friend only knew the half of it.

Jessie Kay arrived at long last, minus West. She was a vision in a fifties-style dress. It was red with black polka dots, a halter top that veed between her breasts and a skirt that flared at her waist and ended just below her knees, revealing a single ruffle. "Hey, y'all. Your day just got made. I'm here!"

Thea and Hillcrest returned to the bar. A smiling Ryanne handed Hillcrest a wineglass and Thea a copper mug. She was having a Moscow Mule without him, he realized. That was *his* drink.

His date.

Thea was all sunshine and light, chatting easily with Hillcrest and her friends. What were they discussing?

She didn't look like she was missing Daniel at all.

"Maybe you could have won your girl's heart...if you didn't have a micropenis," Jude said.

"Or that horrifying problem with impotence," Brock added with a shudder.

"Or those hemorrhoids the size of the Wichita Mountains," Jessie Kay said helpfully.

"Ha ha. When'd you talk to Holly?" Daniel asked.

"She called about an hour ago." Jessie Kay took a drink—gulp—of his beer. "She was being a concerned citizen and thought I, as your best friend in the world, should get you in to see a doctor. I, of course, called your other, less important friends to discuss the best course of action for getting you help."

"Yeah," he said. "I bet."

In the back of the bar, a band carted their instruments to a dais. Ryanne joined them and adjusted the mic while the rest of Thea's group claimed a table in front to watch.

"What do you say we join our girls?" Daniel asked, already marching across the dance floor. He'd told himself he would keep his distance. That he wouldn't approach her until after the date, because he never wanted her to wonder what could have been. But staying away proved impossible. She drew him.

Maybe he drew her, too. Those green, green eyes landed on him and widened. Electrical currents arced between them.

Daniel picked up the pace.

"Oh my gosh, y'all." Jessie Kay clapped as she and the others caught up to him. In an exaggerated side whisper, she said, "Daniel and Dorothea are gonna burn the whole place down, namely because a fire just started in my panties. Someone call West and tell him to forget his work and get down here el pronto!"

When he reached the table, he pulled a seat next to Thea, edging Hillcrest out of the way.

"—getting notes of cedar, chestnuts and raspberry," Hillcrest was saying as he sniffed his wine.

"I'm getting wasted," Thea muttered, draining her mug.

"Mind if we join you?" Daniel asked.

Finally noticing him, a slack-jawed Hillcrest shot out his arm to shake Daniel's hand. "You're Daniel Porter."

"I know," he replied, "but thanks for the update."

The piece of shit didn't take offense but nodded with enthusiasm. "It's so great to see you again, man."

Daniel ignored him, while Thea glanced between them, clearly unsure how to proceed.

Her nails were purple. She was determined.

Determined to do...what?

"I gotta admit I've got a bit of a man crush on you," Hillcrest continued with an easy smile. *First thing I'll do is knock those pearly whites down his throat.* "I was part of the armed guard, and you were something of a legend, even to us. I was so proud to tell everyone we came from the same town. I even—"

Brock pulled a chair behind Daniel and wrapped an arm around the guy's shoulders. "We don't like to talk about military business in front of our women."

Our women, he'd said. Good boy.

"Right, right." Hillcrest ran his fingers over his mouth, miming a zipper, before saying, "My apologies. Oh! Where are my manners? Dorothea, have you met—"

"Yes. She's met everyone," Daniel said. "She's the reason we're here. The reason *I'm* here."

"We're friends," Thea whispered. She cleared her throat. "He works at the inn."

"Oh, that's right." Hillcrest laughed at himself, earning an encouraging smile from Thea. "I'd heard talk, of course, but hadn't put two and two together."

"This is Jude Laurent and Brock Hudson," she added, and Hillcrest clutched his chest as if he were having a heart attack.

"I'm— I— This is…" Hillcrest looked at one, then the other, then the other again, stars in his eyes. "The names of those in your unit were whispered through the ranks and— Sorry. My tongue is running away from me again."

"You are in the presence of greatness," Daniel said, his gaze hot on Thea. "There's no denying that."

She frowned at him before mouthing, *Stop it.*

Jessie Kay caught the exchange and sought to lessen the mounting tension—by sitting on Hillcrest's lap. "Bet you didn't know your hero Danny boy has a micropenis. We're thinking about asking him to get penile enlargement surgery because we're so embarrassed for him."

Thea choked on an ice cube, and confusion pinched Hillcrest's features.

Jessie Kay often had that effect on people.

Soft, haunting music wafted in the background, claiming everyone's attention. Ryanne belted out a shockingly soulful note that put goose bumps on Daniel's arms. She sang about everything left unsaid, everything left undone, and what if there wasn't a tomorrow, no, no, what if there wasn't one, what would we do then?

Had she chosen the song on purpose?

Suddenly all Daniel could think about was everything he hadn't said to Thea, everything they hadn't done to and with each other. If there were no tomorrow, he'd want to spend every second of today with her. She was the person he longed to hold throughout the night; she was the first thing he yearned to see in the morning.

"I mean it. Stop," she whispered to him. "You're making me uncomfortable, looking at me like...like...*that*. I'm on a date. With another man!"

"End it." Desperate to stake a claim, he almost yanked her onto his lap. "Problem solved."

Tremors of anticipation rocked her, but she shook her head no. "I... No. I won't." She licked her lips and turned to Hillcrest. "If you'll excuse me, I need to use the restroom." She stood.

To escape Daniel? Hell, no. That wasn't happening.

"I'll walk you—" Hillcrest began, rising.

"How about you and I get the gang a round of drinks?" Brock threw his arm around the man's shoulders to lead him away. Not that Hillcrest resisted. He stared up at Brock as if he'd hung the moon.

As Thea hurried to the bathroom, Daniel chased after her, hot on her heels. She made it past the door before he caught up with her, so he leaned against the wall just outside, waiting. Five minutes passed...ten. Two women entered and left the bathroom with no sign of Thea. If she'd climbed out the window…

He was about to leave his post to search outside when the door opened. She'd thrown water on her face, droplets clinging to tendrils of her hair. One slithered down her neck and caught in the heart-shaped collar of her shirt.

When she spotted him, she stomped her foot. "I told you to stop it, Daniel, and I meant it. I'm fixing to get angry."

"Get angry, then. I can't stop wanting you, sweetheart."

"You only want me because I keep turning you down. I'm still a challenge for you, admit it."

"We've had this conversation. You're a challenge, but that isn't why I want you." He gave a violent shake of his head. "I don't care how I get you, just as long as I get you."

She rubbed her temples, wilting like a flower that hadn't been watered in days. "You can't do this to me, Daniel. I told you my hard limit. No secret relationship. It's too demeaning for words, and contrary to public opinion—"

"I told my dad."

"—I do have some self-respect. But here you are— Wait. What?"

"I told my dad I want to date you." He took her by the waist and swung her around, then pressed her against the wall. "I want to tell everyone in town you belong to me."

A thousand different emotions flittered over her features. The one he loved most? Hope. "I… I don't understand. What changed?"

"*I* changed. I can't promise forever, and marriage isn't something I'm interested in—with anyone—but I don't like my life without you in it." He stroked the curve of her hip bone with his thumb. "Do you like your life without me in it?"

She only stared up at him with those wide shamrock eyes.

"I'm going to the inn, sweetheart, and I'm getting a room. Consider the slate between us wiped clean. You don't owe me another date, or anything else. If you want to be with me of your own free will, you knock on the door. That's all you have to do. I'll take care of the rest."

CHAPTER EIGHTEEN

Dorothea could only stand in place, rocked to the core, as Daniel walked away from her. He didn't return to the table, didn't say goodbye to his friends. He left the club, just as he'd promised. He was going to the inn, where he would be waiting for her.

If you want to be with me, you knock on the door.

He'd offered her a real relationship. They would be able to hold hands in public, and when someone asked him if he had a girlfriend, he would say yes. As if he was proud to date her.

He could change his mind tomorrow, after they'd had sex and the challenge was gone. With him, that would always be a risk. But...

He'd taken the first step, simply in an effort to please her. How could she not take the second one?

But...

The word continued to echo inside her head. If Daniel's spark for her died, *she* would want to die.

Great risk, great reward.

She trudged back to the table. Both Brock and Jude gave her a searching look. Lincoln West had arrived, and he was cuddled up to his wife. The two were lost in each other, and a deep pang of envy cut through Dorothea.

John frowned at her and squeezed her hand. "Everything okay?"

What to do, what to do? Risk everything, or play it safe?

Daniel hadn't lasted with any of the other women he'd dated. How could Dorothea succeed where they had failed?

Oh, crap. She was doing it again. Thinking less of herself. Self-confidence wasn't just a decision, she realized. It was a daily battle.

Well, fear wouldn't rule her today. She wouldn't let it.

I'm taking the risk!

"John," she said, and sighed. "Will you take a walk with me? Outside?"

Everyone else at the table looked away, suddenly interested in something else. John released a sigh of his own but nodded; they left the dim, soulful atmosphere Ryanne's voice had created and entered the coolness of the evening.

There were no clouds in sight, just mile after mile of twinkling stars.

Silent, they walked through the parking lot...headed toward his car? He already knew.

"You're in love with Daniel Porter," he said without fanfare.

"I am." How strange, admitting the words aloud. Especially to someone other than Daniel. But John deserved the truth. "I didn't want to love him. I hoped another man could help me get over him."

"I understand. I really do. I'm kind of in love with him, too." They shared a laugh, and he added, "To be honest, I'm still not over my ex, and I hoped the same thing. Just seeing you smile did more for me than...well. Anyway. Daniel is a lucky man. And an amazing one. I drooled on him, didn't I?"

"You did, but don't worry, you're not the first." She

bumped him with her shoulder. "There's something about him no one can resist."

They reached John's car, and he fished his keys out of his pocket. "Come on. I'll give you a ride home."

"No, thank you." If she was going to do this thing with Daniel, she was going to do it all the way. That meant a clean break with John. Not that they'd ever been an item. It was just that she knew how she'd feel if Daniel accepted a ride from a woman he'd once been interested in dating. "I'll catch a ride with Jude and Brock."

He leaned down and kissed her cheek. "If things don't work out…"

"I'm going to do everything in my power to ensure they do. I truly wish you all the best, John."

He offered her a sad smile. "Right back at you."

She backed away, and he climbed into the sedan. As he drove off, she made her way back inside the club. Jude and Brock were already halfway to the door. Planning to check on her?

"I need a ride," she said.

"Where's the date?" Jude asked. He looked stressed to the max, but she didn't think it had anything to do with her or John. He'd looked that way the entire time he'd been in the bar.

"He's on his way home."

Brock cracked his knuckles like an evil supervillian. "Good. Saves me the trouble of…chatting with him."

She wagged a finger in his face. "There will be no harming John. He's a good guy."

"Yeah, well, Daniel's better." Brock said the words, and Jude nodded emphatically.

"In some areas, yes," she agreed.

Both men gaped at her.

"What? Don't tell me you haven't noticed his faults," she

said. "Anyway. He's waiting for me at the inn." She lifted an arm in the air and in her best superhero impersonation called, "To the car! We drive like the wind!"

Brock snorted. Jude shook his head, but his frown wasn't as pronounced as before.

Along the way, Dorothea's nerves pitched a bona fide hissy fit. Soon she would be with Daniel. In his room. Alone. They would have sex. He would want the lights on. She would insist the lights stayed out. Would they fight?

Other questions flooded her. Were they just going to jump each other at moment one or were they going to talk first, maybe settle a few details about their relationship?

"Do I need to pull over so you can vomit?" Brock asked, his tone dry.

"Yes!" she shouted, but he kept driving. "Drive to Mexico. I'll call Daniel from the beach." After she'd had a few mai tais.

"No way." Jude shook his head. "You're going to wear our boy out so he'll finally get some sleep."

"He doesn't sleep?"

Neither male responded, but she didn't need their confirmation. She could guess the answer—no—and the reason. PTSD. It must be worse than she'd imagined.

How long had he gone without a solid eight-hour rest? How much stress did he deal with on a daily basis?

"Pedal to the metal," she said, wanting to reach him faster.

Finally they arrived at the inn. Brock parked, and both he and Jude escorted her inside. She looked for Holly, who'd wanted to work this weekend, but found no trace of her sister. Had she already abandoned ship?

Brock patted her bottom. "Go get 'em, tiger. Whatever you do, he'll love it."

Was that his version of a pep talk? "Someone has to stay at reception to—"

"We'll do it," Jude said. "Go on."

She hugged him, then Brock, and neither returned the gesture, but she wasn't upset. They probably weren't used to shows of affection. "Thank you."

She checked the registry for Daniel's room. Her legs trembled as she made her way up the steps to her own room, where she painted her nails glittery white. Then she did it. She marched to his room and raised her hand to knock on the door only to pause.

Was she really going to do this? There would be no going back.

Well, good! She didn't want to go back. She knocked. Hard.

The door swung open a second later, and there he was. Tall and muscled and every fantasy she'd ever had come true. His eyes were hooded, his pupils enlarged. Locks of his hair stuck out in spikes. He looked fierce. The air between them thickened, as if a storm brewed. Lightning seemed to arch through her veins, burning away her nervousness.

She held up her hands and waved her fingers, displaying her polish. "I told John—"

He yanked her against the hard line of his body, his lips slamming into hers, his tongue thrusting into her mouth. As she gasped with shock and bliss, he moved them both backward and pushed the door shut. Then he pushed her against it, crowding her personal space. Heck, she had no personal space. They were practically fused.

He cupped her breasts and kneaded the plump flesh as his thumbs stroked the stiff peaks.

Her desire for him intensified. His mouth—oh, his mouth. His hands. His body. *I want it all. Everything he's willing to give.*

"Off." She jerked his shirt over his head. The collar snagged on the chains hidden beneath. When the material gave, the dog tags and locket fell into place. His bare chest was a bounty. Broad across the shoulders, pecs and abs rock hard; he had the sexiest navel she'd ever seen. A trail of dark hair led to the waist of his jeans, where his fly was already unbuttoned.

Mine. All mine. She drew her nails lightly down his stomach, and he raised his head to peer into her eyes.

"You are a delicious dinner buffet, Porter."

He gave a husky chuckle. "Do you want to eat me up?"

"More than anything."

"I'd say ladies first, but I'm not feeling gentlemanly." He reclaimed possession of her mouth, his tongue owning her. His taste was incredible, everything she remembered but heightened, just like her senses. He was the incarnation of lust and pleasure...

He was addicting...

He tugged at the hem of her dress, and for a moment, she felt frozen solid, her heart nothing but a block of ice in her chest. The lights were on, and that just wouldn't do. She reached blindly for the switch. Contact.

As darkness flooded the room, *Daniel* froze.

He most definitely wanted the lights back on, and she was already desperate to see his chest again. To see the rest of him. But old fears plagued her. What if he rejected her again? What if he compared her to other women? If he found her lacking...

"I want to see you," he said, confirming her fear. His thumb brushed the pulse at the base of her neck. "I've dreamed of you."

"I—" *yes, say yes* "—I'm not ready."

He hesitated before gently kissing her lips. "I know you're scared of my reaction. I screwed things up the first night you showed up at my door, and I'll take this as my penance like a good boy. But, Thea. Sweetheart. Desire for you isn't the problem. I wanted you at 'Do you need more towels?' Thought you were the most exquisite woman on earth. Still think it. Your body was made for mine. More than that, I like you. You make me laugh, something no one else can do.

One day you're going to trust me enough to leave the lights on, and I'm going to pay proper homage to these curves."

With a cry of abandon, she wrapped herself around him. Devoured his lips and tongue.

He picked her up and carried her to the bed and, despite the dark, he had no trouble removing her clothes, ripping them away piece by piece until she was naked. Cool air enveloped her, and she shivered.

She almost cursed as he stripped himself. She would have enjoyed opening her present, because that was what he was. A present to herself. But the only word to escape her was "Yes!" as he lowered himself on top of her.

Fevered skin met fevered skin, burning her chill away. He kissed a path to her breasts to suck on her nipples.

"My sweet babies. I've been missing you. Your mean momma kept you hidden. But don't worry, darlings. I'm going to give her a good tongue-lashing for it."

She wanted to laugh. She wanted to scream. Sex had never been fun, had never been playful or deliciously dirty—and never all at the same time. Sex had been a pleasure with some fondling, some thrusting and a pleasant climax before reaching her favorite part: the cuddling. But Daniel was giving her everything she'd never known she needed, and there was nothing pleasant about it. This pleasure was sharp, and inexorable, and it shot straight to her core.

He played with her nipples until she was writhing, babbling and begging for more. And when he kissed his way down her stomach, her pleasure only sharpened. She couldn't bring herself to worry about her excess softness, didn't care. Just as long as he kept going!

Upon reaching the scars on her abdomen, he stilled. He couldn't see the raised tissues that the fall down the steps—and the subsequent surgery—had caused, but he could certainly feel them. The blood in her veins began to cool…until he licked a scar from one end to the other. She melted against the mattress.

He moved on without asking any questions, kissing around her inner thighs, teasing her with what was to come. Soon she was writhing once again, her head thrashing atop the pillows.

"Daniel."

"I swear I nearly come every time you say my name. It's those lips of yours…that breathy tone. It tells me you'll do anything I want…as long as I do you."

"Yes. Pleeease."

"Please what?" He rested his chin on her pubic bone, his warm breath fanning her belly.

He seemed relaxed, while she was pretty sure she'd lost the ability to form coherent sentences. She gave it a shot, anyway. Anything to get what she wanted, what she needed…what she would die without. "Taste me."

"Taste you where?"

She beat her fists into the mattress, saying, "You know where."

"If you won't utter the word, then you'll have to show me."

Determined to push her past her comfort zone, wasn't he? She slid a trembling hand down her stomach, glided her fingers through the tiny thatch of hair between her legs—he moaned—and tapped the swollen bud now crying for his attention.

His palm found hers, and their fingers linked together. They stayed like that for several heartbeats, lost in the simple delight of holding hands, a bond being forged between them. Aches continued to escalate, plaguing her, and the fever in her blood left her molten inside and out. She drew Daniel's hand to her core and, upon contact, they both sucked in a ragged breath.

"You are liquid fire." He lowered his head.

She held her breath, waiting, waiting.

Waiting.

Lick!

She screamed his name.

He licked her again and again, as if ravenous. "Never tasted anything so sweet. You're like warm honey. *My* honey."

His words…his actions…his sheer masculinity…he surrounded her, drove her need higher, branded her; every part of her responded to every part of him. No doors in her mind remained shut. No windows in her heart remained closed. She was open to him, her every secret fantasy laid bare before him.

He urged her knees farther apart. As far as they could go. Leaving her vulnerable.

"I bet you're real pretty here," he said, his voice strained. He ran a finger through her wetness, and she cried out. "I'm going to be on you every damn day." He *sucked* on her.

The more she writhed, the more pressure he applied, driving her wild.

"Now, Daniel. Darling," she managed to say as she panted. "I don't want you thinking I'm complaining about your technique. It's perfect. You're perfect. But if you don't get to the main event, I'm going to use up all my energy during the opening act."

He stopped. Stopped! Then he released a heavy sigh. "Well, hell, Thea. You know I'm a slave to challenges. How am I supposed to live with myself if I can't make sure you enjoy the main event *more than* the opening act?"

The truth suddenly became very clear. She wasn't going to survive the night.

He got back to work, licking and sucking with an almost brutal determination. Her mind fogged; they were the only two people in existence, this moment the only time that mattered. She struggled to catch her breath, her every pulse point trapped in a wild frenzy, her body nothing but sensation and flame.

Her climax took her by surprise. One second she was grinding against his face, the next she was screaming at the ceiling, her muscles convulsing.

When she came down from the glorious high, Daniel was poised above her.

"I think you're ready for the main event, sweetheart."

The thought of having him inside her, of two beings remade into one, filled her with a longing so intense, she forgot all about her satisfaction. That had been the appetizer. She needed the full meal.

"I am, I really am." She raked her nails down his chest. "Promise."

"Unless you're too tired?" he asked as if she hadn't spoken. "Yeah, you're probably too tired." He straightened, as if to leave her.

She clasped his forearms, holding him in place. "You stop your teasing. You prove you can give me more—give me better. Now."

"Yes, ma'am." He pierced her with a single finger, and her hips bolted off the bed. Then, as she raced toward another stunning climax, her sensitive inner walls clenching around the digit, he added a second one, stretching her; she was so wet, the glide remained easy.

So close, but not yet close enough. "I'm ready?" A question when she'd intended to make a statement.

"Not yet."

She whimpered.

He chuckled, the fierce sound broken by threads of tenderness. "We're together now." In. "A couple. You know that, right?" Out.

Diabolical man! "Yes. Together. Couple."

In. He hooked his finger, and she gasped, her hips once again bolting up of their own accord. "There will be no dating other people." Out.

"No...others...swear."

He was merciless, continuing to torture her, still thrusting in and out, slowly, so danged slowly.

Two could play this game. She reached between their bodies to wrap her fingers around his thick, hard length. It was so wide her fingers couldn't meet in the middle, and so deliciously long. No wonder he hardly blinked about the micropenis comment. He had a macro!

She stroked him, her movements awkward and untried, but he didn't seem to mind.

He praised her. "You're making me feel so good, sweetheart, but it's time for the main event. Only because you've been waiting on it, not because I'm desperate."

If she hadn't been so agonized, she would have laughed.

He left the bed with a strained "Just grabbing a condom. Or six."

Right. Good. But as a modern woman, she had responsibilities of her own. "I've only ever been with Jazz. He's my ex. And after our divorce I got tested. I'm clean. Are..." Wow, this was difficult. "Are you?"

Silence. The bed dipped and Daniel hovered over her, a beam of moonlight filtering through a crack in the curtains and spotlighting him. His expression was infinitely gentle.

"I'm proud of you. You did the right thing. Always ask."

The words gave her pause. Why would she need to ask him again when—

Realization dawned. Always ask her *future* lovers. He might have agreed to date her openly, but he'd been serious when he'd said they wouldn't last. A sick feeling churned at the bottom of her stomach; she ignored it. He wanted her, and he wanted the world to know she belonged to him. That was enough. For now.

"I'm clean," he said. "If you're on birth control..."

"I'm not." There'd been no need.

"Condom on, then."

He would have gone without one if she'd been on the pill?

He must have registered her surprise. "I always wear one. Haven't had sex without one. But one day I want to go bare with you."

Forget her upset. Her heart swelled with love for him. He might think they were doomed, but he trusted her not to betray him.

"I can't get pregnant," she admitted. "Well, that's not one hundred percent accurate. I can, maybe, possibly, but it would be a one in a million chance."

She expected him to ask questions. Instead, he caressed her tattoo, infinitely tender as his fingertips brushed her skin. Then he ripped open the foil packet and slid the latex down his length.

"One in a million is still a chance," he said.

If only. "Bet you're one of those fools who thinks he'll win the lottery."

"Someone has to. And you're about to get lucky, so I don't know why you're complaining about the odds."

She giggled even as she reeled. Apparently she *could* laugh while agonized. "Get inside me. Now, now, now!"

He parted her legs, got into position—and thrust home. Her hips arched to meet him, and she cried out. Oh, the perfection of being filled by him. Her nails sank into his hair and back. The first two strokes burned her, stretching her too wide, but then, oh, then…the magic happened.

CHAPTER NINETEEN

Daniel had entered a state he'd never before known: all-consuming desire. It drove him. It raged inside him, contradicting itself every other second. *Go fast. Go slow.* Contentment and satisfaction beckoned him. *Come closer...* He was going insane, surely, but he'd never been happier. Thea was wrapped around him, hot and wet. No, soaking.

She was soft, and she smelled absolutely amazing. The taste of her sweet, sweet honey still flavored his tongue. He would have given anything to turn on the lights, but she wasn't ready and he wasn't going to push. Not again. He wanted this to be good for her. No, perfect for her, so she would come back for more. So she would *always* come back for more.

Always?

As long as they were together.

He shifted to hook his arms under her knees, forcing her legs to widen, her body to take him deeper. In the dim lighting, he could just make out the crests of her nipples. Those little cotton candy treats. He leaned over and ran one through his teeth.

As she gasped his name, going slow ceased to be an option.

He hammered into her once, twice. Her breasts jiggled under his gaze, and it only fueled his desire. He slid a hand down the inside of her thigh, pressed his thumb over her swollen bundle of nerves.

"Yes! There!" she cried.

He thrust and rubbed, thrust and rubbed. Each action provided a different stimulus, but as he moved faster and faster, the sensations blended into one. She moaned when he applied more pressure, her inner walls constricting, and pleasure ripped through him. She was close; he could get her closer.

He began to thrust harder, faster, until he was a jackhammer. Utterly unstoppable. The legs of the bed scraped against the carpet. Mattress springs creaked. As he peered down at this woman who had obsessed him, a primal sense of possession took root.

"Daniel, Daniel, Daniel," she chanted.

He cupped and kneaded her breasts, pinched her nipples. Her hips writhed as she made delectable sounds he would forever savor. She was the most spectacular picture of feminine pleasure he'd ever beheld.

"Come for me, sweetheart. I want to feel you."

"Yes, yes. Feel you."

He spread his fingers under her ass and lifted, his groin taking over for his thumb, rubbing as he slammed into her core, again and again. She screamed, her entire body bowing. Her inner walls squeezed him just right, and he could hold back no longer. He roared as he jetted into the condom.

When she collapsed on the mattress, he collapsed beside her.

"I think we had another earthquake," she rasped.

He laughed. Gathering enough strength to get up and dispose of the condom was difficult, but somehow he managed. The separation—though short—bothered him. He crawled back into bed and, after draping one of her legs over his and

GENA SHOWALTER261

turning her hips so that they rested against him, he tucked the cover around them, sighing with relief.

She settled her head on his shoulder. "Is the puppet master done?"

"Never." He skimmed his fingers up and down her spine. "Now that we're boyfriend and girlfriend—and one hundred percent exclusive—I expect golden milk every morning and every evening."

"And what will I get in return?"

"The most magnificent headboard ever to be carved."

"No way. I already paid the toll. Use your brain, Porter, and negotiate me something you don't already owe me."

"Very well. But I won't start our negotiations until after you've looked inside the mini fridge."

"Did you put something for me in there?" She sounded surprised and excited.

"Find out." He gave her a little push off the bed.

She took the sheet with her, the material wrapped around her, as she trudged to the fridge.

Dorothea wondered what she'd find inside. Whipped cream to eat off his body? A Red Bull to refuel for the next round of loving? Despite the darkened room, she had no trouble finding her way, knew the layout of every room. She opened the door—and snorted.

"You shouldn't have, Danny boy. All the supplies for golden milk. How amazingly sweet you are—to yourself."

"Failed to notice the bacon-garnished cupcake in back, I see."

Really? She nudged the milk supplies aside and—sure enough. A cupcake with bits of bacon sprinkled on top.

Dorothea had to blink back tears. "Thank you, Daniel."

"Did I mention that as your boyfriend—your exclusive boyfriend—I expect to be served my golden milk every night and every morning?"

"Only ten thousand times. I'm happy to make it for you, but we'll have to go to my room. Yours doesn't have a burner."

He was on his feet a second later, heading for the door. Completely naked! A fact he must have forgotten.

"Wait! You have to dress." She had to dress, too. She scrambled around the room, clutching the sheet close to her chest as she gathered her discarded—and now torn—clothing. Pulling on each item proved difficult with only one hand, but somehow she managed.

"This is almost a deal breaker, sweetheart." He tugged on a pair of jeans, then collected a bag and filled it with the supplies from the fridge as well as her cupcake, which was protected by a plastic case. "I want to keep you naked forever."

Forever? Her eyes widened and she flipped on the lights to study him. He must have realized his slip, because he couldn't hide his sudden scowl.

Her feelings weren't hurt by the negative reaction. Much. He'd already warned her they had an expiration date.

As they strode down the hall, she prayed no one was out and about. Unfortunately, they ran into one of the three patrons. The son of a local, who'd come to visit his pregnant sister. Fortunately, the guy didn't glance up from his phone as he passed them.

Daniel called out, "I don't know if you noticed, but I'm her boyfriend."

Oh, my stars. "Daniel."

At least the patron kept going, lost in his own little world.

"What?" Daniel demanded. "Want me to carry you? You look tried. Like all your energy has been drained by intense lovemaking."

Lovemaking? "No, I—"

"Okay, great." He crouched, fit his shoulder against her middle and lifted her off her feet.

Laughing, she beat at his back. "How dare you treat me this way. I'm your boss."

"I'm your gentleman lover, and gentleman lover will always trump boss." He turned the corner and ascended the staircase to the upper floor.

"Earlier you said you weren't a gentleman. You even proved it! I never got my turn."

"If you're trying to tell me you didn't have an orgasm, I'm going to spank you."

"Not that," she said, and snorted. "The other thing. I didn't get to...you know...taste you."

He missed a step.

The hand on her butt softened, and he began to rub. "Are you pouting, sweetheart? Damn, that's hot." At the door, he set her on her feet. He was smiling his most wicked smile. "You're right. I didn't let you have your turn, and that was my mistake. One I'm going to make up to you." He fished the key out of her pocket and opened the door...only to walk her backward into the room. "We'll negotiate about the golden milk after you've had your turn." He placed the bag of goodies on her coffee table and slowly lowered his zipper, his smile widening. "Go ahead. Devour me."

Dorothea awoke with a smile. Until she realized Daniel wasn't in bed with her...wasn't anywhere in her room or even on the roof. He'd taken off. Why, that dirty piece of—

Oh! He'd left a note, the darling.

Couldn't sleep and didn't want to disturb you, but damn, next time you may just have to deal with being disturbed. Leaving is hell. I like you soft and warm against me.
Yours, D.
PS Where's my golden milk?

She clutched the paper to her chest and sighed. That man. He was everything she'd ever dreamed, but also so much more. But he was hurting himself every time he refused to sleep. She wished she'd worn him out, wanted to give him peace and rest. The way he'd just given her the greatest night of her life.

Her mind replayed some of her favorite moments.

When she'd sucked his length and he'd begged her to take every drop of his climax.

When, in the aftermath, he'd laughingly asked if he tasted better than bacon.

When he'd drawn her a bubble bath and sat behind her, kissing her neck, washing her hair and massaging her back, never once complaining that she wore a swimsuit.

When he'd made love to her while she was bent over the rim of the tub, water sloshing onto the floor, the lights off, per her request.

When she'd curled in bed, exhausted and sore, and he'd fed her aspirin. Then he'd growled, "Can't get enough," and seduced her all over again. He'd been gentle that time, almost loving. But he didn't love her—yet.

Dorothea planned to do everything in her power to win his heart. He wasn't the only one who liked a good challenge.

She traced the outside of the rose tattoo, and a heavy weight settled over her heart. What if she won his heart, and he wanted to get married…and start a family?

Would he be open to adoption?

Whoa! Slow down. You're getting waaay ahead of yourself.

Right. She stood on trembling legs and picked up her cell phone. She'd call him, shiver when she heard his sexy voice, then rail at him for leaving her. One way or another, she would help him fight the demons of his past.

New mental note: research PTSD and the best ways to help a partner deal.

If she called, would she come across as clingy? Their relationship was so new, and they hadn't negotiated any of the particulars. Heck, *she* was new to this.

Okay. No phone call.

Dorothea brushed her teeth, anchored her hair in a ponytail and donned her favorite tank and jogging shorts.

After her run, she would shower. Maybe Daniel would join her.

Daniel. Her boyfriend.

Her phone released a strange buzz. Frowning, she glanced at the screen.

The words *Customers In Lobby* flashed over the screen

What the—

Wait. When Daniel first started working here, he'd mentioned "fixing your security problems as well as your technology problems."

Dang it, she needed to put a stop to all these good deeds of his. She'd done nothing for him, and if she wasn't careful, an imbalance would develop. But what could you do for a man who could do everything for himself? Well, besides make him golden milk? And pleasure his brains out.

Dorothea made her way to the lobby to deal with the customers. Her stomach rolled over when she spotted a sleeping Mrs. Hathaway behind the counter and a suit-clad Jazz in front of it.

Oh, crap. He'd warned her. How could she have forgotten? She should have been prepared.

She wasn't prepared.

The gorgeous Charity Sparks stood beside him, radiant in red. She was speaking to him, but he snapped a retort, silencing her.

Maybe he *had* ended things with her.

Charity flushed and faked a smile, as if his reaction was exactly what she'd wanted.

Dorothea was tempted to back out and get her mother to handle the newcomers. But she wasn't a coward. She'd faced 250 pounds of hard muscle and determination, and she'd won.

Speaking of 250 pounds of hard muscle and determination, she wished Daniel were here for moral support.

I'm smart, strong and—sometimes—confident. I can do this on my own.

She stepped up to the counter and smiled at Jazz. "Hello, Jazz. Charity. How may I help you?"

CHAPTER TWENTY

Daniel had spent the past few hours working on the headboard in his dad's garage. He'd made a lot of progress, but he hadn't been able to finish because he'd had to limit his use of power tools while Adonis and Echo slept. And farted. Unlike his dad, they weren't hard of hearing. But he'd had to stay busy. He wanted to be near Thea, but he'd had no desire to thrash and moan about gunfire and death while in bed with her.

When could he have her again? No one had ever felt so good or hot or wet. So...perfect. Never had he come so hard.

He should have stayed with her. Shouldn't have abandoned her. Shouldn't have let her wake up alone in the bed they'd shared.

He sucked. He would have loved to see her surrounded by morning light. Would have loved to trace her scars, and pray she told him how she'd gotten them...why she only had a one in a million shot at getting pregnant.

She'd lost a baby, hadn't she?

He hated the thought of her in pain.

Desperate to see her, he wrote his dad a note and left it on the kitchen table.

I'll be at the inn. Will you bring Adonis and Echo to me when you visit Anthony? Love you.

He returned to the inn with several pieces of the headboard. No one was up as he carried each one to the theme room. Harlow's murals were coming along nicely. The colors she'd used on the different seasons were vivid and lifelike. In winter, the snow seemed to glitter as it fell, and in summer, waves seemed to ripple through the river.

"I've missed you, Dorothea."

The silkily spoken words echoed down the hall and gave Daniel pause. So did the affectionate tone.

He stalked into the lobby and found a group of four crowded around the counter. One woman, three men. Mrs. Hathaway was slumped in a chair, snoring. No doubt nothing would wake her.

Daniel came up alongside Thea and wrapped an arm around her waist, glad to have her in reach again. He'd missed her more than he was comfortable admitting.

He kissed her temple and said, "Glad to see you're still wearing the white polish."

She trembled against him.

"Can we help you?" he asked the others.

The guy—the ex, he realized. The weatherman. Daniel recognized the polished hair and surfer-boy face. Weatherman was staring at Thea as if she were the answer to all his problems. Which was a major fucking problem.

"Daniel, meet Jazz Connors. He's here to do a story on our town's weather patterns," Thea explained with false cheer. "This is his mistress—oh, I'm sorry, his girlfriend, Charity Sparks."

"Ex," Weatherman said.

Charity cast a nervous glance to the men standing behind

her. "I didn't break them up. They were separated when Jazz and I got together."

"No," Thea said, "we weren't."

"Let's not do this here." Weatherman met Daniel's glare with one of his own. "Who are you?"

Daniel smiled without an ounce of humor. "I'm the boyfriend. And you'll have to excuse my disheveled appearance. I spent the entire night assuaging someone's—and I won't mention any names—insatiable lust."

He expected a reprimand, but Thea surprised him, turning to trace her fingertips down his chest. "I believe we decided your title is gentleman lover."

Hot damn, but he could have kissed her.

What the hell? She belonged to him now. They were in this thing together; they'd decided. He kissed her.

Weatherman gripped the edge of the counter, his knuckles quickly bleaching of color; it was suddenly very clear he still had feelings for Thea.

Daniel understood. Thea was one of a kind. No one had a sense of humor like hers. No one was more kind or caring, no one more giving. No one had better dance moves, or charmed others so easily. No one had a body like hers. No one had lips like hers. She was passionate enough to blow his ever-loving mind. Beautiful in every way.

But she's mine.

The fact that Weatherman had cheated on her and then taken a year to fight for her, well, he'd just proved how stupid he was.

"We talked days ago, and you didn't mention a boyfriend," Weatherman grated.

"You guys talk? Because I thought you'd told your ex to leave you the hell alone." Daniel directed the words to Weatherman, knowing the bastard was trying to drive a wedge of jealousy between him and Thea. Not just stupid. Idiotic.

"Something like that." Her glistening lips pursed. "He calls me. He even used an app to track my phone so he could accost me while I was in the city."

Well, now. If they were dealing with a stalker situation, things were gonna get mean. And by *things* he meant *his temper.*

He made a mental note to ask Brock and Jude to do a background check on the guy.

"He calls you again, he and I are going to have a problem," Daniel said, staring at Weatherman. A grin curved his mouth, this one all bite and malice. "I tend to beat my problems bloody."

Weatherman blanched and grumbled, "So unprofessional."

Dorothea shrugged, all *Daniel's the best man I know.* At least, he hoped. The girl, Charity, paled.

"We're just here to film a three-part segment about the tornadoes, storms and earthquakes the town has experienced in recent times." Weatherman shifted from one Italian loafer to the other. "Also... I thought I could film you while I'm here and present the video to my network. I can help you get the job of your dreams. Like we always planned."

Charity offered Thea a brittle smile. "Don't worry about your appearance. I can help with hair and makeup."

Thea stiffened, and Daniel cursed the blonde with every fiber of his being. If assholes were airplanes, the inn would now be classified as an airport.

"You thinking what the rest of us are thinking?" he asked Miz Charity. "That Thea is going to overshadow anyone who's on camera with her?"

Petting his chest once again, Thea rested her head on his shoulder.

"I... Well... Yes, of course." Charity looked away, saying, "Your inn is so...unique, Dorothea." She ran her finger over the laminate on the counter. "My grandmother used to have this design in her kitchen."

"May I speak with you in private, Dorothea?" Weather-man glanced between her and Daniel. "Please."

No way in hell. Daniel knew the guy wanted Thea back in his bed. And why wouldn't he? The woman had nearly burned Daniel alive. He'd taken her three times, three different ways, and he hadn't gotten nearly enough of her.

Usually at this point in a "relationship," his more violent memories began to plague him. He would move on to a new woman, a new challenge, in need of a new distraction. But he had no glimmer of disconnect this time. He only wanted more of Thea. More of her humor. Her kisses. Her touch. Her breathless moans of surrender. There was nothing sweeter.

Besides, he already had a new and better challenge. Several, actually. Making her smile and laugh—making her happy. The rewards would far outshine any he would find inside another woman.

"A chat won't be necessary," Thea announced, saving him from having to pull the he-man card. "We've said all we need to say to each other."

"Here, let me give you guys the address to the nearest hotel. I think you'll really enjoy the amenities. Namely, you'll get to keep your balls." Daniel reached for a piece of paper.

Thea might have whimpered and whispered, "But the money I'd make…"

Charity looked hopeful. "I didn't know there was a hotel within—"

"No. The nearest hotel is at least twenty miles away," Jazz said, glaring at Daniel. "We'll stay here."

"Wonderful." Blanking her expression, Charity waved her hand through the air. "Here is absolutely…fine."

An-n-nd Jazz continued to glare at him.

"Well, all right, then." Thea inhaled deep, exhaled slow. "Let's see what we have available."

The bell over the door tinkled, and Virgil came rushing inside, dragged by Adonis and Echo.

Gasping for breath, Virgil said, "Here they are. Delivered as requested, son."

Jazz, Charity and company split like the Red Sea. The dogs released a steady stream of barks until they reached the counter, where they promptly jumped up to rest their front paws.

Virgil eyed the newcomers and the array of equipment scattered about the room with suspicion. When his gaze landed on Weatherman, he snapped his fingers. "I recognize you."

Jazz brightened. "You sure do, sir. I'm Jazz Connors." He extended his hand to shake. "I'm chief meteorologist for Channel—"

"No, no, that's not it. You're our sweet little Dorothea's ex-husband."

Now Jazz paled. "I... I'm..."

Virgil slapped his thigh. "Only a real bumble brain can't keep his unmentionable tucked into his unmentionables while he's with a woman other than his wife. An honorable man does everything he can to fix the problems at home *without* straying."

Jazz flinched but recovered quickly. "If I could go back, sir—"

"Yeah, yeah, yeah," Virgil interjected. "If my sister had been born with a pecker, she would have been my brother. Ain't no use wishing for what ain't."

"Mr. Porter, please," Thea said on a groan.

"Now, I'm sorry to burn the ears of a lady, but I can't keep quiet about a grave injustice," the old man said, and Daniel grinned at the singular use of *lady*. "I hope you don't mind, but your dear old momma told me all about your marital troubles, and it made me just about as mad as a donkey chewing on bumblebees. And, honey, if a man is going to commit the crime, he needs to do the time."

"If you'll just let me explain," Weatherman said.

Vigil gave him the stinky side-eye. "If excuses were gooses, we'd all have a happy Thanksgiving. You remember that."

Weatherman was a fool. He'd chosen Charity over Thea. A rotten apple over a lush orange. *His mistake. My gain.*

Thea blinked up at Daniel. "This is really happening?"

"Yes, ma'am."

"Would you stop calling me ma'am?"

"No, ma'am. I have manners. My daddy raised me right."

Virgil beamed at him.

"Um...our room key, please?" Charity looked like a convict intent on escape.

Weatherman cleared his throat, straightened his shoulders and picked up his conversation with Virgil. "The heart wants what the heart wants."

Virgil wasn't interested in excuses. "I think you mean the pecker wanted what the pecker wanted."

"Dad, I love you." Daniel claimed the dog leashes and kissed Thea's gorgeous mouth right there in front of everyone. Kissed her hard, staking a very clear claim. By the time he lifted his head, she was just the way he liked her: breathless and weak in the knees, her frown gone. "I'm gonna miss you. You gonna miss me?"

"Yes, sir," she whispered.

He grinned at her before turning to Virgil. "Come on, Dad. Let's get you to Anthony's before my girlfriend decides I'm not worth the hassle." Weatherman wouldn't do anything untoward in front of his coworkers.

Daniel met Thea's widening gaze; her shamrock eyes were bright. "Call me if you need me for anything. I mean it. Otherwise I'll see you on our run because, yes, the dogs and I are going with you. Also, you owe me a glass of golden milk, and I will collect. With interest."

Dorothea could only nod, caught up in the whirlwind that was Daniel Porter. Was this what life as his girlfriend was going to be like? Every morning she would be trapped in a tumult of sensation, emotion, surprise and longing?

Well, sign her up for an eternity.

"Golden milk," she said. "Check. I'll make it after our run." She'd never had a jogging partner, but she'd always wanted one. "*Our* run. The one we'll be doing together."

"If the ex bothers you, let me know and I'll take care of it," Daniel added, and he wasn't exactly quiet about it. He kissed her again, quickly this time, before taking off with his dad and the dogs.

Her hand fluttered to her chest. What a man.

Jazz turned his glare on her, and Charity offered her a bright smile, this one genuine.

Just think of the money they're going to pay you.

Four guests for four nights at double her usual rate—because why not?

She put everyone on the second floor and passed out keys. "For breakfast, coffee and muffins are free of charge. If you want something more substantial, call room service or visit the dining room to place an order." Now that Carol had returned, the inn could offer hot meals rather than just snacks. "The kitchen is open for lunch and dinner, as well."

"Please, Dorothea," Jazz said. "Talk to me. I have so much to tell you."

Anger flickered in Charity's irises, the edges made ragged by...fear? She was scared of losing him, wasn't she?

Ugh. Why would she want to keep him?

"Jazz!" Holly's voice rang out.

Cheering up, Jazz turned. "Holly!"

Her sister ran to her ex and threw herself into his arms. He twirled her around.

"I've missed you so much," Holly said.

"I've missed you, too, squirt."

Seeing them, Dorothea's heart hurt. When she'd first returned to town, she'd longed for this kind of welcoming reception from her sister. What she'd gotten instead? A bubble pop in her face and a snarled "And I didn't think my life could suck worse."

"Are you staying here?" Holly asked Jazz, ignoring everyone else.

"I sure am." He dangled his key in front of her. "Four nights."

She clapped like the happy child she used to be. "Come on. I'll show you to your room."

There went the progress they'd made, Dorothea thought with a sigh.

Jazz tossed her a do-you-see-how-good-we-can-be-together look over his shoulder. One Dorothea disregarded. He was part of a past she never wanted to revisit. But, no lie, it had felt good, really good, to show her ex how amazing her life had turned out without him. Sure, she hadn't lived all of her dreams, but she was happy, and dang if she couldn't make new dreams.

Unlike the crewmen, Charity didn't follow the pair. She reached over the counter to take Dorothea's hand. "I just wanted to say I'm sorry for the way things happened. I never meant for you... But I loved... I'm sorry," she finished lamely. "And I'd like us to be friends, Dorothea."

Uh, what now?

"I admit I was worried when Jazz pitched your hometown to the network," she continued. "I thought you'd try to steal him away from me, but I can see you have your own man now."

Was this girl for real? She thought Dorothea had her own man now. Now. As if she hadn't before. Where was Charity's moral compass?

"I'll be honest," Dorothea said, extracting her hand "I don't ever see us becoming friends."

Delicate shoulders wilted yet again. "Yeah. I thought you might say that. I didn't mean to insult you or your inn. I was just… I want Jazz to fall in love with me again. He broke up with me, you know? For no reason! I did nothing wrong. I cater to his every whim. I thought maybe if I made him see he doesn't belong here, he'd—"

"I don't want to hear this." And yet she almost asked why Charity wanted to keep a man slimy enough to have an affair, even if the affair had been with her.

"Of course not," Charity said. "I understand. But I really would—"

Dorothea didn't wait for her to finish. She walked around the counter and out of the building, leaving Charity in the lobby. *Shake it off.* She jogged in place for a moment, warming up, breathing in and out with purpose. The sun was shining, a beautiful roll cloud consuming the sky. Birds were chirping.

Her mother was currently pruning the rosebushes in front of the inn, where a plot of grass separated sidewalk from street. "The guests need a pretty view," she liked to say. The buds were starting to bloom and scent the air.

"Morning, my dear," Carol said. A hat shielded her face from the sun's glare.

"Morning, Momma." She made no mention of Virgil's confession. What good would it do? Carol would feel bad for gossiping, and Dorothea would feel guilty for making her feel bad. But lesson learned. Carol couldn't be trusted with her secrets. "I'll be back in about an hour. You've got your phone, right? The guests might ring you for a meal. And if anyone else shows up wanting a room—"

"I'll see to them, don't you worry." Carol wiped her dirt-covered gloves together. "Daniel told me to tell you he's waiting for you at Anthony's, and you aren't to leave him behind."

"Great. Thanks." One step away, that was as far as she got.

"I noticed he stayed the night at the inn," her mother continued.

Tread carefully. "He does that sometimes."

"I didn't just fall off the turnip truck, young lady. I know he stayed in your room."

"Well, we're dating." Openly! "That's going to be happening quite a bit in the near future."

Carol frowned at her. "I hope you know what you're doing. He's—"

"A wonderful man. I know." *And that's my cue to go.* Dorothea kicked off.

When she reached Style Me Tender, she jogged in place, watching as Daniel played with the dogs. He noticed her and smiled a special smile. One she'd never seen before. One she liked to think was for her alone. Rays of sunlight spilled over him, his masculinity on full display.

But the special smile didn't last long. A shadow of concern passed over his features.

Concern for what?

"Hey, Virgil. Hey, Anthony," she said with a wave. The two were at their table, playing checkers.

"Hello again, Miss Dorothea." Virgil padded over to kiss her cheek. "Now, I want you to know something. I'm not sorry for gettin' stern with the pretty boy back there. He did you wrong, and that'll never be okay in my book." His gaze slid to his son. "Not ever. I'll tan the hide of anyone who breaks your heart, and I mean that."

Anthony nodded his agreement, and she wanted to laugh. They were acting like fathers—hers rather than Daniel's. The way fathers were supposed to act.

"That's enough out of you two." Daniel handed her Echo's leash—actually, he presented it to her, as if he were making a point about something—and she gladly accepted. "Get ready for the workout of a lifetime."

"I'm stronger than I look. This pup isn't going to get the better of me."

"Just you wait."

They started off slowly, teaching the dogs to stay at their sides and not buck or lunge when squirrels and cars passed. Soon sweat beaded on her forehead, trickled down her temples. Echo yanked the leash so many times Dorothea lost count, and her arms began to burn more than her legs.

"Okay. You were right. This is not easy." She was already huffing and puffing. "I feel like I'm the one being walked."

They ran another few blocks before the dogs calmed. Huffing and puffing himself, Daniel said, "Are you going to be okay?"

She knew what he meant. Was she going to be okay with her ex and his girlfriend-non-girlfriend staying at the inn, a constant reminder of what she'd lost?

Daniel knew only about the divorce, not her precious Rose.

A whimper escaped her. A whimper Daniel misinterpreted.

"Do you still love him?" The question lashed like a whip.

"I do not."

"You sure? I distinctly remember you telling me that love lasts forever."

"Real love does. With Jazz, I had attachment and gratitude, nothing more." Even back then, her heart had belonged to Daniel. She saw the truth now.

I think you're perfect just the way you are.

It was funny how one sentence—one moment—could impact a life forever.

He stopped and she did the same, realizing they'd come full circle. They were back in front of the salon.

"Why did you look like you wanted to cry?" he asked.

A car drove past and honked. Virgil and Anthony waved at the driver and pretended not to eavesdrop when it was obvious they were straining to hear every word.

"Let's talk about it later." Or never.

No, she had to tell him. He deserved to know the truth. And she needed to be prepared for any reaction. Unconcern. Pity.

Pity might kill her.

He turned away, his posture rigid. "Come on. We should probably return to the inn."

The abrupt change in his mood threw her. What had she done? Besides temporarily deny his request for more information. He'd done the same to her on multiple occasions, and she hadn't thrown a fit.

Men! Were they even worth the hassle?

As Daniel jogged away, sweat trickling between his shoulder blades, his butt tight in his running shorts, his muscles bunching, she sighed. Yes. Yes, they were. At least, this one was.

CHAPTER TWENTY-ONE

The next three days passed in a blur. With the increased number of guests, Dorothea's duties expanded. She cleaned the rooms, did all the laundry and helped her mother in the kitchen. She also hunted for knickknacks for the theme room. As soon as she clocked out, Daniel would take her on a date, every night ending in a different location…or locations— wherever they happened to be when his control snapped. In a dark alley. In his bedroom at his dad's house. In a car, which he parked on the side of the road. Once, he took her to a field of wildflowers and, lit by his truck's headlights, seduced her on the hood.

As they'd lain wrapped together in the dark of night, a full golden moon steeping the moment in romance, he'd said, "I'm running a background check on Jazz. A dirty one, where we dig into all the hidden nooks and crannies."

"Why?" she'd asked. "I mean, other than the obvious. He's my ex, yes, but he has no part in our relationship."

"I don't like the way he's stalking you. What if he's dangerous?"

"He's not." He was just annoying.

More than a dozen times, Jazz had cornered her. Just to talk, he'd said. To explain the terrible mistake he'd made, to make things right with her. He hadn't wanted to cheat on her, he'd added, but he'd *needed* the job—for her, to be the one to support their family; that meant he'd needed Charity's approval. But through it all, he'd never stopped loving Dorothea. Blah, blah, blah.

The only thing he'd said that had gotten her in the feels was Rose's name.

After the fall down those steps, Jazz had visited Dorothea at the hospital. In fact, he was the one who'd called 911. He'd chased after her, had seen her go down. As she was wheeled back for surgery, she told the doctors not to give updates to her soon-to-be ex-husband, and most definitely not to allow him inside her room. The only detail they'd shared with Jazz was Rose's death because, technically, her condition had nothing to do with Dorothea's, and he was the father.

She'd expected, maybe even hoped, he would fight his way in to see her, but he hadn't, and the knowledge had hurt.

Now he was back, claiming he was ready to fight for her.

Why now? What had changed?

"Learned anything incriminating yet?" she'd asked Daniel.

"Only that he cheats on his taxes."

Not exactly surprising.

In another not so surprising turn of events, Holly, who saw Jazz as a surrogate father or goofy uncle, had begun cornering Dorothea, too.

He loves you.

He realized he messed up, and he'll never do it again.

You have to give him another chance.

Dorothea was willing to do anything her sister asked—except that. A life with Jazz would *never* make her happy. But every time she tried to tell her sister the marriage was over for good, Holly had cursed Daniel, then cursed Dorothea herself.

Even Charity had cornered Dorothea. She required relationship help, she'd said, and she wouldn't take no for an answer. Her romance with Jazz had crumbled like a condemned house, and she had no idea what to do. She thought he might be seeing another woman.

Shocker! The man who'd cheated on his wife to be with another woman might be cheating on his girlfriend? What were the odds?

Charity had also asked for Dorothea's help with the town members. Apparently she and Jazz interviewed many of the residents, but no one had given air-able answers to any of their questions.

They support me, Dorothea had realized. Thanks to her mother, news of Jazz's infidelity had spread.

Dorothea understood her mother's reasoning—revenge—but come on! What happened to loyalty?

Lately Daniel was the only one who put her needs above all others.

Which was how he'd almost convinced her to shower with the lights on. In the end, she'd chickened out, using Jude as an excuse. Jude had created a website that would allow her to live stream news about the weather—if ever she decided to do so. Every morning he gave her a crash course in using and maintaining it, and she used the lessons as an excuse to avoid a sexy lights-on shower with Daniel. The refusal irritated him, and she had a sinking suspicion he was now avoiding her.

Despite his loyalty—or maybe because of it?—he never stayed overnight with her at the inn. He always returned to his dad's place. When he returned the next morning, he would be bleary-eyed and cranky.

Only once had she asked him to stay with her, but he'd refused.

"Better this way," he'd said.

"For who?"

"You."

Maybe he was right, but she'd begun to fret. Did he crave his next challenge? Did he regret being with her?

Twice he'd asked her about her scars and her inability to have a baby. She hadn't given him any answers. If he couldn't trust her enough to spend the night together, how could she trust him with her darkest secrets?

To her consternation, her silence only widened the gulf between them.

Dorothea finished cleaning Charity's room, a particularly humiliating task. Not that the news anchor had left any kind of mess. Charity had actually been quite…charitable. She'd picked up her own trash and made sure her dirty towels were piled in the tub rather than strewn across the floor. Jazz hadn't been so tidy, had left soda cans and candy bar wrappers *everywhere*.

Today, Dorothea decided *not* to clean up after him. She'd left clean towels on his bathroom sink and taken off. Considering she'd paid for his schooling, cooked his meals for years while working two jobs, she'd done enough for him.

Ready for lunch, she returned her cart to the storage closet. On her way to the kitchen, she stopped to check out the progress of the theme room.

The door was ajar. Odd. Daniel, Harlow and Jessie Kay wouldn't have forgotten to shut it; there was a sign taped to both the outside and inside, acting as a reminder. And the lock engaged automatically.

Frowning, Dorothea stepped inside—

And screamed. No. No, no, no. Someone had dumped buckets of paint over the beautiful murals. Clumps of red, blue and orange had dripped onto the brand-new hardwood floor. The one of a kind curtains and comforter were shredded, the pieces scattered throughout the room like confetti. The headboard Daniel had exhausted himself carving was gouged from top to bottom and as splattered with paint as the floor.

Who would… Why would… How…

Her mind skipped from question to question without finishing a single one. The horror of the destruction was simply too much to process.

A sob welled in Dorothea's throat as she backed out of the room.

"Daniel," she screamed. One step, two, she began to run. "Daniel!" She didn't care that things were strained between them. She wanted him. She wanted him right now.

Jazz came barreling out of his room, his expression twisted with concern. "Dorothea? What's wrong?"

She bypassed him, shouting, "Daniel!"

"Dorothea," Jazz called. "Let me—"

Her pace increased. Tears burned her eyes and streamed down her cheeks. "Daniel!"

"Thea!" She heard Daniel's gruff, familiar voice a split second before he snaked around the corner and caught her. His strong arms enfolded her, holding her tight. "What's wrong, love? What happened?"

"The paint. The material." Her tears flowed faster as her chin trembled.

"I don't understand." He cupped her cheeks in a gentle grip. Gentle, but forceful enough to ensure she faced him. He'd never looked more tortured. "Help me understand what's going on, and I'll fix it. I swear to you, I'll fix everything."

Finally the sob she'd managed to stave off escaped.

"She was coming out of a room," Jazz said, coming up behind her. He must have followed her. "I—"

Daniel pointed an accusing finger at him. "What did you do?"

Jazz raised his hands, palms out. The color drained from his cheeks. "I did nothing. I only sought to help her."

285

GENA SHOWALTER

"The room," she managed to squeeze past the lump growing in her throat. "Someone trashed the room."

"The theme room?" Daniel asked, his voice now deadly
calm.

She nodded, and oh, the cruelty of the act. The absolute
maliciousness. What had she ever done to deserve this? Who
had she hurt so badly they decided to destroy her dream in
retaliation?

Daniel picked her up, cradling her against his chest. He
kissed her temple before carrying her up the steps without
jarring her.

Inside her room, he eased her onto the bed. "I'll be right
back," he said.

"No. Stay with me." She clutched his shirt, trying to hold
him in place. Clinging was beneath her, and it embarrassed her
to the depths of her soul, but her strength was gone. Zapped.
She would rather have Daniel than her principles.

"I'll be right back, love," he vowed, his voice so tender it
tore something deep inside her. "I just want to look at the
damage."

A moment passed. She forced herself to release him.

After a prolonged hesitation, he disappeared out the door.

I give up. She dragged her knees to her chest, huddling on
the mattress. Shaking. Wallowing.

A cry sounded deep inside her: *Enough!* She'd had to pick
herself up a thousand times before; this would be no different. This wasn't even a big deal. It set her back, sure. Set her
back a lot, even. She couldn't afford new flooring. Harlow
might not be willing to redo the murals, and Jessie Kay might
not be willing to sew new curtains and a comforter. Daniel
would definitely redo the headboard. It was the sheer nasti-
ness of the act that undid her.

Only a few people had unrestricted access to the room.

Harlow, Jessie Kay and Daniel, of course. And Carol and Holly, who had master keys.

Maybe…maybe Harlow had returned to her bullying roots?

As soon as the suspicion formed, Dorothea disregarded it. No way. The expectant mother had changed, and she loved her work. She wouldn't destroy it.

Jessie Kay loved Daniel like a brother and wouldn't hurt him by hurting Dorothea.

Daniel wasn't the kind of man who sneaked around.

Carol hated what Dorothea was doing to the inn, but she hated conflict more. Besides, she wouldn't sabotage her own daughter. Well, not with anything more than gossip. And Holly wouldn't hurt her this way. Like Daniel, she didn't operate in the shadows. She took credit for her work. The good and the bad.

Someone must have picked the lock, then. Jazz? Charity? Or maybe someone Daniel had dated, who was ticked at Dorothea for winning him long-term? Or *longer* term.

But how would that someone have entered the inn and walked the halls without anyone inside the inn noticing? Or the new security system alerting Dorothea's phone?

Okay. So. She had to rethink her list of suspects.

Jazz and Charity were at the top. Jazz could have trashed the room, returned to his own and waited for Dorothea to discover what he'd done. Then, when she screamed, he could have…what? Comforted her in her time of need?

Charity could have done it out of spite.

Another sob racked her, defeat swamping her. *Don't think I can pick myself up this time.*

Just when she'd thought her life was on the right track, happiness finally within her reach, this happened. Something else to knock her down.

This isn't who you are anymore. You will get up and fight!

Yes, but who or what was she supposed to fight?

Start with the misery. Then—the culprit. Whoever committed the crime must do the time.

She quieted. Her puffy eyes burned, and her nasal passages were so swollen she had to breathe through her mouth, but she stood on shaky legs and marched into the hall.

Daniel rounded the corner and stalked toward her, his expression dark and fierce. He held a laptop so tightly his knuckles were white. Despite the menace surely flowing through his veins, he stopped beside her and gently smoothed the hair from her damp cheek.

"You need to see this, sweetheart."

The endearment struck her as odd, even though he'd used it and others many times before. But her head hurt, and she couldn't quite reason out why.

"You know I've been working on your security," he said as he led her back inside the room. He placed the laptop on her desk.

"Yes."

"I put cameras in every hallway." He typed as he spoke, and video feed popped up on the screen. "Last night, Holly showed Jazz the theme room. They were inside three minutes, twenty-two seconds. She shut the door when they left."

"Jazz went back," Dorothea said on a gasp. *The bastard!*

"No." One word, but he'd never sounded more ominous. "But Holly did, soon after Harlow left for lunch."

No. No! "She wouldn't."

Except, on the screen, she watched as Holly entered the theme room alone, a kitchen knife clutched in her hand, her features tight with determination. She stayed inside five minutes and fifty-one seconds. When she left, she was covered in paint splatters.

Dorothea was the next person to enter.

Sickened, she clutched her stomach. "Why would she do

such a thing?" She asked the question, but the answer was obvious. *Why else? To hurt me.*

Maybe Daniel's rage was contagious. One second Dorothea was miserable, the next she was livid, her blood seeming to boil. How dare her sister strike at her like this! Like a good-for-nothing coward. How dare her sister strike at her at all. She'd been hurt enough.

Once again she marched into the hall. Daniel latched onto her wrist to stop her, but she wrenched free and hurried down the steps. At Holly's door, she knocked with so much force she thought she might have cracked the bones in her hand.

Daniel remained behind her, silent.

Holly appeared, and it was clear she'd been crying, her face as red and puffy as Dorothea's. She still wore her paint-splattered clothes.

"You…little…brat." Dorothea threw the words at her sister as if they were weapons. "You're selfish, spoiled rotten and malicious."

Holly didn't waste time with false denials. "I'm sorry."

"You're sorry? You're sorry! Do you know how many times I've apologized to you for going to college like a normal teenage girl? For not wanting to call you when all you ever did was curse at me? How about I forgive you the way you forgave me, huh?"

"I'm sorry," her sister repeated.

"You wanted to hurt me. Well, congratulations. You've hurt me."

"I didn't want to hurt you. I j-just wanted J-Jazz to comfort you. I wanted Jazz to help you repair the room so you guys would get b-back together and—"

"Get it through your stubborn head. I will *never* get back together with Jazz."

Carol must have heard the commotion, because she rushed out of her room…and froze. "Girls?"

"Shut up, Mother," Dorothea snapped. "Go back inside. Or do you need more gossip to spread?"

"I… I thought I was helping you. People needed to know what you'd suffered."

"Shall I tell everyone what *you've* suffered?"

Paling, Carol backed up a step. "You're upset. We're all upset. Let's walk away and calm down. Okay? All right?"

Jazz and Charity raced down the hall.

"Listen to me, Dorothea. Jazz is sorry for what he—" Holly said.

"I don't care!" Dorothea screamed. "You have no idea… You can't imagine…" Another sob welled up and tried to clog her throat, but she gulped it back. She'd been a punching bag most of her life, and she was sick of it. "I can't look at Jazz without remembering everything I've lost."

"Everything you can get back," Holly said quickly.

"No. No! He can't give me back my baby. My Rose Holly." The words slipped out before she could stop them, but she'd been pushed past the point of caring. "She was dead and buried before she ever had a chance to live. And do you know why? Because I caught Jazz having sex with Charity and ran away. I tripped down a flight of stairs and killed my sweet baby girl."

With a gasp of horror, her sister reeled backward. "You named her after me," she whispered. "I knew you were pregnant, knew you'd lost the baby, but I didn't know… I didn't know!"

"It shouldn't have mattered!"

Carol reached for Dorothea, but she sidestepped, widening the distance between them. Accepting comfort was beyond her right now.

Jazz hung his head with shame, and Charity openly cried. Only Daniel remained stoic, as if untouched by the proceedings. And yet in his eyes she saw a fury to rival her own.

"I blame Jazz. I blame Charity. Mostly, I blame myself."
Pain ruled Dorothea, and now that she'd started, she couldn't
stop. "Rose would have been a year old now. Or eight months
if I'd carried her to term."

"I regret that day so much." Jazz reached for her, just as
Carol had done, but once again Dorothea sidestepped.

If he touched her right now, she would claw off his face.
Would punch and kick and knock his balls into his throat.
Maybe kill him. The pain had stripped her of any hope for a
better future, leaving her trapped in a deep, dark pit of despair.

Daniel's calm vanished in a snap. He shoved Jazz against
the wall. "Keep your hands off her or lose them."

Her focus returned to her sister. "You say you weren't trying to punish me, but we both know you're lying."

Holly covered her mouth with a shaky hand. "Dots—
please. *Please.*"

A brutal shake of her head. One step back. "Don't. Just
don't. How many times did I beg you for a modicum of
mercy? How many times did you ignore me?"

"I'm so sorry."

Not good enough. "Everyone says karma is a bitch, but
you certainly gave her a run for her money."

"I'm so sorry," Holly repeated. "Please. You have to believe me."

Dorothea continued backing away. "I didn't just lose my
baby that day, I lost my chance to have a family, and now I
don't think I'll ever want one. All they do is tear you down."

CHAPTER TWENTY-TWO

For the first time, Daniel spent the entire night with Thea. He held her as she cried. When she quieted, he did his best to comfort her as well as make her more comfortable. The lights were extinguished, the room filled with shadows. For once, he didn't resent the lack of illumination. The look on his face might scare her. The look on hers might destroy him.

As much as he'd suffered in life, this woman had endured a thousandfold worse. The loss of a child...given astronomical odds for having another...he couldn't even fathom the depths of her pain.

She remained stiff in his arms, unresponsive and unwelcoming. He was pretty sure she would have asked him to leave if not for the dogs, who were cuddled on her other side, sleeping peacefully. She was curled into them, clinging to them, as if they were a life raft.

He wanted to be her raft, even though he didn't deserve the privilege. The past few days, he'd been distant with her, frustrated that she didn't trust him to see her naked, hungry for her, all while trying to control the emotions she elicited within him. The more time he spent with her, the hotter he burned for her. He craved her constantly, even when she was in his arms. Especially when she was in his arms. He thought about her when she wasn't with him, and he couldn't take his eyes off her when she was.

At some point, her mother came knocking on the door, but he sent her away. Holly came knocking, too.

"Please," the girl said. "I need to talk to her."

"You had your chance. Now you're going to act like a grown-up and wait." He shut the door in her face.

After resettling beside Thea, he kissed her temple.

"By morning the entire town is going to know about..." Her voice quavered.

"No. They won't. I promise you." He'd already spoken to everyone who'd been present during her revelation. Or more accurately, he'd threatened everyone who'd been present. If anyone else found out what Thea had revealed, heads would roll...after bodies were beat black-and-blue. "Do you want to talk about—"

"No."

He stretched out an arm to switch on the bedside lamp. No more hiding in the shadows. "Do it, anyway," he said as light spilled over her. He wondered if her child would have resembled her. Those corkscrew curls and shamrock eyes. Those adorable freckles.

"Why?" she demanded.

"Share your pain with me. Let me help you fight it."

"Share my pain with you the way you share yours with me?" she said with a sneer.

She was...right. Though she'd asked, he'd never really talked about his PTSD. To protect her from the harsh reality of military life, he'd told himself. No reason to burden her with the bleakness of war.

Hogwash, his dad would say. Truth was, the thought of copping to the things he'd done scared the shit out of him.

He'd heard many people say that a little fear was okay, that it was acting despite the fear that made you brave. He disagreed. Fear was never okay. Fear weakened. Fear destroyed. Look what it had done to his relationship with Thea. True bravery was doing what was right, despite the consequences. Fear was simply the enemy in the way.

"I lost friends," he told her. "A lot of friends. And I killed people in the heat of battle. A lot of people. When I sleep, I dream of their deaths. I hear their screams."

As he spoke, she softened against him. "I imagine taking a life is difficult."

In more ways than one. "Before, during and after, it's hell on earth. You end someone's chance to do better, to be better."

"I'm sorry. I'm also grateful for your service. You protected our home."

"You aren't afraid of me?" he asked. "Knowing I'm capable of committing murder."

"Not even a little."

"You aren't disgusted?"

"Only by the farts coming from your dogs."

A surprised laugh woke Echo, who barked before she promptly fell back to sleep. Daniel traced his fingers up and down Thea's arm, something easing inside him. A pressure he hadn't known he'd endured. A weight he hadn't known he'd carried. "I've never really talked about this with anyone."

"Not even Jude and Brock? I bet they understand better than anyone."

"They do, but no. We haven't talked about the past, haven't wanted to burden each other. Sharing with you is…nice." Only a slight pause before he said, "Tell me about Rose."

She went stiff again. "There's nothing else to tell."

"I think there is."

"Well, that just proves you're not nearly as smart as me." A moment later, she withered. "I'm sorry. I'm being cruel, and you don't deserve it." A heavy breath shuddered from her. "I loved her so much."

"Rose is a beautiful name."

"Lovely and delicate, like she was." She sniffled, and the sound just about broke his heart.

"Your tattoo…"

"Yes. For her. An outward sign of my love for her."

He tightened his hold, wishing he could protect her from the world. Even from herself.

"What happened…the way I lost her…it truly was an accident, and might have happened regardless—I was cramping that day. Bleeding, even. But now I'll never know. And… and I loved that girl with every fiber of my being. I miss her. I want her with me."

He had no words. There were no words good enough.

An image flashed through his mind. Thea's belly rounded with *his* child…and it didn't upset him the way he thought it would. And that threw him. Frightened the shit out of him.

No fear. Not anymore.

"I'm so sorry for your loss, Thea." Having memorized every inch of her body, he traced his fingers over one of the scars on her abdomen. Despite the barrier her shirt created, he never missed a single inch of raised tissue.

"I would have given her the best life possible. And if anyone had picked on her the way I was picked on…"

Heads would have rolled.

It had been one tragedy after another for this precious woman, one rejection after another, and yet she'd never waved the white flag. *That* was courage. She possessed a soul-deep strength and a purity of character few others did, both of which mattered far more than outward beauty ever would. Even an outward beauty as magnificent as hers.

"What was the worst thing about high school?" he asked,

steering the conversation to address other hurts she carried. He couldn't help her with Rose, but he could maybe, hopefully, help her with the others.

"Eating alone in the cafeteria. My only friends were being homeschooled, and I had no one to talk to."

Daniel *hated* his teen self. This woman would never eat alone again. He would make sure of it.

"What was the *best* thing about high school?"

"When you told me I was perfect just the way I am."

Gold star, teen self. "You *are* perfect. There is nothing about you I would change."

In a hesitant voice she asked, "Do you want children? One day, I mean. Never mind," she muttered a second later. "It doesn't matter. We're not going to last. Nothing does."

"Nothing does," he echoed, his voice suddenly as hollowed-out as his chest. With five words—*we're not going to last*—she'd somehow hurt him on a level his mind didn't yet understand, even if his heart did.

I think I lov—

Stop! This was an emotionally charged moment. Better to figure out his feelings later.

She needed a distraction, and so did he. "You know," he said to lighten the mood, "before we start dating, I need to know—"

"*Before* we start dating?" she asked primly.

"Yeah. Before we can be classified as an official couple, I need to know who's on your last-supper list."

"One nipple twist, coming up," she said with some of her usual spunk.

Spunk he'd never been so glad to see. "Pass. But you shouldn't make threats you're not going to see through, sweetheart. You love my nipples, and we both know it."

"Hmph. Your nipples are *passable* at best."

He grinned up at the ceiling. Damn, he lo—

Liked her.

"Now tell me about this last supper," she said. "I know about the one our lord Jesus attended, but I'm drawing a blank about my own."

"It's simple. If you were going to die tomorrow, which twelve people would you invite to attend your last meal? And I'm not talking about the people you'd like to poison, so you keep that dream list to yourself."

She snorted. "I don't know who I'd invite. I've never thought about it. What about you?"

"I don't know who you'd invite, either."

Acting fast, she twisted his nipple. "Who would *you* invite?"

"Oh." He pried her fingers off the vulnerable crest. "My number one choice would be you, of course."

"Please. I'm your girlfriend—well, almost your girlfriend, apparently. You have to say that."

"No. You're my girlfriend, so I *get* to say that. There's a huge difference. I'd also invite Jude and Brock and my dad. Both of the pups."

"We can invite animals instead of people?"

"Now, don't you go planning a barnyard dinner, Dorothea Mathis. You only get to invite two animals."

"Why only two?"

"Because I only have two pets."

"So you're making up the rules as you go along. Got it." She drummed her nails against his chest, her features no longer tight with strain. "Who else? You've got six more seats to fill."

He wanted to shout with triumph. *I cheered her up. Me.* "Do I have to pick from the living or can I pick from the dead?"

"Why are you asking me? You're the puppet master, remember."

"Well, well. You finally admit I'm in charge."

"The only thing I'm admitting is that I may not invite you to my dinner," she retorted.

Loving—liking—this teasing side of her, he said, "Someone is just asking for a spanking, isn't she?"

"What is it with the Porter men and spankings? Your dad told me your mom used to spank you when you sassed her. And he recommended I do the same. But he did warn me that you would spank me right back."

"I guess you'll have to spank me and find out. And, Thea? I really hope you spank me." Daniel kissed her temple. "As for my last six guests, I'd have to go with my mom, Santa Claus—"

"Who isn't real."

"I make the rules, remember? I want to know why I never got that miniature racehorse I asked for." He continued. "Also Betty Crocker, Winston Churchill, Moses and Jessie Kay would receive a coveted invite."

"That's a great list." Smug, she said, "Too bad my dinner party will totally blow yours to smithereens."

"Well, well. Look who fancies herself a bona fide party planner. Let's hear your list, Mathis."

"First, I have to know who's picking up the tab for the dinner."

"I will. *If* I'm invited."

"Well, heck. I guess you have to be now. So. You, of course. Lyndie and Ryanne. I think I might even invite Harlow, Jessie Kay and Brook Lynn. Princess Diana for her grace and charm. Marilyn Monroe."

"Why Miss Marilyn?" He noticed her mom and Holly hadn't yet made the cut.

"I want to learn her tricks for enchanting everyone she ever met, as well as everyone else ever born."

"Sweetheart, you don't need any tricks. You've got it nailed."

She gave him another *hmph*. "Jason Momoa. Because wow. Theo James for the same reason. Oh, and Veronica Corningstone and Ron Burgundy, because they are the best news anchors of any generation, ever."

"Ha! Gotta say, that's a whole lot of beefcake at your table."

"But not enough. I'll put Al Roker on the waiting list."

Daniel pretended to think for a moment, then nodded. "All right. Even though you didn't invite the pups—"

"They will be sitting on our laps, so I figured I didn't have to count them."

"—your list passes my test. You are now officially my girlfriend."

She twisted his nipple a second time, not stopping until he yelped.

Laughing now, he pried open her fingers. He brought her knuckles to his mouth, kissed them one at a time, savoring the softness of her skin.

In response, she yawned, the trials of the day finally catching up to her.

"Try to get some sleep now, okay?" he said.

"You staying?"

"I am."

"All night?"

"All night. There's nowhere else I'd rather be."

Cocooned in warmth, Dorothea drifted in and out of a light doze, her mind racing. Love, she realized. Daniel had called her love before. And he'd done it more than once.

She knew she shouldn't read too much into it, but her heart soared. What if he *was* falling for her?

Fantasizing about a future together, she lost track of time but managed to remain cognizant of her surroundings. The mattress springs bounced and squeaked as the dogs jumped down. There was a soft patter of paws, then equally soft sighs.

One thump, then another. She was pretty sure the pair had just sprawled across the floor.

Daniel grunted.

He had spent hours with her, distracting her, making her think and laugh and forget. Every second, his arms had been around her, offering comfort.

Like her, he must have fallen asleep when they'd lapsed into silence. His grunting soon turned to groaning, his body jerking as if he'd been punched or shot.

"No," he mumbled. "No, no."

She'd done her research, as planned, and most PTSD experts agreed it was best to let a nightmare run its course unless it was severe. Then a gentle nudge and a few softly spoken words might be in order. Although, you had to be careful when giving that gentle nudge. The dreamer could attack.

Dorothea decided it would be best to move out of striking distance. If he hit her, even while unconscious, he would hate himself. She stood at the side of the bed and whispered, "Daniel. Daniel, wake up. It's Thea."

His thrashing slowed.

"That's right," she said. "Come on back to me."

The thrashing stopped altogether. With a gasp, he jerked upright. His wild gaze scanned the room. When he spotted her, he stiffened, scrubbed a hand down his face. "I'm sorry. I didn't mean to wake you."

"I'm glad you did." He'd been there for her. Now she would be there for him. She climbed back into bed and cuddled into his side.

"I'm going to go," he said, and made an attempt to stand. "You need your rest."

"So do you." She threw herself on top of him, pushing him back onto the mattress. "If you leave, you'll force yourself to stay awake, and that's not good for you."

"I don't care. It's better than the alternative," he said, but he didn't try to dislodge her.

She rested her head just above his heart. "Guess what? It's your lucky day. Dr. Freckles is in the house, and she's going to take care of you."

His heart kicked into a faster rhythm against her temple. "I thought you hated your freckles."

"I did, but someone keeps telling me how awesome they are. That someone even likes to lick them, so I've decided to embrace them."

"This someone sounds smart."

"He has his moments." She removed his shirt and traced her tongue around his nipple. "He's *very* tasty. Sometimes I just want to eat him up."

He fisted his hands in her hair. "Oh, yeah?"

"Yeah." This time, she grazed his nipple lightly with her teeth. "In fact, I think I'm going to make a meal of him… right here, right now."

"I should do the gentlemanly thing and tell you that you don't have to do this."

"But you aren't a gentleman," she said with a smile. She kissed the center of his chest and drew her tongue all the way to his navel. Then she stripped him to his underwear…drew the material beneath his sac.

"No. I'm not."

"Guess what?" She clasped his erection. He was long and thick. Hard as steel. Lips parted, she traced her thumb over the tip, a bead of moisture rising up to greet her. "I'm very glad about that fact."

He moaned a sound of abject pleasure.

She lowered her head, and as he stiffened with anticipation, she said, "Testing, testing. One, two, three. Is this thing on?"

He barked out a laugh, just as she'd hoped. "It's on. I swear."

It most definitely was, and it was only growing harder by the second. Nearly writhing with the intensity of his need, he waited...waited...for her to run her tongue over the head. The moment she did, he groaned an animal sound and released her hair to grab the sheet, as if he feared getting too rough with her.

"Now, just so you know," she said, batting her lashes at him. Then she gave the tip another lick. As he jerked, feminine power flooded her. "I've never known the touch of a man. I've lived on a deserted island my whole life, and you're the first male I've ever seen. I'm going to do my best to give you pleasure, but I'm afraid I'll fail."

The look he leveled on her suggested he'd never seen a woman, either. Well, not one like her. "I'm an iron-willed explorer and a hard taskmaster. You won't fail, because I won't let you. I knew you were untouched the moment I spotted you in your fig leaf bra and panty set, but I decided to take a chance on you anyway."

What!

"Lesson one. Once you start, do not stop," he said. "When you mess up, and you will, because you're so innocent and all, I'll give you pointers. You're welcome."

Jerk, she thought, trying not to laugh. He'd turned the tables on her, teasing her right back. Well, she would teach him the error of his ways.

Dorothea sucked his entire length into her mouth, earning a roar...and she didn't stop until she'd wrung him dry.

CHAPTER TWENTY-THREE

Dorothea woke alone, no sign of Daniel or the dogs anywhere, but at least she awoke with a smile. After her gentleman lover had come in her mouth, he'd thanked her, embraced her, and she'd thought he'd had every intention of easing the need he'd stoked in her—but he'd fallen asleep instead. She couldn't work up a good upset; for once, his sleep was peaceful.

However, she remained awake and on alert. If he had another nightmare, she would be ready, a blow job engaged.

As sunlight had stolen into the room through the crack in her curtains, fatigue had gotten the better of her and she'd finally drifted off. But she'd ached for Daniel. Oh, how she'd ached.

How she *still* ached.

It's my turn to come.

Rather than going for a run, she locked herself in the bathroom, stripped and hopped in the shower. Afterward, she painted her nails with a white undercoat, and yellow, blue, purple and pink stripes. And, rather than dressing, she donned the infamous raincoat. The last time she'd worn it, she'd been sick with nerves. Now she shook with anticipation.

She was going to trust Daniel with her body. After all, he'd trusted her with his past and she'd trusted him with her greatest heartbreak. He'd had his hands and mouth all over her. Why not his eyes, too?

No more holding back. No more regrets.

She should probably wait, at least until after working hours, but time wasn't her friend. If she lost her nerve...

After tying the belt around her waist, she exited her bedroom. *I can do this.*

A pale-faced Holly waited at the bottom of the stairs. She was chewing on her nails.

Dorothea expected to feel rage, but all she felt was a hollow sensation. "Not now, Holly. Go to school." She tried to pass, but her sister jumped in her way.

"I'm sorry, Dottie. You were right. I've been a spoiled brat. I wanted to hurt you, but I wanted you back with Jazz, too. I thought we could be a real family and this hole in my chest would finally be filled."

"Not now," she repeated. She was too raw, the wounds too fresh. "And don't call me Dottie."

This time, Holly let her pass without impediment when she sidestepped.

"I didn't know," Holly cried behind her. "I didn't know you'd named the baby after me."

Dorothea paused but didn't look back. "You shouldn't have to know to forgive me or feel sorry for me or whatever it is you're doing. What ever happened to *just because I love you?*" She kicked into motion, determined to push the encounter out of her mind. Today was about pleasure, only pleasure. Everything else could wait.

The sound of hammering drew her to the first floor...to the door of the theme room. The open door. She gaped, overcome by shock. The room was bursting with activity. Harlow was painting another mural. Jessie Kay sat on the bed, her head bent over her sewing. Daniel was building a new headboard. He was shirtless, which wasn't fair to Dorothea's hormones. The dogs were at his feet, chewing on his boots. Lyndie and Ryanne were chatting about the upcoming spring festival and picking up strips of tattered comforter. Jude and Brock were sanding the floor.

Tenderness welled inside her. Family wasn't such a bad thing, after all. These people loved and supported her.

Daniel pointed the hammer at Jude. "If you want your skull to remain in its current condition, you'll—" His gaze found Dorothea, and he quieted. He took in her "outfit" and the darkness of his pupils spilled over his irises. "Get out. Get out of the room. All of you. Now. Brock, take the dogs."

His urgency thrilled her, arousing her to a fevered pitch.

"What the hell, man?" Jude grumbled.

"Well, clutch my pearls." Jessie Kay placed her needles and material in a basket. "What's gotten into my sweet Dan— Ohhhhh. I get it now. Our boy wants a little some–some from his girl."

Jude and Brock noticed Dorothea, and Brock smiled a wicked smile. Jude nodded. Laughing, her friends clapped. Dorothea stood her ground, unabashed.

Daniel gave his friends a push. "Out!"

Everyone rushed into the hall. The guys patted her on the shoulder, and the girls winked at her. Daniel never took his eyes off her. She placed the Do Not Disturb sign on the doorknob, stepped deeper into the room and, with a little push, closed the door. The locked engaged.

He took her hand and studied her nails. He kissed her knuckles.

This man...

Her legs grew unsteady as she moved to the center of the room, but her blood practically fizzed like champagne bubbles as she untied the coat. The material gaped open, and cool air kissed her heated skin.

Daniel sucked in a breath. "Off." A croak. "All the way."

I think you're perfect just the way you are.

She shrugged, the material slipping to the floor, leaving her bare. In the bright light of day.

Tension pulsed from him as he walked around her. Slowly. A predator soon to devour his prey. He had on pants, but she was naked, and she experienced a sense of heightened awareness, very conscious of the fact that she was being studied as thoroughly as a science experiment. Her heart raced, determined to win against some invisible competitor. Her nipples puckered. The apex of her thighs ached, and her bones felt as if they were melting.

"Do you know," he began in a husky voice, "how beautiful you are?" He stopped in front of her, so tall and wide he dwarfed her. His gaze burned through flesh and blood and encountered soul. "Exquisite."

The intensity of the moment staggered her, but a tangible weight held her in place.

"And you, Daniel." How to explain the depths of her feelings for him? Her deep admiration for him, spirit, soul and body. "You are amazing. Wonderful. Strong. Sexy. You are magnificent. And *sexy*. You're smart and talented, your carving skills unsurpassed. But it's more than that. You are kind. You care, and it makes others care for *you*. You're protective and...perfect. I think you're perfect just the way you are."

He reached out, his fingers trembling as they brushed over her tattoo, then one of her scars. At the moment of contact, she inhaled sharply; how could a simple touch be so incredibly pleasurable? Easy. Because Daniel was the one who'd touched her. The rasp and heat of his skin, the musk of his scent, the awed look in his eyes—they were her favorite things in the whole world.

"The things you do to me," he said. He bent his head and fit his teeth around her nipple, taking a little nip. Blood rushed to meet him, causing the bud to swell with need. He gave the other one a nip, as well. "The things I'm going to do to you…"

"I hope your energy is high this morning." She shivered. "I've got a little of that insatiable lust you mentioned."

"The job of a gentleman lover is never done." He swept her up in his arms and carried her to the bed. The sheets were chilly as he laid her down, and his tags and the locket were like ice when they clanged against her chest.

She loved the dark smattering of hair on his pecs and under his navel. Loved the bronzed hue of his skin. The tensile strength and sinew he'd earned on the battlefield. She loved *his* scars; they said *I lived, I survived*.

He rubbed his hand up and down his rigid length before he unfastened his pants, maintaining a slow, languid pace, not in any kind of hurry, but savoring every second he spent with her. She loved that, too. They'd sprinted to the finish line before, and as amazing as it had been, this was better. She got to savor him, too.

The pants were kicked aside. Soon his boxer briefs joined the pile. Because the lights were on, she received her first full-length view of him, and—*someone save me*—he was big. Really big. Her X-rated Prince Charming.

She cursed the fear that had kept her from this, from seeing all of him.

"Spread your legs." His voice was nothing but a harsh rasp. "Let me see you."

She obeyed without hesitation, showing him just how wet she was for him. Just how intensely he affected her.

His eyelids hooded as he traced a finger along her aching core. "Look how pink and pretty you are."

Pleasure zinged through her, and goose bumps broke out

all over her skin. "I think I was made just for you," she said, almost drunk on pleasure, remembering when he'd admitted her body fit his.

"That's right. Made just for me. I'm the only one who can have you. The only one who can have *this*." The possessiveness of his tone was almost as potent as his next caress.

"Then take it." Her hips arched up to meet him. A challenge. A dare. "Take it now."

"Oh, sweetheart. You're playing with fire…and I'm going to make you scream for it." He took her hips in his hands and yanked her to the edge of the mattress. After he placed her feet on his shoulders, he dropped to his knees.

So vulnerable. And yet she had never been so turned on.

He leaned in to nuzzle her inner thigh. The stubble of his beard tickled her but also sent a riptide of pleasure zinging through her, and she moaned. He kissed around her core, and waiting for his mouth to reach her where she needed him most was as much agony as ecstasy. Bowing her back, she reached overhead and fisted the pillows, offering herself up to him in every way. Calloused fingers kneaded her breasts before tracing a path of flame down her stomach…but still his mouth remained just out of reach.

She'd told him to take what he wanted. Now she would heed her own advice. She lifted her hips again, higher and higher, until…

Contact.

His tongue swiped out, and she moaned with bliss…rapture. Her head fogged. He fit his hands under her bottom, holding her up as he licked her, faster and faster. When she was crying his name incoherently, he delved his tongue deep, deep inside her to mimic the motions of sex.

"Will never get enough of this," he told her, and replaced his tongue with two fingers. The emptiness was finally, deliciously filled. He sucked on her little bundle of nerves and brought her to a swift and brutal climax.

She screamed to the ceiling, her spasms growing in intensity, racking her entire body. When the last one faded, she sagged against the mattress and tried to catch her breath.

He jackknifed to his feet, his lips glistening in the light. His erection stretched toward her, weeping at the tip.

"We're not even close to being done, love." With one fluid motion, he flipped her to her stomach. The mattress bounced as he worked her into the position he wanted her. On her hands and knees, her bottom in the air. Delicious! His strength and aggression were on Technicolor display, his hunger for her driving him.

"You even have freckles on your back," he said. "I am the luckiest man on this planet."

And she was the luckiest woman. After all her trials and tribulations, Daniel was her reward. "Freckle marks the spot."

He laughed but quickly sobered, too caught up in the moment...the need. Then he leaned over her, his chest pressing against her back. Heat to heat. Skin to skin. His erection teased her opening but didn't enter her.

Warm breath fanning over her nape, he said, "I like having you at my mercy."

"Less gloating, more filling."

A foil wrapper ripped, the sound ramping her up.

He ran her earlobe between his teeth. "I *know* you are perfect just the way you are."

With a shout, he thrust inside her. Pleasure. So much pleasure. Part of her died, part of her came to life.

When he pulled out and slammed back in, the bed rattled. Another wicked sound. She was wet, soaked, and he somehow grew harder, as if he were a sword forged in her fire. Everything was a stimulant. The air. The forcefulness of his breath. The way his fingers dug into her hips. She would be bruised tomorrow, and she would love it; she would remember his possession, and she would smile a secret smile.

He reached around her and caught her swollen little nerves between two fingers. Fingers he scissored. A climax rocked her, swift and sure, her heart practically exploding as her inner walls clenched on him.

His body jerked against her, and he roared her name, coming, coming so hard she *felt* it. She was branded. Forever marked as Daniel's girl.

CHAPTER TWENTY-FOUR

Daniel didn't want to leave Strawberry Valley. He'd begun to dread the arrival of the weekend, when he would have to venture into the city for a job—where he would have to spend an entire weekend away from Thea. But Friday morning arrived on schedule and, because he'd made a commitment, he stayed in.

Jazz and Charity had stuck around longer than anticipated, but they, too, were leaving as soon as they finished filming some kind of segment at the inn. A home-in-the-heartland piece they hoped the network would air to catapult the inn into *the* vacation destination for all Oklahomans. Their way of apologizing to Thea, he was sure.

Since he and Thea had made love in the theme room, he'd spent every night with her. They'd drunk golden milk on the roof while gazing at stars. Sleeping still wasn't his favorite thing, and nightmares still plagued him, but his girl knew just what to do. He always fell back to sleep with a smile.

They'd already said goodbye, before he'd driven to his dad's to pack and get the dogs situated, but damn it, he needed one more kiss.

Virgil was in the kitchen with Adonis and Echo, eating a plate of food Carol had sent over. Daniel joined them, and the dogs rushed over to demand pets.

"Don't forget to—" he began.

"I know, I know," Virgil said. "Take the dogs to Dorothea at seven, when she's done for the day."

"Thank you."

"They're my granddogs. They'd be just fine spending the nights with me."

"Yeah, but she needs them." *Never going to be alone again.* Daniel poured himself a glass of orange juice. "You still thinking I'm not good for Thea?"

"Well, isn't that what *you* think?"

"I...don't know," he admitted. His need for her still scared him, despite his hatred of fear, but he was working on it. He sat at the table and buried his head in his hands. "How did you know Mom was the one for you? That you could risk being with her...one day losing her."

"Easy. I couldn't breathe without her." So simply stated, without fear or reservation. "She was worth any risk."

Jude and Brock strode into the kitchen. Jude was frowning, of course, and Brock looked posthungover and prehungover at the same time.

"Need coffee." Jude scrubbed a hand down his face, revealing cracked and bruised knuckles.

"Rough night?" Daniel asked.

"Ryanne banned Jude from the bar for fighting." Brock pilfered a piece of bacon from Virgil's plate. When Virgil slapped his hand away, he growled, "You should thank me. I'm helping reduce your cholesterol, old man."

"You let me worry about my cholesterol. You worry about the fork you're gonna be wearing if you reach for another piece of bacon."

Brock reached for another piece.

Virgil didn't fork him, but he did grumble under his breath. "You boys are about as useful as a screen door on a submarine. I'm gonna enjoy the peace and quiet while you're gone, yep, that's what I'm gonna do."

After Jude drained the coffeepot dry, the three of them loaded their bags in Daniel's truck.

"You boys be careful now, you hear," Virgil called from the porch, the dogs dancing at his feet.

Daniel saluted him before driving off. "Gotta make a pit stop," he said.

"Let me guess." Jude slipped on a pair of sunglasses. "The inn."

"You are so whipped." Brock, who occupied the front passenger seat, twisted to peer back at his friend. "And so are you. You've been sitting in a dark corner of a bar watching every move the bartender makes like a creeper. I'm embarrassed for you."

"Screw you. Screw you both," Jude snapped, and Brock laughed. "There's talk of a rival bar being built across the street, and how the supposed owner is not a nice man. I'm looking into him. I'm also protecting Daniel's girlfriend's best friend."

Whatever you gotta tell yourself, buddy.

"I'll just be a minute." Daniel parked in front of the inn and jumped out. The sky was a brilliant baby blue, the sun shining.

No one sat behind the reception desk, but he'd linked Thea's phone to the front door, and it was only thirty seconds or so before she rounded the corner. Her dark curls were piled on top of her head, as usual, and her face scrubbed clean of makeup. Those freckles slayed him. Her cheeks were bright with color, and her eyes sparkled as she met his gaze.

"What are you doing here?" She frowned, her hand fluttering to her throat, and he noticed her nails were still striped, indicating her emotions were all over the board. "Is something wrong?"

"Yes, something's wrong. I don't want to go. I've got things to do here." Things he enjoyed. He liked hanging around at the inn, deciding which room patrons would get, monitoring the security feed and working on the theme room. "My boss, also known as the dragon lady, gets pissy when I'm not here to do the hard labor."

She fluffed her hair, actually appearing proud of the new nickname. "Trust me. We'll be fine without you."

"Please. I single-handedly run this place."

She rolled those gorgeous shamrock eyes. "I haven't seen you lugging a cleaning cart around."

"Sweetheart, I don't need a cart. I walk into a room, and the mess hides."

Now she snorted. "Have you always been this full of yourself?"

"It's a recent development. Someone thinks I'm the greatest man in the history of ever, and since she's the smartest person I know, I have to believe her." He should go. He'd already passed the promised minute, but he couldn't bring himself to walk away. Not yet.

She rested her elbows on the counter. "Well, that someone is wondering if anyone has called or emailed about the receptionist position."

"The *assistant* position." He pulled at his collar, suddenly uncomfortable. "Haven't set up any interviews." The same truth he'd given her the last time she'd asked. A truth she would thank him for. So why the hell did he feel so guilty?

"Dang it. I need help, and I thought there were people in this town who needed a paycheck."

"You don't need help. You've got me." He'd gotten only one other call, but he'd told the girl to ring back in three to six weeks. She'd said something about being willing to risk the wrath of the beast, something he hadn't understood and hadn't wasted time questioning. Now an idea hit him. "I wonder if someone warned people away."

Way to shift blame.

"Who would do such a thing?" Her hands fisted and she grated, "Holly?"

"We'll investigate when I return." He leaned over the counter and pressed a hard kiss to her mouth. One that said *Remember me every second I'm gone.*

By the time he lifted his head, her features were luminous. He swore. If he didn't leave now, he wouldn't leave at all. "You'll call me if Jazz corners you again?" he asked her.

She sighed but said, "Yes."

"All right. You better stay safe," he said. "And be ready for me when I get back. Because the first thing I'm going to do—is you."

Lord save me, Dorothea thought, her heart racing as Daniel strode out the door. That man knew how to leave her hungry for more.

She rushed to the door to watch as his truck sped away. When his taillights vanished, she stayed in place, searching the clouds. They were soft, fluffy and white right now, but radar suggested a storm was headed this way, due to arrive tomorrow afternoon; it was supposed to be a doozy, with a high likelihood of hailstorms but only a small chance of tornadoes.

That night, as she lay in bed with the pups, she missed Daniel like crazy. Was *he* missing *her?* She wished he would call her. Strawberry Valley had two earthquakes today. Small ones, but two glasses had broken in the kitchen. Shouldn't he wonder if she had survived?

She already felt as if she loved him more than he loved her—not that he loved her. And that was the problem! She loved while he liked. Their relationship was imbalanced, and her uncertainties were escalating.

In the morning, as she walked the dogs to Style Me Tender, she noticed a greenish hue in the sky. When she returned to the inn, she checked radar. The likelihood of tornadoes had gone up. A lot. As she worked, she continually checked her weather apps and by 10:00 a.m., conditions had worsened. She had an hour, maybe two, before things got superbad.

She returned to her bedroom, worry for Daniel growing. Thankfully, the tornadic activity was localized. Strawberry Valley and the adjacent counties would be endangered while the city would receive only rain and hail.

Next, she checked the safe room in the basement. Bottles of water? Check. A box of flashlights? Check. Blankets, a cordless radio and chairs to sit on? Check, check, check. Jazz and Charity had checked out earlier, leaving their room keys on the counter, and she had only one other guest. There was plenty of space. But not every business in the town square had a safe room, and the owners knew they were welcome here. If everyone showed up, "plenty of" would change to "barely enough," but she wasn't going to worry about that. She would rather be uncomfortable for a few hours than know someone was out there, unprotected.

She sent a text to her sister at school—weekend classes to ensure she graduated. Weather's getting bad. Come home. I'll call the front office & check you out.

Maybe she was being overly cautious, but her gut was shouting *Be prepared*.

Holly texted her right back. Okay, yes. Yes, I'll come home.

How agreeable, she thought with a sneer. Then she sighed. When had she become such a raging witch?

She made the call, as promised, but it went straight to voice mail. Did no one work the front office on Saturday?

She left a message anyway, and a few seconds after she

hung up, her phone buzzed. Someone else had just come through the front door. Or exited. She checked the screen and groaned. Jazz, Charity and the rest of their crew were back.

What now? She trudged to the lobby.

"It's getting worse out there." Jazz wouldn't meet her gaze. "Charity and some of the crew would like to stay until the storm passes. If that's okay."

"Sure," she said. "But what about you?"

"I'm a storm chaser. I'll be filming."

She looked him over. He was dressed in a shirt and jeans, not really camera ready. But then, he wasn't going to film himself.

Excitement bloomed, and she said, "I want to go with you."

"What? No." He shook his head. "You don't have the proper training. You could be hurt."

"I have some training," she grated. Two semesters worth of book smarts.

"But..." Charity glanced between them, worrying her bottom lip between her too-white teeth. "I was hoping you'd stay here, Dorothea. You can help me. The network will be cutting to me just as much as Jazz."

"I'm going, and that's that." Daniel had suggested she film herself and stream it live, and thanks to Jude, her site was ready to go. What better time to get started? Jazz could do his filming, and she could do her own. "I just need to get my family settled in."

At last he met her gaze. Whatever he saw in her eyes convinced him to agree. "You have twenty minutes before I head out. If you're not ready, I leave without you."

"Thank you." She called her mom, who was at a book club meeting at the Rhinestone Cowgirl. She didn't waste time with pleasantries. "Come home and bring the other ladies with you. And bring Virgil, Anthony and the dogs. Looks like we're gonna have ourselves a twister."

"Are you sure? We have storms all the time. I bet this one will pass, too, and we'll—"

"Now! And hurry."

Took a little *over* twenty minutes for everyone to arrive, but Jazz waited. The wind had really kicked up, whistling as it hit the sides of the building. Dorothea gathered the supplies she'd need, filling a large black duffel bag.

"Stay here," she told the masses. "Do not leave." She placed her laptop on a shelf, the screen already set to her webpage, where she would be streaming the feed she captured on her phone. "I'll keep you updated."

Her mom wrung her hands. "Are you sure you should be going out there?"

"Daniel would not be pleased, young lady," Virgil said.

She kissed her mom's cheek, then Virgil's. "I'll be fine, promise. But this is something I've always wanted to do, and I'll be with a...professional." Besides, Daniel would encourage her to live her dream. Right?

She experienced a tendril of unease. *Stay safe*, he'd told her. Meaning *stay put*?

Did it matter? Even if he had issued a flat-out command, so what? Her days of people pleasing were over. Amen.

As she strode to the exit, Holly stepped into her path. "Don't leave. Please, Dot—Dorothea."

Last week she would have been so eager to earn back her sister's affections, she would have done whatever the girl asked. Today? Not so much.

"I'll be back," she muttered, and stepped around the girl.

Jazz was in the lobby, peering out the door. Other storm chasers from other networks would be out there, of course, but they wouldn't know the terrain like she did.

When she sidled up to Jazz, readying her phone, he said, "Are you sure you want to do this? The danger...my liability—"

"I'm sure." She almost added, *"My middle name is Danger,"* but decided she'd sound like a dork, so she kept her mouth closed.

Thump, thump, thump. Clink, clink. The hail had begun to fall.

"The doors are unlocked," he said. "All you have to do is jump in."

His van—with shatterproof windows—was waiting under the portico, she realized.

"You ready?" he asked.

"Ready."

He raced outside, and she followed. Her hair whipped from its knot and slapped her cheeks. The cold and the wet hit her full force, nearly knocking her off her feet, but she kept going.

When she made it to the vehicle, her relief was short-lived. She couldn't get the door open; the wind was too great. Jazz had to help her from the inside. Teeth chattering, clothes plastered to her body, she buckled in.

"Not too late to stay here," he said as he studied the storm in the distance.

And let him hog all the glory? No!

One fact became very clear. He'd never believed in her.

But Daniel did.

"Is that your way of saying you're scared?" she asked.

He looked at her, aghast. "No."

"Then shut up and drive."

CHAPTER TWENTY-FIVE

Daniel took another stroll around the Michaelson Hotel ballroom. Despite the elegance of gilt mirrors, white columns and a freshly polished marble floor, the place lacked the inn's intrinsic charm. But then, he had a feeling no place on earth would ever compare to the inn. His home.

He was beginning to feel like a normal person. Someone who could maintain a stable relationship long-term. He was sleeping at night. He could hear a loud noise without freaking out. And he could almost—almost—believe Thea would stay with him, through good times and bad.

He *wanted* their relationship to last.

He should have called her when he'd first arrived in the city. Then he should have called before he'd gone to bed last night. Hell, he should have called her this morning. Like an idiot, he'd tried to temper his feelings for her.

Things with her were good. Very good. Almost too good.

In his experience, trouble always struck at Too Good O'clock.

Concentrate. You're on a job. The morning gala had bled into a silent auction and lunch buffet, which would ultimately bleed

into an evening party. The ballroom was already crammed
with people. Everyone was decked out in formal wear, the
women sparkling with precious gems, and the men in tuxes.
Even Daniel wore a tux, and the tie was about to choke him,
but he kept his hands at his sides, ready to grab a weapon, if
necessary.

Ten minutes stretched into thirty and thirty into an hour.
A storm erupted outside. Many of the guests pulled out their
phones to check the latest news. Thunder boomed, and hail
began to beat at the windows.

"Daniel, we've got a problem." Jude's voice spilled through
the bud in his ear. "Your dad couldn't reach you, so he called
me."

Jude was in one of the hotel's lavish rooms, watching everything from a makeshift wall of screens. Daniel had turned
off his phone the moment he'd gone on duty.

He missed a step. "Is he okay?"

"He's fine. He and the dogs are in the basement at the inn.
Dorothea has gone out with Jazz, chasing the storm. I've sent a
link to you. It's the website I created for her. She's streaming."

Chasing the storm? What. The. Hell.

"That's not all," Jude said, his voice nothing but doom and
gloom. "Power lines are down in Strawberry Valley, and cell
towers are clogged. I lost touch with your dad."

Daniel spoke into his wrist mic. "Brock—"

"Yep. Heard. You go do what you gotta do, my man. We've
got you covered here."

Daniel rushed into the hallway leading to the lobby and
whipped out his phone. He followed the link, and after several tries, he was able to log on to see video footage of the
storm. A dark sky, black with shades of green. Rain and hail
the size of golf balls poured, the trees whipping in the wind,
limbs breaking. One tree was even uprooted; it danced across
the terrain like a tumbleweed.

In the background, he heard Thea shouting, explaining what was happening. A loud roar had kicked up, as if a freight train was headed straight for her.

He'd lived in Oklahoma long enough to know the sound of an incoming tornado.

"If you live in or around Strawberry Valley, take cover," Thea yelled. "Take cover right now. This is an F-3, at the very least. There's going to be damage. Any homes in its path will be destroyed."

The feed stopped, the screen going blank, and his heart nearly burst from his chest. When he'd told her to live stream, he'd meant from the safety of her room. He hadn't wanted her to go out in the storm and endanger her life. What if he...lost her?

He'd seen death a thousand times, in all its incarnations. Disease. Violence. His granny had died in her sleep with a smile on her face, drifting away peacefully. But he was not prepared for *this*.

Thea had clearly been inside a vehicle, moving away from the coming tornado, which was her only saving grace. If Daniel were with her, he would be shaking her, screaming at her, then covering her with his own body to keep her safe. But she didn't want to be kept safe. She wanted to be in the middle of the action.

"—funnel clouds," he heard her say, the screen alive with images once again. "Yes, yes, they're forming a second tornado, and look! They're dropping! Search the center of the winds. Can you see? Can you see?" She sounded excited.

She wasn't going to be able to escape the worst of the wind or the flying debris. Power lines were flashing as they fell. Damn it! Tornadoes were faster than cars, the absolute worst place to be. The metal could compact, smashing the people inside.

He was roughly two hours away from her. If he left now,

he would reach her after the storm had passed. If he stayed put, he risked not being able to reach her at all. Roads were going to flood, and debris was going to form blockades. That was just the way things worked.

Welcome to Oklahoma.

He pocketed his phone as the website continued to stream, cut out and stream again; he ran outside. No hail, so no problem. But the valet attendants were nowhere to be seen. They were probably inside, staying warm and dry. *They* were smart. At their stand, Daniel shot the lock preventing him from getting his keys. When the cabinet door swung open, he dug through the contents until he found what he needed.

He removed the lid from a nearby garbage can and held it over his head. He ran into the storm, the droplets slamming into the metal. Once he was under the cover of the parking garage, he ditched his shield and picked up the pace. Took him a minute or twelve, but he found his truck and jumped inside.

The engine gunned. Urgency filled him as he pressed the gas. He sped out of the garage and down the street. He was downtown, near Bricktown, where some of the streets were one-way. Construction cones and detours led the way and, yes, certain areas were already flooded. He navigated back roads until he made it to the highway, the rain continuing to fall.

As many combat situations as he'd faced, he should have handled today's danger with aplomb. But he'd never been such an emotional wreck. If Thea was hurt…

He flew down the road, ready to act if he hydroplaned.

The website had gone quiet again. He fished the phone out of his pocket, glanced at the screen. It was blank, and his concern for Thea redoubled, becoming a sickness in the pit of his stomach, acid in his veins, a blade at his throat.

The closer he got to Strawberry Valley, the lighter the rain pitter-pattered, and yet more debris littered the road. Finally he could go no farther. Not in the truck, anyway. Trees, power lines and other vehicles blocked the roadway.

He was only five miles away, roughly half an hour on foot. He parked on the side of the road, jumped out and ran. The air was thick with moisture, the sky growing blue and bright, as if there'd never been a storm. The ground sloshed, his Italian loafers quickly ruined. Like he cared.

A family of four was hiding in a drain, but he didn't stop to chat, only called, "You're safe now." Was Thea? He reminded himself she had some training. She knew what to do. But even experts could make mistakes, and tornadoes were never predictable. The funnel could turn in less than a second, and if you were in the way, you were dead.

He made it to the inn, but she hadn't returned. A crowd had gathered in the lobby, including his dad and the pups, Lyndie, Ryanne, Harlow, Jessie Kay and Holly.

He petted both dogs and hugged his dad, demanding, "Where is she?"

Virgil was pale. "I don't know, son. We lost contact with her."

"Wait! The feed is live again. She's still streaming," Holly said, rushing to his side. As pale as his father, she offered him a laptop.

Jazz must have been holding her cell phone, because Thea appeared on screen. When Daniel saw she was alive and well, relief nearly felled him—but it was the anger rising inside him that he focused on. There was a cut on her cheek and arm, blood dripping. Her hair was soaked, her clothes plastered to her body...but her mud-smeared skin was aglow.

She motioned to the destruction behind her, but he couldn't make out her words.

Daniel searched for visual clues to discern her location and finally spotted something he recognized. One of the only trees left standing was an old oak with a thick base and towering branches. It was on the edge of the town's only park. He'd played under that tree as a child, and he and his friends had notched the bark.

"Be nice to her," Holly pleaded. "Please."

"I can't make any promises," he grated, already heading for the exit.

Carol stepped in his path to stop him. He would have walked around her, but the gentleman his momma raised wouldn't let him.

"You've got your knickers in a twist." She kept her gaze steady on his, determination pulsing off her. "You think Dottie foolishly risked her life."

"I don't think it, I know it."

"Well, that's all well and good, but if you go to her like this, you're going to drive her away or force her to choose you over her life's passion. She's lost so much already. Let her have this. The one thing she loves. Don't try to take it away from her," she pleaded. "Let her be happy."

He moved around her. Screw being a gentleman. Carol had no idea what she was talking about. Thea needed someone to take the storms away from her or she'd pull this shit again. He would rather she live, pissed off at him, than die, happily chasing another storm.

He made his way to the park, where he found her standing beside a van, drinking from a bottle of water. He closed the distance, determination in every step.

"Daniel!" Grinning, she raced over and threw her arms around him. "You're here! Did you check out the webpage? Did you see my report?"

His arms remained at his sides, lest he shake some sense into her. "How could you be so *stupid*, Thea?"

She stepped back, her smile fading. "What are you talking about?"

"Not only did you risk your life, you worried the hell out of your family and friends."

"But I'm fine. Jazz knew what he was doing and—"

He motioned to the cut on her cheek, silencing her. "Not all of you is fine. And the fact that you trusted your ex with your safety—stupid," he repeated.

"Dorothea!" A grinning Jazz bounded over. He was holding up his phone, shaking it. "I sent the network a link to your page, and they loved you. They want to—"

Daniel drew back his fist and punched the bastard in the nose. Cartilage snapped, the man howling with pain, stumbling back and nearly falling into a puddle.

Thea flattened her hands on Daniel's chest and pushed. "What are you doing?"

He paid her no heed, moving around her to get in Jazz's bloody face. "You took her out in the storm."

"And she's safe," the man snarled, his voice nasally as blood poured from his nostrils.

Thea curled her fingers around Daniel's wrist and tugged. "I insisted he take me. I—"

"I don't care," Daniel roared as he spun to meet her gaze. "You could have died out here."

She released him and once again backed away. "I don't understand what's happening. You're the one who suggested I live stream."

"Not from the eye of the storm! You could have died out there," he repeated, then scrubbed a hand down his face. "Storms are like war. An enemy could be waiting at every corner."

"I'm sorry I worried you, but this—"

"No. No buts. Purposely endangering your life isn't okay. Purposely endangering your life to film a storm is worse."

She bristled. "What are you saying?"

He ground his teeth. "I want to be with you. Long-term.

I don't want to worry about the end—losing you to a tornado." Carol had been right about one thing. He was going to make Thea choose. "It's the storms or me, Thea. You can't have both. Pick one. Now."

CHAPTER TWENTY-SIX

Dorothea stared at Daniel, certain she'd misheard. No way would he have told her to pick between storms and him. Right?

So danged wrong.

He was tense, his expression dark. He radiated concern and fury. "Pick," he grated.

How dare he! She loved this man with all her heart, but she would not let him be the dictator of her life. She strove for a let's-be-reasonable tone. "You're worried about me, which is why I'm going to give you a chance to apologize."

As silence stretched between them, her too-fast heartbeat agonized her, keeping her alive but killing her, too. She wasn't ready for their relationship to end. He was finally thinking long-term! But she wasn't going to let him push her around. What kind of future would they have?

If he didn't back down, they were over.

"You're choosing the storms," he said. A hard statement, not a question.

"I'm not. I'm choosing not to cave to such a ridiculous ultimatum."

She'd learned a lot about herself and her future today. Chasing a tornado had been a major rush, there was no doubt about that; her adrenaline had been thumping and pumping. But in order to do it again, she needed the proper equipment. To acquire the proper equipment, she needed to work for a network. Thing was, she liked being her own boss. All her life, she'd fallen into line, and she was done. So done!

And she liked the life she was building here in Strawberry Valley. Working at the inn might not have been her dream or passion in the past, but that didn't mean anything in the present. People changed.

When the storm had passed, she'd found she wasn't as excited about the next one. She'd just wanted to be home, curled up with Daniel. She'd wanted his ring on her finger. Wanted to build a family with him. She had a lot of love to give.

The thought had led to the idea of using her webpage to keep the residents of Strawberry Valley informed about inclement weather, even posting a daily vlog for paying subscribers. A paying job, a delight and a blessing, all rolled into one. She could stay home with her family, share her love and knowledge, help to keep people safe, and never have to venture into the middle of a storm again.

But she told Daniel none of that. If he couldn't accept her without strings, if he was willing to trample on what he thought were her dreams, he wasn't the man for her.

"I will not apologize," he said. "You were reckless and irresponsible and—"

"The network loved it," Jazz interjected. He held a cloth to his bleeding nose. "They want to interview you for a job, Dorothea."

A job she would have wanted yesterday, but moving to the city no longer held appeal. She would have to leave Daniel, the inn, her mom, her sister and her friends. Which she had done before, and she could do again…but she didn't want to.

A muscle ticked beneath Daniel's eye. "Are you going to take the job?"

"It hasn't even been offered yet," she told him.

"And if it is?"

"What would you do if I said yes?" she demanded. *Tell me you'll still love me. Or that you love me even a little. Or that you like me and you'd rather I didn't but you'd support me if I did.* Her gaze beseeched him.

"Then I'd say...we're over."

So simply stated, as if he didn't care one way or the other. This wasn't the sweet Daniel who'd told her how much he would miss her while he was gone. This was a Daniel she'd never met before. Perhaps the one who'd ignored her while he was in the city.

Flattening a hand over her queasy stomach, she said, "Do you want to be over?"

"I don't want to fear for your safety every time it rains. I don't want a long-distance relationship. Like I told you, I don't want to dread the end anymore."

Did he want marriage? Maybe. But... "No, you just want me to forget my needs and focus on yours." Thing was, he didn't want her *enough*. Something she'd always known but had been willing to overlook...for the chance to be with him.

"Don't try to make this about me," he snarled.

"But it is. You made it clear from the beginning we were only temporary." Still her gaze beseeched him. *Tell me you want us to work, no matter what. Fight for us!* "Now you want more, but only if I do things your way. Always your way."

This time he was the one to step back. His hands fisted. "I guess you've made your choice."

Any hope she'd cultivated suddenly withered. Like Jazz, Daniel wasn't going to fight for her.

"Well, all right, then," she said. She blinked back a well of tears. Tears he didn't deserve! "We're over." She turned away.

"Dorothea," Daniel said.

Dorothea. No longer Thea. Tears burned her eyes, but she paused. "What?"

"There's a folder on the computer at the inn labeled Potentials. A handful of people emailed résumés, hoping to get the job."

What! "You said no one had—"

"No, I said I hadn't set up any interviews, and I hadn't."

So he'd misled her. "Why tell me now? To hurt me?"

No response, which was answer enough.

"You're making this easier by the second," she grated.

Jazz watched her with wide eyes.

"Get in the van," she commanded.

He shot Daniel an evil look before obeying. Silent now, she climbed into the passenger seat and slammed the door shut. She kept her gaze straight ahead, probably the most difficult thing she'd ever done, not even glancing at her former boyfriend.

A sob threatened to overtake her, but she suppressed it. Daniel had just shattered her heart into a million little pieces, but not by word or deed would he ever know it. Let him think he was as disposable to her as she was to him.

"Take me back to the inn," she said, using up the rest of her strength.

"Dorothea—"

"Drive!"

The tires sprayed mud in every direction as he put the pedal to the metal. The van motored forward, going over divots and debris.

When Daniel was no longer visible in the mirrors, Jazz tried again. "I'm sorry. I know that was hard for you, but you're getting the better end of the deal. You're free now. You can move without complication. And you're going to love working for—"

"Shut your stupid mouth. For once! You and I are never getting back together. For whatever reason, Charity seems to love you. If you feel the same about her, great. Stop messing around and commit to her. That means no more cheating."

"*She* cheated on *me*," he spat.

Well. His reason for coming to Strawberry Valley finally made sense. He'd hoped to make Charity jealous.

"Cheating speaks of her character flaws, not yours. But the same is true for you. You cheat, you suck. So if you no longer want to make things work with her, cut her loose, don't leave her dangling. And if you lose your job because of it? So the heck what? Get another one."

His hands tightened on the wheel, his knuckles quickly losing color. "You don't understand."

"Because I don't have a network job? Screw you. I paid for your career with blood, sweat and tears. And I had a family. A family I lost. I now have a job I've grown to love." She rested her aching head against the back of the seat. "Do you know why I married you, Jazz?"

"Because you loved—"

"No. Because you were the first guy to pay attention to me. My self-esteem was lower than dirt, and I think you knew that. I think you *liked* that. I did everything you asked, and never tried to impose my will upon yours, because I was too afraid of losing you. But in the end, I lost you anyway, because that's what fear does. It destroys."

Daniel had let his fears destroy their relationship.

He'd been right from the beginning. She was going to lose him one way or another.

Over the ensuing days, SV residents worked together to clean up the streets and patch the buildings affected by the tornado. Though the storms hadn't beat a path through the streets, there'd been collateral damage. Even still, plans for the spring festival continued.

"Though Mother Nature is being a royal witch," Carol had said, "she can't stop us from having fun."

What was fun? Dorothea didn't know anymore. She'd stopped painting her nails; they were devoid of color. A visual reminder of her constant emotional upheaval? No, thanks.

To her consternation, the inn continued to host town meetings about the festival. More and more people were spending the night. She couldn't keep up with the demand because she had yet to hire a new employee.

She refused to ponder the reasons she'd put the hire on hold. If thoughts were drops of water, the amount of introspection she'd done since dating Daniel could fill an ocean. Enough was enough.

Thankfully, Holly came home from school each day and cleaned any rooms Dorothea hadn't yet gotten to.

"I'm sorry you're having to do so much," the girl had said the first day. "When you fired me, I made it clear to the rest of the town that I'd torment anyone who applied for the job."

"I have potential employees." *Just need to let go of the hope that—* No! No introspection! "But even still...fix it," Dorothea had snapped.

"I will. Will you forgive me, then? Please."

"The way you forgave me?"

"I was stupid, but you're smarter than me." Tears streamed down her sister's cheeks. "I have regretted my actions every day."

Regret was something she still battled, and she sympathized. And dang it, she was softening. Could she never hold on to a good mad? "I'm not ever going to get back together with Jazz. He's—"

"I know! And I'm glad. He's an asshole, and you only deserve the best."

Dorothea had drawn in a breath, slowly exhaled it. The tears she'd kept on lockdown since her breakup with Daniel had finally sprung free. She'd sobbed, and Holly had gathered her close. They'd clung to each other the way they used to do as children.

"I'm sorry," Holly had said. "I'm so sorry."

"If you have a problem with me, you come to me. You talk to me."

"I will." Holly had tightened her hold. "Always and forever. I promise."

Always and forever, I'll love you. Words Dorothea had whispered to her sister the day their father had left, and the girl had cried in her arms. She'd wanted Holly to know she could rely on her, no matter what. "Always and forever," she had echoed.

Jazz and Charity had left at last, but other news stations had shown up to interview families that had lost vehicles or trailers. But the only reporter anyone was willing to talk to...was Dorothea. Her webpage had gotten a ton of hits. So many, in fact, that the page had crashed. She'd had no idea what to do, had finally broken down and called Jude.

He'd hung up on her after she'd explained the problem, but he'd also fixed the page.

A thousand times Dorothea had picked up her cell to call Daniel, eager to tell him about everything that had occurred and hear his thoughts. Where was he? What was he doing? She hadn't seen him around. Had he gone back to the city?

She missed him like she would miss her heart or her lungs. Nothing worked properly without him. But nothing would work properly with him, either. With his absence, she'd realized a few more things about herself. Being with a man who always expected the end to come, well, she'd never been able to look forward to the future. She'd had to dread it because nothing had ever been settled, everything up in the air. A wait-and-see situation. Will he or won't he? Would he or wouldn't he?

She was tired of tangling with dread. And sadness. And sorrow. If Daniel had ever liked her, even a little, he would have realized his mistake and come crawling back.

One morning, Dorothea convinced herself she'd been too hard on Daniel and texted him. She told him she wanted to see the dogs. They were hers, too! She'd helped pick them out. But he ignored her, because he was done with her.

And that was for the best. He wasn't good enough for her.

Okay. She was back on the "dislike him" train.

Rather than falling into bed that night, she painted her nails and dragged her sorry butt to the Scratching Post. She needed a distraction. Brock was at a table in back, drinking beer, a woman balanced on his knee.

Dorothea ignored him, staying at the counter with Ryanne and Lyndie.

"You look sad, and I don't know why. Men suck, and you're free," Ryanne said as she wiped down the bar. "I bet Daniel didn't even meet five of the ten commitments."

To be fair, he'd met a lot of them. Then the storm had happened.

Lyndie lifted a shot glass. She'd had several drinks already and was well on her way to Drunkville. "Here, here." She drained the contents, then burped quietly in her hand, her gaze returning to Brock for the hundredth time. "He's so wrong for me. I mean you, Dorothea. Daniel is so wrong for you."

"Did something happen between you and Brock?" Dorothea asked her.

"What? No! Never. He's a man-whore, and besides, he scares me. He has a temper, and one strike from those meaty fists would kill me."

"He wouldn't—"

But Lyndie wasn't done. "Even if he was the calmest person ever born, I'd say no if he asked me out. Because, do you want to know the benefits of dating me? No, because there aren't any!"

Low self-esteem could strike anyone, Dorothea realized, even beautiful strawberry blondes. "The benefit of dating you is that he will be dating you. I could go on, but I'm pretty sure I've already made my point."

Lyndie gave her a small smile. "You know a man like Brock doesn't just enjoy sex, he needs it." She peered into her drink, the smile long gone. "I probably shouldn't admit this aloud, but I hate sex with the passion of a thousand suns."

Dorothea patted her hand. What the heck had her husband done to her? "You haven't liked it in the past, honey. Every man is different. The right one will be gentle and caring, or whatever you happen to need. He could change your mind."

Ryanne wiped the bar with more force. "I love you guys and only want the best for you. Whatever I can do to help, let me know and it's done."

"Love you, too," Dorothea and Lyndie said in unison.

"And right back at you," Dorothea added. "You know what? We're going to drink tonight. Maybe exorcise our demons."

"Good idea." Ryanne poured the three shots.

They clinked their glasses and drained the contents. The amber liquid burned going down but settled sweetly in Dorothea's stomach.

"I loved him," she said, "but he didn't love me back and didn't even like me enough to fight for me. I have to let him go." She held out her empty glass, and Ryanne refilled it. Then she nudged Lyndie's shoulder. "Your turn to tell us what demon you're exorcising."

"Well. I... I stayed with a man who... He hurt me." Lyndie chewed on her bottom lip. "I was afraid of what he'd do to me if I left again. I was afraid of everything. *Am* afraid."

Dorothea hugged her close, aching for her.

Ryanne took Lyndie's fragile hand and flattened it above her heart before refilling their glasses. "My mom slept with not one but two of my boyfriends, so I learned early on never to trust anyone enough to actually have sex," she admitted, and her cheeks darkened. "Then I met the dirtbags here—" she gestured around the bar "—and that was that. Total body lockdown."

What! The roughest, toughest girl in town was a *virgin*?

Dorothea smiled at her. Her first smile since her breakup. "I'm in shock."

"I know," Ryanne grumbled. "I've worked so much I haven't even dated, all to save up for my 'round the world travels."

Ever since they were little girls, the beautiful brunette had wanted to travel to other countries. "Are you hoping to change your virgin status before your first trip? With anyone in particular…like, say, Jude Laurent?"

"No! Of course not." A soft sigh. "Maybe. He's rude, but he's hot. He's quiet, but protective. And he never looks at any other woman but me… I admit I get weak in the knees every time our eyes meet."

"If you decide to go for it, let us be your wingwomen," Lyndie said. "We'll help you nail him good. Or very, very bad."

Ryanne laughed. "To nailing our men, either in bed or to an anthill!"

They held up their drinks and clinked the rims, then drained the contents. Again Dorothea experienced a burn and a sweet settling. Her inhibitions began to melt away, her head hazing.

"So what do we do now?" Lyndie asked.

"Yeah," Ryanne said. "What do we do?"

"Now," Dorothea told them, "we dance and sing and live stream it on my webpage. We deserve to be happy, dang it, and we're going to show the world!"

CHAPTER TWENTY-SEVEN

Daniel sat at the desk in his bedroom, sober for the first time since his breakup with Thea. The dogs were asleep on his bed, and his dad was out on a date with Carol Mathis, of all people. He doubted the date had anything to do with romance, though. The two were probably plotting ways to get Daniel and Thea back together.

Well, that wasn't going to happen. He wouldn't be second place in her life while she was first in his.

Is she really first?

Yes!

Since their breakup, he hadn't slept and he'd barely eaten. Fatigue and hunger had hounded him. He'd drunk, and then he'd drunk some more, trying to keep his mind off his girl.

Not my girl. Not anymore.

His PTSD was back in full force, his mind a wealth of land mines, always ready to blow.

Earlier Thea had texted him about wanting to see the dogs, but he had yet to respond. Every time he'd tried, he'd started writing in all caps. HOW COULD YOU DO THIS TO—

He rubbed at the ache above his heart, hating her, hating himself. His life had gone to hell in a handbasket.

Jessie Kay wasn't speaking to him. His dad only ever sighed at him, and Daniel had begun to worry about his health. Virgil often rubbed at his chest, as if pained. The only people who'd remained normal around him were Jude and Brock. Jude was as grumpy as ever, and Brock was drinking too much. As evidenced by the call Daniel had received half an hour ago.

"You by a computer?" the guy had asked, anger crackling in his tone, even as he slurred his words. Music played in the background.

"I am." His laptop had been only an arm's length away.

"Check out Dorothea's webpage."

Just hearing her name made his internal pain worse, and he'd cursed. But he'd also hung up and obeyed. And then he'd watched as Thea had the time of her life with her friends. He was still watching.

She laughed. She drank. She danced. Then she laughed, drank and danced some more.

Fury brewed. He didn't like his life without her, while she clearly loved hers without him. She'd already moved on. Her nails were purple; she was determined.

Why hadn't she started her new job in the city?

Why hadn't she hired a new employee?

Again and again, Daniel almost swiped up his keys and drove to the Scratching Post. He craved her. His eyes wanted to see her live and in person. His mouth wanted to taste her. His hands wanted to touch her. His ears wanted to hear her voice.

But he stayed where he was. There was a hollow sensation in his chest. One he'd battled many times before, after his mom died and every time he'd lost a friend in battle.

Deep down, he understood why he had to deal with it

now. Thea hadn't died, but their relationship sure had. She'd chosen the fucking weather over him. The weather! Daniel Porter couldn't compete with a tornado.

So this is what true rejection feels like. This was what she'd endured most of her life.

The contents of his stomach—what felt like barbed wire, buckshot and broken glass—churned together.

On the screen, as a strobe light flashed, a man came up behind Thea, hoping to dance with her. Daniel slammed the laptop shut before he did something stupid. Like break speed records to get to the bar and beat the man to death.

Actually, why not? Releasing a little steam might do him some good. He leaped to his feet and grabbed his keys. Careful not to wake the dogs, he sneaked out of the house. But as soon as he was enclosed in his truck, the engine running, he slammed his fists into the steering wheel, going nowhere fast.

A car pulled up to the curb, and Brock basically fell out of the passenger seat. The driver—a woman—begged him to stay with her, but he shut the door midsentence and headed toward the house, a six-pack in hand.

"Daniel!"

Daniel rolled down the window. "Over here."

Brock changed directions. He stumbled a bit, but eventually managed to settle into the cab with ease. "Came home to help you." He lifted the beer. "Here. Drink."

"I'm trying to sober up."

"Now isn't the time for that kind of nonsense. Why did you let Dorothea go, anyway? She's your preferred vice, yeah?"

"I think she was my salvation." The words left him before he could think, before he could decide if they were true. Of course, they *weren't*. He relied only on himself.

"Then again, I gotta ask. Why did you let her go?"

Good question. One he didn't want to answer. "Does it matter? You'll support me, whatever the reason."

"Do you know me at all? I will never blindly support anyone, not even you and Jude. You make a stupid decision, and I'm going to call you on it. So I ask for the third time. Or is it the sixth? I've lost count. Why did you let her go?"

"Because I'm stupid." He punched the steering wheel so hard the top bent backward. "Because I'll lose her one day anyway. Either she'll walk out on me or she'll die."

"Uh, hate to break it to you, buddy, but I'm going to die, too. So is Jude and your dad and everyone you know. Did no one tell you death is hereditary? It's going to happen to all of us at some point or another. None of us are getting off this planet alive."

Daniel narrowed his eyes at him. "Is this the part where you tell me I need to overlook my fears and focus on the here and now?" Once, he'd proudly boasted about having conquered all his fears. What a fool. "That I need to enjoy life while I can?"

"Hell, no." Brock finished his beer and crunched the can into a small ball. "Haven't you heard? Misery loves company, so I happen to like you just the way you are."

Daniel snorted. "Speaking of miserable company, where's Jude?"

"Investigating something to do with the bar about to be built across from the Scratching Post."

He wished his friend would watch over Thea and prevent her from going home with some random guy. She had needs, and she was single. She could do whatever she wanted, with whomever she wanted, and there was nothing Daniel could do about it. "Tell me something to make me feel better about the choice I made," he said, rubbing his chest. The ache was worse.

"Easy. A woman is a woman is a woman. They are all the same. You'll meet someone else. Tonight, if you want. I've got the number of a real hot—"

"I'm going to stop you there, because you're an idiot and you're wrong. A woman isn't a woman isn't a woman. They are different." Thea was unlike any other woman he'd ever known. She was a soothing balm to his wounds. She was sweet to his sour, kind to his grumpy, soft to his hard. She was the light to his dark, and when he was with her, life made sense. He had a purpose.

"Do you love her?" Brock asked.

Love. The word echoed in his mind. Was this love? He hadn't let himself wonder before. Now he couldn't stop.

He loved his dad and the dogs, Jude and Brock, but what he felt for Thea was so different. Much more intense. "Maybe. Probably. Lord knows I've tried not to."

"That's because you're stubborn like Jude."

And unhappy. Jude used to whisper a prayer as he'd knelt over his dying brothers and sisters. Right there on the battlefield while enemy fire still rained, he'd held hands and cried, as if every life was precious. He hadn't prayed or cried since his wife and twins had died. He'd shut down in so many ways.

What would Daniel do if Thea died in a storm?

Actually, she could be hit by a car. Or struck by an illness. Fall to a random act of violence. He could lose her any number of ways, whether they were together or not. So why not spend what time they had left together?

But none of those ways were purposely sought out. And that was the word he couldn't get past. *Purposely.*

The next morning, Daniel sat outside Style Me Tender as his dad and Anthony played checkers, the dogs running around their table and chairs. The sun was shining brightly. The town had done a good job of cleaning up after the tornado, and the publicity the storm had brought had only helped the economy. People from all over the state and even other states were flooding in for the spring festival, which kicked off tomorrow.

The inn must be overrun. How was Thea handling the

excess work? Just fine, if last night was any indication. She hadn't seemed stressed at all.

His hands fisted.

Virgil sighed wistfully and made his next move on the board.

"Dad," he said. "Cheer up. Please." If his heart problems worsened because of this, guilt would kill *Daniel*. This was what he'd hoped to avoid.

"Thought you'd wise up by now and go get your woman," Virgil grumbled. "But nooo. I had to go and learn I'd raised a boy so dumb he couldn't pour piss out of a boot if the instructions were written on the heel."

Anthony said, "I think he's remained single because he's afraid of disappointing you." His dark eyes landed on Daniel. "You aren't the only one who watches and learns, kid."

"Well, he needs to get over it." Virgil moved a red checker across the board. "I can handle a little disappointment. What I can't handle is seeing my only son destroy his life."

"It's not destroyed," Daniel grated. Was it? "Dad, you didn't think I belonged with Thea. Darkness and light can't coexist or some shit?"

"Who says you and Dorothea can't both be light? She made you happy. You did the same for her. Why don't you buck up and deal with it."

Daniel rubbed his chest. The pangs had been coming more frequently.

He began to pace in front of the table. As minutes ticked by, men and women passed him. No matter their sex, they shook their heads, tsked or whispered about his stupidity.

Broke our sweet Dorothea's heart, he did.

Damn it! *She* had broken *his* heart. Why couldn't they see that?

The thought brought him to a screeching halt. His heart. The very thing paining him. She *had* broken it, which meant he *had* fallen in love with her. Not maybe, not probably, but definitely.

He loved her. Loved her madly, passionately and completely. She had become his everything. His reason for waking up every morning. His reason for smiling. His reason for breathing.

His reason for being.

And yet he'd let her go. He'd practically pushed her away.

What was he going to do about it? What *could* he do?

He needed to clear his head. To think. "I'm taking off, Dad. Gonna take a little time."

"Great. But before you go, son, do us all a favor and pull your head out of your ass."

Nice. "I'll do my best." Daniel called the dogs, but they ignored him in favor of tugging at his dad's shoelaces.

He loped down the street all by his lonesome. When he turned the corner, his chest started aching again. Thea! She was jogging toward him.

This was his first real-time sighting since the breakup, and his body reacted without a command from his brain. His legs stopped working, his muscles going from lax to clenched in point two seconds. Thea stopped, too. Even across the distance, he could see the dark circles under her eyes—eyes that were filled with a hundred different emotions. The frontrunners were regret, sorrow, anguish and hope. Her skin was pale, and there were tangles in her hair. Her nails were bare again, and the lack of polish bothered him.

Only a second passed, but at least ten different scenarios about how this could play out whisked through his mind. His favorite? She threw her arms around him, covered his face with kisses and promised never to chase another storm.

Her dark curls were pulled back in a ponytail, and her beautiful curves encased in a tank and running shorts. Loyal Thea, as faithful to her run as her mailman was to delivering her mail. Come rain, sleet, hail or sunshine, she'd be trek-king the sidewalks.

Thea didn't approach him. Instead, she raised her chin and kicked back into motion.

His hope withered to ash.

Say something. Tell her you love her. Win her back!

And send her off during the next storm?

He moved forward at a clipped pace, his heart desperately trying to leap from his chest…and passed her without say-ing a word.

CHAPTER TWENTY-EIGHT

The first day of the spring festival arrived. As a kid, Dorothea had awoken on this day with a smile, knowing she would soon be enjoying fried desserts of every kind and hopefully winning a giant stuffed toy. Today, she hadn't awoken at all because she hadn't gone to sleep. She'd stayed up all night crying.

Daniel had finally been spotted, and he hadn't cared enough to even say hi. He'd washed his hands of her.

Not good enough to keep him.

No. She refused to believe that. The breakup had nothing to do with her, and everything to do with his fears of losing someone else. And that had been his problem all along.

She remembered the night she'd spent at the Scratching Post, dancing with Ryanne and Lyndie. Jude had shown up at some point and cornered her. She'd been buzzed, but his first words had sobered her up in a hurry.

"You want Daniel, you're going to have to fight for him."

She'd bristled with indignation. "Why can't he fight for me? When is it my turn to be the prize?"

"You *are* a prize. He's miserable without you."

Was he? "Good!"

"He's afraid of losing you, and your desire to chase storms has only exasperated that fear."

"If he allows that fear to dictate his decisions, then he's not *worth* fighting for."

Jude had left her in a huff, mumbling under his breath about fools too stubborn to see the gift they'd been given.

After she'd spent the night throwing up in a toilet, wishing Daniel had been there to hold her hair and bathe her and tell her everything would be all right, she'd actually considered going to him. Then she'd thought, *What the heck? I'll do it!* When they'd ended things, they'd both been driven by adrenaline and fury. They needed to talk, and if he was as miserable as she was, maybe they *could* work things out.

But halfway to his dad's house, she'd realized her mistake. She could fight for him, but she couldn't fight his fears for him. They could get back together, but their relationship would still be fractured, and they'd end up splitting again.

Now Dorothea crawled out of bed and into the shower. Hot water sluiced over her but failed to melt the ice that had taken up residence in her bones. *Have to let Daniel go. For real and for good.*

She would have fun today, dang it. The inn was filled to capacity, every room but the theme room taken—it still wasn't done. Towels, soaps and snacks had been set up in the dining room, and Mrs. Hathaway would be sleeping at the counter, just in case.

When Holly had passed out flyers containing a pledge not to hurt anyone who interviewed for the reception position, four other people had applied for the job.

Dorothea knew the second she made a hire, any hope of Daniel coming back would die.

It needs *to die.*

Fighting tears, she dressed, applied sunscreen and lip gloss, and dried her hair on the lowest, coolest setting. Less frizz and softer curls that way. She'd come to embrace who she was. She may not possess the standard beauty, but she *was* beautiful.

Purple nails. Perfect.

With a nod at her reflection, she exited the bathroom, intending to find her sister and mom and head to the festival. But she had no need to search—both Holly and Carol sat on the roof, drinking hot chocolate and whispering worriedly.

Dorothea sat beside her sister and confiscated her mug, taking a sip, moaning with delight. Warm chocolate was the ultimate indulgence.

"What are you guys talking about?" she asked. As if she couldn't guess.

"Virgil called me," Carol said. "Daniel is at the festival with his friends."

Holly rested her head on Dorothea's shoulder. "We can spend the day here. Yeah. Let's spend the day here. I'm afraid if I see him, I'll murder him. Save me from a life in jail."

Her heart squeezed painfully, but she patted the top of her sister's hand. "No murders today. We can't allow the actions of someone else to dictate ours. We're going, and we're behaving."

Since the festival was held in the town square, all they had to do was walk outside the inn, and they were in the thick of the activities. Booths had been set up along both sides of the street. The food trucks she'd dreamed about were intermixed with a thousand different games, each one incorporating strawberries in some way.

She saw people she knew and people she didn't. Though she didn't feel like smiling and waving, she did both.

"Look! Gourmet doughnuts!" Holly twittered with excitement. "Do you think they have anything with coconut?"

"Let's find out."

Arm in arm, they made their way to the truck in question

and took a place at the end of the line. A few minutes later, she heard a familiar male voice behind her and stiffened.

"Well, this isn't awkward at all." Brock.

A grumble from Jude was the only response, but Dorothea felt a hot gaze on her back. Tensing with dread, she turned—

And came face-to-face with Daniel.

He and his friends had taken the spot directly behind her, and as they stared at her, her heart thudded against her ribs. The sun, which had so lovingly embraced her when she'd exited the inn, suddenly deep-fried every inch of her.

"Dorothea," he said with a stiff nod.

Dorothea again. Ouch! Well, she could do him one better. "Mr. Porter."

He flinched, but she experienced no satisfaction.

"Aren't you supposed to be out there working security?" she asked. "You know, putting yourself in danger for your job."

His eyes narrowed. "I'm on a break. And I can wear Kevlar to protect myself from a bullet. What can you wear to protect yourself from a twister?"

Holly spun, a good-sized helping of anger taking the place of her excitement. "Wow. Look at the piece of shit the cat dragged in." She jammed a finger into Daniel's shoulder. "Can Kevlar protect your balls from my knee? I don't think so. Now hit the bricks, Porter. This town isn't big enough for the both of us. Get gone. Fast."

He was too strong to be budged. "You're as pleasant as always, I see," he replied, his features twisted into a sneer.

Hey! "You don't talk to my sister with that tone," Dorothea snapped. "Do it again, and you won't be talking for a week."

"Or ever. Because I'm your worst nightmare, boy-o." Holly fronted on him. "I cut first and ask questions never."

He looked between them, astonishment registering. "You forgave her," he grated to Dorothea.

"Yeah. So? What business is it of yours?"

"Now, girls." Carol tugged Holly back to her side and put her nose in the air. "We all know Mr. Porter is severely brain damaged. Let's not tax his limited mental capacity with big words." She looked him straight in the eye and, as if she were speaking to a toddler, said, "Go. Away."

Dorothea wanted to cheer. The woman who hated confrontation was doing a dang good job of confronting. And since their own confrontation, she'd been a better mother all the way around. She'd encouraged Holly and Dorothea to talk, and she'd helped around the inn more.

Daniel's focus remained on Dorothea. "Why aren't you in the city?"

"Why would I be in the city?"

"You know why. The job you couldn't live without."

"I didn't take the job because I didn't want it," she said, and turned away. Let him stew on that!

For several seconds, he said nothing. Then he bit out, "If you didn't want the job, why the hell did you choose storm chasing over me?"

Without looking at him, she replied, "I didn't choose storm chasing over you. I chose freedom from a dictator. You demanded I do things your way or no way, and you weren't willing to talk to me about your concerns. Why would I ever want to be with you?"

Another round of silence stretched out. The line shortened, and she moved forward, but now her limbs were quaking. A showdown with Daniel had been destined to happen sooner or later, but she hadn't been prepared for what it would feel like. This hurt. This hurt bad.

"If everyone will excuse us, Thea and I are going to have a quick word." He grabbed hold of her hand and whisked her away.

Holly sputtered. Brock said something to quiet her.

"Let me go," Dorothea snapped.

"Hell, no. I made that mistake once already." He dragged her through the crowd and back inside the inn.

He was going to try to get back together with her, wasn't he?

Once the door closed, she wrenched free. "Don't do this, Daniel." She rubbed the skin where he'd touched her, trying to ease the burn he'd left behind.

His anger was gone, not a vestige of it remaining. His posture was yielding, open, his golden gaze beseeching. The way hers had once beseeched him, without success.

"I shouldn't have commanded you like a soldier and expected you to comply," he said. "I'm sorry."

"Of course you're sorry. You got your way. I won't be chasing storms."

"Thea—" He reached for her.

She jumped out of range. "Before you showed up tossing commands like they were pennies, I'd already realized I could live my dreams from the comfort of my home. I'm going to be a stay-at-home weather girl, and I'm going to do it without you in my life." There! Take that!

Despite her words, he looked at her with hope, and it only made her want to slap him. "I was so afraid of losing you. I wasn't thinking clearly."

"Maybe you weren't thinking clearly," she grated, "but you lost me anyway."

"Don't say that. I've been a mess ever since we broke up. I can't eat or sleep. I miss you. I think about you all the time. I...love you."

After everything he'd done and said to her, he was finally ready to admit his feelings? Well, of course he was; he'd gotten his way. No job in the city, no chasing storms. She laughed bitterly. Nothing had changed—for her. Their relationship was still fractured. Knowing he loved her fixed nothing.

"Too little, too late, Daniel." The anger leached out of her, leaving only sadness. "I will always know there are strings to your love. I'll worry about losing you if I don't do things your way. With that, on top of your worry about losing me again, we'll never be happy."

Sweat beaded on his forehead. "I know I messed up, but I wasn't worried. I was being proactive."

Oh, the lies we tell ourselves. "You *were* worried, and you *are* worried. I reached out to you, Daniel. I tried to talk to you. I took steps to win you back. You did nothing. Wait. That's not true. You threw me away like so many others have done. As if I meant nothing."

His skin pulled tight around his eyes and mouth. "I couldn't fight for you because I was busy fighting for my sanity. And I didn't answer your text because I hoped to save myself from drowning in my misery."

"Or you wanted to punish me. Meanwhile, you left me drowning in *my* misery."

He blanched. "I'm sorry," he repeated. "I'm so sorry. I just... I was trying to avoid future hurts."

"That's the thing. You can't avoid hurts. They're going to come one way or another. That's life."

"Thea—"

"It doesn't matter, anyway," she interjected. "I told you. We'll always be worried about losing each other, and I don't want to live that way."

He grabbed her by the shoulders, holding tight, as if sensing she was about to bolt. "If I could go back..."

"But you can't."

"I'm worried, yes. I admit it. But I'll deal."

Not good enough, she thought, and oh, her heart was breaking. "I'm sorry. I'm not putting my trust in you again. You're the same man today that you were when you broke up with me. You haven't changed."

"Thea." He framed her jaw with his hands, his thumbs

dusting over her cheeks. "Please. My dad is upset about the breakup. He wants us to be together as desperately as I do."

It was the total wrong thing to say, heralding the return of her anger. "Have you fooled yourself into thinking you love me just because your dad wants us together?"

"No. No!" His grip tightened. "I know how I feel about you."

He kissed her then, smashing his lips into hers. An act of desperation. She opened for him, because she was used to opening for him and because she wanted needed his kiss more than she needed her next breath…and because she was saying goodbye.

She wrapped her arms around him and kissed him back with all the love trapped inside her. For one minute, two, three, she savored the feel of his heart thundering against hers. Finally she rubbed herself against his erection, knowing it would be the last time—and pulled away.

She was panting, and so was he. He reached for her, but she backed away.

"You haven't changed, but I have. I'm not the girl you started dating," she said softly. "That girl couldn't see her worth. This one can. And I'm worth more than you're willing to give. I'm worth everything—because that's what I'm willing to give."

"Thea—"

"What if I want to move to the city one day? I do want to finish school. I might decide then that I do want to work for a network. I might decide I want to storm chase again." Holly would move out of the inn one day to start her adult life. Carol might decide she wanted the inn back.

And what would Dorothea have then? Her vlog, but not much else.

"Thea—"

"No, Daniel. You said it yourself. We're done." With that,

she walked away from him, and she didn't look back. The past was the past. It was time to march toward the future. And if that future didn't include Daniel—that was okay. She would be okay.

Loving a man didn't mean depending on him for her happiness. That was why Ryanne's mom still searched for contentment but never found it. Loving a man meant sharing, caring and being better together. And if you weren't better together or at least *fighting* to be better—

You needed to be apart.

Tears splashed down her cheeks, but she exited the inn, certain she was doing the right thing.

CHAPTER TWENTY-NINE

Had she done the right thing? Dorothea wondered for the thousandth time that day. She'd spent several hours at the festival with her mom and sister, but she hadn't eaten a single treat, and she hadn't played any games. Now, as darkness descended outside and residents returned home, her mind demanded to know where Daniel was and what he was doing. The rest of her demanded she run—no, sprint—to his side.

She loved him with all her heart. And now, without him, she felt as if she'd been ripped apart. As if she'd lost something precious, something she would never have again. But...

Of course she'd done the right thing. Her reasons were valid. If things got bad, and they would at some point, she couldn't trust him to stay with her.

A knock sounded at her door a split second before Holly marched inside her room. "All right, enough moping."

"I'm not moping."

"Sis, I can hear you pacing three flights down." Her sister stooped in her closet and grabbed a bag she began filling with Dorothea's clothes. "Get your crap in order. Mom and

I are taking over the inn for an entire week, starting tomorrow. You, missy, are going on vacation."

"You have school."

"Nope. Next week is spring break. Besides, I've turned in all my overdue homework. I'm making straight Cs now! Practically Bs. Or close to getting *one* B. In art."

"Oh, Holly. I'm so proud of you." And she meant it. Before, Holly had been making Ds and Fs. "But I'm still not vacationing." Where would she even go? "This is our busiest time of year."

"Which is the perfect time for you to get away." Holly zipped the bag, which was overflowing, bits of cloth catching in the metal teeth. "I've already talked to Dane Michaelson about letting you use a room at his hotel, free of charge. He was happy to comp everything, including spa treatments, as long as I never again threatened to give his stepdaughter a makeover."

"You didn't."

"Oh, yes, I surely did. For once, someone is going to take care of you. Clean your room for you. Deliver food to you. You will rest, and you will relax. Maybe you'll even sleep with a pool boy. I don't know. That's for you to decide."

Dorothea nearly choked on her tongue.

"You can't say no. Lyndie and Ryanne are going with you. But they're coming over tonight to keep you from running away. That's right, you're having a slumber party. The three of you will leave at 6:00 a.m."

Dorothea drew her sister close for a hug. "Thank you."

"You're amazing. The best person I know. And if Daniel doesn't realize that, he doesn't deserve the privilege—the honor!—of being your man."

"Maybe he does. He said he loves me."

"So? Did he *show* you he loves you?"

Well…

She shook her head.

"So there you go. There's your answer." Holly dropped the bag beside the door. "If the pool boy isn't your type, call maintenance and pretend you need help with your TV. When he shows up at your door, you can be naked. That's, like, what happens in every porno ever made."

"No, it's not." Scandalized by her sister, and her own inadvertent admission that she knew what happened in pornos, she said, "What do you know about pornos, young lady?"

"I work at an inn, sis. I can charge movies to other people's rooms. What do you think I know?"

Oh, sweet heavens. She kissed her sister's cheek. "When I get back, we are washing your mind out with soap."

Daniel answered his phone with a snapped "What?"

"Dottie is leaving at six tomorrow morning, and she'll be gone for a week," Holly said in lieu of a greeting. "If you want her, you better prove it before then, because Jazz used to tell her that he loved her, but his actions always proved the opposite. If you don't show up, I'll make it my mission in life to bury you—literally." She hung up. A specialty of hers.

He stared at his phone. Or his two phones. Why were there two? Oh, well. He stuffed the device back in his pocket and finished his newest shot of whiskey. He'd lost track of how many he'd had. Ryanne wasn't on duty at the Scratching Post, so she wasn't here to limit his intake with her wit and charm—and when that failed, her snide remarks. *You don't want another whiskey, cutie. You want a coffee. Mmm. Coffee. So good! Oh, you don't want coffee? Well, too bad. Drink it before I ram the mug down your throat.*

Before she'd taken off, she'd said, "She's too good for you!"

"If you're talking about Thea—" he'd begun.

"No. I'm talking about the alcohol. Use your brain, dummy."

"—you're right."

He'd messed up. He'd messed up badly, and he could think of no way to fix it.

Thea was a smart girl, brilliant, and she'd done what was best for her. How could he have gotten angry about something like that? He should always want what was best for her, whether that meant moving to the city or staying here and chasing storms. More than that, he should have done everything in his power to *become* the best. Anything for her, because she was everything to him.

He'd lamented about Thea putting storms first, but hadn't he put his fears before her? He'd told himself he'd beaten the fear of losing her, that he was only being practical, but as Thea and Holly had said, his actions had proved otherwise.

He'd been a total asshole. And why? Because he'd tasted rejection, blaming everyone but himself.

Brock, who sat beside him, signaled for another round. "Go ahead. Drink up. Learn what your life will be like if you continue on this path."

Jude, who sat on his other side, watching with unreadable eyes, finally piped up. "Who called?"

"Holly. She's going to bury me." He told his friends about Thea's trip.

"That…can't be right," Jude replied, and scratched his chest. "She wouldn't leave you."

"Well, she is, and I deserve it. My dad was right. My head has been up my ass."

Brock patted his shoulder. "It's still there, buddy, or you'd already be at the inn."

Frowning, Jude stood. "If you'll excuse me…" He walked away. Women smiled coquettishly at him, and men stepped away from him. He ignored them both and pressed his phone to his ear, making a call.

Daniel drained his next whiskey. "Thea liked me. Might have even loved me."

"So she doesn't have very good taste. So what?"

Daniel glared at him. "She has perfect everything."

His friend held up his hands, palms out, all innocence.

The bar was crowded tonight, filled to the brim with out-of-towners. In the morning, they'd visit the festival, which would be raging the entire weekend. They would have fun, and they wouldn't know or care that he had lost the love of his life.

"Well, I declare. Daniel Porter." Nails traced up his back. "Is that really you?"

He turned to frown at a pretty blonde and flipped through his mental files. She looked familiar, yes, but still he couldn't place her. "I'm sorry, but I don't..."

Laughing, she waved a hand through the air. "I'm Madison. Madison Clark."

The cheerleader from high school? The one Thea had seen him making out with inside the band room? "Madison Clark. Of course." Her skin was sun-kissed, but she was thin, too thin. Like the women he used to date. Skin and bones without the softness he'd come to crave.

"I'm in town for the festival." Her hand fluttered to her shoulder, the hand that would have borne a ring if she'd been married. "I come every year, but this is the first time I've seen you. And to think, I was actually going to skip this one. I didn't want to risk any more bad weather, but now I'm so glad I continued the tradition."

Had she been kind to Thea or had she been one of her tormentors?

Tormentors, he thought, remembering the day Harlow had threatened Thea with whipped cream. Madison had laughed as Thea had blushed.

He stared at her, never uttering a word.

"Come over here and meet me," Brock said to her. "He's a mean drunk, but I'm a very, very nice one. I'm also eternally single, so you'll never have to worry about one of my exes. A word of warning, though. I have no respect for women or men or anyone, not even myself. But damn if we won't have fun together."

She looked between them before arching a brow in Brock's direction. "You're one of those bad boys my momma warned me about, aren't you?"

"Oh, honey. I'm the baddest."

"Well, I'm not going to sleep with you."

"How about a dance, then?" Before leading her off, Brock leaned over to whisper to Daniel, "You owe me."

Yeah, yeah, yeah. Like Brock was really suffering. Daniel drained another glass of whiskey.

Jude returned as a wave of dizziness rolled through him.

"I'm spinning," Daniel told him.

"You're also going to spend the rest of your life without Dorothea. Tomorrow she's going on vacation with her friends, and she's going to find herself a new man. A palate cleanser, I guess you could say. And when she returns, she's going to start over with a clean slate. You'll be nothing but a distant memory."

"I'm no one's memory," he snapped, hating the thought of Thea with anyone else.

"You're no one's prize, either," Jude said.

Bastard. "I'm strong. A natural-born protector."

"So are others."

He scowled at his friend. No, his *former* friend. "I'm handsome." Thea had said so. Had said he was the most beautiful person she'd ever seen.

"Physical beauty fades."

"I'm…" What? Honorable? Kind? Loyal? Brave? Not even

close. And those were the things that mattered. They were the things he wanted in his woman. The things Thea already was.

Damn it. He needed to get out of here. He jumped to his feet, the chair falling behind him. Despite the music playing in the background, he heard a loud thud. The people around him leaped out of the way.

"What the hell is wrong with you?" a familiar voice growled. The ex-husband. "First you break Dorothea's heart, then you hit me with a chair."

"What are you doing here?" Daniel demanded.

"Holly called me. Said—"

"Move along." Jude stepped in front of the guy, his body vibrating with oncoming rage. If he gave in to that rage… bad things would happen.

Weatherman must not have sensed the danger. He stepped closer. "I'm not going anywhere. I came here to tell you how badly you've messed up."

Daniel remained in place, his hands fisting. "How badly *I* messed up?"

Weatherman added, "You're just like me, you know."

"I *never* cheated on her, and I never will. I would rather die."

"What you did was worse. You had her heart, something I never did, and you stomped on it."

With a roar, Daniel leaped over the table. His fist connected with Weatherman's nose, and blood spurted. But Weatherman didn't yelp or run away. He threw a punch of his own, and Daniel's brain banged into his skull, a loud ring erupting in his ears.

As the ring quieted, he heard Jude say "—next one will cost you."

"No," Daniel said. Both he and Weatherman deserved a beating for the way they'd treated Thea. "I've got this."

"You don't have anything but a bleak future," Weatherman snapped. "Trust me. I know."

"Shut up if you want to live through this," Brock snapped. He must have abandoned Madison and raced over.

"Too late. He's got to die." Once again, Daniel threw himself at Jazz. They punched and kicked at each other, falling over tables and chairs. Glass shattered. They rolled across the floor, and sharp pains cut across his back.

Cheers reverberated. He continued to punch and kick, but he was having trouble seeing. His coordination was off, he realized, punching nothing but air. He had warm fluid in his eyes—blood?—and wiped his face with a throbbing hand.

Weatherman was...being held down by Jude.

"Let him go." Daniel stomped over, or tried to. Brock wrapped strong arms around him and forced him to the floor.

He reclined there, the rage burning out of him until he was nothing but a panting, bleeding husk with a racing mind.

Thea was the best thing to ever happen to him, and she was right. He hadn't fought for her.

Nothing mattered more than her, and yet he'd allowed fear to direct his steps and order his path. He'd been so worried about losing her that he hadn't done anything to keep her.

He'd told her he wanted her and had thought he'd laid himself bare for her. As bare as she'd been the night she'd come to his room and dropped her coat. But he hadn't. Not really. He'd kept the armor around his heart, and she'd known it. She'd had compassion in her eyes, and it had finally begun to crack. He was shamed. He'd sent her away that first night with harsh words and the fresh sting of rejection, yet she had offered him forgiveness and sweetness and everything right in a world gone wrong. And still he'd done nothing to keep her.

As a teen, he'd seen a glimpse of her worth when she'd stood before Harlow, her head held high. He'd told her, *I think you're perfect just the way you are.* And she had been. She was.

But he'd still focused his attention on other girls. Girls who would sleep with him. Girls who would never be part of his future. Easily had, easily forgotten. Just a bit of fun. But fun like that never lasted.

Since his return, he'd stuck to the same pattern, looking for distractions. But he didn't need distractions. He needed Thea. She was his safe place. His light. She chased away the darkness.

If he couldn't be the right man, he didn't deserve the right woman.

He'd tried to fit her in the same box. First, temporary. Then permanent but only on his terms. Well, no more. Thea was the right woman. The only woman. He still wasn't worthy of her, and he still deserved to lose her, but he wasn't going to lie down and accept what he deserved. Not anymore. He was going to fight for what he wanted. Finally. He was going to be the right man.

"I have to go to her. Have to win her."

"Hallelujah." Brock helped him sit up and patted his shoulder. "I will help you win her, but first I'm going to take you to the hospital. You're bleeding—everywhere."

"No. No." He shook his head, and dizziness returned with a vengeance. His jaw hurt. "Have to…inn…go."

Darkness joined the dizziness and, with a single yank, managed to pull him into the abyss. He knew nothing more.

CHAPTER THIRTY

Her car wouldn't start.

Dorothea's bags were stuffed in the trunk, right beside Ryanne's and Lyndie's. They had been ready to go for the past hour.

Her mom and Holly hovered in front of the inn, throwing out advice as she stared under the hood at machinery she couldn't identify.

"Maybe it's the rotator cuff?" Carol suggested.

"Or the thingamabob. You know, the thing with circles," Holly said.

Ryanne and Lyndie stood beside her family, offering equally useless advice.

Lyndie: "Tell the car you love her. She'll stop trying to punish you."

Ryanne: "Tell the car to RIP. Because she's dead. Forever."

Ryanne could rebuild an engine—and had! If she said the car was dead, it was dead. And yet neither girl offered the use of her own car. Did they not want to go on this freebie vacation?

"You sure Brad Lintz wasn't at the auto shop?" she asked.

Since he and his girlfriend had broken up a few weeks ago, he'd been living there. According to local gossip, he hadn't left more than twice.

"I'm sure," Holly said. "I looked everywhere, even shouted his name."

"Then it's settled. We'll wait until he returns, and you'll use the time to make sure you packed everything you need." Carol wiped her hands together in a job well done. "I'm certain you don't have enough clothes."

"I plan to eat my weight in dessert," she replied. "I don't need anything but a T-shirt and a pair of sweatpants."

"What about a swimsuit?" Holly asked. "How are you going to seduce the pool boy if you don't take a swimsuit?"

"If I decide to go swimming, I can buy—"

"Well, look who's talking like she's Miss Richie Rich." Carol tossed her arms up in exasperation. "Buying a new swimsuit when you have a perfectly good old one?"

What the heck was going on?

"What about snacks?" Lyndie asked, joining the madness. "A road trip isn't a road trip without snacks."

"Funny, but you failed to mention the importance of snacks before now," Dorothea grated.

A pause. Then her friend blurted out, "Blood sugar!"

Seriously? "You don't have low blood sugar."

Ryanne frowned at her. "I can't believe you can be so cavalier about a possible medical condition our friend may or may not have developed late in life."

All right. Dorothea'd had enough. "What's going on?"

Holly looked at the screen of her phone, and her shoulders rolled in. "It's seven freaking o'clock."

"I know!" Dorothea had been ready to leave right at six, as commanded, but first Lyndie had claimed to have a case of that "raging diarrhea you once experienced, remember? I bet you were contagious."

Dorothea had replied, "Contagious…several weeks ago? Even though I never had it?"

Her friend had responded with "Some germs need time to incubate. And you could have been a carrier and just not have known it." Then she'd spent the next fifteen minutes in the bathroom.

The street and sidewalk were filling as people arrived to man their booths at the festival, which would kick off in about an hour. If they weren't gone before then, they wouldn't be leaving until tomorrow.

Gasps of horror suddenly rang out, and the growing crowd parted.

"Out of my way," a familiar voice demanded. "Out of my way!"

Daniel?

Relief radiated from her family and friends.

"Daniel," she whispered, horrified. He wore a bloodstained hospital gown, some of that blood fresh, wetting the paper-thin material. One of his eyes was swollen shut, and there were knots and bruises all over his face. His knuckles were cracked and scabbed, and there was an IV tube hanging from the inside of his elbow.

His desperate gaze landed on her. "Don't go," he said, his voice ragged. "Please." He stopped in front of her car. "I'm not letting you go. Or if you do go, I'm following. My place is with you. You are my home, and I'm fighting for you."

She took a step toward him, only to go still. No matter how much she wanted to comfort him, she couldn't give him false hope. "What happened to you?"

"A little skirmish at the bar. It's not important." His gaze moved to Ryanne. "I'll pay for damages."

"You're danged right you will," Ryanne said, but she didn't sound upset. She sounded relieved.

A skirmish? Dorothea took another step, stilled. "Are you okay?"

"Not yet, but I will be. If you can find it in your heart to forgive me." He wavered with more dynamism. The wildest part? Despite his weakness, he was still a force to be reckoned with. "I woke up in a hospital room with Jude and Brock at my side, but not you. I only wanted you. I *only* want you."

Hospital? Her heart thudded against her ribs. "Maybe you should return."

"I love you, Thea."

She licked her lips. "Don't do this. I can't—"

"I love you. I love you so much it's a sickness inside me. No, no, that's not true. It's the only thing that's healing me from the sickness I've carried for far too long."

She swallowed the lump growing in her throat and looked around. Her mom and sister were grinning. Ryanne and Lyndie were crying. This was actually happening?

"You deserved an apology before. After the storm," he continued. "I didn't give it to you then. I gave you one yesterday, but for all the wrong reasons. I was sorry you'd left me. Sorry I missed you so much. Sorry I couldn't function without you. The truth is, I'm sorry I allowed fear to lead me. I'm so sorry, love. I fought my feelings for you when I should have fought to keep you."

She had to swallow again.

"If you want to chase storms, I'll be your driver. If you don't want me to be your driver, I'll have a hot meal waiting for you at home. If you want to move to the city, I'll move with you. There are no conditions to my love. I will love you even if you hate me. I will love you forever. If you decide to take a chance on me—and I'm begging you to take a chance—we can adopt as many kids as we want. I'm on board for a big family."

Her hand fluttered to her throat, where emotion continued to coagulate. Resist him. She had to resist him. "The future will never be assured. What happens when your fears come back?"

"I'm sure they will, but we will fight them. Together. And we will win. You will always and forever be my prize. My life isn't right without you."

Dang him! He was telling her everything she'd ever wanted to hear.

Resist?

"I love you, Dorothea Valentina Mathis, and I want you now and always. I want to marry you and spend the rest of my life proving just how much you mean to me. I'm not worthy of you," he said. "I know this, but I'm going to do everything in my power to change that. I'm going to fight for you, every day, in every way."

"Say yes," someone shouted. Another voice she recognized. The crowd was still gathered around them, though Dorothea had somehow been oblivious; they parted, revealing a smiling Virgil.

In that moment, the misery Dorothea had been stroking like a lover finally just evaporated. She couldn't have it and have Daniel, and she would much rather have Daniel. She'd accused him of clinging to his fears, but hadn't she done the same?

"Wait just a sec, sis. Don't you dare say yes to this man." Holly strode to her side and faced Daniel with all her customary sass on display. "Not until he promises a few things."

Tenderness welled inside her. "Right," she said, doing her best to appear stern. "You want me, Daniel Porter, you're going to have to negotiate with me."

Hope gave way to undiluted joy, dancing in his eye and lighting his entire face. For several seconds, he clearly tried his best to tame his expression, but he failed. "You're right. We need to negotiate. So here are my terms. You'll hand some of the inn's responsibilities to me. Let's face it, love, I've got better people skills and—"

"What! You do not have better skills!"

He snickered at her. "Thing is, I like the work. I feel like I've finally found my place. And I've already spoken with Jude and Brock about taking a behind-the-scenes role at LPH. I can work from the inn and take care of customer service for both of us. As for you, love. You will compliment me at least once a day. A woman isn't the only one who needs praise, you know. And I insist, I absolutely insist you take my last name when we get married. I don't care how much you protest, there will be no hyphens for you."

"I never—"

"Also, we'll take equal responsibility for Adonis and Echo. They're part of our family."

The first of their children, she thought, that well of tenderness expanding.

He looked to Brock and Jude. "Am I forgetting anything?"

His friends stepped from the crowd. They'd been here all along? Her skills of observation amazed her. But in her defense, she'd been pretty wrapped up in Daniel.

"Yes," Brock said. "You're forgetting about the sex."

"Sex. Right." Daniel nodded. "Three times a day is the bare minimum for us. And the lights will be on."

"Sweet fancy Moses." Her mother fanned her face.

Lyndie and Ryanne gave her a thumbs-up.

Holly sighed. "He's offering you a gold-star mediocre deal you probably shouldn't pass up."

Excitement shivered through Dorothea as she focused on the man she loved. "I've heard your terms, Daniel, but before I can even consider giving us a chance," she couldn't help but tease him, "you'll hear mine. You'll finish the theme room. In fact, you'll finish *all* the theme rooms. On top of guest satisfaction at the inn, you'll be responsible for helping me clean

the rooms until we're flush enough to hire someone else...
and you'll do it shirtless. In fact, go ahead and throw out *all*
your shirts. Oh, and you'll cheer me on as I finish school online and continue to grow my website."

"Yes, absolutely yes," Daniel rushed to say. "I agree to everything."

Whoa. Hold up. "You're not going to try to change my
terms?"

His expression turned deadly serious as he said, "This is too
important. If you want it, you get it—as long as I get you."

Her insides turned molten, and she just about died of happiness right then and there.

"The inn is my home," he added, "and I'm willing to beg
for the privilege of working there. Plus, you'll be paying me
in kisses, so I'll be the richest man in town."

Every time he spoke, she melted a little more. "Daniel—"

"I will fight for you, Thea. Always."

He *was* fighting for her, she realized. He was willing to
give up anything and everything to be with her.

Her resistance had never stood a chance.

With a sob, she threw herself in his arms. He stumbled
back, but if the contact pained him, he didn't show it, holding on to her tightly.

"I love you," she told him. "I love you so much."

He pulled back to frame her face in his hands. Tears were
welled in *his* eyes. "You love me?"

"I do. I really do."

A radiant smile glowed down at her. "I would spin you
around, but I'm pretty sure I've already torn open most of
my stitches."

"Daniel! We need to get you back to the hospital."

"No," he said. "I'm right where I want to be."

"A wedding," Carol called. "There's going to be a wedding! A big one!"

Dorothea pressed her forehead against Daniel's chest and moaned. "Momma—"

"She's right," Daniel said. "I want to marry you, and I want a big wedding. The whole town will witness my pledge to love you forever. We'll even invite Jazz. I want him to realize you're mine, and I'm never letting you go."

Embarrassment gave way to pleasure. "All right. Yes. I'll marry you."

"I'll plan everything." Carol clapped her hands. "It will be absolutely perfect!"

"That's right. It will be perfect," Holly piped up, "because I'll spend my time stopping Mom."

Dorothea and Daniel shared a smile. He might consider her the prize, but she felt like the one who'd won.

"One last thing." Brock pressed something cold and metal in her palm. "Daniel wanted you to see this, but he dropped it in his haste to get to you."

She glanced down and saw the locket. It was open, the picture of Daniel's mother staring at her from one side, a picture of Dorothea's face staring at her from the other.

Her gaze zipped to Daniel. "When did you have this done?"

"This morning. The main reason I was late."

"You knew I was leaving?" she asked.

"Holly called me."

Well. Now the delay was starting to make sense. Her family and friends had her back. The girl who'd once felt alone now had a strong support system. Could life get any better?

"Guess I can fix your car now," Ryanne said, holding up a... Dorothea had no idea. The thingamabob, maybe.

"I'm going to make you happy, Thea. I'm determined." Daniel gazed at her with adoration and awe, as if he couldn't believe how blessed he was.

Yes, life could get better.

She would be spending every day of hers with the man

she loved—the man who loved her right back. The man who hadn't just said the words but had proved it with action. "I'm going to make you happy, too."

"I hope we're included in that happiness," Brock said. "Because we are a package deal."

"I figured as much," she said with another laugh.

"Just don't go getting any matchmaking ideas," Jude groused.

"Too late. You're a project. You both are." She reached out and patted both their shoulders. "But that's okay. Daniel and I have decided you're worth the effort."

"Oh, you and Daniel decided?" Brock arched a brow at her. "When was this?"

"Just now." She fluffed her hair. "I don't know if you heard, but what makes me happy makes him happy."

"It's true." Daniel kissed her lips gently, tenderly. "Always and forever, it's true."

Always and forever. Dorothea melted against him.

"I'm going to make sure your nails are only ever painted yellow, pink, gold or white," he said. "Mostly white."

She laughed. "We're going to have a good life together, aren't we?"

"The very best," he vowed.

★ ★ ★ ★ ★

If you liked Dorothea and Daniel's story, don't miss the next book in THE ORIGINAL HEARTBREAKERS *series,* CAN'T LET GO, *coming soon from Gena Showalter and* HQN *Books.*

Turn the page for a sneak peek at Ryanne and Jude's story!

"I need to speak with you. Privately." Jude took Ryanne's hand and hauled her into the nearest alley. He backed her into the brick wall and loomed over her, his narrowed eyes glaring daggers. "I told you there would be consequences for your actions."

This was the closest Ryanne had ever been to Jude, and she was having trouble catching her breath. Her blood heated, and her skin tingled. Little quivers spread through her torso.

"Screw your consequences." Led by desire rather than logic, she wrapped her arms around his neck and combed her fingers through his hair. Trust had always been a problem for her, but not here, not now. No man was more loyal than Jude Laurent.

"What are you doing?" he grated, his ragged tone practically a caress.

"I don't know exactly." She licked her lips, reveling as his eyes followed the motion. "I've never done this before. I have trust issues, and I don't date."

He went still. "Don't date...ever?"

"Well, not in a long while. My last official date happened two and a half years ago."

Now he stiffened. "Were you cheated on?"

As she toyed with the ends of his hair, the usually icy man didn't relax, but he didn't push her away, either. Growing bolder by the second, she plucked at the collar of his shirt, her nails scraping lightly over his skin. "Twice my mother slept with my boyfriends," she admitted. "And the things I've seen at the bar…" She nibbled on her bottom lip, then asked, "What about you? How long since you—"

"Two and a half years," he interjected.

Ohhh. They had more in common than she'd realized. And the fact that they'd remained alone for the exact same amount of time, well, the odds had to be astronomical. Some people might even call it fate.

"Jude?" What was she asking him? What did she want from him?

Only everything.

Her pulse points throbbed.

"Don't do this." He took two steps back.

"Do what?" She grabbed hold of his shirt and tugged him forward—he wasn't leaving her, not now. He wore a metal prosthesis today, and the impromptu action caused him to stumble.

She opened her mouth to tell him she was sorry but suddenly found herself plastered against his chest, speaking beyond her. Their gazes locked. Again he stopped breathing. And so did she…

"I should go," he rasped, but remained in place. He braced his palms flat on the brick, caging her in. His body heat enveloped her, sizzling waves of agony and need washing over her nerve endings, and she knew. Knew what she had asked of him, what she wanted from him.

A kiss. Here and now. Before he remembered how much he missed his family.

"Don't freak out, okay?" she told him. Then she cupped

his face and yanked him down, pressing her lips against his. His soft, sweet lips...

He stiffened all over again before jerking away—but just as before, he didn't leave. He glared at her, panting now. She was panting, too, the scent of him filling her nose. Musk and oranges with a subtle floral note. Not feminine but strangely, deliciously, masculine. A whimper escaped her. She was hungry for him, so danged hungry. No, she was starved.

"You freaked out," she accused.

He closed his eyes for one second, two, before focusing on her with unwavering hatred...but also fiery lust. "You surprised me."

She'd surprised herself!

Okay, she had a choice to make. Continue on, perhaps stoking the hatred as well as the lust, or walk away, never knowing what could have been.

No contest. She had to know.

Slowly, giving him time to process her intention, she leaned forward to nip at his lower lip. "Did I also turn you on?"

With a growl, he dived on her, devouring her, his hunger a perfect match to her own. Their tongues dueled, creating a hot tangle of desire. Her nipples crested into hard buds, and the apex of her thighs ached, liquid need pooling between her legs. As her bones melted, passion surged through her, flooding her. She arched her hips and groaned. Contact! Her throbbing core rubbed against the long, thick length of his erection.

In the midst of the kiss, he shed his aloof veneer, a winter coat he no longer needed, the sun finally peeking out from behind storm clouds. He seemed to shed a thousand pounds of anger and sadness and even pain. She *felt* their absence, the temperature of his skin heating; arousal had burned everything else away.

Groaning in raw frustration, he stepped closer, forcing her

spine flush against the brick wall, smashing his chest into hers. Cold behind her; heat in front of her. The warring temperatures bombarded her with sensation, creating a tornado in her bloodstream. Inhibitions were the first casualty.

She and Jude were outside, in a public setting, but so what? This man disliked her most of the time. So the heck what? He kissed her as if she was his last meal. As if she was the air he needed to survive. As if she alone held the key to his happiness.

"Ryanne." He kicked her legs apart. The move lacked finesse, and yet it electrified her from head to toe. He ground his shaft between her legs, currents of passion searing her veins.

She wanted to strip him. She wanted to climb him—ride him. She wanted to feel him inside her, moving, thrusting... pounding. Finally she would experience everything a man had to give her. Everything *this* man had to give.

"More," she demanded, pulling at the hem of his shirt. The moment her fingers touched the blistering silk of skin covering his rock-hard abs, her knees nearly buckled. She might have gone two and a half years without a kiss or a hot-and-heavy make-out session, but she couldn't go two more weeks...two more days...two more freaking minutes without Jude.

"You taste like strawberries, buttercup," he rasped. "You smell like strawberries, too. How is that possible?"

"I've lived in this town most of my life. I'm only shocked I don't taste and smell like pineapples. *Dummy*," she teased, nipping at his bottom lip.

He chuckled. A husky, rusty chuckle, but a chuckle nonetheless. It shocked them both. In unison, they stilled. Once again their gazes met, locked. His pupils were blown, what remained of his irises glittering and wild. His cheeks were flushed, his nostrils flaring every time he inhaled.

So beautiful. Not ready for this to end. Ryanne traced a trembling fingertip along the seam of his lips. Such soft lips for such a hard man.

His eyelids narrowed, and he stepped back, severing every point of contact. A scowl darkened his features.

Well, crap. Was he about to blame her for what just happened? Would he vow never to come near her again?

She braced for whatever vitriol he planned to unleash. But all he did was take another step back and wipe his mouth with the outside of his hand. Then horror replaced his scowl and he took another step back...and another. The silence cut deeper than a knife.

"Jude," she said. "Care enough to tell me what you're feeling." *Please.*

"I don't," he croaked. "I don't care." Without another word, he spun on his heel and stalked off, disappearing around the corner.

Ryanne remained in place, stunned and hurting. Deep breath in, out. Her heartbeat refused to slow, and her bones were still too hot to solidify.

Whatever thoughts had tumbled through Jude's mind, well, they obviously tormented him. Did he think he'd betrayed his wife? Maybe. Probably. She'd died two and a half years ago, and he'd gone two and a half years without touching another woman.

A pang of envy cut through Ryanne, and she cringed. *I'm jealous of a dead woman?*

Had Jude stopped allowing himself to enjoy life because his family was gone?

Maybe. Probably, she thought again.

His wife was gone, and she wasn't coming back. He was alive and well. He deserved happiness.

Whether he knew it or not, whether he would admit it or not, Ryanne had helped him today. With a single kiss, she'd given his body new life. She knew it, felt it—in more ways than one.

Pleasure and hope collided, zinging through her as she remembered the feel of his shaft between her legs. If she could turn him on once, surely she could do it again…